Dear Reader,

I am delighted to introduce you to the first book in my thrilling new project, The Black Cobra Quartet. The concept evolved from wondering what happened to the soldiers who fought alongside the Cynster cousins in their cavalry troop at Waterloo. The answer is:

Five of them went to India to serve with the army of the East India Company under the direct command of the Governor-General of India, who in 1822, gives all five a mission: do whatever it takes to bring a fiendish villain, the Black Cobra, to justice.

One of the five gives his life to secure the vital evidence. The other four swear to avenge him by getting that evidence back to England and into the hands of Royce Varisey, now Duke of Wolverstone, the one man powerful enough to bring down the Black Cobra.

You didn't think you'd heard the last of Royce and the members of the Bastion Club—or their wives—did you? And, of course, our four latest heroes appeal to their old comrades-in-arms, the Cynster cousins, for assistance, too. The result is four action-packed adventures ranging from Bombay to Norfolk, filled with danger, passion, and intrigue, with an exciting cast of fresh new characters walking onto a stage peopled by many you already know.

The Prelude begins in India, after which our four heroes part, three carrying decoys and one the vital original evidence back to Royce in England by four very different routes. Each book in the quartet tells the tale of one journey—and of the lady and the love each hero discovers along the way.

Each of our heroes is due to reach England in the days leading up to Christmas, 1822. Join me in following them through the perils and pleasures of their journeys, which culminate in a wonderful joint Christmas you won't want to miss.

So read on and let the Prelude take you to India in 1822, and then sit back and enjoy the journey of Colonel Derek Delborough in *The Untamed Bride*.

Happy reading!

Stephanie Laurens

By Stephanie Laurens

The Untamed Bride

Coming Soon

The Elusive Bride

Bastion Club Novels

Mastered By Love • The Edge of Desire
Beyond Seduction • To Distraction
A Fine Passion • A Lady of His Own
A Gentleman's Honor • The Lady Chosen
Captain Jack's Woman

Cynster Novels

Temptation and Surrender • Where the Heart Leads
The Taste of Innocence • What Price Love?
The Truth About Love • The Ideal Bride
The Perfect Lover • On a Wicked Dawn
On a Wild Night • The Promise in a Kiss
All About Passion • All About Love
A Secret Love • A Rogue's Proposal
Scandal's Bride • A Rake's Vow
Devil's Bride

STEPHANIE LAURENS

The Untamed Bride

THE BLACK COBRA QUARTET

AVON

An Imprint of HarperCollinsPublishers

AVON BOOKS
An Imprint of HarperCollins*Publishers*
10 East 53rd Street
New York, New York 10022-5299

Prelude
to
The Black Cobra Quartet

India, 1822

March 24, 1822
East India Company Headquarters, Calcutta, India

J can't stress how important it is that we behead this fiend." Francis Rawdon-Hastings, Marquess of Hastings and Governor-General of India for the last nine years, stumped back and forth behind his desk.

The five officers at ease in the elegant rattan armchairs arranged before the massive mahogany expanse in the Governor-General's study sat silent and still; Hastings's passage was the only movement stirring the heavy, humid air.

The old man's color was high, his fists clenched, the muscles in his shoulders and arms taut. Colonel Derek Delborough, Del to all who knew him, seated at one end of the row of chairs, eyed the signs of his commander-in-chief's agitation with cynical detachment. It had taken Hastings long enough to summon him and his men, Hastings's personally appointed special officers.

Behind Hastings, the white plaster wall was broken by two teak-framed windows shaded by the wide balcony beyond yet already shuttered against the burgeoning heat. Hanging between, a portrait of the king, painted when he'd still been Prince Florizel and the darling of Europe, stared out over this outpost of English wealth and influence. The room was amply endowed with rosewood tables and teak cabinets, many intricately carved and inlaid, glowing in the light that seeped through the shutters to glint off myriad ornate brass fittings.

Airy, spotlessly clean, richly and exotically appointed, the room possessed a timeless serenity underlying its utilitarian function, much like the subcontinent itself, a large portion over which Hastings now ruled.

Immune to any soothing ambience, Hastings continued to pace heavily. "These depredations on our convoys *cannot* go on—we're losing face with every day that passes, with every attack that goes unanswered."

"I understand"—Del's own drawl was the epitome of unruffled calm, a sharp contrast to Hastings's terse tones—"that the Black Cobra's activities have been escalating for some time."

"Yes, damn it! And the Bombay station didn't think it worthwhile reporting, let alone *acting*, until a few months ago, and now they're bleating that the situation's beyond them." Pausing by the center of his desk, Hastings exasperatedly rifled a stack of documents, fanning out a selection before pushing them across the polished surface. "These are some of the recent reports—just so you know what anarchy you're heading into."

The four men seated to Del's right glanced his way. At his nod, they reached out and took one of the documents each; sitting back, they perused the reports.

"I've heard," Del went on, reclaiming Hastings's attention, "that the cult of the Black Cobra first reared its head in '19. Does it have any previous history, or was that its inception?"

"That was the first inkling we had, and the locals in Bombay hadn't heard of it before then. No saying it hadn't been lurking in some backwater somewhere—God knows there's enough of these secretive native cults—but there's no reports, even from the older maharajahs, of its existence prior to mid-'19."

"A *de novo* cult suggests the arrival of a particular leader."

"Indeed, and it's him you'll need to eliminate. Either that, or do enough damage to his forces"—Hastings flung a hand at the documents the other four were reading—"the rabble he uses to murder, rape and pillage, to make him scurry back under whatever rock he slithered out from."

" 'Murder, rape and pillage' hardly does the Black Cobra justice." Major Gareth Hamilton, one of the four officers who served under Del, glanced up, his brown gaze pinning Hastings. "This reads more like deliberate terrorization of villages, which suggests an attempt to subjugate. For a cult, that's ambitious—an attempt to seize power beyond the usual bleeding of money and goods."

"Establishing a yoke of fear." Captain Rafe Carstairs, seated three seats along from Del, joined Gareth in tossing the report he'd read back on the desk. Rafe's aristocratic features showed evidence of distaste, even disgust, which told Del that the contents of the report Rafe had read were truly dreadful.

All five of them seated before Hastings's desk had seen human carnage unimaginable to most; as a group they'd served through the Peninsula campaign in the cavalry under Paget, then been in the thick of the action at Waterloo, and had subsequently taken commissions with the Honorable East India Company to serve under Hastings as an elite group of officers deployed specifically to deal with the worst uprisings and instabilities the subcontinent had thrown up over the past seven years.

Seated between Gareth and Rafe, Major Logan Monteith's lip curled as, with a flick of his tanned wrist, he sent the report he'd read skating to join the others on the desk. "This Black Cobra makes Kali and her *thugees* look civilized."

Beyond Rafe, the last and youngest of their five, Captain James MacFarlane, still faintly baby-faced even though he was twenty-nine, leaned forward and carefully laid the document he'd perused with the others. "Has Bombay no clue as to who's behind this? No trail—no associates, no area in which the Cobra has its headquarters?"

"After more than five months of active searching, Bombay has precisely nothing beyond a *suspicion* that some of the Maratha princelings have been drawn into clandestinely supporting the cult."

Rafe snorted. "Any fool could have predicted that. Ever since we slapped them down in '18, they've been spoiling for a fight—*any* fight, they're not particular."

"Exactly." Hastings's tone was acid, biting. "As you know, Ensworth is now governor in Bombay. He's performing well in all other respects, but he's all diplomat, no military man, and he freely admits that when it comes to the Black Cobra he's in over his head." Hastings's gaze raked them, coming to rest on Del. "Which is where you gentlemen come in."

"I take it," Del said, "that Ensworth isn't going to get his nose out of joint when we ride into his patch."

"On the contrary—he'll welcome you with open arms. He's at his wits' end trying to reassure the merchants while simultaneously balancing the books for London—not easy when every fifth convoy is plundered." Hastings paused, and for a moment the strain of managing the far-flung empire India had become showed in his face. Then his jaw firmed, and he met their gazes. "I can't overstate the importance of this mission. The Black Cobra *has to be* stopped. Its depredations and the atrocities committed in its name have reached a level that threatens not just the Company, but England herself—not just in terms of trade, but in stature, and you've all been here long enough to know how vital the latter is to our nation's continuing interests. And lastly"—with his head he indicated the reports on his desk—"it's India, and the people in those villages, who need the Cobra removed."

"No argument there." Rafe came out of his characteristic lounge and rose to his feet as Del and the others did.

Hastings let his gaze travel over them as they ranged shoulder-to-shoulder before his desk, a solid wall of red in their uniforms. They were all over six feet tall, ex-Guardsmen all, hardened by long years of battle and command. Experience etched their features, even MacFarlane's; worldly knowledge colored their eyes.

Satisfied with what he saw, Hastings nodded. "Your mission, gentlemen, is to identify and capture the Black Cobra, and bring him to justice. You have a free hand as to ways and means. I care not how you do it, as long as justice is seen— and known—to have been done. As usual, you may draw on the company's account, and on its troops as seems fit."

Typically it was Rafe who put their collective thoughts into words, albeit his words. "You mentioned beheading." His tone was light, his habitual ineffable charm on show, as if he were at some tea party and speaking of croquet. "With cults that's usually the most effective approach. Can we take it you would rather we went direct for the leader—or are we to play cautious and try to defend the convoys wherever possible?"

Hastings met Rafe's guileless blue eyes. "You, Captain, wouldn't know caution from your elbow."

Del's lips twitched; from the corner of his eye, he saw Gareth's do the same. Rafe, nicknamed "Reckless" for good cause, merely looked innocent, continuing to meet Hastings's cynical gaze.

Hastings humphed. "Your supposition is correct. I expect you to target the Black Cobra specifically, to identify and eliminate him. For the rest, do whatever you can, but the situation is urgent, and we can no longer afford caution."

Again Hastings's gaze raked them. "You may interpret my orders in whatever way you wish—just bring the Black Cobra to justice."

August 15, five months later
The Officers' Mess
The Honorable East India Company Bombay Station

"Hastings did say we could interpret his orders as we wished—that we had a free hand as to ways and means."

Rafe settled his shoulders against the wall behind him, then raised one of the glasses the barboy had just set on the table, and took a long draft of cloudy amber beer.

The five of them—Del, Gareth, Logan, Rafe and James— were seated around the corner table they'd claimed as theirs in the bar off the officers' mess. They'd chosen that table because of its amenities, namely that it commanded an uninterrupted view of the entire bar—the enclosed front verandah of the officers' mess—as well as the maidan beyond the verandah steps. In addition—the table's principal recommendation—with thick stone walls at their back and along one side, there wasn't anywhere anyone could stand unobserved by them, inside or out, and overhear their low-voiced discussions.

The bamboo screens fitted between the verandah's front pillars were presently lowered against the late afternoon sun and the dust stirred up by a troop of sepoys engaged in parade drills, leaving the bar wreathed in cooler shadows. A distant hum of conversation rose from two groups of officers seated further down the long verandah; the clink of billiard balls wafted from an alcove off the verandah's far end.

"True." Gareth claimed a glass. "But I doubt the good marquess envisioned us going around him."

"I can't see that we have any choice." Along with the other three, Logan looked at Del.

Staring into his beer, Del felt their gazes, looked up and met them. "If, as we believe, the Black Cobra is Roderick Ferrar, then Hastings won't thank us for bringing him the news."

"But he'll still act on it, surely?" James reached for the last glass left on the tray.

Del glanced at him. "Did you notice the portrait behind Hastings's desk?"

"The one of Prinny?"

Del nodded. "That's not company property, but Hastings's own. He owes his appointment to Prinny—pardon me, His Majesty—and knows he can never forget it. If, presuming we can find it, we take him incontrovertible proof that Ferrar is our villain, we'll place him in the invidious position of having to decide which master to appease—his conscience, or his king."

Frowning, James turned his glass between his hands. "Is Ferrar really that untouchable?"

"Yes." Del's voice was reinforced by Gareth's, Logan's and Rafe's.

"Hastings is beholden to the king," Del explained, "and the king is beholden to Ferrar senior, the Earl of Shrewton. Furthermore, although he's Shrewton's second son, Ferrar is widely known to be his father's favorite."

"Rumor," Rafe said, leaning on the table, "has it that the king is in Shrewton's pocket—not a situation all that hard to believe—so unless there's some animosity between Hastings and Shrewton that no one knows of, odds are that Hastings will feel obliged to 'lose' any evidence we find."

Logan snorted. "Hell—I wouldn't be surprised if some of the gold the Cobra is skimming off John Company's profits isn't, in a roundabout way, ending in His Majesty's pocket."

"Hastings," Gareth reminded them, "was very insistent that we 'bring the Black Cobra to justice.' He didn't instruct us to capture him and deliver him to Bombay." He looked at Del, arched a brow. "Do you think Hastings might suspect, and this—using us—is his way of gaining justice without offending his royal master?"

Del's lips twisted cynically. "The possibility has crossed my mind. Consider—it took us a bare two weeks to realize the Black Cobra either had someone in the governor's office here, or else was himself a member of the governor's staff. After that it took what?—six weeks?—of watching and noting which convoys were attacked to narrow it down to Ferrar. As the Governor of Bombay's second adjutant, he and only he had knowledge of all the convoys attacked—others had the details for some, but only he had routes and times for all. Hastings has similar information stretching back for months. He has to have at least some suspicion of who's behind the Black Cobra cult."

"Hastings," Rafe said, "also knows when Roderick Ferrar took up his appointment here—in early '19, five or so months before the first known appearance of the Black Cobra and his minions."

"Five months is long enough for a sharp lad like Ferrar to see the possibilities, make plans, and gather said minions," Logan said. "More, as the governor's adjutant, he's had easy and officially sanctioned contact with the disaffected Maratha princelings—the same hotheads we now know have secretly ceded the Black Cobra their private robber gangs."

"Ferrar," Del said, "reported to Hastings in Calcutta before joining the govenor's staff here—a position our contacts back in Calcutta confirm he specifically requested. Ferrar could have had a position with Hastings at headquarters—it was his for the taking, and what eager-to-advance-in-the-company youngster wouldn't rather work for the great man himself? But no, Ferrar requested a posting to Bombay, and was apparently quite satisfied with the second adjutant's desk."

"Which makes one wonder," Gareth said, "if the principal attraction of said desk was that it was the entire subcontinent away from Hastings's potentially watchful eye."

"So, James, m'lad"—Rafe clapped the younger captain on the back—"all that suggests that instructing us to 'bring the Black Cobra to justice,' and to use whatever means we deem necessary to do it, is very likely a shrewd politician's way of taking care of the matter." Rafe met the others' eyes. "And Hastings knows us well enough to be sure we'll do his dirty work for him."

James glanced at the others' faces, saw they all thought the same, and reluctantly nodded. "All right. So we bypass Hastings. But how do we do that?" He looked at Del. "Have you heard anything from England?"

Del glanced along the verandah, verifying that no one else could possibly overhear. "A frigate came in this morning, with a very thick packet for me."

"From Devil?" Gareth asked.

Del nodded. "A letter from him, and rather more from one of his peers—the Duke of Wolverstone."

"Wolverstone?" Rafe frowned. "I thought the old man was next thing to a recluse."

"He was," Del replied. "The son—the current duke—is another matter. We know him—or rather know *of* him—under another name. Dalziel."

The other four's eyes opened wide. "Dalziel was really Wolverstone?" James asked.

"The then-Wolverstone's heir, apparently," Del replied. "The old man died late in '16, after we got here."

Gareth was counting years. "Dalziel must have been retired by then."

"Presumably. Regardless, as Duke of St. Ives, Devil knows the new duke well. After reading my letter explaining our predicament, Devil showed it to Wolverstone, reasoning there could be no one better placed to advise us. If you recall, Dalziel was in charge of all British agents on foreign soil for a decade and more, and knows every trick when it comes to couriering sensitive information across the continent and into England. More, as Devil went to literary lengths to point out, Wolverstone is the peer best-placed to oppose Shrewton. Wolverstone owes the king nothing—if anything, the shoe is on the other foot, and His Majesty is well aware of it. If Wolverstone presents evidence that Ferrar junior is the Black Cobra, there'll be nothing the king or Shrewton will dare do to derail the wheels of justice."

Rafe grinned. "I always knew there was a reason we agreed to form a troop with the Cynsters at Waterloo."

Gareth smiled reminiscently. "They were damned fine soliders, even if they weren't regulars."

"In the blood." Logan nodded sagely.

"And their horses were worth killing for," Rafe added.

"We covered their backs often enough, so now they're returning the favor." Del held up his glass, waited until the others touched the rims of theirs to his. "To old comrades-in-arms."

They all drank, then Logan looked at Del. "So has Wolverstone given us the required advice?"

Del nodded. "In detail. First, he confirmed that he's willing to take any proof we turn up and present it through the proper channels—he has all the contacts and the standing to do that. However, he makes it plain that to take down Ferrar junior, said proof will have to be incontrovertible. It has to be clear, instantly obvious, unequivocal, not circumstantial, not something that requires interpretation, let alone knowledge of the situation, to make sense."

Gareth mumured, "So it has to be something that incontestably implicates Ferrar directly."

"Exactly." Del set down his empty glass. "Once we have that proof—and Wolverstone was very clear there is no point in proceeding without the right proof—but once we have it, then he's already put in place a . . . for want of a better word, campaign, a detailed plan of action for us to follow to bring the proof safely to England, and into his hands." Del glanced at the others, lips curving wryly. "Looking over his plan, it's not hard to see why he was such a success in his erstwhile occupation."

"So what are the details?" Logan leaned his arms on the table, his interest plain. The others, too, were waiting.

"We're to make copies of the proof, and then separate and independently make our way home—four carrying copies and one carrying the original. He's sent five sealed letters— five sets of instructions—one for the original, the other four for the decoys. Each letter contains the routes each of us should take back to England and which ports we should use—once we land, there'll be men of his waiting to escort us further. They—our escorts—will know where each of us is to go once in England."

Logan's lips had curved. "I take it Wolverstone's a firm believer in sharing information only with those who need to know?"

Del smiled. "The way we're to handle this, while each of us will know what we're carrying—decoy or original—and what route we'll be taking home, we won't know what any of the rest of us have, or the others' routes. Specifically, the only one who'll know who is carrying the original, and what route they'll be taking home, what port they'll be heading for, is the one of us who draws the original." Del eased back from the table. "Dalziel wants us to draw lots, then immediately part."

Rafe nodded. "That's safer all around." He glanced around the table. "His way, if any of us are caught, we can't give the others away." Face and voice both uncharacteristically sober, he placed his empty glass carefully on the tray. "After the last months of chasing the Black Cobra's gangs, seeing the results of their methods firsthand . . . it's only wise to ensure that if they do take any of us, the others will be safe. We can't tell what we don't know."

A moment passed in silence, each recalling the atrocities they'd seen while leading troops of sowars on raids into the hinterlands and hills, chasing the Black Cobra and the robber gangs that formed a large part of the cult's forces, searching for the evidence—the incontrovertible, irrefutable proof they needed to bring the reign of the Black Cobra to an end.

Gareth drew a long breath, let it out with, "So, we find our proof, then we take it home." He glanced at the others. "On leave, or are we finally resigning our commissions?"

Rafe passed a hand over his face, as if wiping away the stark memories of a moment before. "I'll resign." He, too, glanced at the others, reading faces. "We've all been thinking about it—chatting, joking, but considering nonetheless."

"True." Logan spun his empty glass between his fingers. "And after these last months—and the months to come until we get the proof we need—by the time we do, I'll have had more than enough." He looked up. "I'm ready to go home permanently, too."

Del nodded. "And me." He looked at Gareth.

Who nodded. "I've been campaigning all my adult life—as have all of you. I've enjoyed the campaigns, but this, what we're doing here now, is no longer campaigning. What this country needs isn't military, not cavalry and guns. It needs rulers who rule, and that's not what we are." He glanced at the others. "I suppose what I'm saying is our role here is done."

"Or will be done," Del amended, "once we take down the Black Cobra."

Rafe looked at James. "What about you, stripling?"

Although he'd been one of them since before Waterloo, James was the baby of the group. There was only two years in age between him and Rafe, yet in experience and even more in temperament the difference was immeasurably greater. In knowledge, attitude, and sheer hardened command, Rafe was as old as Del. Rafe had remained a captain by choice, had turned down promotion the better to merge with his men, to inspire and lead. He was a remarkable commander in the field.

Del, Gareth, Logan and Rafe were equals, their strengths not exactly the same but equally respected, each by the others. James, no matter the actions he fought in, the atrocities he observed, the carnage he witnessed, still retained some vestige of the apple-cheeked innocence he'd had when he'd first joined them, a youthful subaltern in their old cavalry troop. Hence their paternalistic affection, their habit of seeing him as much younger, of ribbing him as a junior officer, someone whose welfare they still felt compelled to keep a watchful, if distant, eye on.

Now James shrugged. "If you're all resigning, then I will, too—my parents will be happy to see me home. They've been hinting for the last year that it was time I came back, settled down—all that."

Rafe chuckled. "They've probably got a young lady picked out for you."

Entirely unruffled as he always was by their ribbing, James merely smiled. "Probably."

James was the only one of them with parents still living. Del had two paternal aunts, while Rafe, the younger son of a viscount, had countless connections and siblings he hadn't seen in years, but like Gareth and Logan, he didn't have anyone waiting for him in England.

Returning home. Only James had any real home to return to. For the rest of them, "home" was a nebulous concept they would have to define once they were back on English soil. In returning to England, the older four would, in a sense, be venturing into the unknown, yet for himself Del knew it was time. He wasn't surprised the others felt the same.

He signaled the barboy for another round. When it came, and the boy withdrew, he lifted his glass. "India has made us wealthy, given us more than we ever otherwise would have had. It seems only right to pay the country back by taking down"—glancing at Rafe, he grinned—"by beheading the Black Cobra, and if, as it seems, that will lead us back to England, then that, too, seems fitting." He met the others' eyes. "We're all in this together." He raised his glass, held it out for them to meet it with theirs. "Here's to our eventual return to England."

"Home," Rafe echoed, as the glasses clinked.

They all drank, then Gareth, ever practical, asked, "So how are we faring getting our proof?"

They'd spent the last three months—ever since they'd convinced themselves that Roderick Ferrar, second adjutant to the Governor of Bombay, had to be the Black Cobra—trying to turn up evidence of Ferrar's secret identity, all to no avail. Each now reported their latest forays into what was fast becoming known as "Black Cobra territory," each thrust aimed at uncovering some trail, some clue, some solid connection back to Ferrar. All they'd uncovered were terrorized villages, some burnt to the ground, others with empty huts and no survivors, with evidence of rape and torture all around.

Wanton destruction and a liking for violence for violence's sake were fast becoming the Black Cobra cult's trademark, yet despite all the carnage they'd waded through, not a single piece of evidence had emerged.

"He's clever, I'll give the bastard that," Rafe said. "Every time we find one of his cultists, they've got their instructions from someone else, who they either don't know, or, if they can point a finger, the trail only leads to some other local—"

"Until eventually you hit one who again doesn't know." Logan looked disgusted. "It's like that game of whispers, only in this case, no one has any clue who whispered first."

"The way the Indians relate to one another—the caste system—plays into the Black Cobra's hands," James said. "The cultists unquestioningly obey, and never think it unreasonable that they know nothing about their masters— just that they are their masters, and so must be obeyed."

"It's a veil," Gareth said. "The Black Cobra operates from behind a deliberately maintained veil."

"And being a cult wreathed in all the usual mystery," Rafe added, "the cultists think it only right that the Cobra is never seen, never directly heard—for all we know he sends out his orders on bits of paper passed through that damned veil."

"According to Wolverstone and Devil," Del said, "the entire Ferrar family is widely known to be viciously exploitative—that's why the Earl of Shrewton is in the position he's in. In that respect, Roderick Ferrar seems very much a twig off the same trunk."

"So what's next?" Rafe asked.

They spent the next half hour, and another beer, discussing the villages and outposts they thought worth a visit. "Just riding up, flag waving, will be seen as a challenge," Logan said. "If we can provoke a response, perhaps we'll capture someone with some useful knowledge."

"Getting them to talk will be another matter." Rafe glanced at the others. "It's that yoke of fear—the Black Cobra's got their tongues well-leashed with fear of his retribution."

"Which," James added, "is admittedly ghastly. I can still see the man I cut down last week." He grimaced.

"Nothing we can do other than press harder," Del said. "We need that proof—the incontrovertible evidence implicating Ferrar. Gareth and I will concentrate on trying to shake something loose through Ferrar's contacts with the princelings—we'll start interviewing those he's had dealings with via the governor's office. Given his temperament, he has to have made enemies—with luck one might talk, and resentful princelings are more likely to than villagers."

"True." Logan exchanged a look with Rafe and James. "Meanwhile, we'll keep on stirring up dust in the villages and towns."

"If nothing else," Gareth said, "that should keep the fiend's focus in the field, not closer to home, and give Del and me a bit of cover."

James pulled a face. "You'll have to count me out for the next few weeks—apparently I've drawn a duty-mission. The governor has requested that I take a troop up to Poona and escort his niece back to Bombay."

The others all made commiserating noises as they pushed back from the table and rose.

Rafe clapped James on the shoulder. "Never mind—at least you'll get a chance to put your feet up for a few days. And most of the memsahibs and their darling daughters are spending the monsoon season up there. Who knows? You might even find some engaging distraction."

James snorted. "What you mean is that I'll have to attend formal dinners and make small talk, then dance with giggling girls who bat their lashes, while you and Logan have all the fun chasing the Black Cobra and routing cultists. Thank you, but I'd rather be doing something useful."

Rafe laughed and slung an arm around James's shoulders. "If Logan or I get any cultists to talk, you'll be back in time to help follow up."

"Yes, but just think how boring my next weeks are going to be." Together with Rafe, James headed for the archway leading outside. "I'll deserve something extra-promising when I get back."

Smiling at James's angling for his pick of the missions when he returned from Poona, Del ambled beside Gareth and Logan as they followed the other two outside.

September 2, eighteen days later
East India Company Barracks, Bombay

A hot, dry wind blew relentlessly across the maidan, swirling the dust kicked up by the sepoys practicing formation,
marching as the sun slowly bled in the west.

On the verandah of the barracks, Del sat in a low-slung
wooden chair, feet up on the extendable arms, glass in hand
as, with Gareth similarly at ease beside him, he waited for
the others to join them. Logan and Rafe had been due to
return from their most recent sorties today, and James was
expected back from Poona. It was time to take stock again,
to decide what next to try.

Logan had ridden in with his troop half an hour ago.
Covered in dust, he'd reported to the fort commander, then
crossed to the barracks. Climbing the shallow steps to the
verandah, he'd shaken his head grimly before Del or Gareth
could ask how he'd fared, then gone into the barracks to
wash and change.

Del watched the sepoys drilling tirelessly on the parade
ground, and felt the weight of failure drag. The others, he
knew, felt the same. They'd been pressing relentlessly—in
Rafe's case, increasingly recklessly—trying to pry loose the
vital evidence they needed, but nothing they'd learned had
been sufficient to meet Wolverstone's criteria.

What they had learned had confirmed that Ferrar and no
other was the Black Cobra. Both Rafe and Logan had found
ex-cultists who once had been high in the organization, but
had grown jaded with the Cobra's vicious rule and had successfully fled the Cobra's territory; they'd verified that the
Black Cobra was an "anglo"—an Englishman—moreover
one who spoke with the refined and distinctive accents of
the upper class.

Combined with their previous grounds for suspicion, as
well as the documents and guarded comments Del and Gareth
had managed to tease from various Maratha princelings, there
was absolutely no doubt that they had the right man.

Yet they still had to prove it.

A heavy bootstep heralded Logan. He slumped in a chair alongside them, let his head fall back and closed his eyes.

"No luck?" Gareth asked, although the answer was obvious.

"Worse." Logan didn't open his eyes. "Every village we rode into, the people were cowering. They didn't even want to be seen talking to us. The Black Cobra has them in its coils and they're frightened—and from all we saw, with good reason." Logan paused, then continued, voice lower, eyes still closed, "There were examples of the Black Cobra's vengeance impaled outside most villages—women and children, as well as men."

He drew a shaky breath, then sat up and scrubbed both hands over his face. "It was . . . beyond ghastly." After a moment, he glanced at the other two. "We have to stop this madman."

Del grimaced. "Did you see Rafe?"

"Only early on. He headed further east, up into the hills. He was hoping to find the edges of the Cobra's territory, to see if any village was resisting in the hope they'd trade information for assistance."

Gareth humphed. "Searching for a fight, as always." It was said without rancor.

Logan looked out across the maidan. "Aren't we all?"

Del followed his gaze to where, far beyond the open fort gates, a dust cloud drew steadily nearer.

By the time the cloud had passed through the distant gates, it had resolved into Rafe at the head of the troop of sowars he'd commandeered for his mission.

Just one look at Rafe's face as he drew rein some yards away to spare them the inevitable dust was enough to answer their most urgent question. He hadn't fared any better than Logan in gaining evidence of the Black Cobra's identity.

Handing his reins to the sergeant, Rafe walked to the verandah, weariness—nay, exhaustion—in every line of his long frame. Eschewing the steps, he came to the railing beyond which they sat, crossed his forearms upon it and laid his tousled and dusty blond head on his arms. His voice reached them, muffled, strangely hoarse. "Please tell me that one of you found something—*anything*—we can use to stop this fiend."

None of them replied.

Rafe's shoulders slumped as he sighed, then he lifted his head and they saw his face clearly. Something more than dejection haunted his eyes.

Logan shifted forward. "You found something."

Rafe dragged in a breath, glanced back to where his troop were dispersing, nodded. "At one village where the elders had already bowed to the Black Cobra's demands—did you know he's taking half—*half!*—of what they scratch and eke out of their fields? He's literally taking food from the mouths of babes!"

After a moment, he went on, "There was nothing for us there, but one of the younger men lay in wait for us as we were riding on—he told us of a village further east that was resisting the fiend's demands. We rode there as fast as we could."

His gaze on the maidan, Rafe paused. His voice was lower, gruffer, when he went on, "We were too late. The village had been razed. And there were bodies . . . men, women, and children, raped and mutilated, tortured and burned." After a moment he continued, voice still lower, "It was hell on earth. There was nothing we could do. We burned the bodies, and turned back."

None of the others said anything; there was nothing they could say to take the haunting vision, the knowledge, away.

Eventually Rafe drew a massive breath and turned to face them. "So what's happened here?"

"I returned empty-handed," Logan volunteered.

Del glanced at Gareth, then offered, "We've learned more—been told much more—but it's all hearsay. Nothing we can put before a court—nothing good enough to take home."

"That's the positive side," Gareth said. "On the negative,

Ferrar now knows beyond doubt that we're watching him. Investigating him."

Logan shrugged. "That was inevitable. He couldn't be oh-so-clever and yet miss the fact we're here, on Hastings's direct orders, and with no mission we've seen fit to divulge."

Rafe nodded. "At this point, it can hardly hurt. Perhaps knowing we're after him will make him careless."

Del humphed. "So far he's been unbelievably shrewd in keeping everything unincriminating. We've turned up even more of those documents, more or less contracts he's enacted with various princelings, but the cheeky sod always uses his special Black Cobra seal on the correspondence, and he signs with a mark, not a signature."

"And his writing is English-grammar-school-standard," Gareth added. "It could be any of ours."

Another moment of glum resignation passed, then Rafe asked, "Where's James?"

"Not in yet, apparently," Del replied. "He's expected today—I thought he'd be in earlier, but he must have been held up."

"Probably the lady didn't approve of riding above a sedate canter." Rafe managed a weak smile, then turned back to the maidan.

"There's a troop coming in," Logan said.

The comment focused all eyes on the group approaching the gates. It wasn't a full troop, more a mounted escort riding alongside a wagon. It was the slow, steady pace the small cavalcade held to, as much as the somber deliberateness of the sowars, that told them this wasn't good news.

A minute ticked past as the cavalcade drew nearer, cleared the gates.

"Oh, no." Rafe pushed away from the railing and started across the maidan.

Narrowed eyes locked on the cavalcade, Del, Gareth and Logan slowly came to their feet, then Del swore and the three vaulted over the railing and headed after Rafe.

He waved the cavalcade to a halt. As he strode down the wagon's side, he demanded to be told what had happened.

The head sowar, a sergeant, dismounted and quickly followed. "We are very sorry, Captain-sahib—there was nothing we could do."

Rafe reached the tail of the wagon first and halted. Face paling under his tan, he stared at what lay in the bed.

Del came up beside him, saw the three bodies—carefully laid out, but nothing could disguise the mutilation, the torture, the agony that had preceded death.

Distantly conscious of Logan, then Gareth, ranging behind him, Del looked down on James MacFarlane's body.

It took a moment to register that beside him lay his lieutenant and the troop's corporal.

It was Rafe—who of them all had seen more of the Black Cobra's lethal handiwork than any one man should ever have to bear—who turned away with a vicious oath.

Del seized his arm. Simply said, "Let me."

He had to drag in a breath, physically drag his gaze from the bodies before he could raise his head and look at the waiting sowar. "What happened?"

Even to him, his voice sounded deadly.

The sowar wasn't a coward. With creditable composure, he lifted his chin and came to attention. "We were more than halfway back on the road from Poona, when the Captain-sahib realized there were horsemen chasing us. We rode on quickly, but then the Captain-sahib stopped at a place where the road narrows, and sent us all on. The lieutenant stayed with him, along with three others. The Captain-sahib sent the rest of us all pell-mell on with the memsahib."

Del glanced at the wagon bed. "When was this?"

"Earlier today, Colonel-sahib."

"Who sent you back?"

The sowar shifted. "When we came within sight of Bombay, the memsahib insisted we go back. The Captain-sahib had ordered us to stay with her all the way to the fort, but she was very agitated. She allowed only two of us to go with her to the governor's house. The rest of us went back to see if we could help the Captain-sahib and the lieutenant." The sowar paused, then went on more quietly, "But there were only these bodies left when we reached the place."

"They took two of your troop?"

"We could see where they had dragged them away behind their horses, Colonel-sahib. We didn't think following would do any good."

Despite the calmness of the words, the outward stoicism of the native troops, Del knew every one of them would be railing inside.

As was he, Gareth, Logan, Rafe.

But there was nothing they could do.

He nodded, stepped back, drawing Rafe with him.

"We will be taking them to the infirmary, Colonel-sahib."

"Yes." He met the man's eyes, nodded. "Thank you."

Numbly, he turned. Releasing Rafe, Del led the way back to the barracks.

As they climbed the shallow steps, Rafe, as usual, put their tortured thoughts into words.

"For the love of God, *why*?"

Why?

The question rebounded again and again between them, refashioned and rephrased in countless ways. James might have been younger than the rest of them, but he'd been neither inexperienced nor a glory-hunter—and he wasn't the one they called "Reckless."

"So *why* in all hell did he make a stand, rather than at least *try* to escape? While they were moving, they had a chance— he had to have known that." Rafe slumped in his usual chair at their table in the officers' bar.

After a moment, Del answered, "He had a reason—that's why."

Logan sipped the arrack Del had ordered instead of their

usual beer. The bottle stood in the center of the table, already half empty. Eyes narrowed, he said, "It had to have been something about the governor's niece."

"Thought of that." Gareth set down his empty glass and reached for the bottle. "I asked the sowars—they said she rode well, like the devil. She didn't hold them up. And she tried to veto James's plan to stay behind, but he pulled rank and ordered her on."

"Humph." Rafe drained his glass, then held out his hand for the bottle. "So what was it? James might be lying in the infirmary very dead, but damned if I'm going to accept that he stayed back on a whim—not him."

"No," Del said. "You're right—not him."

"Heads up," Rafe said, his gaze going down the verandah. "Skirts on parade."

The others turned their heads to look. The skirts in question were on a slender young lady—a very English lady with a pale, porcelain face and sleek brown hair secured in a knot at the back of her head. She stood just inside the bar and peered through the shadows, noting the groups of officers dotted here and there. Her gaze reached them in the corner, paused, but then the barboy came forward and she turned to him.

But at her query, the barboy pointed to them. The young lady looked their way, then straightened, thanked the boy and, head high, glided down the verandah toward them.

An Indian girl swathed in a sari hovered like a shadow behind her.

They all rose, slowly, as the young lady approached. She was of slightly less than average height; given their size, and that they were all looking as grim as they felt, they must have seemed intimidating, but she didn't falter.

Before she reached them, she halted and spoke to her maid, instructing her in soft tones to wait a little way away.

Then she came on. As she neared, they could see her face was pale, set, features tightly, rigidly controlled. Her eyes were faintly red-rimmed, the tip of her small nose pink.

But her rounded chin was set in determined lines.

Her gaze scanned them as she came to the table, circling, not on their faces, but at shoulder-and-collar-level—reading their rank. When her gaze reached Del, it stopped. Halting, she lifted her eyes to his face. "Colonel Delborough?"

Del inclined his head. "Ma'am?"

"I'm Emily Ensworth, the governor's niece. I . . ." She glanced briefly at the others. "If I could trouble you for a word in private, Colonel?"

Del hesitated, then said, "Every man about this table is an old friend and colleague of James MacFarlane. We were all working together. If your business with me has anything to do with James, I would ask that you speak before us all."

She studied him for a moment, weighing his words, then she nodded. "Very well."

Between Logan and Gareth sat James's empty chair. None of them had had the heart to push it away. Gareth now held it for Miss Ensworth.

"Thank you." She sat. Which left her looking directly at the three-quarters empty bottle of arrack.

With the others, Del resumed his seat.

Miss Ensworth glanced at him. "I realize it might be irregular, but if I could have a small glass of that . . . ?"

Del met her hazel eyes. "It's arrack."

"I know."

He signalled to the barboy to bring another glass. While he did, Miss Ensworth fiddled below the table's edge with the reticule she'd been carrying. They hadn't truly noticed it before; Miss Ensworth was neatly rounded, softly lush, and none of them had noticed much else.

Then the boy delivered the glass, and Del poured a half measure for her.

She accepted it with a strained almost-smile and took a small sip. She wrinkled her nose, but then gamely took a larger dose. Lowering the glass, she looked at Del. "I asked at the gate and they told me. I'm very sorry that Captain MacFarlane didn't make it back."

His face like stone, Del inclined his head in acknowledgment. Hands clasped on the table, he said, "If you could tell us what happened from the beginning, it would help us understand." *Why James gave up his life.* He left the last unsaid, but the others clearly heard it. He suspected Miss Ensworth did, too.

She nodded. "Yes, of course." She cleared her throat. "We started very early from Poona—Captain MacFarlane was very insistent, and I wasn't averse, so we left at sunrise. He seemed keen to get on, so I was surprised when we ambled at a quite ordinary pace at first, but then—and I realize now it was as soon as we were out of sight of the town—he dug in his heels and from then we went at a cracking pace. Once he realized I could ride . . . well, we just rode as fast as we could. I didn't understand why—not then—but he was riding alongside, so I knew when he saw the riders chasing us—I saw them, too."

"Could you tell if they were private militiamen, or were they robbers?" Del asked.

She met his gaze directly. "I think they were Black Cobra cultists—they wore black silk scarves tied about their heads and wound around their faces. I've heard that's their . . . insignia."

Del nodded. "That's correct. So what happened once James spotted them?"

"We rode even faster. I assumed we would simply outrun them—we'd seen them on a curve so they were some way back along the road—and at first that's what we did. But then I think they must have cut across somewhere, because suddenly they were much closer. I still thought we could outrun them, but then we came to a spot where the road passes between two large rocks, and Captain MacFarlane stopped. He gave orders for most of the sowars to go on with me and make sure I got to the fort safely. He and a handful were going to make a stand and hold the cultists back."

She paused, dragged in a breath, then remembered the glass in her hand and drained it. "I tried to argue, but he would have none of it. He drew me aside—ahead—and gave me this." From beneath the table, she drew out a packet— a blank sheet of parchment folded and sealed about other documents. She set it on the table, pushed it toward Del.

"Captain MacFarlane asked me to bring this to you. He said he had to make certain it reached you, no matter the cost. He made me promise to get it to you . . . and then there wasn't time to argue." Her gaze fixed on the packet, she drew a shaky breath. "We could hear the cultists coming—ululating, you know how they do. They weren't far, and . . . I had to go. If I was going to bring that to you, I had to leave then . . . so I did. He turned back with a few men, and the rest came with me."

"And you sent them back when you came within sight of safety." Gareth spoke gently. "You did the best you could."

Del put a hand on the packet and drew it to him. "And you did the right thing."

She blinked several times, then lifted her chin. Her gaze remained fixed on the packet. "I don't know what's in that—I didn't look. But whatever it is . . . I hope it's worth it, worth the sacrifice he made." At last she lifted her gaze to Del's face. "I'll leave it in your hands, Colonel, as I promised Captain MacFarlane I would."

She pushed back from the table.

They all rose. Gareth drew back her chair. "Allow me to organize an escort for you back to the governor's house."

Gareth's gaze touched Del's, and he nodded. No sense taking any unnecessary chances with Miss Ensworth.

Their interaction had passed over Emily Ensworth's head. She nodded graciously to Gareth. "Thank you, Major."

Then she inclined her head to Del and the other two. "Good evening, Colonel. Gentlemen."

"Miss Ensworth." They all bowed, waited as Gareth led her away, then resumed their seats.

They stared at the packet lying on the table before Del. Without a word, they waited for Gareth to return.

The instant he did, Del picked up the packet. Removing the outer sheet, he laid it flat, revealing it was blank. It had been wrapped around a single document, a letter, the seal already broken.

Del unfolded the letter, briefly scanned. After a quick glance around, he leaned on the table and, voice low, read the contents aloud.

The letter was addressed to one of the more influential Maratha princelings, one Govind Holkar. It began innocently enough, with nothing more sinister than social news revolving about what was loosely termed the younger Government House set. But after those first paragraphs, the tone of the letter changed to one of offer, a blatant inducement to persuade Holkar to commit more men and resources to the Black Cobra cult.

The further he read, the more Del frowned. Reaching the end, he concluded with, "And, as usual, it's signed with the mark of the Black Cobra."

Letting the letter fall through his fingers to rest on the table, Del shook his head. "This isn't anything more than we've already got—than James knew we already had."

Gareth reached for the letter. "There has to be something more in it—something concealed."

Del sat back, feeling oddly dead inside, and watched while Gareth silently went through the letter. Then Gareth raised his head, grimly shook it. "If there is, I can't see it."

Logan took the letter, read it, then, with a swift shake of his head, passed it to Rafe in his corner.

It didn't take Rafe long to scan the single sheet. He slumped back in his chair, the letter held in one hand at arm's length. "Why?" He shook the letter. "Damn it, James, *why* did you give your life for this? There's nothing here!"

Rafe flung the letter toward the table. It flipped and landed upside down. He scowled at it. "That's not worth—"

When he said nothing more, Del glanced at him and saw him staring, as if mesmerized, at the letter. As if it had transformed into their nemesis.

"Oh, Lord," Rafe breathed. "It can't be." He reached for the letter.

For the first time in all the years he'd known him, Del saw Rafe Carstairs's hand shake.

Rafe lifted the letter, held it closer to his face, staring. . . .

"It's the seal." Voice firming, Rafe leaned forward and turned the letter, held it so the seal, largely intact, was on a level with the others' eyes. "He's used his own seal. Bloody Ferrar finally made a mistake, and James—youthful-sharp-eyes-and-even-sharper-wits James—caught it."

Gareth reached out and took the letter. He was the most familiar with Ferrar's seal; he'd been the one to go through the man's desk. He studied the imprint closely, then looked up and met Rafe's eyes. Nodded. "It's his." The suppressed excitement coming off both of them was palpable.

Del asked, "Could he say someone had stolen the seal and used it to implicate him? One of us, for instance?"

A slow smile spread across Gareth's face. He looked at Del. "That won't wash. It's a seal ring, and it never leaves Ferrar's pinky. In fact, short of him losing the finger, it can't. All the clerks and secretaries at Government House know that—he makes quite a show of his lineage and its accoutrements. The whole office knows about his seal ring—and there's not another like it in all of India."

"Could it have been duplicated?" Logan asked.

Gareth handed him the letter. "See what you think. And anyway, why would anyone bother?"

Examining the imprint, Logan grunted. "I suppose that's why people use seals, but you're right—this has curlicues, swirls, and they look like they're cut to different depths. It wouldn't be easy to duplicate."

"It doesn't matter," Rafe said. "What matters is that *we* know that's real—and so does the Black Cobra." He met the others' eyes, excitement plain in his. "And I've just realized the true beauty of Wolverstone's plan."

Del frowned. "What? Beyond being the most effective way for us to get this back to England."

Rafe checked their surroundings, then leaned in, forearms on the table. He spoke soft, low, quickly. "He told us to make copies, and then separate and head home. What do you think Ferrar's going to think—and do—once he learns we've done that, as of course he will? You said it yourself—he knows we're investigating him. Suddenly, without warning—worse, immediately after James's death at the hands of the Black Cobra—we up stakes and resign, something we've been thinking of, but no one else knows that. And, to cap it off, we all head home by *different* routes. What will he think? What will he do?"

Logan had caught his enthusiam. "He'll think we've found something that incriminates him."

"And he'll come after us, and by that very action prove the validity of our evidence." Del nodded. "You're right." He looked at the others, met each gaze. "Gentlemen, thanks to James, we have our proof. Thanks to Devil Cynster and Wolverstone, we have a plan and know what we have to do. Thanks to Hastings, we have the freedom to do as we wish. I vote we follow the plan, carry out our last orders, and bring the Black Cobra to justice."

While Del had been speaking, Rafe had recharged their glasses. They each claimed theirs.

"To success," Del said, raising his glass.

"To justice," Gareth offered, putting his glass alongside.

"To James MacFarlane's memory." Logan raised his glass to the other two.

They all looked at Rafe.

Who raised his glass to theirs. "To beheading the Black Cobra."

They clinked, then drained their glasses.

Setting them down with a snap, they rose and left the bar.

September 14, twelve days later
Bombay

They met in the back room of the Red Turkey Cock, a smoke-filled tavern down a minor side street in one of the seedier native quarters of Bombay.

The tavern's back room was a small square chamber with no window, the only entrance the doorway behind the scarred bar through which they'd entered. Logan, the last to arrive, let a bamboo screen rattle down to the floor behind him, a sufficient impediment to interested eyes. With Gulah, a massive ex-sepoy, manning the bar, and the otherwise flimsy walls reinforced by countless boxes and crates stacked against them, they weren't too worried about interested ears.

"I don't think I was followed." Logan sounded disappointed as he slipped onto the last of the four rickety chairs set about a square wooden table.

"I don't think I was either," Gareth said. "But in this district, four anglos like us will be noticed and remembered—the Black Cobra will hear about our meeting without a doubt."

"Ferrar knows something's up." A grim smile curved Del's lips. "He knows we've resigned, and isn't swallowing the gossip that we're all devastated because of what happened to James. He's been asking questions about our plans for the future."

"Perhaps he'd like to recruit us?" Rafe said. "Come to think of it, that's a tack we never tried."

"Because he'd never believe it. The man isn't just a cold-blooded killer—"

"Torturer, maimer, fiend," Rafe supplied.

"—he's clever, and cunning, and a great deal too powerful. So"—Del looked at Gareth—"are we ready to move against him?"

Gareth reached down, lifted a woven basket from the floor beside his chair, and set it on the table. His chair squeaked as he reached into the basket and lifted out four wood-and-brass cylindrical scroll-holders. "As ordered. The subcontinent's version of a diplomatic pouch."

The scroll-holders were identical, each about ten inches long and a bit more than two inches in diameter. Formed from strips of rosewood clamped together by brass bands, their lids were secured by a complicated set of brass levers of varying length and thickness.

They each took a holder, fiddled. "How do you open them?" Logan asked.

"Watch." Setting the basket back on the floor, Gareth picked up one holder and deftly moved the six levers, one after the other. "It has to be done in that order, or the metal teeth inside don't disengage. Try it."

They all practiced. Gareth insisted they worked at it until they could open and close the holders by touch alone. "You might need to at some point—who knows?"

Rafe reached across and took the holder Gareth held, compared it with the one he'd picked up. "They truly are identical."

"I don't think anyone could tell them apart." Logan looked at Del, then Rafe. "So we have the holders. Now for what goes in them."

From his pocket, Del drew the sets of instructions Wolverstone had sent. "Five packets." He separated out one with *Original* scrawled across a corner. "That one goes with the real letter. These"—he fanned out four identical packets—"are the decoys' instructions. But we only need three."

Now that James was gone.

They all looked at the four letters. Rafe sighed. "Shuffle the four, I'll select one, and we can open it and see what form of instructions we're going to find when we open our own sets later."

"Good idea." Del shuffled the four packets, held them out. Rafe drew one and handed it to Logan.

Logan took it, opened it, scanned the sheets inside, then handed them on to Gareth. "Comprehensive, but not specific, of course. The route we should follow, but no dates, no specified modes of travel. He does specify which English port we're supposed to head for—Brighton, in this instance. Apparently we'll be met by two men, Dalziel's ex-operatives, who will have our route through England and our ultimate destination, neither of which are included here."

Del nodded as he received the sheets from Gareth. He scanned them, then handed them to Rafe, who exchanged them for four slim packets he'd pulled from his inside coat pocket. "The three copies and the original." Rafe cast a cursory glance over the now-to-be-discarded set of instructions while Del and the other three carefully unfolded and compared the copies and the original.

Reaching the end of the instructions, Rafe looked up. "We should destroy this."

Logan held out his hand. "I'll burn it." Rafe handed the folded sheets over.

Del and Gareth had lined up the four scroll-holders across the table. They laid one instructions packet and one letter before each holder, making sure the original letter with its incriminating seal was paired with the appropriately marked instructions.

"As per Wolverstone's directions," Del said, "I sent him word we were putting his plan into action. It went ten days ago by fast frigate, so he'll know we're heading home in good time to have his men waiting at the ports."

Rafe reached out, drew the nearest scroll-holder, letter and instructions to him, and set about opening the holder. "Now we do as he suggested and draw lots—in this case, scroll-holders." He proceeded to carefully roll the letter and instructions and insert them into the holder.

The others followed suit, smiling faintly, all knowing that Del had been about to try to pull rank and argue that he should take the original.

He wouldn't have succeeded—they'd resigned their commissions effective from this morning. They were all in this together, and equals in all ways now.

Reclosing his holder, Rafe asked, "Where's that basket?"

Gareth hauled it back up. Rafe took it, dropped the scroll-holder he'd packed inside, then collected the holders from the others as they reclosed them, sealing in the letters and instructions.

"Right." Rafe stood, closed the top of the large basket

with his hands, then shook and rattled the holders, mixing them. With one last flourishing swirl, he set the basket down in the middle of the table and sat again.

"All together," Del said. "We reach in, each takes a holder at the same time, whichever is closest." He met the others' eyes. "We don't open them here. We leave this room together, but from the moment we pass through the door of the Red Turkey Cock, we go our separate ways."

That morning, they'd moved out of the barracks. Over the years, each had gathered small households who traveled with them; those households were now packed and waiting, ready to leave, but all in separate locations.

They exchanged one last glance, then sat forward, reached into the basket. They waited until each of them had grasped one of the cylindrical holders, then, as one, drew them forth.

"Right," Rafe said, his gaze locked on his holder.

"Wait." Gareth swept the empty basket from the table, and replaced it with a bottle of arrack and four glasses. He splashed pale amber liquor into each glass, then set the bottle down.

They each took a glass and rose.

Del held his out. "Gentlemen." He looked at each of them in turn. "To our continued health. Godspeed, and may luck be with us."

They knew the Black Cobra would come after them; they knew they'd need all the luck they could get.

Gareth raised his glass. "Until we meet again."

"On the green shores of England," Logan added.

Rafe hesitated, then raised his glass. "To the death of the Black Cobra."

They all nodded, then drank, drained their glasses and set them down.

They turned to the doorway. Lifting the bamboo screen, they ducked beneath it, walking out into the smoky bar.

Picking their way past rickety tables, they reached the open tavern doorway and moved out onto the dusty steps.

Del halted and held out his hand. "Good luck."

They all shook hands, each with the other.

For one last instant, they stood and simply looked at each other.

Then Rafe stepped down into the dusty street. "May God and St. George be with us all." With a last salute, he walked away.

They parted, each disappearing by a different route into the bustling city.

September 15, two nights later
Bombay

"We have a problem."

The voice fitted the setting, the clipped, aristocratic accents appropriate to the beauty, the elegance, the wanton luxury pervading the enclosed courtyard of the discreet bungalow tucked away on the fringe of the fashionable district of Bombay.

No one seeing the house from outside would look twice. The street frontage was unremarkable, like many others nearby. But on entering the front foyer, one was struck by a sense of subdued elegance, yet the front reception rooms—the rooms those who called socially might see—were nothing more than quietly refined, restrained and rather spare.

Not quite soulless, yet the chosen few who were invited further quickly sensed a different ambiance, one that filled the senses with ever-increasing richness.

It wasn't merely a show of wealth, but a deliberately sensual display. The further one penetrated into the private rooms, the richer, more wantonly yet tastefully luxurious the furnishings, the more artful, and graceful, the settings.

The courtyard, surrounded by the private rooms of the owner, was the apogee of restful, sensual delight. A long tiled pool glimmered in the moonlight. Trees and shrubs lined the whitewashed walls, while the open windows and doors gave access to mysteriously dark and inviting comforts. The exotic perfume of a temple flower tree wafted in the night breeze, the shed blossoms lying like snippets of the costliest silk scattered on the stone paving.

"Oh?" A second voice answered the first through the cool dark.

The speakers were on the extended open terrace that jutted from the owner's private sitting room into the courtyard. The second speaker reclined on a sofa piled with silk cushions, while the first paced the edge of the terrace, his bootheels creating a quiet tattoo—one that held a certain tension.

A third man watched silently from an armchair beside the sofa.

The night's shadows cloaked them all.

"Damn Govind Holkar!" The first speaker paused to rake a hand through thick hair. "I can't believe he left it this long to send word!"

"Word of what?" the second asked.

"He lost my last letter—the one I sent over a month ago trying to persuade him to give us more men. *That* letter."

"By lost, you mean . . . ?"

"I mean that it went missing from the desk in Holkar's room at the governor's palace in Poona while that damned hound of Hastings's, MacFarlane, just happened to be there, waiting to escort the governor's niece back to Bombay."

"When did this happen?" The second voice was no longer so languid.

"On the second of the month. At least that's the day Holkar realized the letter was gone. That was also the day MacFarlane left Poona with his troop and the governor's niece at dawn. Holkar sent his cultists after them—"

"Don't tell me." The until-then-silent man's baritone rumbled, a contrast to the others' lighter voices. "They killed MacFarlane but didn't find the letter."

"Exactly." The first speaker's voice dripped frustrated ire.

"So that's why we killed MacFarlane—I did wonder." The second speaker's cool tones showed little emotion. "I take it they didn't learn anything pertinent from him before he died?"

"No. But one of the sowars who made a stand with him eventually revealed that MacFarlane gave the governor's niece a packet before sending her on." The first speaker held up a hand to keep the others from interrupting. "I got word from Holkar only this morning—when he realized the letter had reached Bombay, he decamped to Satara, *then* he sent me word."

"We can deal with Holkar appropriately later," the second speaker put in.

"Indeed." Anticipation colored the first speaker's voice. "We will. However, once I knew about the letter, I had Larkins see what he could ferret out from the governor's staff. Apparently, Miss Ensworth, the niece, was greatly distressed when she rode in, but later that afternoon, she took a maid and went to the fort. The maid was overheard saying that, on learning at the gates of MacFarlane's death, the lady searched out Colonel Delborough, found him in the officers' bar, and gave him a packet."

"So there's no reason to pursue this Miss Ensworth. Even if she read the letter, she knows nothing of any worth."

"True." The first speaker added, "And that's just as well, because she's leaving any day to return to England."

The second speaker waved. "Ignore her. So Delborough has the letter, and Holkar is therefore compromised. All his own fault. We'll just have to find another source of men, and the way our recruitment efforts have been progressing lately, I can't see Holkar as any great loss."

Silence fell, but it was strained, pregnant with unresolved tension.

The first speaker broke it. "That's not why we have to get the letter back."

The man with the deeper voice spoke again. "Why bother? It's not as if Delborough can make anything more of it than of the other missives of ours his little group has gathered.

They don't contain anything to link you, personally, with the Black Cobra. Any suspicion he bears is simply that— suspicion. Suspicion he won't dare air."

"It's not what's *in* the damned letter that's the problem." Again the first speaker raked a hand through his hair. He turned from the other two, pacing again. "It's what's *on* the damned letter. I sealed it with my personal seal."

"*What?*" The second speaker's voice was incredulous. "You *can't* be serious."

"I am. I know I shouldn't have done it, but what chance was there this letter of all letters—going to Poona—would end back in Bombay, in Delborough's hands?" The first speaker spread his arms. "It's bizarre."

"But what possessed you to write a letter from the Black Cobra and use your own damned seal?" The baritone's accents were sharply condemnatory.

"It was necessary," the first speaker snapped. "I had to get the letter off that day, or we would have lost another week— you'll remember we discussed it. At the time we were desperate for more men, Delborough and his cohorts were making life difficult, and Holkar seemed our best bet. We agreed I should write, and it was urgent. But the Poona courier decided to leave early—the officious beggar actually had the gall to stand in my doorway and watch me finish the letter. He was itching to leave—if I'd ordered him out, told him to close the door and wait outside, he would have left. He was looking for any excuse to go without my letter."

Still pacing, the first speaker twisted the signet ring on the little finger of his right hand. "Everyone in the office—the damn courier included—knows about my seal ring. With him standing there, I could hardly reach into my pocket, draw out the Black Cobra seal and use it—with him watching my every move. In the circumstances, I decided using my own seal was the lesser of all evils—it's not as if Holkar doesn't know who I am."

"Hmm." The second speaker sounded resigned. "Well, we can hardly allow you to be exposed." The second speaker exchanged a glance with the baritone. "That would definitely put a dent in our enterprise. So"—gaze reverting to the pacing man, the second speaker briskly stated, "we'll just have to locate Delborough and get this incriminating letter back."

September 16, the following night
Bombay

"Delborough and his three remaining colleagues, together with their households, left Bombay two days ago."

Silence greeted the first speaker's terse announcement. Once again the three conspirators had gathered in the night-shrouded courtyard—one on the sofa, one in the armchair, the other pacing the terrace above the glimmering pool.

"Indeed?" the second speaker eventually said. "That's disturbing. Still, I can't see Hastings acting—"

"They haven't gone back to Calcutta." Reaching the end of the terrace, the first speaker swung back. "I told you a week ago—they've resigned! They are, by all accounts, heading back to England."

Another lengthy silence ensued, then the baritone inquired, "Are you sure they're even bothering with this letter? Easy enough to miss a seal, especially if concentrating on the information inside. They've laid hands on similar letters before, and known well enough such documents would get them nowhere."

"I'd like to believe that—that they've given up and are on their way home—believe me, I would." The first speaker's agitated pace didn't ease. "But our spies have reported they met in a back room in some seedy bar in town two days ago. When they came out, each was carrying one of those wooden scroll-holders the locals use to ferry important documents—and then they parted. Went their separate ways. Those four have been together since long before they reached these shores—why would they each go home by completely different routes?"

On the sofa, the second speaker sat straighter. "Do you know which way each has gone?"

"Delborough's done the obvious—he's taken a ship of the line to Southampton. Exactly as if he were simply heading home. Hamilton took a sloop to Aden, as if he were ferrying some diplomatic communication along the way—but I've checked, and he isn't. Monteith and Carstairs have vanished. Monteith's household is due to leave shortly on a company ship for Bournemouth, but he's not with them and they don't know where he is. Their orders are to go to an inn outside Bournemouth and to wait there until he comes. Carstairs has only one man, a Pathan who's as loyal as they come, and they've both disappeared. I've had all the passenger and crew lists combed, but there's no sign of anyone who might conceivably be either Monteith or Carstairs leaving Bombay by sea. Larkins believes they've gone overland, or at least by land to some other port. He's put men on their trail, but it'll be days, perhaps weeks, before we hear if they've located them."

"What orders did you give those you sent after them?" the second speaker asked.

"To kill them, and anyone with them, and above all, to retrieve those bloody scroll-holders."

"Indeed." A momentary pause ensued, then the second speaker said, "So we have four men heading to England—one with the original document and three presumably as decoys. If the letter with your seal gets into the wrong hands in England, then we'll face a very serious problem indeed."

The second speaker exchanged a glance with the man in the armchair, then looked at the first speaker. "You're right. We have to get that letter back. You did precisely right in loosing our hounds and sending them on the hunt. However . . ." After another glance at the other man, the second speaker continued, "I believe, in the circumstances, that we should head home, too. Should our hounds fail us, and Delborough and the other three reach England's shores, then given the bounty the Black Cobra brings us, it would be wise for us to be there, close to the action, to ensure the original letter never gets into the hands of anyone likely or able to interfere with our enterprise."

The first speaker nodded. "There's a fast frigate just in from Calcutta. She'll be sailing the day after tommorrow for Southampton."

"Excellent!" The second speaker rose. "Secure passage on it for us and our staffs. Who knows? We might reach Southampton in time to welcome the importunate colonel."

"Indeed." The first speaker smiled thinly. "I'll take great delight in seeing him receive his just reward."

The
Untamed Bride

One

December 11, 1822
Southampton Water, England

*D*el stood on the deck of the *Princess Louise*, the twelve-hundred-ton East Indiaman on which he and his small household had left Bombay, and watched the Southampton docks draw steadily nearer.

The wind whipped his hair, sent chill fingers sliding beneath his greatcoat collar. From horizon to horizon, the sky was an unrelieved steel-gray, but at least it wasn't raining; he was thankful for small mercies. After the warmth of India, and the balmy days rounding Africa, the change in temperature as they'd headed north over the last week had been an uncomfortable reminder of the reality of an English winter.

Artfully angled, the ship surged on the tide, aligning with the dock, the distance between lessening with every moment, the raucous cries of wheeling gulls a strident counterpoint to the bellows of the bosun as he directed the crew in the dicey business of bringing the heavy ship alongside the timber dock.

Del scanned the dockside crowd waiting to greet those on board. He was under no illusions; the instant he stepped off the gangplank, the Black Cobra's game would be afoot again. He felt restless, impatient for action—the same compulsion he was accustomed to feeling in those moments on the battlefield when, with his horse skittish beneath him, held on a tight rein, he would wait with his men for the order to charge. The same anticipation rode him now, yet with sharpened spurs.

Contrary to his expectations, the trip had been anything but uneventful. They'd sailed from Bombay only to fall foul of a storm, which had left them limping down the African coast with one of their three masts crippled. Once they'd reached Cape Town, repairs had taken three full weeks. While there, his batman, Cobby, had ferreted out the information that Roderick Ferrar had passed through a week ahead of them, on the *Elizabeth*, a fast frigate, also bound for Southampton.

He'd taken note, and so hadn't fallen victim to the knives of the two cult assassins left in Cape Town who had subsequently joined the *Princess Louise* as crew, and lain in wait for him on two separate moonless nights as they'd sailed up the west coast of Africa.

Luckily, the cultists had a superstitious aversion to firearms. Both assassins were now feeding the fishes, but Del suspected they'd merely been scouts, sent to do what they could if they could.

The Black Cobra itself lay ahead of him, coiled between him and his goal.

Wherever that proved to be.

Gripping the railing of the bridge deck, which, as a senior company officer—albeit resigned—he'd been given the freedom, he looked down at the main deck, to where his household staff—Mustaf, his general factotum, tall and thin, Amaya, Mustaf's short, rotund wife who served as Del's housekeeper, and Alia, their niece and maid-of-all-work—sat on their piled bags, ready to disembark the instant Cobby gave the signal.

Cobby himself, the only Englishman in Del's employ,

short of stature, wiry, quick and canny, and cocky as only a cockney lad could be, stood by the main railing at the point where the gangplank would be rolled out, chatting amiably with some sailors. Cobby would be first among the passengers to disembark. He would scout the immediate area, then, if all was clear, signal Mustaf to bring the women down.

Del would bring up the rear, then, once they'd assembled on the dock, lead the way directly up the High Street to the Dolphin Inn.

As luck would have it, Wolverstone had nominated the inn Del habitually used when passing through Southampton. He hadn't, however, been there for years, not since he'd set sail for India in late '15, just over seven years ago.

It felt like more.

He was quite certain he'd aged more than seven years, and the last nine months, while they'd been hunting the Black Cobra, had been the most draining. He almost felt old.

Every time he thought of James MacFarlane, he felt helpless.

Seeing more scurrying below, hearing the change in the bosun's orders, feeling the slight bump as the padding slung along the ship's side met the dock, Del shook off all thoughts of the past and determinedly fixed his mind on the immediate future.

Sailors leapt down to the dock, hauling thick ropes to the capstans to secure the ship. Hearing the heavy rattle and splash as the anchor went down, then the squealing scrape as the railing was opened and the gangplank angled out, Del headed for the companionway to the main deck.

He swung off it in time to see Cobby scamper down the gangplank.

Reconnaissance, in this instance, wasn't simply a matter of scanning for those with dark skins. Southampton was one of the busiest ports in the world, and there were countless Indians and men of other dark-skinned races among the crews. But Cobby knew what to look for—the furtiveness, the attention locked on Del while attempting to remain inconspicuous. If there were cultists waiting to strike, Del was confident Cobby would spot them.

Yet it was more likely the cultists would watch and wait—they preferred to strike in less populated surrounds where escape after the event was more assured.

Del strolled to stand with Mustaf, Amaya and Alia. Mustaf nodded, then went back to scanning the crowd; he'd been a sowar—a cavalryman—until a knee injury had seen him pensioned off. The knee didn't discompose him in other ways; he was still a good man in a fight.

Alia bobbed her head, then resumed casting shy glances at the young sailors who rushed back and forth along the deck.

Amaya looked up at Del with liquid brown eyes. "It is very very cold here, Colonel-sahib. Colder than my cousin's house in Simla in the winter. I am being very very glad I was buying these shawls from Kashmir. They are just the thing."

Del smiled. Both Amaya and Alia were well wrapped in the thick woolen shawls. "When we stop at a big town, we'll have to get you some English coats. And gloves, too. They'll help keep out the wind."

"*Ai*, yes—the wind, it is like a knife. I am understanding that saying now." Amaya nodded, plump hands folded in her lap, thin gold bangles on her wrists peeking from beneath the edge of one shawl.

Despite her sweet face and matronly disposition, Amaya was quick-witted and observant. As for Alia, she would instantly obey any order from her uncle, aunt, Del or Cobby. When necessary, the small group operated as a unit; Del wasn't overly worried over having Amaya and Alia with them, even on the upcoming, more dangerous leg of their journey.

Regardless, knowing the Black Cobra cultists' vindictiveness, he wouldn't take the chance of leaving the women anywhere, even with Mustaf to guard them. To strike at him, the

Black Cobra was perfectly capable of wiping out his household, simply to inspire fear, and to demonstrate his power.

Human life had long ago lost all meaning for the Black Cobra.

A shrill whistle pulled Del's attention back to the dock. Cobby caught his eye, snapped a jaunty salute. *All clear.*

"Come." Del took Amaya's arm and helped her to her feet. "Let's go down and head for our inn."

Cobby had commandeered a man with a wooden cart. Del waited with the women while their luggage was ferried down the gangplank and loaded in the cart, then he set off, leading the way off the dock and straight up High Street. The Dolphin wasn't far; Mustaf followed with the women close behind, with Cobby bringing up the rear, ambling alongside the carter, eyes constantly shifting this way and that as he chatted.

As Del walked up the street, he found his gaze drawn downward—to the cobbles that covered the ground, to the first steps he was taking on English soil after so many years away.

He wasn't sure what he felt. An odd sense of peace, perhaps because he knew this time his travels were over, a sense of anticipation over what his new and as yet unstructured future might hold, all tinged with a healthy dose of apprehension over what lay between this moment and being able to get started on shaping his new life.

Their mission to bring the Black Cobra to justice.

He was in it now. There was no going back, only forward. Ahead, through whatever fire the opposition might send his way.

Raising his head, he filled his lungs, looked about. It felt exactly like the moment after the charge began.

The Dolphin was a town landmark. It had stood for centuries and been refurbished several times; it currently sported two wide bow windows fronting the street, the solid front door in between.

Del glanced back along the street. He couldn't see any

likely cultists, but there were plenty of people, carts, and the odd carriage thronging the cobbled thoroughfare—plenty of cover for anyone watching.

They would be watching.

Reaching the inn, he opened the door and went inside.

Securing suitable rooms was no difficulty; his years in India had left him very wealthy and he wasn't of a mind to stint either himself or his small household. The innkeeper, Bowden, a solidly built ex-sailor, responded appropriately, cheerily welcoming him to the town and summoning lads to help with the luggage as the others joined Del in the foyer.

With the rooms organized and their bags dispatched, and the women, Mustaf and Cobby following the luggage up the stairs, Bowden turned to Del. "Just remembered. I've two letters waiting for you."

Del turned back to the counter, brows rising.

Reaching beneath it, Bowden produced two missives. "The first—this one—came on the mail coach nearly four weeks ago. The other was left last evening by a gentleman. He and another gentleman have looked in every day for the last week or so, asking after you."

Wolverstone's escorts. "Thank you." Del accepted the letters. It was midafternoon, and the inn's public rooms were quiet. He sent an easy smile Bowden's way. "If anyone should ask for me, I'll be in the tap."

"Of course, sir. Nice and quiet it is in there at present. Just ring the bell on the bar if you need anything."

With a nod, Del sauntered into the dining room and through an archway into the tap, a cozy room toward the back of the inn. There were a few patrons, all older men, gathered about small tables. He went to a table in the corner where the light from the rear window would allow him to read.

Sitting, he examined the two missives, then opened the one from the mystery gentleman.

The lines within were few and to the point, informing him that Tony Blake, Viscount Torrington, and Gervase

Tregarth, Earl of Crowhurst, were holding themselves ready to escort him further on his mission. They were quartered nearby and would continue to call at the inn every evening to check for his arrival.

Reassured that he would be moving forward, in action again soon, he refolded the letter, tucked it inside his coat, then, mildly intrigued, opened the second missive. He'd recognized the handwriting, and assumed his aunts had written to welcome him home, and to ask and be reassured that he was, indeed, heading up to Humberside, to the house at Middleton on the Wolds that he'd inherited from his father, and that remained their home.

As he unfolded the two pages, crossed and recrossed in his elder aunt's spidery script, he was already composing his reply—a brief note to let them know that he had landed and was on his way north, but that business dealings on the way might delay him for a week or so.

Reading his aunt's salutation, followed by an enthusiastic, even effusive, welcome, he smiled and read on.

He wasn't smiling by the time he reached the end of the first page. Laying it aside, he deciphered the rest, then tossed the second sheet on the first and quietly, but comprehensively, swore.

After staring at the sheets for several minutes, he gathered them up, rose and, stuffing the sheets in his pocket, made his way back to the inn's foyer.

Bowden heard his footsteps and came out from his office behind the counter. "Yes, Colonel?"

"I understand a young lady, a Miss Duncannon, was due to arrive here some weeks ago?"

Bowden smiled brightly. "Yes, indeed, sir. I'd forgotten— she asked after you, too."

"Indeed. I take it she's left and headed north?"

"Oh, no, sir. Her ship was delayed, too. She didn't get in until last week. Quite relieved, she was, to learn you'd been delayed, too. She's still here, waiting on your arrival."

"Ah. I see." Del suppressed a grimace and started making

plans. "Perhaps if you could send word to her room that I've arrived, and would appreciate a moment of her time?"

Bowden shook his head. "No use at present—she's out, and she's taken her maid with her. But I can tell her as soon as she comes in."

Del nodded. "Thank you." He hesitated, then asked, "Is there a private parlor I might hire?" Somewhere where he and his unexpected burden could discuss her onward journey.

"I'm sorry, sir, but all our parlors are presently taken." Bowden paused, then said, "But it's Miss Duncannon herself as has the front parlor—perhaps, seeing she's waiting to see you, you might wait for her in there?"

"An excellent notion," Del responded dryly. "And I'll need to hire a carriage."

But again Bowden shook his head. "I'd like to oblige, Colonel, but this close to Christmas all our carriages are spoken for. Miss Duncannon herself took the last of our post chaises."

"Fortuitous," Del murmured. "I was wanting the carriage for her."

"Well, then." Bowden grinned. "All's well."

"Indeed." Del pointed to the room to the right of the foyer. "The front parlor?"

"Aye, sir. Go right in."

Del did, shutting the door behind him.

With white plaster walls and heavy timber beams crossing the ceiling, the parlor was neither overlarge nor cramped, and boasted one of the wide bow windows looking out on the street. The furniture was heavy, but comfortable, the pair of chintz-covered armchairs well-supplied with plump cushions. A highly polished round table with four chairs stood in the middle of the room, a large lamp at its center, while a crackling fire sparked and flared in the grate, throwing welcome heat into the room.

Gravitating toward the hearth, Del noticed the three watercolors above the mantelpiece. They were landscapes depicting green pastures and meadows, lush fields and richly canopied trees beneath pastel blue skies with fluffy white clouds. The one in the middle, of rolling heathland, a vibrant patchwork of greens, caught his eye. He hadn't laid eyes on such landscapes for seven long years; it seemed odd to gain his first sense of home via pictures on a wall.

Glancing down, he drew out the letter from his aunts; standing before the fire, he scanned it anew, searching for some insight into why the devil they'd thought to saddle him with the duty of escorting a young gentlewoman, daughter of a neighboring landowner, home to Humberside.

His best guess was that his doting aunts had some idea of playing matchmaker.

They were going to be disappointed. There was no place for a young lady in his train, not while he was a decoy for the Black Cobra.

He'd been disappointed when he'd opened the scroll he'd selected and discovered he hadn't picked the original letter. Nevertheless, as Wolverstone had made clear, the missions of the three decoys would be vital in drawing out the Black Cobra's men, and ultimately the Black Cobra himself.

They needed to lure him into striking, and for that they needed to reduce his cultists sufficiently to force him to act in person.

Not an easy task, yet by any reasonable estimation it should be within their collective ability. As a decoy, his role would be to deliberately make himself a target, and he didn't want any extraneous young lady hanging on his arm while he was so engaged.

A tap on the door had him hesitating, then he called, "Come."

It was Cobby.

"Thought you'd want to know." Hand on the knob, his batman hovered by the door he'd closed. "I ducked back down the docks and asked around. Ferrar arrived over a week ago. Interesting thing is he had no bevy of natives with him—seems there was no room left on the frigate for more than him and his man."

Del raised his brows. "Definitely interesting, but no doubt he'll have had cultists coming in on other ships."

Cobby nodded. "So you'd think. But it does mean he won't necessarily have all that many just at present. Might have to resort to doing his own dirty work." Cobby grinned malevolently. "Now wouldn't that be a shame?"

Del smiled. "We can but hope."

He nodded a dismissal and Cobby left, closing the door behind him.

Del glanced at the clock ticking on a sideboard. It was already after three, and what daylight there was would soon fade. He fell to pacing slowly before the fire, rehearsing suitable words with which to break the news to Miss Duncannon that, contrary to his aunts' arrangements, she would be heading north alone.

It was well after four o'clock, and he'd grown increasingly impatient, before a feminine voice in the foyer, well modulated yet with an unmistakably haughty tone, heralded the return of Miss Duncannon.

Even as Del focused on the parlor door, the knob turned and the door swung inward. Bowden held it open to permit a lady—not so young—in a garnet red pelisse, her dark auburn hair swept up and tucked under a jaunty hat, who was juggling a plethora of bandboxes and packages to enter.

She swept in, her face alight, a smile curving lush red lips, as Bowden hurriedly said, "I believe this is the gentleman you've been waiting for, miss."

Miss Duncannon abruptly halted. Animation leaching from her face, she looked across the room and saw him. After a moment, her gaze slowly meandered upward, until it reached his face.

Then she simply stared.

Clearing his throat, Bowden retreated, closing the door behind her. She blinked, stared again, then baldly asked, "*You're* Colonel Delborough?"

Del bit his tongue against an impulse to respond, "You're *Miss* Duncannon?" Just one look, and his vision of a biddable young miss had evaporated; the lady was in her late twenties if she was a day.

And given the vision filling his eyes, why she was still a miss was beyond his comprehension.

She was . . . *lush* was the word that sprang to his mind. Taller than the average, she was built on stately, even queenly, lines, ripely curvaceous in all the right places. Even from across the room, he could tell her eyes were green; large, faintly slanting up at the outer corners, they were vibrantly alive, awake and aware, alert to all that went on around her.

Her features were elegant, refined, her lips full and ripe, elementally tempting, but the firmness of her chin suggested determination, backbone and a forthrightness beyond the norm.

Duly noting that last, he bowed. "Indeed—Colonel Derek Delborough." *Sadly, not at your service.* Quashing the wayward thought, he smoothly continued, "I believe your parents made some arrangement with my aunts for me to act as escort on your journey north. Sadly, that's not possible—I have business to attend to before I can return to Humberside."

Deliah Duncannon blinked, with an effort dragged her senses from their preoccupation with shoulders and a wide chest which should by all rights have been encased in a uniform, replayed his words, then abruptly shook her head. "No."

Moving further into the room, she set her boxes and bags on the table, distractedly wondering whether a uniform would have increased his impact, or lessened it. There was something anomalous in his appearance, as if the elegant civilian garb was a disguise. If the intention had been to screen his innately vigorous, even dangerous physique, the ploy had failed miserably.

Freeing her hands, she reached up to extract the long pin securing her hat. "I'm afraid, Colonel Delborough, that I must insist. I've been waiting for the better part of a week for you to arrive, and I really cannot journey on without a suitable escort." Setting her hat on the table, she swung to face the recalcitrant ex-colonel—significantly younger and immeasurably more virile than she'd envisioned him. Than she'd been led to expect. "It's quite unthinkable."

Regardless of his age, his virility, or his propensity to argue, for her, it was, but the last thing she intended to do was explain.

His lips—mobile and distractingly masculine—firmed. "Miss Duncannon—"

"I expect you're imagining that it will simply be a matter of bundling me into a carriage with my maid and household, and pointing north." Pausing in the act of removing her leather gloves, she glanced at him and caught a telltale twist of those disturbing lips; that had, indeed, been precisely what he'd planned. "I have to inform you that that's very definitely not the case."

Dropping her gloves on the table behind her, she lifted her chin and faced him squarely—staring down her nose as well as she could given he was more than half a head taller than she. "I must insist, sir, that you honor the obligation."

His lips were now a thin line—one she wanted to see relax and curve into a smile . . . what was the matter with her? Her pulse thrummed in her throat, her skin prickled with unexpected awareness, and he was still a good six feet away.

"Miss Duncannon, while regrettably my aunts overstepped their authority in seeking to oblige a neighbor, I would, in normal circumstances, do all in my power to, as you phrase it, honor the commitment they made. However, in this instance, it is entirely—"

"Colonel Delborough." She hauled her gaze from his lips, for the first time met his gaze directly, deliberately locking her eyes on his. "Permit me to inform you that there is no reason you could advance, none whatever, that will induce me to excuse you from escorting me north."

His eyes were dark brown, richly hued, unexpectedly intriguing, fringed with the longest, thickest lashes she'd ever seen. Those lashes were the same color as his burnished, lightly waving hair—a sable more black than brown.

"I regret, Miss Duncannon, that that is utterly impossible."

When she set her chin, retreated not an inch, but kept her gaze meshed unwaveringly with his, Del hesitated, then, far more aware than he wished to be of her sinfully sensual mouth, stiffly added, "I'm presently on a mission, one vital to the country, and must see it to its conclusion before I'll be free to indulge my aunts' wishes."

She frowned. "But you've resigned your commission." Her gaze slid to his shoulders, as if confirming the absence of epaulettes.

"My mission is civilian rather than military."

Her finely arched brows rose. Her gaze returning to his face, she considered him for an instant, then, in a deceptively mild—sarcastically challenging—tone, said, "So what do you suggest, sir? That I wait here, at your convenience, until you *are* free to escort me north?"

"No." He struggled not to clench his teeth; his jaw was already tight. "I would respectfully suggest that, in the circumstances, and at this present season with much less traffic on the highways, it would be perfectly acceptable for you to head north with your maid—and I believe you mentioned a household? As you've already ordered a carriage—"

Her green eyes flashed. "With all due respect, Colonel, you are talking through your hat!" Belligerent, determined, she stepped forward, face tipping up as if she intended to go nose-to-nose with him. "The notion of me traveling north, in this season or any other, with no suitable gentleman arranged and accepted by my parents as escort, is quite simply ineligible. Unacceptable. Absolutely 'not done.' "

She'd come so close that a wave of tempting warmth slid over the front of him, cascading down to heat his groin. So long had it been since he'd experienced such an explicit reaction he was, for just an instant, distracted enough to simply stand and enjoy it, drink it in. . . .

Her gaze abruptly shifted to his left. She was tall enough to see over his shoulder. He saw her focus, saw her gorgeous jade-green eyes widen—then flare.

"Good God!"

She seized his lapels and dragged him, hauled him, tumbled him down to the floor.

For one crazed instant, his brain interpreted her actions as lust gone wild—then the reverberating explosion and the tinkle of shattered glass raining down upon them jerked his wits back to reality.

She had never left it. Trapped half beneath him, she wriggled and squirmed to get free, her horrified gaze locked on the shattered pane.

Slamming a mental door on the effect of her curvaceous form bucking beneath him, he gritted his teeth and pushed back to his knees. After a quick glance out of the window at the stunned crowd milling in the darkened street, he got to his feet, and was assisting her to hers when the door slammed open.

Mustaf stood in the doorway, saber in his hand. Cobby stood beside him, a cocked pistol in his. Beyond them towered another Indian, swarthy and tall—Del stiffened instinctively. He started to step in front of Miss Duncannon, only to have her hand on his arm hold him back.

"I'm quite all right, Kumulay." Her small, warm hand still resting on Del's bicep, she looked up at him. "It wasn't me the man was trying to kill."

Del met her eyes. They were still wide, her pupils dilated, but she was utterly in control.

A hundred thoughts churned through his head. Every instinct screamed "*Chase!*" but this time that wasn't his role. He looked back at Cobby, who had lowered his gun. "Get ready to leave immediately."

Cobby nodded. "I'll get the others." He and Mustaf drew back.

The other man—Kumulay—remained in the open doorway, his impassive gaze locked on his mistress.

Del glanced at her. Met the green shards trained on his face.

"You are *not* leaving without me." Each word was carefully enunciated.

He hesitated, giving his mind one more chance to come up with an alternative, then, jaw set, nodded. "Very well. Be ready to leave within the hour."

"Finally!" More than two hours later, Del shut the door of the post chaise Miss Duncannon had been farsighted enough to hire, and dropped onto the seat beside his unlooked-for charge.

Her maid, Bess, an Englishwoman, sat in the corner on her other side. Along the seat opposite, in a colorful array of saris and woollen shawls, sat Amaya, Alia and another older Indian woman and two young girls, the latter three all members of Miss Duncannon's household.

Why she had a largely Indian household he had yet to learn.

The carriage rocked into motion, rolling ponderously up the High Street. As the vehicle tacked around Bargate, then headed on toward the London road, Del wondered, not for the first time over the last two and more hours, what had possessed him to agree to Miss Duncannon traveling on with him.

Unfortunately, he knew the answer, and it was one that left him with no other possible course. She'd seen the man who'd shot at him—which meant the man had almost certainly seen her.

Given cultists rarely, if ever, used firearms, that man was most likely Larkins, Ferrar's gentleman's gentleman and his master's most trusted aide, or Ferrar himself. Del's money was on Larkins.

Although Cobby had questioned all those who'd been standing in the street, still stunned and exclaiming over the shooting, no one had seen the man with the gun well enough to describe, let alone identify. All they'd learned was that, as expected, he'd been fair-skinned.

That the Black Cobra had struck so immediately and decisively had been a surprise, but on reflection, were he in Ferrar's shoes, Del might have mounted a similar preemptive gambit. If he'd been killed, the ensuing chaos might have proved sufficient for Ferrar to gain access to his room and baggage, and the scroll-holder. It wouldn't have played out that way, but Ferrar didn't know that. Regardless, Del was perfectly sure that if it hadn't been for Miss Duncannon's quick thinking—and actions—he would very likely be dead.

It was nearing seven o'clock. The night was dark, the moon cocooned in thick clouds. The carriage lamps beamed through the chill darkness as the four horses reached the macadam of the highway and lengthened their stride.

Del thought of the rest of their combined households, traveling with the bulk of their luggage in two open wagons, all Cobby had been able to hire at such short notice.

At least they were away, on the move.

And they knew that Larkins, and presumably therefore Ferrar, were close, and chasing him. The enemy had broken cover and engaged.

"I can't understand," Deliah said, "why you insisted nothing be said to the authorities." She spoke quietly, her voice sliding beneath the repetitive thud of the horses' hooves; she had no wish to communicate her dissatisfaction to anyone other than the man beside her. "Bowden said you paid for the windowpane but insisted nothing more be made of the incident." She waited an instant, then demanded, "Why?"

She didn't turn to look at him. The interior of the carriage was a sea of shifting shadows; she couldn't see well enough to read anything from his face—and she'd already realized that only showed what he wanted it to.

Silence stretched, but she waited.

Eventually, he murmured, "The attack was linked to my

mission. Can you describe the man with the pistol? It would help."

The vision she'd seen through the window was etched in her mind. "He was somewhat above average height, wearing a dark coat—nothing all that fashionable, but decent quality. He had on a dark hat, but I could see his hair was close-cropped. Beyond that . . . I really didn't have time to note every detail." She let a moment tick past, then asked, "Do you know who he was?"

"He sounds like one of the men linked with my mission."

"Your 'mission,' whatever it might be, doesn't explain why you refused to alert the authorities to the action of a felon—any more than it explains why we're racing away in the dead of night, as if we'd taken fright." She didn't know much about Colonel Derek Delborough, but he didn't seem the sort to cut and run.

He answered in a bored, superior tone. "It was the right thing to do."

"Humph." She frowned, disinclined to let him stop talking. His voice was deep, assured, his accents—those of a man accustomed to command—strangely soothing, and after the excitement of the shooting, she was still on edge. Her nerves were still jangling. She grimaced. "Even if you didn't want to draw attention to yourself, you might at least—"

Del transferred his gaze to the unrelieved darkness outside. He'd glanced at her, seen her grimace, seen her lips pout . . . and felt a nearly overwhelming urge to shut her up.

By sealing those pouting lips with his.

And finding out how soft they were, and what she tasted like.

Tart, or sweet? Or both?

Quite aside from the audience lined up on the opposite seat, he felt reasonably certain any such action would result in him receiving at least one boxed ear. Probably two. Yet having her sitting beside him, her hip less than an inch from his, her shoulder lightly brushing his arm with every rocking motion of the carriage, the warmth of her bathing his side, was a temptation to which his body was shamelessly responding.

The search for the Black Cobra had consumed him for months; he hadn't spared the time to dally with any woman—and it had been far longer since he'd been with an Englishwoman, and never with a termagant of Miss Duncannon's ilk.

None of which explained why he was suddenly so attracted to a harridan with lips for which the most experienced courtesans would trade their souls.

He blotted out her voice, her insistent, persistent prodding, focused instead on the heavy rhythm of the horses' hooves. Leaving Southampton with all speed had been what he'd had to do, no matter how much it had gone against his grain. If he'd been carrying the original letter, then the necessity of keeping it out of Ferrar's clutches would have trumped any inclination to give chase.

If he'd stood and fought—tried to hunt down Larkins, even dallied to set the Watch on Ferrar's trail—Ferrar would have guessed that he wasn't all that concerned with the contents of the scroll-holder he carried. And then Ferrar would have shifted his attention, and that of his cultists, from Del to one of the others.

Were the others ahead of him, or were they yet to land in England?

With luck Torrington and Crowhurst would know. He'd left a short note for them with Bowden.

Given the hour, and the falling temperatures, and that more than half their number were traveling exposed, they couldn't go far. For tonight, Winchester was his goal.

He prayed he'd be able to resist the impulses provoked by the feminine muttering from beside him long enough for them to reach it.

The Swan Inn in Southgate Street proved sufficient for their needs.

Miss Duncannon predictably grumbled when he refused to stop at the larger Pelican Hotel. "There's so many of us to accommodate—they're more likely to have room."

"The Pelican is largely timber and lathe."

"So?"

"I have an unreasoning fear of waking to a house in flames." The Black Cobra's men had been known to use fire to flush out those they were chasing, without the slightest thought for any others who might get caught in the ensuing blaze. Climbing out of the carriage in the yard of the Swan, Del considered the inn, then turned to hand his burden down. "The Swan, however, is built of stone."

Taking his hand, she stepped down, paused to look at the inn, then, expressionless, looked at him. "Stone walls in winter."

He glanced up at the roof, to where multiple chimneys chuffed smoke. "Fires."

She sniffed, lifted her skirts, climbed the steps to the porch and led the way through the door the innkeeper was holding wide, bobbing and bowing as they passed.

Before Del could take charge, she did, sweeping to the inn's counter and stripping off her gloves. "Good evening." The innkeeper scurried around the counter to attend her. "We need rooms for us all—one large chamber for me, another for the colonel, four smaller rooms for my staff and two more for his staff, and the colonel's parlor maid can room with my lady's maid—that's wiser, I think. Now, we'll all want dinner—I know it's late, but—"

Del halted just behind her—she knew he was there—and listened to her rattle off orders, directions and instructions, more or less without pause. He could have stepped in and taken over—he'd intended to—but as she was making such an excellent fist of organizing their combined party, there seemed little point.

By the time the luggage had been unloaded and ferried inside, the innkeeper had sorted out their rooms, arranged for a private parlor to be prepared for them, and sent orders to the kitchen for their meals. Del stood back and watched a round-eyed maid lead his charge upstairs to her chamber, then he turned to the innkeeper. "I need to hire two more carriages."

"Of course, sir. Dreadfully cold already, and they say there's worse to come. I don't have any carriages free myself, but I know the stableman at the Pelican—he'll oblige me, and I'm sure he'll have two he can let you have."

Del raised his eyes to the top of the stairs—and met Miss Duncannon's direct green gaze. She said nothing, however, but with a faint lift of her brows, continued on into the gallery. "Thank you." Returning his gaze to the innkeeper, he arranged for the members of his household and hers to be given whatever they wished from the tap, then left the now deserted foyer to climb the stairs to his room.

Half an hour later, washed and brushed, he was in the private parlor when Miss Duncannon entered. Two maids had just finished setting a small table for two before the fire; they retreated with bobbed curtsies. Del strolled to hold a chair for his charge.

She'd removed her pelisse, revealing a garnet-red gown trimmed with silk ribbon of the same hue, over which she'd draped a finely patterned silk shawl.

Sitting, she inclined her head. "Thank you, Colonel."

Strolling to his chair on the other side of the table, Del murmured, "Del." When she raised her brows, he explained, "Most people I know call me Del."

"I see." She considered him as he sat and shook out his napkin. "As we're apparently to be in each other's company for some time, it would be appropriate, I suppose, to make you free of my name. It's Deliah—*not* Delilah. Deliah."

He smiled, inclined his head. "Deliah."

Deliah struggled not to stare, struggled to keep her suddenly witless mind functioning. That was the first time he'd smiled at her—and she definitely didn't need the additional distraction. He was ridiculously handsome when serious and sober; when his lips softened and curved, he was seduction personified.

She, better than anyone, knew how dangerous such men were—especially to her.

The door opened and the maids reappeared, ferrying a soup tureen and a basket of bread.

She nodded her approval and the maids served. Deliah eyed the soup with something akin to gratitude, inwardly congratulating herself for having ordered it. One didn't need to converse while consuming soup. That would give her just a little more time to whip her unruly senses into line.

"Thank you." With a nod for the retreating maids, she picked up her spoon and supped.

He reached for the bread basket, offered it.

"No, thank you."

He smiled again—damn him!—and helped himself; she looked down at her soup and kept her gaze on her plate.

It had taken her all of the short journey, and most of the half hour she'd spent out of his sight, to untangle the skein of emotions besetting her. She'd initially attributed her skittering nerves and breathless state to the shock of finding herself looking down the barrel of a pistol, even if the gun hadn't been pointed at her.

The shot, the subsequent flurry, the rush to leave, the unexpected journey during which he'd remained stubbornly uncommunicative over his mysterious mission—the mission that had led to him being shot at—were all circumstances that might naturally be considered to have contributed to her overwrought state.

Except she'd never been the sort to allow circumstances—no matter how dire or unexpected—to overset her.

In the quiet of her chamber, she'd finally unravelled her feelings sufficiently to lay the truth bare—it had been that moment when she'd found herself on the wooden floor with his hard body covering hers that was the root of her problem. The source of her skittishness.

If she thought of it, she could still feel the sensations—of his weight pinning her, hard muscles and heavy bones trapping her beneath him, his long legs tangling with hers, his heat—then the searing instant of . . . whatever it had been that had afflicted her. Hot, intense, enough to make her squirm.

Enough to make her treacherous body yearn.

But she didn't think he knew. She glanced at him as he laid down his spoon.

He caught her eye. "I should thank you for taking charge of the domestic organization."

She shrugged. "I'm accustomed to managing my uncle's household. It's what I've been doing in my years away."

"Jamaica, I believe my aunt wrote. What took you there?"

Setting down her spoon, she leaned her elbows on the table, lacing her fingers and viewing him over them. "Originally I went out to visit my uncle, Sir Harold Duncannon. He's the Chief Magistrate of Jamaica. I found the climate and the colony to my liking, so I stayed. As time passed, I took charge of his household."

"Your servants are Indian—are there many Indians in Jamaica?"

"These days, yes. After the slave ships stopped, many Indian and Chinese workers were brought in. All my staff were originally with my uncle's household, but over the years became more mine than his, so I gave them the choice of staying in Jamaica or coming to England with me."

"And they chose England." Del broke off as the maids reappeared. While they cleared the first course and laid out platters of succulent roast beef, roast potatoes and pumpkin, ham, and a jug of rich gravy, he had time to consider what her staff's loyalty said of Miss Deliah—*not* Delilah—Duncannon.

"Thank you." She nodded graciously to the maids, and they departed. Before he could frame his next question, she fixed her gaze on him. "You, I gather, have been with the East India Company for some time."

He nodded, picking up the serving fork. "I've been in India for the past seven years. Before that, it was Waterloo, and before that, the Peninsula."

"Quite a lengthy service—am I to take it you're retiring permanently?"

"Yes." They served themselves, and settled to eat.

Five minutes passed, then she said, "Tell me about India. Was the campaigning there the same as in Europe? Massed battles, army against army?"

"At first." When he glanced up and saw her plainly waiting for more, he elaborated, "Over the first years I was there, we were extending territory—annexing areas for trade, as the company describes it. More or less routine campaigning. Later, however, it became more a case of . . . I suppose you could say keeping the peace. Keeping the unruly elements in check to protect the trade routes—that sort of thing. Not really campaigning, no battles as such."

"And this mission of yours?"

"Is something that grew out of the peacekeeping, as it were."

"Being something more civilian than military?"

He held her gaze. "Indeed."

"I see. And will pursuing your mission necessitate you leaving me behind at some point well south of Humberside?"

He sat back. "No."

She arched her brows. "You seem to have experienced a quite dramatic change of heart regarding my presence consequent on you being shot at. I'm not sure I see the connection."

"Regardless, you see me resigned to your company—I'm waiting on confirmation of our exact route, but I believe we'll need to spend a few days, perhaps a week, in London."

"London?"

He'd hoped she'd be distracted with thoughts of shopping—she had been out of the country for years, after all—but from the calculation in her eyes, he could tell she was trying to see what going to London told her of his mission.

"Incidentally," he said, "why Jamaica?"

After a moment, she shrugged. "I was in need of new horizons and the connection was there."

"How long ago did you leave England?"

"In '15. As a colonel, were you in charge of a . . . what? Squadron of men?"

"No." Again she waited, open curiosity coloring her eyes and her expression, until he added, "In India, I commanded a group of elite officers, each of whom could take command of company troops and deal with the constant small insurrections and disturbances that are always blowing up in the subcontinent. But tell me, was there much of a social circle in . . . Kingston, isn't it?"

She nodded. "Yes, Kingston. And yes, there was the usual social circle of expatriates, much like any colony, I expect. How was India in that regard?"

"I was stationed mostly in Calcutta—the company headquarters are there. There were always balls and parties in the so-called season, but not so much of the matchmaking one finds at Almack's and the like."

"Indeed? I would have thought—"

They continued to trade question and answer as they progressed through the courses. Del tried to ascertain why she'd felt the need for "new horizons" while avoiding falling into the conversational pits she dug and revealing more than she needed to know about his mission.

He might have to take her with him to ensure her safety, but he intended to do all in his power to keep her ignorant of and entirely separate from his mission, and as far as possible out of the Black Cobra's sight.

It was only after they'd risen from the table and together walked out of the parlor and up the stairs that he realized he'd spent an entire evening alone with an unmarried lady, doing nothing more than talking, and he hadn't even thought of being bored.

Which he usually was. Thus far in his life, women, even ladies, had fulfilled one and only one role; he'd had very

little interest in them outside that sphere. Yet although he'd
focused on Deliah's luscious lips far too often for his comfort, he'd been too engaged in their mutual interrogation—
her quick wits had ensured he'd had to keep his own about
him—to dwell on her sexual potential, much less act on an
attraction that, he was surprised to discover, had not just survived the last hours but had, if anything, grown.

She paused outside the door of the chamber next to his
and glanced up at him. Her lips curved lightly—a genuine
smile tinged with a hint of appreciation and a soupçon of
challenge. "Good night . . . Del."

He forced his lips into an easy smile. Inclined his head.
"Deliah."

Her smile fractionally deepened, but her tone was entirely
innocent when she added, "Sleep well."

Del stood in the shadowed corridor and watched the
chamber door close behind her, then he slowly walked the
few paces to his own, reasonably certain that her last wish
was very unlikely to be granted.

Two

December 12
The Swan Inn, Winchester

el was woken from a slumber every bit as restless as he'd predicted by Cobby rattling the bedcurtains.

"It's morning, believe it or not. Gray as the grave, and equally cold. Whatever passes for sun these days it's not up yet, but there's two gentlemen downstairs waiting to see you—Torrington and Crowhurst."

Del grunted. He pushed back the covers and rose, stretched, suppressing a shiver at the chill in the air. "Tell them I'll be down directly."

"Aye, sir."

Del washed, quickly shaved, then dressed in the clothes Cobby had left warming by the fire. A quick glance out of the window showed a drear landscape bathed in pearl-gray light. No snow had yet fallen, and it wasn't raining. Good enough weather for traveling.

Downstairs, he passed Cobby in the foyer.

"In the parlor, they are. Thought I'd get breakfast served, seeing you were on your way."

With a nod, Del strolled on, opened the parlor door, and

walked in to find two large gentlemen enthusiastically addressing plates piled with ham and sausages. Both looked up, smiled, and rose as he approached.

Both must have been in the Guards at some point—there was a certain set to their shoulders, a similarity in their long, tall frames.

The dark-haired, black-eyed one held out his hand with a smiling nod. "Delborough, I take it. I'm Torrington."

Del shook hands.

"Gervase Tregarth." The second man, with amber eyes and curly brown hair, likewise offered his hand. "Also known as Crowhurst."

Del smiled. "Call me Del." He took a seat facing them, his gaze lowering to the platters. "I haven't had a real English breakfast in over seven years. Is it any good?"

"Excellent." Torrington picked up his fork. "Very good ham. I'm Tony, by the way—Tony Blake."

"Blake." Del helped himself to the ham and three sausages. "There was a Blake behind enemy lines after Corunna."

"That was me. Old days long gone. Not much call for those sort of larks these days, not for any of us."

"Which," Gervase said, reaching for the coffeepot, "is why you'll find us all very grateful for this chance to get back into some action, no matter how briefly. Civilian life has its challenges, but they aren't quite the same."

Just those few exchanges put Del entirely at ease; men like these he understood, because they thought like him.

"We heard," Tony said around a mouthful of ham, "that you had a spot of bother at the Dolphin."

"Indeed—it seems the Black Cobra is aware I'm here, and ready, even eager, to engage."

"Excellent." Gervase grinned. "Reassuring to know the action's already underway."

"So," Del said, "what word do you have from Wolverstone?"

"Who," Tony informed him, "is likewise grateful, but, as usual, is keeping his cards exceedingly close to his chest.

We're to head into London, and spend a few days making noise and seeing what cult forces we can draw out. Royce has left the timing to us, but once we feel we've done all we can in the capital, we're to head to Cambridgeshire, to a house called Somersham Place."

"I know it," Del said. "Devil Cynster's home."

"Where," Gervase said, "Cynster will be waiting with a crew of other Cynsters. The idea is to lure the Black Cobra to strike at you while there—no reason the cult would know how many ex-Guardsmen are in the house."

Del chewed, nodded. "So it'll be an ambush of sorts."

"Exactly." Tony refilled his coffee cup, and sat back.

Del arched a brow at them both. "Do you know if any of the others have reached England?"

Tony shook his head.

"I sent word last night to Royce that you'd landed," Gervase said, "and that we'll proceed as planned. As far as we've heard, you're the first home."

Del hesitated, then said, "About proceeding as planned, we have a slight complication—an unexpected addition to our group." He told them of Miss Deliah Duncannon, and briefly explained why he hadn't been able to leave her behind.

Tony winced. "Last thing we need, to have to act as nursemaid to a sweet young thing all the way through London and into Cambridgeshire."

"At least we'll be able to hand her over to the Cynster ladies once there," Gervase said.

Del tried to imagine Deliah Duncannon being "handed over." Or nursemaided. Couldn't.

He was searching for words with which to correct their misapprehension that Deliah was "a sweet young thing" when Tony continued, "Still, I suppose it'll just be a matter of leaving her with her maid and your people, well out of the action." Setting down his empty cup, Tony reached for the coffeepot. "As we should get on the road in the next hour or so, I daresay the first step is to send a message up to this Miss Duncannon's maid to get her mistress awake."

"Miss Duncannon is already awake."

The frosty words brought them to their feet as the door—which Del now realized hadn't shut properly behind him—swung fully open to admit Deliah, ready for the day in a gray carriage dress, and transparently unimpressed.

Just how long she'd been standing outside the door was impossible to guess.

Del quickly made the introductions, which she acknowledged with a haughty air. Both Tony and Gervase bowed over her hand, endeavoring to appear cheery and charming. Del held a chair for her, while the others recommended the ham and sausages, which she waved away as a maid bustled in with fresh toast and a teapot.

"Thank you." Deliah smiled at the maid, claimed a slice of toast, then fixed her eyes on Del's guilty friends. "So how far do you plan to travel today?"

She'd addressed the question to Tony. He looked to Del, but she refused to follow his gaze and continued to look at him inquiringly . . . as she'd hoped, he felt compelled to answer.

"We should reach London late this afternoon."

She nodded. "And then into Cambridgeshire." When they exchanged quick glances, she added, "In time. A few days, maybe more?"

They didn't correct her, so she nodded again, supposition confirmed. She nibbled her toast, then poured her tea and took a sip, all the while noting the telltale signs of their uncertainty over what to say to her, letting it grow. She set down her cup. "About this mission—what are the relevant details?"

All three shifted. The other two looked at Del, and didn't look back at her. Eventually, Del said, "Our . . . commander, for want of a better term, isn't one to encourage the unnecessary sharing of information."

She raised her brows. "Indeed? And does this commander know of my existence—that I've unwittingly been drawn into his scheme?"

"No."

"Then he can't have made any decision against informing me of its details."

Del met her limpid green gaze, held it. The others were leaving the question of her continued ignorance up to him. If she'd been a man, he would have told her and enlisted her aid. But she wasn't a man—very definitely wasn't—and every instinct he possessed came down firmly on the side of leaving her ignorance uninformed, unrelieved. "Be that as it may, there's no reason for you to . . ."

Her tight smile was a warning. "Bother my pretty little head about it?"

Brazen, he nodded. "Something like that." He wasn't going to be intimidated into surrendering his position.

She held his gaze—again he had the impression they were standing toe-to-toe, certainly will-to-will, and once again found it inexplicably arousing—then she transferred her gaze to Tony. "As it appears we'll be spending a number of days in London, where are you intending to stay?"

The sudden shift in attack caught Tony unprepared. "Ah . . ." He glanced at Gervase, then briefly at Del before saying, "We had thought to put up at our private club, but now . . ."

"I take it it's a gentlemen's club?" she asked.

"Of a sort, but our wives also stay there when visiting town."

Her brows rose. "Indeed?" She appeared to consider, then shook her head. "I don't think any *private* establishment will do."

Del fully expected her to circle back to what she really wanted to know about—his mission. He cut in. "We can discuss the possibilities in the carriage." He glanced pointedly at the clock on the mantelpiece. "We should get underway as soon as possible."

She looked at him, then smiled. "Of course." She set down her empty cup, laid aside her napkin. With regal grace, she rose, bringing them to their feet. She inclined her head as she turned to the door. "Gentlemen. I'll be ready to leave in an hour."

They stood and watched her glide to the door; she opened it, then shut it quietly behind her.

"I assume," Gervase said, "that we're supposed to understand that she's not a cypher to be ignored."

Del snorted. "More that she's not a cypher—and *will not be* ignored."

"Well? Are you going to tell me or not?"

Head back against the squabs, eyes closed, arms crossed over his chest, Del supposed he should have expected the question. "Not."

He didn't bother opening his eyes. They'd left Winchester half an hour before, and were now bowling along the highway toward London. There was, however, a pertinent difference between their present journey and that of the evening before—today he and she were alone in the carriage. Her staff and his were following in the two carriages immediately behind, the three conveyances traveling in convoy. Gervase and Tony, the lucky sods, were on horseback, riding parallel to the road, close enough to keep watch, yet not so close that they would scare away any of the Black Cobra's men who might be tempted to stage an attack.

Del didn't think an attack at all likely. Even in this season, this highway was too busy, with mail coaches and all manner of private vehicles constantly bowling along in both directions. The Black Cobra cultists preferred less populated surrounds for their villainy.

"Where are the other two?"

He slitted open his eyes and saw her peering out of the carriage window.

"They said they'd ride with us, but I can't see them."

He closed his eyes again. "Don't worry. They're there."

He felt her sharp glance.

"I'm not worried. I'm curious."

"I've noticed."

Her gaze heated to a glare; even with his eyes closed he felt it.

"Let's see if I have this right." Her tone was the epitome of reason and sense. "You arrive in Southampton and take rooms at an inn, then discover you've been elected to be my escort and promptly try to divest yourself of the responsibility. Then someone tries to shoot you, and you immediately up stakes and quit said inn—even though your people have only just settled in and it's already evening—to rattle all of what?—ten miles?—further along the road. And by the next morning, you've acquired two . . . should I call them *guards*?"

His lips quirked before he stilled them.

She saw, humphed. "Are you going to tell me what this is all about?"

"No."

"Why? I cannot see how it would hurt for me to know what it is you're carrying—information or something more tangible—and what you want to do with it, who wants to stop you, and why."

At that he opened his eyes, turned his head and looked at her. Met her irritated green gaze. She'd guessed so much . . . he set his jaw. "It's better if you don't know."

Her eyes slitted, her lips thinned. "Better for whom?"

He wasn't, when it came to it, all that sure. Facing forward, resettling his head, he murmured, "I'll think about it."

And closed his eyes again.

He felt the heat of her temper focus on him, but then she shifted on the seat, and blessed silence descended.

It lasted. And lasted.

Eventually he opened his eyes enough to send a careful look her way.

She was sitting in the corner of the carriage, leaning against the side, watching the fields flash past. There was a faint frown on her face, and her lips were . . . just slightly pouting.

Minutes ticked by, then he forced his gaze forward and closed his eyes again.

* * *

They stopped for lunch at a small country inn in the village of Windlesham. Deliah had been unimpressed when he'd refused to halt at any of the major posting inns at Camberley but instead had directed the coachman to the much smaller—and therefore much safer—country village.

Tony and Gervase would hang back, keeping watch to see if they could spot anyone following. But as the Black Cobra had to suspect Del would make for London, he, Tony and Gervase were all of the opinion that it was more likely there would be watchers planted at vantage points along the road to report his passage to their master.

If Tony or Gervase could spot such a watcher, they might be able to follow the man back to the Black Cobra's lair. As the game stood, any information on the Black Cobra's forces would be welcome, while information on the Black Cobra himself would be gold.

Del climbed down from the carriage before the Windlesham Arms, and after a swift look around, handed Deliah down. She continued to grumble, which in her case was more like acerbic verbal sniping, which Del found amusing, although he was careful not to let his appreciation show.

But after the innkeeper bowed them into a pretty parlor with lace curtains and comfortable chairs, and then proceeded to serve an excellent meal, her griping ceased. By the time he escorted her back into the main tap and paused by the bar to settle the account, she was entirely appeased, and in a relatively mellow mood—not that she would admit it.

Lips curving, Del chatted to the barman while he waited for the innkeeper to tot up the damage.

The tap was half full. Rather than stand beside Del and be covertly studied by the occupants, Deliah wandered to an archway where a pair of glassed doors gave onto a small courtyard. Gently rolling lawns lay beyond; in summer, the area would, she suspected, be dotted with the trestles and benches she could see stacked to one side under a row of leafless trees.

Nearer at hand, a narrow bed ran along the wall of the inn, full of hellebores in bloom. It had been so long since she'd seen the so-called Christmas roses on impulse she opened the door and went out to admire them.

The plants were old, large, and carried many spikes of large, nodding white blooms. Some were even spotty. She bent down the better to see.

And heard a soft rush of footsteps coming up the lawn.

Straightening, she started to turn—just as a large man seized her from behind.

She screamed, struggled.

A second man tried to help the first, tried to hold her still as the first attempted to clap a hand over her mouth.

She ducked her head, jabbed an elbow back hard—into a flabby stomach. The first man gasped, then wheezed.

The second man swore and tried to haul her away from the inn as the first man's grip faltered.

She dug in her heels, dragged in a breath, and screamed again. Wrenching one arm free, she struck wildly at the second man.

Del erupted from the inn. Kumulay and Mustaf were on his heels.

The second man swore, and fled for his life.

The first man wasn't as fast; he was still clutching her, still wheezing. Del grabbed her free arm with one hand. His other fist flashed past her shoulder.

She heard a sickening crunch, then the large man's grip on her eased and fell away.

Del pulled her to him, to his other side. Peering back, around him, she saw the man who'd seized her laid out unconscious on the flagstone path.

Then every man and woman who'd been in the tap came pouring out—to see, exclaim, ask questions, demand answers.

Del suddenly found himself and Deliah surrounded by a well-meaning throng. Many seemed to think Deliah would be in imminent danger of collapse, presumably from overwrought sensibilities, an assumption she seemed to find as mystifying as, and rather more irritating than, he did.

Questions, solicitude and sympathetic outrage came from all sides; it took vital minutes to calm everyone down.

Finally Del looked up and saw Mustaf and Kumulay striding back up the lawn. Mustaf shook his head, gestured with his fingers—the man had had a horse waiting.

They'd intended to grab Deliah and take her somewhere. Del's mind supplied the where—wherever the Black Cobra or his lieutenant was waiting.

He swallowed a curse, looked for the man he'd laid out— then clamped his lips shut on an even more virulent oath.

The man had vanished.

Teeth gritted behind an entirely false smile, he tightened his hold on Deliah's arm and started steering her through the crowd, toward the front of the inn.

Having noted the disappearance of the man, and Del's direction, Mustaf and Kumulay went to summon the others and ready the carriages.

It was another twenty minutes before they were once again underway, and rolling out of the no-longer-so-sleepy village.

Del slumped back against the seat, finally registered the throbbing in his left hand. Lifting it, he saw he'd split the skin over one knuckle. He put the injured joint to his mouth.

Deliah noticed, frowned, then she looked ahead. Lifted her chin. After a moment, she said, "I believe your commander, whoever he is, would agree, now, that I have a right to know."

Del grimaced. He glanced at her profile; her lips weren't pouting—they were set in a grim line. "I don't suppose you'd accept that those men were merely footpads—itinerants looking for an easy mark?"

"No."

He sighed.

"If I'd known I stood in any danger of attack, I wouldn't have gone out of that door." She turned her head, met his eyes. "You can't not tell me—it's too dangerous for me not to know."

He held her gaze for a moment, then looked ahead, filled his lungs. And told her.

Initially he gave her a carefully edited description of the Black Cobra and his mission. She seemed to sense his prevarications and refused to let them lie, verbally pulling and prodding until she'd extracted an account a great deal closer to the full picture from him.

He inwardly winced as he heard himself tell her about the manner of James MacFarlane's death, and of the evidence he'd given his life to get to them.

"Poor boy—how utterly dreadful. Yet at least he died a true hero—I imagine that would have been important to him. And this is the evidence you and your friends are endeavoring to ensure gets into Wolverstone's hands?"

"Yes."

"And part of the plan is to make the Black Cobra attack, so he can be caught and thus implicated entirely independently of the evidence itself?"

"Yes."

She was silent for a moment, then said, "That's a very good plan."

He'd expected her to be appalled, and then horrified, frightened, even terrified by the very real threat of very real and nasty danger—something she certainly wouldn't have missed. Yet while she'd been as appalled as he'd imagined, horror, fright and terror didn't seem to be in her repertoire; if he'd had any real doubts that she was made of sterner stuff, her immediate focus on the salient points of his mission had slain them.

After another, longer silence, she looked at him, met his eyes. "I will, of course, help in whatever way I can—you have only to ask. As the Black Cobra clearly views me as part of your entourage, there's no sense in attempting to keep me distanced from your mission."

He managed to hide his reaction. He could think of any

number of reasons to keep her separate from his mission, all of which made excellent sense to him, but he hadn't attained the rank of colonel without having some idea of how to manage others—although he'd never tried his hand at managing a termagant before. "Thank you." With an inclination of his head, he accepted her pledge of help; if he'd tried to refuse it, to quash the enthusiam burning in her green eyes, her resolve to assist would only have hardened. Instead, he could use her commitment as a subtle lever to keep her under control—to channel her contribution into safe arenas.

Speaking of which . . . "We still haven't decided where to stay in London." Brows rising, he relaxed against the seat. "Do you know of any place that might suit?"

December 12
Grillon's Hotel, Albemarle Street, London

"See?" Deliah stood just inside the foyer of fashionable Grillon's Hotel, and watched Del survey the critical amenities— the single handsome staircase leading to the upper floors, the dining room to one side, the parlor to the other, and directly opposite the main entrance, the only entrance from the street, the wide counter behind which two young men stood, ready to deal with any request from guests, all under the eagle eye of an older gentleman in a uniform sporting gilt-embroidered epaulettes. In addition, there were not one but two uniformed doormen manning the portal. "It's the perfect place for us to stay," she murmured. "Not only is it in the heart of London, but Grillon's reputation is based on security and propriety—they would never permit anything so gauche as an attack of any sort to occur on the premises."

Del had come to the same conclusion—the ex-solider behind the counter was watching him steadily, and the doorman who had shown them in had yet to return outside. He nodded. "All in all, an excellent choice."

He walked forward. Deliah glided beside him, her long

legs allowing her to keep pace easily. The head clerk behind the counter straightened, all but coming to attention; after decades in the army, Del's bearing inevitably gave him away.

"Can we help you, s—"

"I'm Miss Duncannon." Deliah laid her gloves on the counter, waited until the clerk looked her way. "I require a room for myself, and accommodation for my staff. Colonel Delborough"—with one hand she waved at him—"will also require a room—"

"And also has various stipulations to make." Del caught her eye when she glanced at him, captured her gaze and pointedly held it. "As I am escorting you north at your parents' request, it might perhaps be appropriate for you to consider me *in loco parentis*."

She blinked at him.

His smile took on an edge. "Perhaps you should allow me to organize our rooms."

She frowned.

Before she could argue, he looked at the clerk. "Miss Duncannon will require a suite overlooking the street, preferably with no balcony."

The head clerk consulted his list. "We have a suite that might suit, Colonel—it's on the first floor, but is some way from the stairs."

"That will do admirably. I'll want a bedchamber myself, on the same floor, between the suite and the stairs."

"Indeed, sir." The head clerk conferred with one of his underlings, then nodded. "We have a room four doors closer to the stairs, if that would suit?"

"Perfectly. We also require two more bedchambers for two gentlemen who will arrive in the next hour or so. Viscount Torrington and the Earl of Crowhurst. They would prefer to have rooms as close as possible to the stairs."

Gervase and Tony were watching the carriages from further along the street; once they saw they were indeed staying at Grillon's, they would head to the Bastion Club to check for any messages, then return to join them.

After more conferring, the head clerk said, "There *are* two single bedchambers that face the head of the stairs, but they overlook the lane. They're rarely requested . . ." The clerk looked his question.

Del smiled. "They will suit us perfectly. In addition, as I'm returning from service in India, and Miss Duncannon is returning from an extended sojourn in Jamaica, we're both traveling with household staff."

"That will pose no difficulty, sir. Not at this time of year. If I might suggest, I can consult with your staff directly as to what arrangements might be best?"

Del nodded. "My batman is Cobby, and . . ." He looked at Deliah.

With a slight frown, she supplied, "My majordomo is Janay."

"Excellent—I'll speak with Mr. Cobby and Mr. Janay. I take it your carriages are outside?" When Del assented, the clerk dispatched his underlings to direct the carriages into the mews, then came around the counter. "If you'll come this way, Colonel, Miss Duncannon, I'll show you to your rooms. Your bags will be brought up momentarily."

The next hours went in the inevitable bustle of settling into their rooms. The suite—something Deliah wouldn't have thought of to request—was commodious. Both the large sitting room and her adjoining bedchamber had wide windows overlooking the street. Contrary to her expectations, Del had managed the arrangements perfectly well. While she dressed for dinner, she thought again of the stipulations he'd made, a clear indication of how seriously he took the threat of the Black Cobra.

She sat at the dressing table and let Bess have at her hair.

Deftly rewinding the long tresses into a neat knot, then anchoring it atop Deliah's head with a tortoiseshell comb, Bess nodded at her in the mirror. "Just as well I didn't put all your evening gowns in the big trunks."

Deliah grimaced; most of her clothes, along with all her

other baggage, were traveling north by carter. "How many do we have?"

"This, and the emerald silk." Bess set in the final pin. "There." She stood back. "Perhaps if there's time while we're in town, you might get another. If we're going to some duke's house, even for a few days, you'll need it."

"We'll see." Deliah rose; she paused by the cheval glass and checked the fall of her plum silk gown, with its raised waist and scalloped neckline. Satisfied, she headed for the door to the sitting room.

They'd arranged to have dinner in the suite. Approving the menu was something Del had left to her. Janay and Cobby would serve the meal, leaving them free to discuss their plans.

Walking into the sitting room, she found Del standing by the window looking out over Albemarle Street. He turned as she entered; for an instant he seemed surprised to see her, then a knock on the door had them both turning that way.

"Come," she called.

The door opened to admit Tony and Gervase. Both nodded rather vaguely, absorbed with scanning the room, taking note of the window and the door to her bedchamber, before surveying the table laid ready for dinner, the comfortable armchairs set before the hearth, and the excellent fire.

Brows rising, Tony strolled forward. "Not a place I'd have picked, but it seems very well suited to our needs. Our rooms are right by the stairs, and we saw where yours is—couldn't have been better."

Del glanced at Deliah. "The accolades are due to Miss Duncannon—Grillon's was her suggestion."

Both Tony and Gervase smiled and half bowed to her.

The door opened again. Seeing Janay bearing a tureen, Deliah waved to the table. "Pray be seated, gentlemen. Dinner is here."

Del held a chair for her. She sat, with Gervase on her right, and Tony opposite.

Janay served the soup, while Cobby offered bread. When they setttled to sup, the two men left to fetch the next course.

"I have to say," Gervase murmured, "that I never thought I'd ever stay here, bastion of the prim and proper that it is." He glanced at Deliah. "We formed the Bastion Club late in '15, more or less immediately we returned from the Continent, and for those of us without houses in town—like Tony here, and me—it's become our London base over the last years."

"We originally set it up as a gentlemen's club," Tony explained, "but we all married in '16, over a period of about eight months, and our wives elected to use the club, too."

"Gasthorpe, our majordomo, and his staff adjusted very readily." Gervase grinned. "They've even coped with children on occasion."

They were just making conversation, but Deliah wanted to know more. "How many club members are there?"

They explained, and when she probed further, elaborated. The more she heard of their families, their pasts, their presents, the more she understood of their connection to the people on their country estates—an evolution from the protectiveness that must have driven them into the services years before—the more she relaxed with them. The more she trusted them.

The fruit platter had been decimated. As Cobby and Janay cleared the table, she glanced curiously at Del. She'd trusted him from the moment they'd met.

She knew better than to trust her instincts where men were concerned—especially handsome men who made her pulse race—yet there was no denying there was something very steadying, very steadfast, about Colonel Derek Delborough.

In lieu of port, Del told Cobby to fetch a bottle of arrack from his bags, Gervase and Tony having voiced a wish to sample the Indian version of brandy.

Tony glanced at Gervase, then looked at Del. "Perhaps we

should repair to your room." He turned his charming smile on Deliah. "We should discuss strategy, which will no doubt bore Miss Duncannon to tears."

Deliah smiled, equally charming. "On the contrary, Miss Duncannon is all ears." Her smile took on an edge. "I know all about the Black Cobra—or at least all I need to. You and Gervase may speak freely."

Tony and Gervase exchanged a swift, surprised, not entirely approving look, then glanced at Del.

"Two men tried to abduct Miss Duncannon during our halt at Windlesham."

Tony and Gervase straightened. "That," Gervase said, glancing at Deliah, "is not good news."

"You didn't manage to capture them?" Tony asked.

Briefly, Del described what had happened. "After that, as Miss Duncannon—"

"Please call me Deliah—it's simpler, and we're clearly all in this together."

Del inclined his head. "As Deliah subsequently observed, given that the Cobra has demonstrated he definitely has her in his sights, it was too dangerous for her not to know what, precisely, was going on." He met her gaze. "Incidentally, did you get any hint that there were others nearby—the man who shot at me, for instance?"

"No—it was just the two you saw. I don't think there were any others close."

"Can you describe both men? The rest of us barely saw the one who fled."

She complied, painting a picture sufficiently detailed to have all three men frowning.

"It sounds very much as if the Black Cobra is hiring locals to assist him—specifically to act against us so that there's no chance he or his lieutenants will be implicated." Del's gaze rested on Deliah. "You described the man who shot at me in Southampton—thinking of that now, I can't be sure if he was Ferrar's man Larkins, or a local hired to do the deed. If you saw him again, would you recognize him?"

"Definitely," Deliah averred. "I looked directly at him, and there were only ten yards or so between us."

And that, Del thought, very possibly explained the attack on her. Ferrar would also know that kidnapping her was a surefire way of pulling him into pursuit—pulling him away from his defined route, deflecting him from his mission.

"Given the current state of play"—he chose his words carefully—"you shouldn't venture outside—anywhere in public—without at least one of us in close attendance."

When he glanced at her, he was surprised by her ready nod. As if sensing his latent suspicion, she arched a brow. "After all you've told me, I have no wish to become a . . . guest of the Black Cobra."

"No, indeed." His expression stripped of all levity, Tony looked at Del. "I should mention that while Gasthorpe and his minions are desolate to have missed the pleasure of putting you up, they're always delighted to play supporting roles in our little adventures. Consequently, they're presently throwing themselves into watching the hotel and scouting out the surrounding streets for any hint of our pursuers."

"I take it you saw no potential lookouts during the journey?" Del asked.

Gervase grimaced. "We saw no Indians, or even tanned Englishmen. We did, however, see numerous shifty characters watching the carriages roll by, but there was no way of telling those reporting to the Black Cobra from the others. No one worth following."

The three men fell silent.

Deliah eyed each face, then prompted, "So what are our plans?" When no one rushed to speak, she suggested, "Perhaps you might reiterate what you wish to achieve over our sojourn in town?"

"We want," Del said, "to leave the Black Cobra guessing whether or not I'm carrying the original or a copy of the evidence. If he learns I've got a copy, he'll lose interest in me and swing his focus onto the other three. We don't want to give him that option. The way I interpreted Wolverstone's plan, part of the intent was to force the Black Cobra to fight on four different fronts, either simultaneously or at the very least in rapid succession."

Gervase nodded. "That's correct—weaken him by forcing him to spread his troops thin."

"So," Del continued, his gaze on the table, "we keep the scroll-holder safe—that's taken care of, and given Grillon's security, it's as protected as we can make it. We don't need to do anything more on that front, so that's our defensive aspect covered. As for the rest, we should do what we can to assess the strength of the Black Cobra's forces—has he imported many cultists into the country, as we assumed he would, or has he got just a handful, and that's why he's hiring locals? Is he using locals because it's easier, or because he has no choice?"

He glanced at Tony and Gervase. "The Black Cobra's modus operandi is to smother opposition—he usually relies on numerical advantage and expendable troops to win any encounter. The cult preaches that death in the service of the Black Cobra brings glory. Strategically, he's accustomed to attacking with an excess of men. It would help—a lot—to know if he has a large number here, held in reserve to date, or if lack of numbers will force him to play the game more craftily."

Tony nodded. "So we need to draw him, or at least his forces, out. We need to metaphorically wave the standard and dare him to come and take it—we need to taunt and tempt, just as we would on a battlefield."

"Which," Gervase said, "fits with Royce's orders to spend some time making noise in town, attracting, then fixing, the enemy's attention, drawing as much down on our heads as we can handle before we go haring north to Somersham Place, with any luck drawing a goodly number of cultists with us, into an ambush there." He shrugged. "Standard procedure, all in all."

They spent some time discussing options as to what might serve as "waving the standard."

"I should at some point call at East India House," Del said, "if nothing else to give Ferrar a sleepless night—he'll at least feel forced to check that I haven't shown anyone there the letter."

"You could add in visits to Whitehall and to Guards' Headquarters." Tony reached for the now half empty bottle of arrack. "The latter is somewhere he might find difficult to penetrate."

Deliah shifted in her chair. She could envision what they were suggesting and could see a potential problem, but she didn't want to point it out. Better they saw it themselves.

Gervase frowned. "We can do all that, but I fear it's all going to look too guarded. Too obvious. He'll watch, but he won't come into the open."

Precisely. Deliah cleared her throat. "If I might suggest . . . the one element in your plan that the Black Cobra couldn't have anticipated is me." She glanced at Del. "Not even you knew I would be traveling with you. But he now knows I'm with you, and that you are, for some reason unknown to him, acting as my escort. If we —you and I—start going about town on the sorts of excursions a provincial lady—a flighty, demanding provincial lady—would be expected to go on, he'll assume those excursions are driven by me, not you, that they're about what I want to do, not about you trying to draw him out.

"And just think." Seeing the sudden interest in their eyes, she let her own mounting enthusiasm show. "We can go for walks in the parks, shopping in Bond Street and Bruton Street, visiting the museum—and at this time of year fashionable London is almost deserted. He's unlikely to mount an attack in Whitehall, or outside the Guards, but outside a dressmaker's shop in Bruton Street? In the park as the shadows are lengthening? There's no reason for him to think such excursions are traps, not if you're escorting me."

Gervase slowly nodded. "That could work."

Del thought it might, too, but felt distinctly reluctant. It hadn't escaped him that, no matter her innocent I'm-merely-being-helpful attitude, Deliah had inserted herself into the heart of the action.

More, she'd made the worthiness of the excursions dependent on her.

Tony, too, waxed enthusiastic. "You could break up the fashionable excursions with those places Del mentioned—all places the Black Cobra would expect him to go." He paused, then nodded. "That should work—we have to make the enemy believe he has a chance of success if we want him to risk his men."

Del listened while the others discussed fashionable excursions with the potential to tempt an attack. He had to agree with their strategic assessment; Deliah's presence would lure the cultists into discounting any chance of a trap. And although he inwardly disapproved of her exposure to potential harm, he would be beside her, and Tony and Gervase would be close, ready to come to their aid.

Still. . . .

It was late, and they'd been traveling. With a decent list of excursions to mull over, they agreed to make their final arrangements in the morning, and rose to go to their rooms.

Tony and Gervase made their goodnights and strolled out. Del followed them to the suite's door, Deliah beside him.

He stepped into the corridor, then paused and glanced back at her.

She raised her brows. "What?"

He hesitated, then said, "Just because I've agreed to your involvement doesn't mean I'm in any way thrilled at the notion of you being exposed to danger, much less to the machinations of the Black Cobra."

She returned his regard levelly. "You'll be every bit as exposed to the same danger. And when all is said and done, you're not that much harder to kill than I am."

He frowned. Before he could correct her, she started to shut the door.

"Good night, Del."

Her soft words reached him, then he was left staring at the closed door.

December 12
Shrewton House, London

The drawing room of Shrewton House in Grosvenor Square was exactly as Alex had imagined it. Of course, the family was presently not in residence, and all the furniture was shrouded in holland covers, yet even in the shadowed gloom with the chandeliers unlit, the proportions of the room, the elegant appointments, were evident.

Alex sank onto the chaise Roderick had uncovered, and watched him pacing before his ancestral hearth. More correctly, *their* ancestral hearth—they could all lay claim to it. Their servants had set a fire blazing, driving the frigid chill from the air.

Roderick grimaced. "Grillon's might be unsuitable for a direct attack, but at least we can keep watch on them there easily enough."

"And"—Daniel subsided, languidly elegant, into a still shrouded armchair—"I seriously doubt Delborough is naïve enough to imagine he can advance his cause by showing the letter around East India House, or even Whitehall." Daniel looked at Roderick. "He knows your connections."

"Regardless," Roderick returned, "we'll watch."

"Indeed." Unshakably calm, Alex asked, "Meanwhile, what is Larkins doing about retrieving Delborough's letter?"

"His man inside Delborough's party is still there—a lucky break. Larkins is confident his man will find the letter and bring it out."

"But Larkins isn't simply relying on this thief of his, is he?" Daniel asked.

"No. If he sees a chance to take a hostage—the lady, for example—he'll act. And if for any reason he judges the letter has passed beyond our reach, unattainable by any means, he'll kill Delborough." Roderick continued to pace. "We'll watch and attack if an opportunity presents—aside from all else, it's what Delborough will expect, and the attacks will keep him focused outward, not on his own household."

"M'wallah tells me that Larkins isn't using our men." Alex made the statement and waited for an explanation.

Roderick nodded. "I thought it best, at least while we're shorthanded and the rest of our men are still arriving, that wherever possible Larkins should use local hirelings, rather than risk our own forces."

Alex smiled. "An excellent call." It always paid to compliment Roderick when he got things right. "So where are the others—our far-flung cultists?"

"We've got groups waiting in every south coast port, and those on the east as far north as Whitby. There are assassins with each group, and of course we have men on the trail of the other three. Given their varied routes and the impossibility of correctly predicting which English port they'll eventually use, I've given orders that, should they make it alive and still carrying their scroll-holder to any of the embarkation ports on the Continent, the first thing the men following them should do is inform us immediately." Roderick glanced at Daniel, then Alex. "That way, we'll have warning and time enough to get a suitable welcome in place."

"A welcome that has yet to be successful in Delborough's case," Alex coolly pointed out.

"We didn't have our usual complement of men available when Delborough arrived, but with a man inside his household, and the good colonel dallying in London with his mystery lady, we'll succeed." Roderick paused and once again glanced at Daniel, then Alex. "Regardless of retrieving all four letters, we should ensure that the couriers—all four of them—do not escape unscathed."

Alex smiled coldly, a chilling sight. "I agree entirely. We wouldn't want anyone to think we'd lost our fangs."

Three

December 13
Grillon's Hotel

They gathered over breakfast in the sitting room. The suite, Deliah admitted, was a strategic advantage for which Del had foreseen the need. They had to meet with Tony and Gervase to discuss their plans, but wanted to avoid being seen in public with their secret guards.

They quickly decided on their program for that day.

"Some of Gasthorpe's lads will be assisting," Gervase said, "so don't be surprised if they join in any fight."

"How will we know who they are?" she asked.

Tony smiled. "They'll be fighting on our side."

She would have made some retort, but Gervase quickly went on, "Gasthorpe sent word—a message from Royce." He nodded at Del. "You are the first one home, but Hamilton's reached Boulogne—he's expected to cross the Channel in the next few days."

"That's good news." Del felt a quiet relief knowing Gareth had made it that far unscathed.

"All is, we're told, in place for him to be met when he sets foot on English soil, but as usual Royce has omitted to mention where that will be." Gervase smiled resignedly. Del and Tony did, too.

Deliah asked, "Did this commander of yours say anything further?"

Gervase pushed his empty plate away. "Only that we should proceed as planned and draw out the cultists in London." He glanced at Del. "The letter's safe?"

Del nodded. "It's never left unattended."

"Right, then." Tony rose, gave his hand to Deliah and gallantly assisted her to her feet. "Let's get cracking. First stop, Bond Street."

"It's been years since I was here," Deliah said.

As she was standing with her nose all but pressed to the window of Asprey, Jewellers to the Crown, and had spoken without lifting her gaze from the sparkling display, Del had guessed as much. Her arm in his, she'd all but towed him down Albemarle Street, into Piccadilly and around the corner into Bond Street. Pretending to be dragging his heels hadn't been difficult.

Yet it was amusing—and revealing—to realize that the part she was playing, that of a provincial lady fascinated by and determined to enjoy all the typical London delights, wasn't all pretense.

She finally dragged her bright gaze from the scintillating array and looked further up the street. "There are more jewelers, aren't there?"

He pointed out Rundell & Bridge, further along on the other side of the street; all bustling determination, she towed him over. Given the entertainment, he had to make an effort to look suitably bored. They halted before the well-known jeweler's windows; while she examined an arrangement of necklaces, he glanced at her face.

No pretense; she coveted the sparkling gems as much as any other lady. He started to wonder what else might be revealed when, as per their plan, they continued on to the Bruton Street modistes.

His attraction to her hadn't waned, which he found rather strange. She was domineering—or would be if he let her be—opinionated, wasp-tongued and a great deal more willfully independent than he was comfortable with, yet she'd become a part of his mission—unwittingly and through no fault of her own—and was now assisting, a contributing player in the game, and somewhere beneath his reluctant resignation, he was grateful. Grateful it was her, with all her innate confidence, and not some wilting, shrinking, typical genteel young miss, who would cling and require constant reassurance, effective lead in his, Tony's and Gervase's saddlebags.

Holding to his ennui, he cast an idle—in reality acute—glance back along the street. Without hurry, he returned his gaze to the window. "We're being followed, by locals."

"The two men in brown coats back down the street?"

He hadn't seen her look, much less notice.

She shifted and pointed, apparently through the window. "I think he—the man in a shabby bowler behind us—is watching us, too."

Del focused on the reflection in the big window. Decided she was right. "They won't close in along here—there are too many people to make any attempt on us."

"Bruton Street should be much less frequented at this hour."

Del made a show of sighing, then tugging on her sleeve. When she turned, he pointed further up the street. She shook her head, and instead pointed to Bruton Street, off to their left. Pantomiming resigned frustration, he reluctantly escorted her that way.

They turned into Bruton Street. The man in the bowler crossed the mouth of the street, then also turned down it on the opposite side.

Deliah walked along, studying the plaques announcing various modistes and the gowns displayed in narrow windows alongside—watching the bowler-hatted man trail them.

Beside her, Del murmured, "The other two have just turned the corner, so once again we have three."

"I wonder how they think they're going to blend in in this neighborhood."

"I suspect they think we're oblivious."

She humphed, then stopped before the next modiste's window. "I've been away for so long, I have no idea which modiste is in favor. I don't even know what the latest styles are."

"There's no point looking to me for assistance." After a moment, he added, "Didn't you see any of the latest fashions in Southampton?"

"I wasn't paying attention—I was just filling the time."

"By shopping?"

"What else was I to do? Inspect ships?" Recollecting, she added, "Perhaps I should have—ships would undoubtedly have been more interesting."

"I thought all ladies shopped whenever the opportunity presented."

"I shop when I need something—I generally have better things to do."

It wasn't so much the comment as her tone that jarred Del's memory. He'd never met her before Southampton, but he had heard of her. Heard tales of her when she, and he, had been much younger. She'd been the local tomboy, the bane of her mother's existence, as he recalled.

She'd noticed his abstraction. "What?"

He glanced at her, met her eyes. "Did you really tie a bell to Farmer Hanson's bull's tail?"

Her eyes narrowed, then she looked ahead. "I wondered if you would remember."

They walked on to the next modiste's window.

"So did you?"

"Martin Rigby dared me to, so yes, I did." She frowned at him, waved at the window. "You really have no recommendation—no preferences?"

He glanced along the street. The salons lining it were all similar. "None."

"In that case, I'll just pick one." She walked on, then halted before a window showcasing a simply cut but stylish gown of blue silk. "No ruffles, no frills, no furbelows. And a French name. This one will do."

Reaching for the door beside the window, Del read the brass plaque fixed to the wall beside it. "Madame Latour." He opened the door, held it.

As she passed through, Deliah murmured, "I haven't caught sight of our guards or their helpers."

"I suspect they're a trifle more expert in the art of unobtrusively trailing people. Don't worry—they'll be there."

A bell had jangled overhead when the door opened. Finding herself facing a narrow set of stairs, Deliah started to climb. A young assistant appeared at the top, smiling and bobbing in welcome.

"Good morning, ma'am. Sir. Please." The girl waved them through an open door. "Go through. Madame will be with you shortly."

It was barely ten o'clock, unfashionably early, so it was no great surprise to find no other patrons gracing the salon.

What was a surprise was Madame herself. She emerged from behind a curtain, a slim young woman, pale-skinned, with brown hair sleeked back in a tight bun and large hazel eyes. Madame was young—younger than Deliah. And after her first words, a heavily accented greeting, it was obvious Madame was no more French than Deliah was, either.

She pretended not to notice. "Bonjour, madame. I have this week returned from a prolonged sojourn overseas and am in dire need of new gowns." Gently reared young woman impoverished by harsh circumstance was Deliah's assessment of Madame. "I liked what I saw in your window. Perhaps you could show me what else you have?"

"*Absolutement.* If madame would sit here?" Madame gestured to a satin-covered sofa, then glanced at Del. "And monsieur your husband, also?"

Deliah glanced at her escort. "The Colonel is an old family friend who has kindly consented to accompany me north."

She sat, and watched Del amble across the salon.

He smiled, charmingly, at Madame. "I've agreed to assist and lend my opinion." So saying, he sat beside Deliah, elegantly at ease, and looked inquiringly at Madame.

Who stared back as if unsure just what she'd invited into her salon.

Deliah couldn't blame her. He was large, and although he was wearing civilian clothes, nothing could cloak his military bearing, that dangerous, suggestively rakish aura that hung about him.

Thus far she'd managed to keep her skittering nerves within bounds and her reactions to him hidden. She'd even managed largely to ignore them, or at least not allow them to dominate her mind. Now . . . whether it was the heightened contrast of having him beside her, large and so brashly masculine in such an intensely feminine setting, she didn't know, but she was suddenly highly conscious of the tension that rode her, compressing her lungs, distracting her senses and setting her nerves flickering.

Still, as long as he didn't realize. . . .

She gestured to Madame. "Pray proceed."

Madame blinked, then bowed. "Ma'am. I have a number of styles available, suitable to be worn from morning to evening. Does madame wish to start with the morning gowns?"

"Indeed. I need gowns of all types."

With a nod, Madame whisked behind the curtain. From where they sat, they could hear a whispered conference beyond.

Still too aware of the hard heat beside her, Deliah glanced at the windows. "Those look over the street."

"True, but it's too soon to check. If they see me looking out all but immediately, they'll get suspicious."

Madame chose that moment to reappear, two gowns on her arm. Her little assistant staggered in her wake, bearing an armload of garments.

"First," Madame said, "I would suggest this." She held

up her first offering, a plum-colored morning gown in soft cambric.

What followed was an education. Del relaxed on the sofa and watched. Watched Deliah respond to Madame's designs, and Madame grow steadily more confident. The youthful modiste presented each gown, holding it aloft to recite and display its features. Deliah would then either accept or decline to allow it to be added to the pile for her to try on. She asked questions, most of which were a mystery to Del, but apparently made excellent sense to Madame. Within minutes, Deliah and the modiste had established a rapport.

Regardless, it wasn't until they reached the evening gowns that Del realized Deliah was sincere in her intention to buy a number of Madame's creations. She'd already added to her pile for further consideration a sleekly simple gown in pale green silk that even he could tell would look stunning on her, and was debating between a gown of soft gold satin and another of a delicate shade of sky blue.

"Try them both."

Madame shot him a grateful smile.

Deliah looked at him, faintly shocked.

"If you'll come into the dressing room, ma'am, we can see if these selections will suit."

"An excellent idea." Del couldn't resist adding, "I'll be waiting to give you my views on each."

Deliah's eyes narrowed. She flicked a glance toward the windows. "Shouldn't you be keeping an eye out for our friends?"

"It's too soon yet to look for them."

She wanted to argue, but with Madame hovering, she rose and allowed herself to be shepherded beyond the curtain.

Del sat back and prepared to enjoy himself. Tony and Gervase, supported by the legendary Gasthorpe's men, would be in place outside by now, but waiting a trifle longer would give the Black Cobra's minions time to grow bored and careless.

The curtain rattled back, and Deliah came out arrayed in a morning gown of some pale gold material with small emerald green leaves liberally sprinkled over all. She looked like Spring personified. With nary a glance for him, she walked to the corner of the salon where four mirrored panels were arranged to allow ladies to view the gowns they wore from several different angles.

Deliah turned this way and that, her gaze following the lines of the gown, from the tightly fitting bodice to the trim raised waist, to where the skirts caressed her hips before falling to sway about her very long legs.

Del's gaze followed hers. Lingered. Appreciatively. "Very nice."

She stiffened, glanced at him in the mirror.

Then she turned to the hovering modiste, nodded curtly. "Yes—I'll take this one."

Without again glancing his way, she stalked past him and back behind the curtain.

The parade that followed left Del questioning his sanity in remaining to view it and simultaneously pleased he had. While the more rational, logical side of his brain continued to insist she was nothing more than a female his aunts had thrown in his path, someone to be smiled at courteously and deposited safely back with her parents in Humberside, another, more primal side was far more viscerally interested in her on a personal, not to say primitive, level.

Of course, he couldn't resist giving her his opinion on her appearance in the various gowns. Couldn't resist giving himself the excuse to run his eyes down her evocatively feminine length, from her nicely rounded shoulders, bared by the evening gowns, over the womanly swells of her breasts, the subtle curve of her neat waist, her sweetly rounded hips, and the fascinating length of her long legs.

The sum of her made his mouth water.

He would have suffered in relative silence had she not reacted. Had she not, after the first faint blush rose in her cheeks, decided to torment him. After modeling a carriage gown, to which, admittedly with his gaze fixed on the tightly fitting frogged bodice, he'd given his verbal stamp of approval, she'd shot him a look, whisked back behind the curtain, a definite tinge in her cheeks, then minutes later swanned back out in a gown of flame-colored silk and a temper equally fiery.

The fabric clung to every curve like paint. Man of the world that he was, that wouldn't, normally, have affected him all that much.

She, in that gown, in a mood part anger, part reaction, and all challenge, did. She swished, she swanned, she glided and pirouetted. Played to the mirror, to her gaze, and his. Then, over her shoulder, she glanced at him and brazenly asked his opinion.

He met her gaze and equally brazenly gave it. "Revealing. You should definitely indulge in that one." As he had no wish to shock Madame, he didn't specify exactly what he was recommending she indulge in, yet Deliah comprehended his meaning.

Her eyes glittered, then she looked back at the mirror, shamelessly twirled some more. Then she nodded decisively. "Yes, I believe I will."

With that, she swayed back behind the curtain.

Deliah let the silk gown slide down her body, felt its caress like a lover's hands, and knew responding to his blatant interest was madness.

A madness she hadn't felt for years. No—a madness beyond anything she'd felt before.

There was . . . something in the way he looked at her. Something that made her feel heated. Wicked. Wanton.

She'd known from her first sight of him that he was dangerous. That he could connect, draw forth, lure *her*—the real her—from the cavern she'd hidden in for seven long years. She hadn't told him why she'd gone—been sent—to Jamaica, that an old scandal had been to blame. That she'd been seduced, then betrayed, by a viscount's son on a repairing lease. That, innocent and wantonly passionate, she'd given her heart as well as her body, only later to learn that for him it had all been merely a challenge, a way to fill the time.

Her parents had railed, her father especially, church elder that he was. She'd had it drummed into her, in so many ways, that her inner self was *bad*. That she had to hide it, subdue it, suppress it at all costs.

She'd been packed off to Jamaica, and she'd never felt that inner self stir again. She'd thought it had died—of shame, of rejection.

Of imprisonment without succor.

Thanks to Colonel Derek Delborough, she now knew otherwise.

But while part of her rejoiced, the wiser, more cautious side of her foretold disaster.

Yet she was sick, so sick, of being only half alive.

So she let Miss Jennings—Madame Latour as she'd styled herself—slip the next gown, the gold satin evening gown, over her head. It fell with a soft *swoosh* over her limbs. She surveyed the effect in the mirror, as Miss Jennings, with pins between her lips, nipped and tucked.

The particular shade of gold made her skin glow like the costliest pearl, made her hair appear more intensely garnet-red.

She looked . . . like a king's ransom.

Lips curving, she turned and glided out to show Del, who sat like a pasha relaxed on the sofa, his eyes—richly dark and intent—locking on her, tracing her curves as, with flagrant disregard of his regard, she swept to the mirror. And performed.

Like a houri. A very English houri, yet a houri nonetheless. Del was finding it increasingly hard to catch his breath, to breathe freely. With effort he maintained his pose, his façade of relaxed ease, even though every muscle in his body had long ago tightened with sheer lust.

He was almost certain she knew.

Then she swirled, hips circling beneath the shimmering

satin, and let her gaze meet his in the mirror, sending a shot of heat straight to his groin . . . oh, yes, she knew. She definitely knew.

Teeth gritted behind his easy smile, he waited until she slipped behind the curtain to stand, to force himself to walk to the window—to ease his mounting discomfort and try to get his mind back on the game he was supposed to be playing.

Away from the game he'd rather be playing with her.

Standing to one side of the window, he looked down on the street. The two men in brown coats and the man in the shabby bowler had given up waiting separately. They were standing, pretending to be chatting, on the pavement opposite Madame Latour's door. The occasional, surreptitious glances they cast toward the door foretold their plan.

Perfect.

Looking up the street, he saw a lounging figure chatting—with much greater success at projecting nonchalance—with two street sweepers. Tony.

And on the other side, the man leaning against the wall just this side of Bond Street and talking to two lads was Gervase.

Everyone was in place. It was time for action.

He turned from the window as Deliah swept back in.

In a pale green gown that nearly stopped his heart.

Deliah saw him by the window—instantly her need to tweak his nose fell away. "What is it?"

He held her gaze, then, as Miss Jennings followed her through the curtain, reached into his pocket. Pulling out his fob watch, he glanced at it, then tucked it back. "Time's getting on."

For one long instant, he let his eyes—his hot gaze—slide, long and lingeringly, over her body, over the pale green silk that clung lovingly to her form . . . then he raised his eyes, captured hers. Nodded. "That's my favorite. I'm going to go down and hail a hackney while you change."

With that, he strode for the door.

She started after him. "*Wait*—" But he was already gone.

Beneath her breath, she swore, then turned to Miss Jennings. "Quickly. I have to get out of this and into my clothes."

Miss Jennings fluttered after her as she strode back behind the curtain. "If you're late, I can pack them and send them on—"

"I'll be back in a few minutes to make my selection. Here, hurry—help me out of this!"

Miss Jennings jumped, then responded to the voice of one used to giving orders. With her help, Deliah climbed out of the green silk, flung it aside and scrabbled through the welter of gowns for her own. "Damn him! I should have guessed he'd do this."

Miss Jennings was entirely at sea. "Has he left you?"

"No, of course not. He thinks . . . oh, never mind. Here—do up my laces." As Miss Jennings's shaking fingers complied, Deliah added, "And don't worry—I'll be taking the gowns."

She heard the young modiste haul in a huge breath, then her fingers steadied.

The instant the laces were cinched and tied, Deliah reached for her pelisse. As she shrugged it on, she heard a distant shout.

Grabbing her reticule, she dashed out of the dressing room and hurried to the window. She looked out. The street seemed empty, but she couldn't see the pavement directly before the shop; an awning obstructed her view. All she caught were glimpses of a shifting mass of arms and shoulders.

Turning, she flew out of the open doorway and onto the stairs. Clattering down as fast as she could, she tugged her pelisse properly on, fumbled with the buttons.

Heart racing—what was going on outside the door?—she was almost at the bottom of the stairs when the door opened.

Breath catching in her throat, she looked up.

Del filled the doorway.

She tried to halt her precipitous rush. Her heel snagged in her pelisse's hem, jerking one shoulder—she twisted, lost her balance.

Pitched forward.

Straight into his arms.

Del stepped forward to catch her. Heard the door he'd sent swinging shut snick behind him just as she landed flush against him, and every sense he possessed focused, intent and hungry—suddenly ravenously hungry—on her.

On her long, tall, undeniably feminine form plastered to his.

On the warmth of her curves, on their lush promise.

On her face, jade eyes wide with shock.

Lips, rosy red and luscious, parted. . . .

Because she'd been above him, they were face-to-face, those luscious lips level with his.

He saw them shift, form words.

"What happened? Are you all right?"

He felt her hands grip his arms. When he lifted his gaze to her eyes, hers searched, urgently, almost frantically. The emotion lighting the jade was simple, undisguised concern.

She cared.

No woman had for decades.

Her lips firmed, then parted again. Her fingers gripped, and she tried to shake him. "Are. You. Hurt?"

He'd been struck—that he knew—but not by any fist.

She drew breath, her luscious lips parted again—and he knew he had to answer. So he did. In the most appropriate way.

He bent his head, covered her ruby lips with his.

Kissed her, not as he might any gently bred young lady but as he'd longed to kiss the houri who'd taunted him for the last hour.

Her lips had been parted. He took her mouth with no by-your-leave. Simply waltzed in and laid claim . . .

And ended reeling. Sinking. Drowning.

Captive to an exchange too potent for excuses, too primitively powerful to ever be denied.

Too urgent to be brought to any quick and neat end.

His arms cinched tight, hauling her against him, locking her there—where she belonged. He felt her hands on his shoulders, then in his hair.

Felt—knew—when she succumbed to the compulsion, to the desire that suborned all reason, to the unrelenting thud of passion in his veins.

Their veins.

The sensation was so heady Deliah was helpless to resist. To pull away, retreat to safety, to step back. Instead, she plunged in.

Into the temptation of his hot demanding mouth, into the whirling vortex of desire that had seized the unlooked-for moment to manifest between them—the cumulative promise of the last hour's teasing; the nascent passion they'd both been deliberately prodding flared to urgent life between them.

She kissed him back, flagrantly demanding, joyously inciting, her inner self racing ahead, free of all restraint.

Wantonly enticing. Abandoned and eager.

Del sensed it, tasted her unleashed passion, and urgently wanted more.

But . . . wrong time, wrong place.

Some distant spark of sanity assured him that was so. With regret, he forced himself to draw back; only by reminding himself of all he would eventually gain did he manage to rein in his hunger, soothing it with promises of ultimate gluttony. That she would, at some time—the right place and the right time—appease his hunger, feed it until he—it—was utterly sated was, to his mind, an engagement already inscribed in stone.

Easing back from the kiss, he lifted his head and looked down into dazed jade eyes, took in her oddly blank, faraway expression—and knew a moment of intense satisfaction.

At last he'd found a surefire way to manage the willful woman.

A way to tame her, to bring her to him, to his bed. . . .

The sound of a throat clearing hauled his mind from that attractive track, from dwelling on the satisfaction having her beneath him would bring. Looking up, he saw Madame Latour and her assistant peering rather warily down.

"Pack up the gowns—all that were tried on—and send them to Miss Duncannon at Grillon's. You may send your account to me there."

Madame's face lit. She bobbed a curtsy. "Thank you, Colonel. Miss Duncannon. You won't be disappointed."

He was sure he wouldn't be. He had plans for that pale green dress.

Looking down at Deliah, he set her on her feet.

She opened her mouth, but before she could speak, he asked, "Are you ready to go on?"

She blinked, hearing, correctly, the latent triumph in his tone.

Remembering what had brought her rushing down the stairs, Deliah swallowed, nodded. She wasn't yet sure she had command of her voice.

By the time he'd led her outside—where all appeared normal and utterly mundane—and she'd finished buttoning her pelisse against the increasingly biting wind, settling her reticule and gloves, then had taken his arm and begun strolling beside him, her wits had started to function again— enough to have her wondering if perhaps he'd kissed her, at least in part, because the modiste had been watching.

That didn't seem convincing, not even to her, but if furthering their roles wasn't his motive, she'd rather not think of what was.

Shouldn't think of what was, or might be.

She was shocked enough by her own motives—by the reemergence of the wanton inner self she'd thought she'd buried, or at least bludgeoned into weakness, long ago.

With him, that side of her wasn't weak at all. She was going to have to be on guard henceforth; she couldn't return to England after all these years, supposedly reformed, only to fall victim to her own desires with the first handsome man who crossed her path.

Admittedly, he was exceedingly handsome. But still. . . .

He'd been the first man to kiss her, at least like that, in more years than she cared to count . . . actually, in all her life.

After a moment, she blinked, inwardly shook her head. She was looking ahead down the street—and seeing his lips.

She needed to concentrate on the here and now. Replaying his last words . . . she frowned. "I can't accept gowns from you. It wouldn't be proper."

He glanced her way, but she didn't meet his eyes.

"What do you imagine I'm going to do with them? The least you can do is take them off my hands. Better yet, consider them a perquisite of helping me pursue the Black Cobra. Believe me"—his tone hardened—"it's a small price to pay."

"In that case, you can let me pay for them—I'm more than flush enough to buy my own gowns."

"That's not the issue. I can't countenance you paying for the necessaries to continue our ruse. This is my mission, not yours. My responsibility, not yours."

Those last two points were ones Del felt sure he needed to stress—and often. In every possible way.

She grumbled, "I can't see how those evening gowns could be deemed necessary."

"Oh, they are. Believe me, they are." They—and the visions of her in them—were going to keep him going through the coming days. His reward, as it were, for weathering the difficulties keeping her with him had already caused, and those yet to come.

"They'll come to a pretty penny—you do realize that?"

"After all my years in India, I'm wealthy enough to rival Croesus, so your concern on that point, while appreciated, is unnecessary."

She humphed. Eventually she said, by way of conceding,

"Just be warned that that last evening gown alone will cost a small fortune. Madame may be young, but she values her work highly."

"Rightly so." He felt doubly triumphant that he'd won that round—won the right to pay for her gowns. He should, he knew, be exceedingly wary about such a reaction, but he was too busy wallowing in the victory to let such considerations dim his mood. "A workman is worthy of his hire, and all that. But your point is duly noted—I promise not to expire of shock."

She gave an unladylike snort, then fell silent.

He strolled on, with her on his arm, and imagined seeing her in that pale green gown. Wondered how he might arrange it.

Some paces on, the fact that she'd been perfectly willing to part with "a small fortune" of her own registered. But her family wasn't wealthy, and he was fairly certain she couldn't have inherited more than a competence from any relative, not without his aunts mentioning it.

Now he thought of it, she was traveling with an entire household, staying at major inns, hiring carriages and private parlors—and she hadn't even paused to consider the cost of putting up at Grillon's. He'd be picking up the bill there, but she hadn't known that, and still didn't.

She was wealthy. But how?

"Did you and the others catch any of those men?"

Her question shook him out of his abstraction. "Yes." They'd reached Berkeley Square. Halting, he glanced around, one comprehensive survey, then turned to her. "And as there appear to be no more following us, we're going to take a detour."

"Oh? To where?"

"The Bastion Club."

Four

T he club wasn't far. The hackney Del had hired halted outside a house in a street south of Hyde Park.

Standing on the pavement beside Del while he paid off the jarvey, Deliah owned to considerable curiosity over the strange "private gentlemen's-cum-family" club she'd heard so much about. Number 12 Montrose Street was a solid house, not dissimilar to those flanking it. As they walked up the neatly paved path to the front porch, she could see nothing to distinguish it from any other gentleman's residence.

The front door opened as they ascended the porch steps. A neat, rotund individual in the garb of a majordomo— somewhere between a butler's regulation black tails and a gentleman's gentleman's less formal attire—stood waiting to greet them, a delighted smile on his kindly face.

"Colonel Delborough?"

"Indeed. And this is Miss Duncannon. I believe Torrington and Crowhurst are already here?"

"Indeed, sir. I am Gasthorpe." He bowed them in, then took Del's greatcoat. "If we may be of assistance at any time, sir, please do not hesitate to call upon me and the staff here."

Deliah elected to keep her pelisse on. "Torrington and Crowhurst told us of this place." While the underlying ambiance of the house was sparse and rather plainly severe, a vase of hothouse blooms rioted on the hall table, their color and freshness drawing the eye, softening the décor. There was a lace doily beneath the vase, and numerous other little touches that spoke of female, rather than only male. "I understand it was originally just for the gentlemen, but clearly that has changed."

"Oh, yes, miss—we often have the ladies to stay these days. Once the gentlemen wed—indeed, even before, during their various adventures—we were called upon to accommodate their ladies."

She was curious. "You don't seem to mind."

"I will admit I was initially trepidatious, but now we look forward to the families descending—quite keeps us on our toes."

Deliah smiled. "I can imagine."

"Torrington and Crowhurst?" Del inquired.

"Yes, sir. They're awaiting you downstairs with the captured miscreants." Beaming at Deliah, Gasthorpe gestured to the room to the right of the front door. "If you would care to wait in comfort in the parlor, miss, I will bring up a tea tray directly."

Deliah glanced, once, at the room beyond the open door, then, brows rising, looked at Del. "I'm not in the mood for tea, but I do want to see these men. I'll come with you."

Del had hoped that Gasthorpe might manage to deflect her, but wasn't truly surprised that he'd failed. Stifling a resigned sigh, he nodded. "Very well." He'd long ago learned not to fight unnecessary skirmishes but to save his powder for the important battles. He looked at Gasthorpe. "Lead on."

Gasthorpe looked uncertain, but he took his lead from Del and, without argument, turned and led them to a set of stairs at the back of the front hall.

Waving Deliah ahead of him, Del followed her down. The stairs led to spacious kitchens. Gasthorpe led them through and into a narrow corridor, off which several storerooms lay. He paused outside one. With his hand on the latch, he turned to them. "This is one of our holding rooms."

As Gasthorpe opened the door, Del drew Deliah back and entered first. He halted just inside, then moved further in, allowing her to follow.

Deliah took in the occupants of the small room in one glance. Tony and Gervase sat with their backs to the door, on straight-backed chairs before a plain wooden table. On the other side of the table, three ruffians slouched on a bench. Hands tied before them, they propped against each other, shoulder to shoulder.

All three looked rather the worse for wear. Two sported blackening eyes. The other had a nasty bruise on his chin. All three looked uneasy, restless and uncertain.

Tony and Gervase glanced at Del and her as they entered; both started to rise, but she waved them back to their seats. She and Del remained standing behind them.

Subsiding and turning back to the table, Tony gestured to their captives. "We've been chatting with these gentlemen." Despite the easy tenor of his words, there was a definite suggestion of steel beneath. "They don't seem to know very much about anything, but we thought we'd wait for you before getting to specifics."

Standing inside the now closed door, Deliah viewed the three ruffians and was glad of the three gentlemen between her and them. For all they were tied and clearly off-balance, they were hulking brutes with rough menace in their beady eyes—all of which had fixed on her.

Regardless, she felt perfectly safe. The three gentlemen were more than a counter to the louts; the menace that rolled off their elegant selves was of an infinitely more lethal variety.

And the louts knew it.

That the pecking order was established and recognized

was immediately made clear. When Del asked who had hired them, the louts answered readily.

"Geezer came to our tavern—it's in the East End. Said he were looking for men to grab a woman as was giving him trouble. He'd make it worth our while. All we had to do was grab her, and bring her to him tonight, and we'd get ten sovereigns."

"Ten sovereigns?" Deliah was incensed. "That's insulting!"

Del sent her a quelling look.

"How did you know which lady to grab?" Gervase asked.

The lout in the middle looked at Deliah. "He said she were tall, with dark red hair, a real looker—and she was staying at Grillon's."

Deliah crossed her arms. "What, exactly, were you supposed to do with me after you seized me?"

"He made it sound easy." The lout on the left sniffed. "Didn't say nuffin 'bout you havin' guards. All we had to do was snatch you off the street, and being careful not to damage the goods, bring you to the tavern tonight. He said to sit in a corner, an' keep you quiet 'til he arrived."

Deliah was tempted to ask how they'd thought to keep her quiet.

"Describe this man," Del said.

The louts grimaced, looked at each other. Then the one in the middle shrugged. "Nothing special about him. Could be anyone."

"Not helpful," Tony murmured, and the louts paled.

"How tall was he?" Deliah asked.

The louts looked at her. "Maybe an inch or so taller'n you, miss. Ma'am." The middle lout glanced at Del. "Not so tall as the gentl'man."

Deliah nodded. "What about his clothes?"

The lout grimaced. "Middling. Not one thing nor another."

"He wasn't a toff, that's certain," one of the others put in.

"Nay—he weren' even a gentl'man, though he spoke well enough."

"Describe the man's hair," Deliah said. "What color, and how was it cut?"

The louts looked at her, then one answered, "Brown hair, longish."

Deliah glanced at Del. "Not the man in Southampton."

"Nor the two at Windlesham." Del looked at the ruffians. "Where's this tavern?"

The three shifted on the bench, exchanging glances. Then the one in the middle—the leader—looked up. "What's in it fer us if we tell you?"

It was Tony who answered. "It's simple enough. Tell us where the tavern is, and after we keep your appointment for you, we'll hand you over to the authorities for attempted thieving, rather than attempted kidnapping. In other words, your choice is between transportation, or hanging."

The three exchanged another, longer glance, then the leader sighed. "All right. It's the Blue Barrel in Cobalt Lane."

Leaving the three louts in Gasthorpe's custody, the four of them repaired to the library upstairs. A comfortable room on the first floor with large leather armchairs and numerous side tables, it was the perfect venue for discussing developments, and planning their next move.

"Tony and I will keep their appointment this evening," Gervase said. "We'll see who turns up, and if we're lucky, follow them back to the Black Cobra's lair."

"I doubt it'll be that simple," Del said. He glanced at Deliah. "Ferrar clearly wants to use you as hostage for the letter."

"Presumably," Tony said, "he sees that as an easier option than making a direct try for it."

"Which," Gervase added, "tells us he's engaged—that we have his attention—which, after all, is the crux of our mission."

"That, and reducing his forces." Del frowned. "So far, we've only seen locals—hirelings."

"Perhaps," Deliah said, "I should play the part of captive

hostage this evening?" She looked at the three men. "I'll be perfectly safe, because you'll be my captors."

For one instant, she glimpsed horror in all three pairs of eyes, then their expressions blanked.

"No." Del's tone was unequivocal, unassailable.

Deliah met his eyes, read his absolute opposition. Shrugged. "All right." She didn't harbor any ambition to visit an East End tavern, much less run the risk of meeting the Black Cobra; she'd only made the offer because she'd felt she should.

All three men looked at her, searched her face for a moment more, as if not quite certain of the sincerity of her agreement, then Del looked at Gervase. "So what should we do to fill the rest of the day?"

What could he do to ensure she was distracted? Just the thought of her sitting in some seedy tavern, a hostage waiting to be collected by the Black Cobra, had shaken him—in a way he wasn't accustomed to being shaken. He'd never felt possessive about any other woman, let alone a lady, let alone a lady like her. If given the choice, he would have elected to go with Gervase and Tony to the tavern that night, but now . . . he didn't dare leave her to her own devices. Who knew what she might take it into her head to do? All in the name of being helpful, of course.

Despite his mission being to flush out the Black Cobra, he knew beyond question that his place was with her. Guarding against any possible threat to her.

Tony and Gervase seemed to be thinking along similar lines. In short order, between them they decided on an afternoon of excursions that might, or might not, draw out the cult's forces, but would definitely occupy Deliah's time.

December 13
City of London

"Is that it?" Deliah peered out of the hackney at a long stone building with an impressive façade of Doric pillars fronting

Leadenhall Street. The pillars were crowned by a pediment with numerous carved figures.

"East India House," Del confirmed. "The London headquarters of the Honorable East India Company."

"They take themselves very seriously, don't they?"

"Indeed. Wait until you see inside. I've heard the new skylight is quite something."

After letting Gasthorpe feed them luncheon in the dining room of the club, they'd hailed two hackneys and set out for the city. Del and Deliah were in the first carriage, while Tony and Gervase followed in the second. While Del and Deliah went inside, Tony and Gervase would watch from the street to see if any likely-looking characters took an interest.

Their hackney halted before the steps leading up between the pillars. Del descended, after one glance around handed Deliah down, then paid off the jarvey. He turned to find Deliah, head back, staring up at the frieze above the pillars.

"Is that Britannia? And Tritons on sea horses?"

"As you remarked, the company considers itself an august institution." Taking her arm, he led her up the steps and through the massive doors, which attentive doormen in the uniforms of sepoy regiments leapt to hold wide.

Inside, massive braziers glowed, taking the chill from the marble walls and floors. Deliah halted, staring around. "The word that springs to mind is *opulent*."

"And this is merely the foyer." He steered her on through a massive archway into a huge chamber that rose fully three stories high. It was lit by a large, domed skylight. Niches on the wall held marble statues; glass-fronted cabinets displayed jeweled Indian artifacts, and gold and silver plate.

Halting, Deliah looked around. "Simple words fail me. I take it they wanted everyone to realize how profitable trade with India is?"

"I suspect that was a large part of the motivation." Del glanced around, looking for familiar faces. "This is the Grand Court Room. We're going to visit the main rooms, see who's here, chat with some." He looked at her. "It would help if you would smile and hang on my arm. And, if possible, remain silent."

Deliah arched her brows, but twined her arm in his and endeavored to keep a light, airy smile on her face.

They started promenading. There were many others about, and while some hurried past with papers in their hands, or were deep in serious discussions, most seemed to be socializing—discussing business, perhaps, but without any specific intent.

Some among the gathering—mostly officers in the uniforms of various regiments, but others in civilian attire—recognized Del. All evinced surprise as they shook his hand. "What brings you home?" was the common first question.

One, Deliah noted, he didn't actually answer. Instead, he spoke of when he'd arrived, and asked after others who might be there that day. When a few in uniform asked after his colleagues, he admitted some others were also expected home any day.

It didn't take long for Deliah to realize that, with her hanging as directed, sweetly smiling on his arm, those who spoke with them leapt to the obvious conclusion.

When they moved on through an archway into the next room, she leaned close and murmured, "You're deliberately letting people imagine that you came home to marry me."

He glanced at her, met her eyes. "It's easier than telling the truth."

She mulled over that for a moment, then asked, "Why? Why not say you're here to lay evidence against the Black Cobra? There's no reason to keep it secret, is there? The Black Cobra already knows."

"True. But my mission is to draw the cultists out, not to encourage a horde of well-meaning others to become involved. Many of those here know of the Black Cobra's villainy and would be happy to assist in bringing him down. Yet playing this sort of game is the same as cooking—having too many cooks doesn't help."

Another gentleman approached to speak with Del. Deliah continued to smile while she pondered his words.

The room they were now in, the New Sale Room, was decorated with pilasters and paintings of scenes of Indian commerce. Curious, she let her eyes feast, while her mind turned over their situation.

They continued to stroll, and the New Sale Room gave way to the Old Sale Room, with statues of various dignitaries. She made out Lord Clive and Sir Eyre Coote among them. Although she listened to Del's exchanges, they added little to what she already knew of him, other than establishing that he was held in high esteem, by the miltary men especially, but by the civilians, too.

They eventually strolled on into what Del told her was the room of the Committee of Correspondence. The large chamber held portraits of past governors-general, the Marquis of Cornwallis and Warren Hastings among them. Of more interest to her was the large number of paintings depicting views of Indian scenery that lined the walls.

At last, after more than an hour, they returned to the grand foyer.

Before she could talk herself out of it, Deliah turned to him and said, "I realize now that my insisting you escort me home to Humberside has made your mission that much more difficult—more complicated."

She knew he hadn't intended to include her among the "well-meaning others," that he'd accepted her help and her place in their little group of conspirators, but he would have preferred to be rid of her from the start . . . and if that kiss this morning had demonstrated anything, it was that she couldn't trust herself—her inner self—when it came to him, when he was anywhere near.

Dragging in a quick breath, she lifted her chin. "So I'll apologize for that, and if it will make your mission easier, you can leave me here, in London. I can go and stay with my old governess for a few days, until you go on to Cambridgeshire and lead the Black Cobra away. Then I can make my way home. I'll have Kumulay and the rest of my household with me. It'll be perfectly safe."

"No." Del didn't even think before the answer was on his lips. He paused, frowning. Reminded of her earlier insistence on propriety—something he now knew was uncharacteristic—he had to wonder why she'd acted as she had and clung so tenaciously to his promised escort, but he set that conundrum aside for later. He had to quash her latest suggestion; his instinctive response was to reject it out of hand. Which he'd done. Now he needed to assemble his rationalization. His explanation.

His excuse.

He'd managed to keep his expression impassive. His eyes locked with hers, he stated, "You had your chance to bow out of my mission at the beginning, but now you're a part of it—an integral part as far as the Black Cobra is concerned—so you have to stay with me and see it through to the end."

Only then would she be safe. Regardless of what might develop between them—and after this morning he was increasingly certain something would—there was no way this side of Heaven he would let her out of his orbit to be exposed to the malicious vindictiveness of the Black Cobra.

She held his gaze, studied his eyes, considered his words, then inclined her head. "If that's what you truly wish, then I'll stay."

He was unprepared for the relief that swept through him.

Entirely satisfied—she hadn't wanted to step back but had felt honor-bound to make the offer—Deliah looked around again, thinking of the large number who'd come to talk to him. "Isn't there *anyone* in the company you can warn about the evidence, about the Black Cobra himself?"

"If there was, I would, but as the culprit's Ferrar, there's no one in the company I feel confident would—or could—see justice done. Ferrar's father, the earl, is a director, and he almost certainly has too many of the other directors in his pocket. That's his way of doing business."

Del swept the foyer one last time, then took her arm.

"Come. We've spent enough time here—talked to enough people to have Ferrar wondering."

Deliah looked at him. "Is he here?"

"No, but various associates are. News of my visit will do the rounds. The Black Cobra will hear."

He escorted her outside, onto the pavement in front of the building.

When he halted and pulled out his fob-watch, she glanced across the street and saw Tony lounging, with Gervase further along. "Where to now?"

Replacing his watch, he said, "It's just after three, and the afternoon is fine. So how would a lady of your ilk pass the time?"

Deliah wasn't averse to an amble in Hyde Park. Not only was she happy to stretch her legs over the lush lawns but as the female half of the ton—or at least as much of it as remained in the capital in that season—was arrayed in its customary splendor in the carriages drawn up along the Avenue, there was plenty to catch her eye.

Strolling beside her, Del noticed her absorption. "I thought you weren't all that interested in the latest fashions."

"I'm not." Her eye caught by a particularly fine crepe gown—very bravely worn considering the icy breeze that rattled the bare branches—she answered absentmindedly. "I'm more interested in the materials themselves."

A moment passed. "Why?"

She blinked, realized what she'd said. Glanced at him, and saw from the intentness in his eyes that he wasn't likely to accept an evasive answer. And truly, why should she conceal her success? Especially from an ex-East India Company man. "I . . . have an interest—a commercial interest—in cotton."

His brows rose.

She hurried on, "My primary investments are in sugar-cane, but I recently had an opportunity to buy into cotton farming and importation, and I did. Consequently, I'm interested in the degree to which cotton is used compared to wool or silk."

He was now regarding her with fascinated interest. "You invest?"

Ladies weren't supposed to, of course, but she was tired of hiding her light under a bushel. Tired of pretending to be a woman she was not. She nodded. "My uncle encouraged me to learn the ropes. While he's terribly conservative in some ways, in others, he's quite progressive. And, of course, in Jamaica it's not so unheard of for ladies to be involved."

She glanced at Del, wondering if he'd prove to be one of those gentlemen for whom the very notion of ladies being involved in making money was simply scandalous.

"What sort of company is it? Has it been operational for long? And are the returns as good as with sugarcane?"

His questions came thick and fast. Absorbed with answering, she strolled on beside him. The shrewdness behind his questions suggested he had more than a passing understanding of investing. Even more reassuring, he demonstrably viewed her involvement with respect, not derision.

She couldn't recall ever discussing business in such depth with anyone other than her longtime brokers, now far away in Jamaica.

They came to the end of the Avenue, and he paused, then steered her across the carriage drive into a secluded walk leading deeper into Kensington Gardens. The gravel path was lined with thick borders backed by a row of even thicker bushes. "Keep talking," he murmured.

"Are they following us?" When he nodded, she asked, "How many?"

He listened. "Three, I think. At least."

"Are Tony and Gervase near?"

"Back behind the trees to our north. They'll be keeping pace on that side."

They walked on, chatting of this and that, no longer paying

attention to their words. Along one side, other paths joined theirs, but the bushes along the north side continued in an unbroken line.

"They're being rather furtive," he eventually said. "Which suggests they might, at last, be cultists, rather than hired locals."

By mutual unspoken accord, they slowed. Deliah, too, heard stealthy rustling following them along the line of bushes.

"They're still there," she murmured, "but we're nearly at the end of the path."

Del looked ahead. The path ended, opening onto a wide lawn, thirty yards ahead. Taking Deliah's elbow, he slowed further. "We need to lure them out."

Even as the words left his lips, the sound of giggles and light voices eagerly chatting came from behind them. Glancing back, they saw a party of very young young ladies and their attending beaux step onto the path a good way back.

The rustling ceased abruptly.

Deliah exchanged a look with Del. "Perhaps they'll take one of the other paths and leave this one."

Del's jaw firmed. "Let's keep walking."

They did, slowly ambling, but the giggling, lighthearted party continued on the same path, drawing ever nearer.

Defeated, deflated, Del and Deliah reached the end of the path and stepped out onto the open lawn. They walked a few paces to one side and halted. The giggling party came out of the walk and, with exclamations of delight at the vista, continued on.

Once the chattering had died, Del glanced at Deliah. "We could head back the same way. Give them another chance at us."

She nodded. "Let's."

They did, but there were no more rustlings in the thick bushes.

Whoever had been stalking them was gone.

Reaching the end of the walk, they stepped out onto the

carriage drive. Looking north along it, they saw Tony standing chatting to Gervase under a large tree. Gervase looked their way, gave a very slight shake of his head.

"Come on." Grim-faced, Del took Deliah's arm. "We may as well go back to the hotel."

December 13
Grillon's Hotel

An hour and a half later, Del headed for his room. He and Deliah had repaired to the suite. She'd ordered tca, then Tony and Gervase had joined them.

There had been elusive shadows lurking in the bushes along the path. Tony and Gervase had hung back, watching, waiting for the shadows to make a move before they closed in, but suddenly the shadows had frozen, then drifted away.

They'd been locals, however, not Indians, not cultists. And their wariness suggested that the Black Cobra was now hiring better-quality help.

Not a good sign.

Reaching his room, Del opened the door and went in. Cobby was there, preparing his bath. Closing the door, Del shrugged out of his coat. He frowned abstractedly as he laid it aside. "I have an errand for you."

"Aye?"

"I need tickets to some event or other—the opera, theater— whatever's on. For Miss Duncannon and myself."

"For this evening?"

"Yes."

"Does the lady like music?"

"I have no idea." Del drew off his cravat. "Any entertainment will do. Just find me something that might distract her."

And him.

"If you've all you need here, I'll go see the lads at the desk."

Del nodded. Cobby left.

Stripping off the rest of his clothes, Del sank into the hip bath. The water was steaming. Leaning back, he closed his eyes.

Gervase and Tony were on their way to the tavern to keep watch for the Black Cobra's man.

His duty tonight was to keep Deliah safe, yet after the events of their long day, spending the entire evening with her alone, in private, was the very definition of unwise.

Quite aside from that startling kiss and the sense of unfinished business in the way it had ended—on which he'd dwelled more than once during the day—there was the associated problem of the debilitating effect having her with him, literally beside him, while being stalked by the Black Cobra's minions was having on his control.

It was a constant abrasion, a relentless weakening.

He didn't like even the thought of her going into danger; having her beside him, knowingly taking her along with him, was a form of subtle torment. Something inside him, some part he'd rarely had to deal with and had rarely crossed, let alone provoked, invariably reacted, as if her being in danger was a grave and gross oversight on his part.

And it—that other side of him—prodded him, hard, to correct that oversight. To do something to ensure she wasn't exposed. At all. Not just to ensure she was safe but to unequivocally take her out of the action so there was no chance she'd ever be in any danger at all.

He could imagine how she'd react if he let that part of himself loose, let it guide him.

The response she evoked in him was extreme, ridiculous in one sense, and by and large not something he understood. But he had too much on his plate with his mission, with the Black Cobra, to spend time thinking of it, thinking through it, now.

He just had to find ways to deal with it—to manage it for now. Later, once the mission was over, once the Black Cobra was caught, he'd have time to work through it and assuage it, but not yet. Not now.

When it came down to it, his mission was not proceeding well. They were drawing out the Black Cobra's minions, but those minions were local hirelings, not cultists, yet it was the cultists he needed to remove.

They were the deadly ones, the ones with no rules, no lines they, in the Black Cobra's name, would not cross. His decoy's mission was to reduce their number so that the others following would have fewer to face.

That was the crux of his mission, and in that, he was failing.

Sangay stuck his nose out of the alley door of the fancy hotel. The icy wind whipped in, made him shiver uncontrollably, but the alley was empty. He had to go now.

Slipping outside, he shut the heavy door, then, sucking in a breath, holding it against the chill, he crept down the alley, away from the street at the other end, toward what he'd heard the other servants call the mews—the area for carriages and horses at the rear of the building.

The hotel stable was further along, tucked behind the bulk of the hotel itself. Reaching the mews, he peeked around the corner and saw the usual huddle of grooms and stableboys gathered outside the open door of the stable, warming their hands at a glowing brazier.

He wished he could spend a few minutes getting warm, but he dared not. He needed to get back to the docks. He prayed to Ganesh every hour that his ship would still be there, somewhere in the huge waterways around what they called the Pool of London.

It wasn't really a pool, not to Sangay's way of thinking. But he had to make it back, or he'd never see India, or his mother, again.

Sliding unobtrusively around the corner, hugging the deepening shadows along the wall, he crept soundlessly away from the stable, away from the hotel. He'd been safe enough there, warm enough there—he'd been fed enough there for the first time in his short life. But he didn't dare stay.

The man would come for him, he knew. He had to go before he found him.

His slippered feet made no sound on the cobbles. As the distance from the hotel grew, he risked going a little faster. Memory of the man drove him on. He might have been just a cabin boy, but he'd been an honest boy, a good boy. He didn't want to become a thief, but if the man caught him again. . . .

He started running.

Reaching the end of the mews, he swung around the corner—and ran into a wall of muscle and bone.

He staggered back. Before he could regain his balance, a hand closed on his collar. He sucked in a breath, ready to protest his innocence, when from a long way above him a dark voice growled, "And just where do you think you're going?"

Fear shot through him. He squeaked, tried to squirm loose, but the grip on his collar tightened. The man shook him like a rat.

Shook him until he was gasping, choking.

Then the man's other hand caught his chin, forced his face up until he found himself staring into a dark-featured scowl. It wasn't the frown that terrified Sangay—it was the man's pale eyes.

"Let me remind you, boy, what will happen if you don't do as I say." The words were low, a rumble. "I'll have your mother strung up and slow-roasted over a fire. She'll scream and beg for mercy—mercy no one will grant her. Before she dies—and I assure you that won't be soon—she'll curse your name, curse the day she brought such an ungrateful whelp into this world." The deep rumble paused.

The cold fist of fear tightened, choking Sangay.

"On the other hand," the dark voice continued, "if you do as I say, your mother will never know anything about any fire, any excruciating pain, any horrible, terrible, god-forsaken death."

On the last word, the man shook him again. "So, whelp—your choice." The man all but snarled, "Which will it be? Will you get back into that hotel and fetch the wooden scroll-holder I sent you for, or do I kill you now and send a message back to India on the first tide?"

"I'll do it! I'll do it, sahib!" Sangay could barely get the words out through his chattering teeth. When the man abruptly let him go, he staggered, then stood, and hung his head. "I will do as you say."

No choice. He could barely breathe for sheer terror.

"So, have you looked? Done anything at all since Southampton?"

"Oh, yes, sahib, yes. I have been searching through all the general baggage, sahib, but there's no scroll-holder there. It must be kept with the baggage the colonel-sahib keeps in his room, or perhaps with the bags his man Cobby keeps with him. Or the colonel-sahib might be carrying it with him, only I don't think he is because I have looked closely and I cannot see how such a thing would fit beneath his coat."

"I doubt he'll carry it with him."

"Perhaps"—Sangay brightened—"it is in the memsahib's bags?"

The man eyed him, then nodded. "Perhaps. You search everywhere until you find it, understand? But try to do it without being caught. We've a few days yet. Better you look until you find it, then bring it to me, rather than you get caught before you get your hands on it—understand?"

Sangay bobbed his head repeatedly. "Yes, sahib. I'm to stay hidden until I find it—no one must know I am looking for this thing."

"That's right. You do that, and no one will touch your mother—remember that. Now, what do you know about the other two gentlemen who go out when the colonel does? They seem to be guarding him."

"Yes, sahib-sir—they are friends of his." Sangay screwed up his face. "I have not heard their names well enough to say them, but they are at the hotel, too, in other rooms on the same floor."

"Are they, indeed?" The man fell silent.

Sangay shivered, unobtrusively shifting from one foot to the other. Carefully he tucked his hands under his arms and hugged himself, bowing his thin shoulders away from the wind.

"Keep an eye on those two, but you'd best keep out of their way. But how have you been hiding yourself?"

Sangay shrugged. "The colonel-sahib's people think I'm one of the memsahib's servants, and her people think I'm a one of the colonel-sahib's servants."

The man looked at him through narrowing eyes. "Very clever. You're quick, I'll give you that. Just don't be forgetting your maataa won't be able to escape the Black Cobra."

Sangay shivered. "No, sahib. I won't be forgetting that."

"Good. Now get back in there and find the scroll-holder. Once you do, all you need do is come out and slip away—I'll be watching. I'll come and meet you."

"Yes, sahib. I will be getting back now." Receiving a nod of assent, Sangay turned and, head down against the biting wind, slipped back around the corner, then walked slowly, despondently, back along the alley.

He hadn't thought it possible, but he felt even more miserable, even more filled with black despair. All he could do was do as the man told him, and pray to the gods that something would happen—to the man, perhaps?—to save him from the nightmare his life had become. And to save his maataa, too.

Five

*D*el was still in the bath when Cobby returned.

"Found just the thing." Cobby shut the door. "A recital at St. Martin-in-the-Fields. It's only a short hackney ride away."

Del considered, nodded. "Perfect." He closed his eyes, laid his head back again. "Get tickets."

"Don't have to. It's free, apparently. You can just walk in."

December 13
St. Martin-in-the-Fields, Trafalgar Square

He should, Del realized, have registered what Cobby's words meant. As he escorted an eager Deliah through the crowd thronging the old church's wide porch, he berated himself for not having seen the danger.

Yes, they could simply walk in—and so could anyone else.

He glanced at Deliah, wondered—again—if he should suggest they leave. Once again, he held his tongue. The light in her face, in her jade eyes, stated louder than words that she was looking forward to the performance.

Reaching the main doors, she led the way in, going straight through the foyer and into the nave. She started down it, looking right and left, evaluating the available seats. Taller than she, Del could see over the crowd clogging the aisle. Taking her elbow, he steered her to two seats in a pew two-thirds of the way down the nave.

Excusing herself to the well-dressed lady in the corner of the pew, Deliah slid past and on, then, leaving space for Del, sat and arranged her skirts.

After taking note of the unquestionably innocent couples filling the pew behind theirs, Del sat, then surveyed those in the pew ahead.

All safe enough.

Despite the season, the majority of the crowd were tonnish, the rest mainly gentry or well-to-do merchants. But he'd spotted a few less savory sorts hanging about the fringes of the crowd, and the rear pews were jammed with shabby coats and unkempt figures.

Deliah had picked up a printed program in the foyer. Consulting it, she commented excitedly and knowledgably about the various airs and sonatas to be performed by the small chamber orchestra. Clearly she enjoyed music and had been starved of this type of entertainment over the years she'd been away.

So had he, but this particular entertainment he could have done without. Far from feeling relaxed, every sense he possessed was on high alert. His eyes incessantly scanned, his ears constantly sorted through the babel around them, listening for accents that weren't English, or tones that boded ill.

If he'd been the Black Cobra, this would have been an opportunity too good to pass up. Whether the fiend had realized Tony and Gervase were their guards, he had no idea. Cobby had confirmed that the reputation of Grillon's for absolute discretion with respect to their guests was well deserved; it was unlikely the staff had spoken of the connection between his party and the two gentlemen. But if the Cobra did know, then this excursion—just Del and Deliah alone at night, without even Cobby, Mustaf, or her bodyguard Kumulay—was tailor-made for the Cobra's purpose. He didn't even need to seize both of them; either would do.

The orchestra started to file in. There was a rush to fill the last seats as the musicians settled on the chairs arranged before the steps to the altar.

An expectant hush fell, then the conductor appeared, walked to his lectern, bowed to the audience, then turned to his players and raised his baton.

A lone violin began to sing, then the other instruments joined in. Even in his state of battle-ready alert, Del felt the music swell and take hold. He glanced at Deliah.

And didn't look away. She was caught in the music, swept away on the tide. Her eyes glowed with pleasure; her luscious lips had curved, parted.

She was oblivious, enchanted by the music. He was enthralled, ensorcelled by her.

As the music continued, the pieces flowing one to the other with only the barest pause to allow the musicians to readjust their sheets, he tried to remain attuned to their surroundings, watchful, alert to any potential danger, yet she— her face, her radiant expression, those lips that had from the first enticed—held a far stronger fascination.

A fascination that was rapidly approaching obsession.

The battle within wasn't one he was destined to win. In the end, he surrendered, let his eyes feast, and left whatever might come later for later.

The entire concert passed without incident. If Deliah was at all aware of his tension she gave no sign.

It was raining when, one couple amid a sea of others, they reached the edge of the porch. The hackneys were doing a roaring trade. Taking Deliah's hand, Del stepped onto the wet steps just as a hackney pulled into the curb below. He immediately hailed it. The driver saluted with his whip.

"Come on." Del hurried Deliah down the steps, opened the hackney's door and helped her in, then followed and sat beside her. Raising his arm, he pushed up the hatch. "Grillon's, Albemarle Street."

"Aye, sir. Quite a lot of traffic, so don't worry if we're a bit slow."

Letting the hatch fall, Del sat back. Nothing had occurred. Perhaps the Black Cobra wasn't watching as closely as he'd feared.

"That was lucky." Deliah looked out of the window. "It looks like it's been pouring, although it's easing up now."

She then launched into an enthusiastic analysis of the performance, waxing lyrical over the first violin's solo and the artistry displayed by the principal cellist. Del inwardly smiled, closed his eyes, and let her words roll over him. She was safe and happy, ergo so was he. The evening had gone without a hitch, providing distraction for them both, filling the hours safely.

They would return to the suite, perhaps share a drink—tea for her—then they would retire, in amity with the world, to their respective beds.

All safe.

Deliah's fingers closed about his wrist. He realized she'd stopped speaking, had been silent for a few minutes. He opened his eyes.

She was staring out into the night, then, her fingers tightening warningly, she leaned close, murmured, "This is not the way to Albemarle Street."

He looked out of the hackney window. It took a moment to see enough through the drizzle to get his bearings, then he softly swore. They were on the Strand heading deeper into the City, the opposite of the direction in which they should have gone. No matter the traffic—and the carriage was stopping and starting, barely crawling—there was no sense at all in the jarvey taking this route.

Del took Deliah's hand in a firm grip. Through the shadows he whispered, "Be ready to jump out behind me."

She squeezed his fingers in reply, shifted to the edge of the seat.

He waited until the next snarl of traffic forced the hackney to a rocking halt. Silently opening the door, he slipped out onto the pavement, turned and smoothly lifted her down, then quietly shut the door just as the carriage jerked forward again. His concentration fixed ahead, the jarvey hadn't noticed his lighter load.

Taking Deliah's hand, Del strode quickly back the way they had come. Courtesy of the rain, there were few people on the streets, no cover as they hurried back along the Strand. If the jarvey looked around. . . .

Passing the third hackney lined up behind theirs, Del glanced at the carriage—and saw two pale faces staring out at them.

Surprised. Shocked.

"Damn!" He clutched Deliah's hand tighter. *"Run!"*

He dragged her on with him, hauled her alongside, glanced back as a "Hoi!" rang out.

Two—no, *three*—burly men jumped out of the hackney and started pounding along the pavement after them.

Deliah had taken a quick glance, too. Catching up her skirts, she started to run in earnest. "Come on."

The slick, wet pavements made running dangerous, but they had no choice. With her gown, two petticoats and the skirts of her heavy pelisse swinging about her legs, her reticule banging against one knee, she raced as best she could along the thankfully level flagstone pavement of the Strand.

Del's hold on her hand helped steady her, yet even without looking she knew their pursuers were closing the distance.

"Now I remember why I always preferred breeches in situations such as this."

"Sadly, there's no time to change."

"No breeches, either."

"That, too."

A silly exchange, but it confirmed how desperate their straits truly were. From the sublime to the horrendous had taken mere minutes; her mind had yet to catch up. But it was long after ten o'clock on a wet winter's night. Although there was plenty of carriage traffic still about, there was almost no one on foot. No support, no succor, and nowhere to make a stand.

Del suddenly changed direction, urging her up a side street heading away from the river. She agreed with the sentiment—the river wasn't a wise destination—but for a moment she worried the lane they'd taken would prove to be a dead end.

But no. The murk ahead was cut by a beam of light, then they heard the rattle as a carriage rumbled along the street at the upper end of the lane.

"Thank God." Deliah looked down and put her mind to keeping up, and not slipping on the wet paving stones as Del raced them up the lane.

Neither she nor he could resist a glance back.

The three men were too close, and gaining rapidly. They were all hulking brutes. One was carrying a club.

They were more than two-thirds up the lane, but with the men closing ever more rapidly, ever more determinedly, they weren't going to reach the street beyond.

A pace ahead of her, Del abruptly stopped, hauled her up to him, then pushed her on. "Go! As fast as you can, then to the left. I'll catch up."

Releasing Deliah, Del swung to face the men.

They grinned, and fanned out as they came on.

Behind him, he heard Deliah's retreating footsteps. At least she was away; if either of them were going to fall into the clutches of the Black Cobra, he'd much rather it was he.

The bruiser in the middle was the one with the club. He slowed, smiled evilly, then stepped in and swung the club at Del's head.

Wondering who had taught the man to fight, Del stepped inside the swing, grabbed the man's arm with one hand, his throat with the other, and used the man's own momentum to heave him into the man on his right.

They both went down heavily in a tangle of limbs, heads cracking against the stone gutter.

Del swiveled to face the third man—and found himself instinctively leaping back from a knife.

Cursing his own stupidity in coming out unarmed, he shifted, backing, assessing his opponent and the long-handled blade he held. A distraction was what he needed.

He'd reached that conclusion when he saw a shadow shift behind the man.

His blood turned to ice as he saw Deliah creeping up behind the man—he'd told the damn woman to run!

Quickly he looked back at the man—leapt back from another swipe.

Deliah rose behind the lout and clouted him over the head with her reticule.

Caught totally by surprise, the man yelped and instinctively ducked.

Del stepped in, seized the hand with the knife, then smashed his boot into the side of the man's knee.

There was a vicious crack and the man went down, howling and clutching his leg.

Del glanced at the other two. They were groggily trying to get to their feet. They didn't appear to be able to focus yet.

He didn't dare take them on with Deliah there.

Turning, he grabbed her hand and tore up the lane. She struggled to keep up, but did, without complaint.

In the mood he was in, that was just as well.

They weren't out of the woods yet.

They reached the end of the lane and stepped into a wider street. Looking left, he saw the spires of St. Martin-in-the-Fields rising through the low-hanging fog, and thanked heaven for a military man's sense of direction.

He glanced back down the lane, then pulled Deliah on toward the church.

Assessing the possibilities.

The two bruisers he'd left mobile were up and heading their way, in a very much grimmer mood. And he and Deliah were still too far away from the church precincts to trust in reaching them safely.

They needed a place to hide, and they needed it now—before the two chasing them reached the street and saw them. The place didn't need to be perfect, just somewhere the two brutes wouldn't think to look. . . .

Ahead, a row of hackney carriages materialized through the murk. If they took one . . . they risked their pursuers catching up with them in the traffic crawling around Trafalgar Square and all the way to Grillon's.

With renewed urgency, he hurried Deliah along, scanning the buildings they raced past. Praying they would reach the carriages in time.

Reaching the nearest hackney, he halted, tossed the jarvey a sovereign. "Don't ask why—just drive, as fast as you can, down Piccadilly. Go!"

The jarvey blinked, but was already lifting his reins to set his coach rolling.

At least the voice of command worked on some.

One glance back showed their pursuers had yet to reach the street. Tightening his grip on Deliah's hand, he swung her toward the buildings, hurried and harried her into a small alcove before a locked door. He pushed her into the shadows, then crowded in, too, just as the two men came out of the lane.

He looked at Deliah—just as she opened her mouth.

Felt her breasts press against his chest with the breath she'd drawn in.

Seizing her other hand, too, he ducked his head and shut her up.

By kissing her.

Hard.

He shifted into her, trapping her against the brick wall of the alcove. His greatcoat was dark, his trousers were, too, and so was his hair, which currently reached his collar. With his head bent, with her trapped before him, completely shielded by his body, they should be all but invisible in the shadows. Not even her pale face could catch a stray gleam from the smoky street flares.

He hoped, he prayed. . . .

He had to fight the distraction of her lips beneath his, ignore the temptation to taste her, try to blot out the sensation of her exceedingly feminine body pressed along the length of his, and concentrate, focus all his senses, on what was happening in the street behind his back.

Through the sensual storm hazing his brain, he heard the bruisers' pounding footsteps near, heard them halt, swear at the retreating carriage, then he heard them—yes!—hail the next hackney in line and clamber up, calling orders to follow the other carriage.

He didn't lift his head when the carriage door slammed, not even when the horses' hooves rang in the street. He didn't pull back from the kiss and risk a look until the retreating hoofbeats were fading.

The hackney with their pursuers was disappearing into the murk at the end of the street.

They were safe.

Registering Deliah's silence, he looked back at her. Despite the shadows, he fell into the dark pools of her wide, stunned eyes. He felt the quick rise and fall of her breasts, mashed against his chest. Saw her lips, lush and ripe, full and parted in the poor light. Beckoning.

He saw the tip of her tongue glide over her lower lip, making the lusciousness glisten.

He didn't need to kiss her again, yet he did.

It wasn't a simple kiss but one fueled by anger, and relief. And by something he didn't understand—that something she and only she evoked, and set pounding in his blood.

Her lips had been parted; he filled her mouth, stole her breath, then gave it back. Deliberately lingered, tasted, explored.

He tightened his fingers on hers, kept their hands safely

locked, arms down, even though every instinct pushed him to free his hands and seize her, hold her, bring her close— much closer.

He wanted her, and that want was open, undisguised, there in every bold stroke of his tongue, in the demanding pressure of his lips on hers. In the hard ridge that pressed against her belly. Deliah had no difficulty reading his desire, recognizing it—along with the response that raced through her, hot, instinctive, and strong.

She wanted him, and that was dangerous.

Dangerous with a capital *D*.

Yet she couldn't back away, pull back—end this unwise kiss. Because she didn't want to. Because there was, it seemed, no force within her powerful enough to counter the pull of it, and him.

Once again, Del found himself in the unaccustomed position of having to force himself to end a kiss—a kiss that promised so much more, that left him aching and hungry for much more. A "more" he now was certain he could have, but while this, it seemed, was the right time, it absolutely wasn't the right place.

Drawing back from the exchange, limited though it had been, was hard enough. Lifting his head, he looked down into her face, at the lashes that fluttered, then lifted, revealing eyes clouded with rising passion. Her lips were lightly swollen, sheening from his kiss.

Stepping back was much harder, losing the elementally feminine cushion of her curves, an evocative softness that had cradled his hard frame. Easing back, subduing his rising clawing need, took more effort than he'd imagined, but he finally moved back, then, releasing one of her hands, he turned and stepped out of the alcove.

After checking they were indeed safe, he drew her out, too, without a word led her to the nearest hackney, opened the door, and helped her in. He looked up at the jarvey. "Grillon's."

Climbing in, he shut the carriage door and dropped onto the seat beside her.

He didn't say a single word on their journey back to Grillon's—and neither did she.

By the time the hackney pulled up outside the hotel, Deliah had recovered her composure, but her pulse was still pounding.

With suppressed anger, and unslaked passion.

She recognized both, and knew which was the safer to address. While she could understand, even without his explanation, why he'd kissed her the first time, she couldn't explain, and didn't want to think about, why he'd kissed her again. The second time.

That second, much more thorough time.

Sweeping into the hotel's foyer, she regally nodded to the clerk behind the desk, then continued without pause up the stairs and down the corridor to the suite.

Del, of course, followed; she heard his heavy footsteps closing in from behind. Reaching the suite, she threw open the door and swept in.

He strode in on her heels and shut the door with force.

Halting, she whirled on him, temper sparking. "Don't you *dare* upbraid me for coming to your aid. I'll do it again in such circumstances."

"No. You won't." Eyes already narrowed, he walked toward her—only halted when he stood directly in front of her with a bare inch between her breasts and his chest, so she had to tip her head back to meet his eyes.

Eyes that snapped with a temper to match hers. "You will never, ever, disobey my orders again. If I tell you to go on, you will—without hesitation."

She narrowed her eyes back. "No. I won't. I'm not one of your subordinates you can order around. Whatever the situation, I'll do as *I* think best."

Del felt his jaw lock. He fisted his hands against a nearly

overpowering urge to seize her and shake some sense into her. It was a moment before he could trust himself to speak. "If you wish to continue to be a member of this group—to assist in my mission—you will henceforth do exactly as I say."

One finely drawn dark brow arched. Maddeningly. "Or what?"

He had to stop and think.

When he didn't immediately answer—not because he couldn't answer but because, belatedly, wisdom had caught his tongue, and he couldn't immediately think of a response it would be safe to utter—her eyes, her expression, hardened, and she went on, "I'm not some flunky, or some private who has to jump to do your bidding. What's more, if you recall, I offered—only this morning—to step away from this enterprise, but you insisted that, having commenced it, I had to see it through to the end. So I am—I will. However, I didn't agree to transform into the sort of weak-kneed twit with more hair than wit who runs away and leaves you to deal with not one, not two, but *three* assailants—one armed with a club, another with a knife!"

She flung up her hands. "Why are you even lecturing me about this? We're here, we're safe—isn't that the important thing? Aside from all else, I'm my own person. I'm twenty-nine, for heaven's sake! I've sailed to Jamaica and back, more or less on my own. I've been an adult, my responsibility and no one else's, for a very long time!"

"Which is undoubtedly my problem." Del tried to shut up, but something—*that* something—was riding him hard. He met her glare for glare, leveled a finger at her nose. "This habit of yours of putting yourself in danger has got to stop!"

"*Me* putting myself in danger? Pray tell, *who* insisted we go to the recital tonight? And yes, I enjoyed it, thank you very much, but taking me there doesn't give you the right to dictate to me!"

"You're a female—one in my care. Your parents' request for me to act as your escort makes you my responsibility."

Lowering his finger, he jabbed it at her sternum. "It's my job to protect you."

Her eyes narrowed to flinty shards. "Indeed? Is that what that kiss was about then? The *second* kiss. *Protecting* me?"

Deliah heard her voice rise—abruptly remembered the kiss in Madame Latour's narrow hall, the more recent exchange, and her helpless reactions. She searched his eyes, all dark, hot and heated. Heaven help her, he was infinitely more dangerous to her than any thug.

Luckily, he didn't know it.

So she could look down her nose and scornfully state, "I am not yours, not in any way—you don't need to feel responsible for me!"

Fueled by a senseless, witless fury that he'd only kissed her to keep her safe—to continue their roles before the modiste, to stop her making a sound tonight, and even tonight's second kiss she felt sure he'd have a sensible reason for—she whirled and stalked into her bedroom.

The door had been left ajar. Passing through it, she shoved it closed behind her.

Waited to hear it slam.

It didn't.

On a stifled gasp she swung around—to see Del, his face like a thundercloud, storming after her.

Fury boiled through her veins. She straightened to her full height, raised one arm and dramatically pointed to the door, opened her mouth to order him out—

He grabbed her pointing hand, jerked her hard against him.

His head swooped.

And he covered her lips with his.

Six

C rushed them. Hauled her into his arms and held her as if he were trying to absorb her into his body.

He kissed her in the same way.

As if he wanted to devour her. To own her, claim her.

Have her.

In every imaginable way.

Deliah sank her hands into his hair and kissed him back. With equal fervor, equal need.

Their wills met and merged in a clash of fire and passion. Of instant conflagration and fiery need.

The anger that had driven her converted in a heartbeat to something more potent, to a compulsion that thrummed in her blood, that filled her head with dizzying desire, that burgeoned, erupted and swept her on.

Her inner self seized control, and it wanted, needed, yearned.

For more. For this. For what it had been starved of for so long.

He angled his head, ruthlessly, relentlessly deepened the kiss, and she pressed against him, into him, and met him caress for caress.

She remembered this, the heat, the urgency.

Yet this time there were flames and fire, and heady desperation.

Del sensed the same, knew beyond doubt that he ought to stop, that if he'd been wise he'd never have kissed her.

Yet he'd had to.

He had to show her because she refused to see, had to demonstrate unequivocally in the most indisputable way that she was *his*—his in more ways, deeper ways, than could ever be needed to justify his right to protect her.

He wrenched his mouth from hers. "*This* is why I need to keep you safe."

Safe from the Black Cobra. Safe from all danger.

Safe. And his.

She blinked up at him, jade eyes drowning in a glory of passion. Then her grip on his head tightened and she hauled his head down, hauled his lips to hers. Catapulted them both into a blazing inferno.

An eruption of molten desire shook him—snared him, lured him.

If he'd been able to think . . . yet he couldn't, not with her hands gripping his skull, not with her lips ravenous beneath his.

Not with her tall, curvaceous figure provocatively plastered along the length of his.

She wanted, incited, and he broke, seized, took. Claimed her mouth, then, holding her tight within one arm, raised a hand to her breast and claimed that, too.

Her response was instantaneous, undeniable, encouraging— a murmuring moan trapped in her throat. Her fingers tightened in his hair as his fingers played, learned. Seduced.

Deliah felt the wanton within her rise, felt her blossom and bloom with every evocative touch, with every heavy thrust of his tongue against hers, every increasingly flagrant caress.

No matter her memories, it had never been like this. Never so fiery, never so fraught. She'd never been so desperately needy.

Even through her pelisse, his knowing hands made her breasts swell and ache, a sweeter, sharper ache than she recalled. Griffiths, the bastard, had never made her feel like this. There was no comparison.

This was new, and she had to have. Better, more; she had to know. She reached for the buttons of his coat as he reached for hers.

The next minutes went in a blind flurry of hands and grasping, greedy fingers, of passion escalating degree by inexorable degree as this garment, then that, slid away.

Tugged, pulled, ripped away.

And blind need took over—infected them both, drove them, fired them.

His hands found her skin, hard, hot and urgent. Hers found his, greedy and grasping. The muscled expanse of his chest, his heavy shoulders, the shifting muscles of his back.

Then his lips left hers, slid lower. His mouth fastened over one nipple and she arched, cried out.

Discovery and demand, yielding, then seizing, insisting and commanding, they traded caresses, shared and challenged, uninhibitedly answered the other's call.

Until they rolled on the bed, skin to naked skin, long limbs tangling, hands sculpting, urging, fingers searching.

Finding.

She arched beneath him as he stroked between her thighs. Lips locked with his, she burned, her hands gripping his sides, urging him over her.

Into her.

He complied. Lifting over her, he parted her thighs with his, spread them wide, set his hips between, and with one powerful thrust joined them.

She lost her breath. Every nerve in her body sparked, then whipped taut. She gasped, might have cried out, the sound muffled by their still rapacious kiss.

He withdrew and plunged in again, deeper still, steel encased in velvet shafting into her body.

And the wild ride began.

Pagan in its power, it held her, compelled her. She danced

beneath him, rode with him, through the flames, straight into the heart of the fire.

And they burned. Hotter, more intense than anything she'd dreamed, a fiery need blossomed at her core. Relentlessly, ruthlessly, he fed and stoked the blaze. . . .

Until that need became her all, until it throbbed beneath her fingertips, pounded in her blood, burned beneath her skin.

Silk and passion. She was that and so much more. Del had never known such urgency, such all-consuming, unwavering compulsion to have a woman—to take her and be damned. Regardless—despite—any and all restrictions.

Despite every last one of his rational reservations.

It was madness—this driving desperation, this compulsive conviction. Its claws were sunk deep, not just in his flesh but into his psyche, his soul.

He couldn't live without having her—some part of him had accepted that as indisputable fact. That primitive side rejoiced as he pinned her beneath him, as her curves—those bounteous curves he'd coveted from first sight—cushioned him, cradled him. As, her long legs spread, she took him in, arched and took him yet deeper, all scalding slickness and wet, clinging heat.

She was tight, tighter than he'd expected, the walls of her sheath clutching, clamping, fisting him.

Taking him.

Lids heavy, breath coming in panting gasps, barely able to see, he was beyond all control, but so was she. This might have been unwise, but he didn't care—and, thank God, neither did she. If he'd had any doubts, the half-moons her nails were scoring in his skin had banished them.

She was with him, urging him on even as he reached for her knees, and drew first one, then the other, to his hips, opening her to even deeper penetration. She only gasped, clung, rocked beneath him ever more evocatively, wordlessly pleading for release.

The roar in his blood grew, drowning out all but the need to have her climax. To see her surrender, to take her to the very peak of desperate sexual need, then tip her over into sexual bliss.

To feel her beneath him as he did, to sense that moment of absolute surrender.

To see her face, her expression, in the instant ecstasy took her.

He thrust deeper, faster, harder, more powerfully as he felt her rise.

Her fingers bit into his arms as she arched. She gasped into his mouth as her nerves drew that very last fraction tauter.

Then she shattered.

She came apart beneath him on a strangled cry, a sound that satisfied one of his needs. He'd expected to hold back, to take more of her, yet her convulsing sheath clamped tight, and she took him with her, pulled him over the precipice's edge and on.

Release swept him; he couldn't deny it. His roar muffled in the curve of her throat, he thrust deep and let go.

And joined her.

Felt her arms close around him and tug him down, wrap about him and hold him close as oblivion rolled in, over, and enveloped them.

For long moments, the heat held them, blessed and golden, a gentle sea.

Slowly, inexorably, satiation swept in, infusing them as they spiraled down, and drifted back to earth.

To the unexpected, unanticipated intimacy of each other's naked arms.

December 14
Grillon's Hotel

Deliah woke to a gray morning and the rattling of coals in the grate. Heart leaping, she glanced at the bed beside her—only to discover it empty.

The bed was a four-poster, and at some point in the night

Del must have drawn the curtains along one side and across the end; she could see the window and the leaden sky, but the hotel maid at the hearth couldn't see her.

Or the rumpled, crumpled disaster of the bed.

Bess would be up shortly and undoubtedly would notice, but Deliah had no intention of explaining. Indeed, thinking back, she wasn't sure she could.

How did one rationalize something so far beyond reason?

She spent two minutes trying, then gave up.

Aside from all else, she could not bring herself to regret a single moment of the night, something Bess would detect, and that would only lead to more questions. Difficult, prickly questions given Bess knew her history with gentlemen and was every bit as protective as Del wished to be.

Would he regret—was he already regretting—the interlude, their unanticipated explosion of mutual madness? Of shared insanity.

She knew he hadn't intended it any more than she had, but they'd clashed, kissed fierily, and that had been that.

The firestorm of passion sparked by that kiss had swept over them and cindered all caution, and reduced all inhibitions to insubstantial ash.

The result . . . had been glorious.

Lying in the enfolding warmth, she replayed each scintillating moment, at least those she could recall.

Quite enough to heat her cheeks, to have her shifting beneath the sheet.

Then she remembered what had happened later, when he'd woken her in the depths of the night.

He certainly hadn't behaved like a man burdened with regrets.

If he had been, he wouldn't have . . . done it all again.

Only more slowly, and with much greater attention to detail.

Her body thrummed just from the memory.

The maid had left; the fire was crackling. She heard the door open, and Bess's quick, light steps. Tossing back the covers, she froze, then set her chin, wrapped the loose sheet about her naked self, and swung her legs out of the bed.

"Good morning, Bess." Sheet trailing after her, she walked out from around the bed. "Have you seen my robe?"

Despite her best efforts, she couldn't wipe the smile from her face.

Bess stared at her, mouth open, for one long moment, then simply said, "Oh, my God."

Washed, brushed and wearing one of the walking gowns that had been delivered from Madamae Latour's salon, Deliah strolled into the sitting room of the suite in an entirely amiable mood.

Over the matter of the gowns she'd decided not to cut off her nose to spite her face. She'd accept them for now, but later she would insist on paying Del in full. In money.

But she needed gowns to wear now. Not anticipating a prolonged halt on their journey north, she had a few carriage gowns, and not much else. She'd charged Bess with shopping for chemises, stockings and similar necessities while she was out tempting the Black Cobra with Del.

He was in the sitting room, seated at the table breaking his fast with Tony and Gervase. At sight of her, all three started to get to their feet. She waved them back. "No—stay where you are."

While the others subsided, with a careful look, Del pulled out the empty chair between his and Tony's. With an airy nod and a light smile, she thanked him and sat.

She looked at Tony as Del resumed his seat. "So," she asked, reaching for the teapot, "did anything come of your watch at the tavern?"

If Del could be a man of the world and evince no telltale sign of the hours they'd spent rolling naked in her bed, then she could do the same.

From the corner of his eye, Del watched her sip tea and nibble a slice of toast and marmalade as Tony and Gervase recounted their disappointingly uneventful evening.

"The Cobra or his minions must have been watching from

outside the inn, waiting to see if their hirelings brought a woman." Gervase shook his head. "We thought of hunting to see if we could spot them, but in that neighborhood there are simply too many seedy characters."

"And they *all* look suspicious," Tony said.

Grimacing in commiseration, Deliah set down her empty cup. "So what are our plans for today?"

They discussed their options for drawing the cultists out.

Del had already told Gervase and Tony of the excitement following his and Deliah's attendance at the recital. They'd been troubled, and not a little disgusted to have missed the action. They'd resolved they wouldn't again leave Deliah and him unwatched while out of the hotel. However . . .

"We need to make it easier, more attractive for them to approach—to come out of hiding and make some move." Gervase looked at Del and Deliah. "The museum's a warren—it might appeal to them."

They all agreed that the museum and its many rooms was worth a try.

Del stirred and shot a glance at Deliah. Tried to keep all expression from his face. "It's too early yet to go to the museum." He switched his gaze to Tony and Gervase. "I think I'll take a stroll to Guards' Headquarters. Laying more false trails can't hurt."

"That," Deliah said, laying aside her napkin, her gaze on Tony and Gervase, "sounds eminently sensible. You two can follow and keep watch. I'll wait here until you get back, then we can go to Montague House."

Tony and Gervase agreed readily.

Del inclined his head.

And told himself he had no grounds on which to feel sensitive, let alone irritated, by his recent bedmate's unaffected manner, by the lack of any hint of susceptibility, or consciousness in her attitude to him.

She was behaving exactly as he should want her to behave. Neither Tony nor Gervase had detected any change in the air between him and her.

Because there wasn't any. At least, none to be detected. Even by him.

Despite all, he'd expected *something*—a tremble in her fingers, an almost imperceptible change in her breathing—some indication of her heightened awareness of him.

Entirely against his better judgment, he wanted to speak with her—just to jog her memory of the heated hours they'd shared last night—but all four of them rose from the table and, instead of giving him a chance to hang back and exchange those few words, with an airy wave, Deliah headed for her bedroom.

Leaving him to quit the suite with Tony and Gervase, in a distinctly disgruntled mood.

His mood hadn't improved when he returned to Grillon's from visiting the Guards, then taking a quick swing through Whitehall and the Home Office, just to set a few more spectral cats prowling around their pigeon.

Nothing of any moment had been achieved. There'd been no one worthwhile confiding in at any of his stops, and neither Tony nor Gervase had spotted any cultists, although they were sure he'd been followed by at least three different locals working as a team—keeping watch, but too wary to try any direct attack.

Regardless, after last night, if he was to escort Deliah on another foray in which he and she would play welcoming targets, he wanted something a little more lethal than his cane.

His swordstick would feel better in his hand.

Tony and Gervase had elected to wait outside, hanging back at the corner of the street. Although he'd known they'd been close, even he hadn't always been able to spot them.

Reaching the top of the stairs, he turned and made for his bedchamber. He'd change his cane for his swordstick, then collect Deliah and leave for the museum.

He was still some way from the door to his room when it opened. The Indian boy who was part of Deliah's household came out. The boy shut the door and, without seeing Del, walked off down the corridor in the opposite direction, no doubt making for the servants' stairs at the end.

Slowing, Del watched him go, then, reaching his door, opened it and went in.

Cobby was there, folding shirts. He looked up as Del closed the door. "Any luck?"

"No." Del tossed him his cane, which Cobby deftly caught. "I thought I'd take my swordstick."

Cobby grinned. "By the wall beside the door."

Del turned, saw it waiting, and grunted. Picking it up, he paused. "Did Miss Duncannon send a message?"

"No. Haven't heard from her, nor seen her, since breakfast."

"What was her boy doing here, then?"

"Sangay? He just looked in to see if I had anything for him to do—any errands or the like. Probably looking for an excuse to get outside."

Del humphed, nodded. He refocused on the swordstick in his hand. "So it's off to the museum to trawl for cultists. Wish us luck."

"I would, only I'm not sure which way that should go. Do you want them to hang back and let you live peaceably, or come at you and try to slit your throats?"

"The latter." Del turned to the door. "At the moment I could definitely do with engaging a cultist or two."

Or three. By the time he and Deliah reached the museum, Del was itching for a fight. He knew the sensation well, but never before had it been provoked by a woman, a lady. And all because she was behaving absolutely perfectly.

Except. . . .

He'd spent the short hackney ride to Montague House lecturing himself on the absurdity of wishing her to change into some different, more delicate type of female, the sort prone to displaying her sensibilities. That might make reading her, and managing her, easier, but it would conversely make his life a great deal more difficult.

And he didn't truly want her to change. He wanted. . . .

If she'd noticed his abstraction, she'd given no sign, but had commented happily on the sights as they'd crossed the town into Bloomsbury. Now she stood in the museum foyer scanning a board listing the current exhibits. "Where should we start? I rather fancy the Egyptian gallery. I've heard it's quite fascinating."

"The Egyptians it is." He waved her on.

Discreet signs directed them up the stairs. As they climbed, she glanced at him, then asked, "How did your visit to the Guards go?"

It was the first she'd asked of it—which, now he thought of it, was unlike her. Perhaps she wasn't as unaffected—as undistracted—as he'd thought?

"I found a few friends to chat to, but it was all for show. I didn't even mention the Black Cobra."

At the top of the stairs, he touched her elbow and indicated another sign down a corridor. They started toward it.

"I know you've resigned your commission, supposedly permanently, but was that merely for this mission? Will you rejoin when it's over, perhaps serve in some other capacity? Or are you truly retiring from the field?"

He thought as they strolled. "The latter was my intention, and still is. Talking to the others today only confirmed that—the reasons for that."

"Which are?"

An interrogation again, but gentler. He sensed she truly wanted to know. And after last night . . . "I'm thirty-five. My service has shown me much of the world, and also brought me significant wealth. Militarily, there are few challenges remaining—not for field officers such as myself. It's time I came home and tried my hand at new challenges."

"In Humberside?"

He felt his lips curve. "In Humberside, strange as that may seem."

Her nose tipped upward. "It doesn't seem strange to me."

And that, he thought, was interesting—revealing. Despite

her travels, it seemed she, too, had a special place in her heart for the county of her birth.

Before he could turn the tables on her, she asked, "So what form do you imagine this Humberside challenge will take?"

They'd reached the Egyptian gallery; side by side, they turned into it. A succession of smaller connected rooms opening off a central hall, it was tailor-made for an ambush. The silver head of his swordstick felt reassuring in Del's hand. Taking Deliah's elbow, he steered her toward the first of the large statues in the hall, one of Isis that towered some eight feet tall. "Let's examine the statues in this room first, going down this side, then up the other. That'll give them a moment to find us. Then we can go through the smaller rooms and see if we can tempt them to make a move."

She nodded. Dutifully considered Isis, and read the description inscribed on a plaque beside it.

"So," she said, as they moved to the next statue, "what do you plan to do on your return to Middleton on the Wolds?"

His lips quirked. "You've missed your calling—you should have been an interrogator."

Her brows rose haughtily. "I take it you don't know the answer."

"Not entirely. I'd toyed with the idea of resigning for some time, but beyond going home to Middleton on the Wolds, I hadn't got to the stage of making more detailed plans, then this mission arose, and as part of it I resigned. So no, I haven't any fixed intentions beyond going home."

"But it's your house, isn't it?" She glanced at him. "Delborough Hall, where your aunts live?"

"Yes." He steered her on. "They've been keeping the place—house and estate—running while I've been away, more or less since my father's death. But from their letters I gather they're eager for me to take up the reins, something I did wonder about."

"Indeed. They've been mistresses there for decades. They might not have wished to surrender control."

"Apparently now peace has been established, they're keen to travel and see all the sights the wars prevented them from seeing."

She smiled. "From what I remember of them, they'll thoroughly enjoy harassing some poor courier-guide."

The notion made him grin.

They'd reached the end of the main hall. Glancing up the long room, he saw a number of other people, including two men who didn't seem the sort to spend their hours studying ancient statuary. "I believe"—he turned back to Deliah— "that we've collected two watchers, but sadly, they're not cultists."

"But they might be . . . what's the term? Scouting? For the cultists. Mightn't they?"

"They might. Let's go back along this side—we'll pass them as we go up the room, then we'll turn into the first rooms on our right."

She nodded, and obligingly glided beside him as they perambulated up the room, stopping at every statue to admire and exchange comments.

As they left the main hall for the minor rooms, she returned to her earlier interrogation. "You don't seem the sort to be a gentleman farmer." She glanced at him. "Or at least, not to be satisfied with being only that."

Very true. "I've been thinking, what with Kingston so close, and York and Leeds not that far away, that I might look into investing in manufacturing. Manufacturing what, I'm not sure." He glanced at her. "Textiles, perhaps."

She dipped her head. "There are all those mills about Leeds. I had wondered if there might be a market for cotton there."

"And silk."

"Actually, there are a number of combinations of silk and cotton that are quite valuable commercially." Her skirts swished as she paused by a glass case housing pieces of pottery. "Are they still following us?"

"Yes. And they're drawing closer."

"Hmm. Then again, these rooms are smaller."

"True."

They continued ambling, and their watchers continued to follow, close enough to observe them, but not close enough to pose a physical threat. They seemed intent on watching only, thus giving Del no excuse to react.

Whether it was the possibility of impending danger abrading his protectiveness, or the airy nonchalance of her replies, or, loweringly, that he remained acutely aware of her, of the body he'd spent hours possessing thoroughly through the night that now seemed so elusive, drifting close yet beyond his reach, he didn't know, but her continued apparent imperviousness, her insensibility to his nearness, his presence by her side, pricked him, increasingly on the raw.

Enough to have him reach for her, his hand brushing the side of her breast as he wound her arm with his.

He detected the faintest tremble, the slightest quiver in her breathing, but her serene smile never faltered. A second later, she was enthusing about some ancient scroll.

Once started, he couldn't seem to stop. Some part of him interpreted her refusal to let any sensual awareness of him show as a challenge, even though his rational mind knew he should be grateful. Instead, as he guided her deeper into the labyrinth of smaller rooms surrounding the main hall, he let his hand linger at the small of her back. Her breath caught. When she tried to move away, he moved with her, letting his palm brush upward, then slide down.

She sucked in a breath, tighter, more constrained, and shot him a sharp, if wary, glance.

Wariness wasn't what he wanted. When she stopped before another glass case and stared in apparent rapt contemplation, he slipped his arm from hers and stepped behind her, his palm trailing from her waist down over her hip, and around to, as he stood behind her watching her reflection in the glass, lightly caress the swell of her derriere.

This time she sucked in a more definite breath, caught her

lower lip between her teeth, then looked up—and glared at him.

Her breasts swelled more definitely. She glanced swiftly across the room to where the two watchers were pretending to examine a wall plaque, then swung to face him. "What are you doing?"

Her hissing tone was music to his ears. She was no longer so unaffected.

He opened his eyes wide. "Me? Nothing."

"Nothing?" Eyes narrowing, she prodded him in the chest. When he stepped back, she swept past and, with more of a swish than a glide, headed toward the next open door. She spoke over her shoulder in an irritated whisper. "Just because I lost my head last night doesn't mean I'm going to—"

"Acknowledge it?"

She shot him an angry glance as he drew near. "Acknowledge what? And how?"

He halted just inside the doorway. The room was more of a small alcove; it had only one door, the one at his back. Returning his gaze to her face, he replied, "Acknowledge that you transformed into a veritable houri, and that you enjoyed every minute of what I did to you."

"A *houri*? Nonsense!"

"Trust me, I know a houri when I have her beneath me."

She nearly choked. "What about *you,* and what I did to you?"

"You want me to acknowledge that?"

"Why not? If you want me to do the same?"

He studied her for an instant, then nodded. "Very well."

She frowned. "Very well what?"

He reached back and closed the little room's door.

Her eyes flared wide. "What are you doing?"

He caught her arms, stepped back so his shoulders were against the door, then yanked her to him. Met her eyes as he lowered his head. "I'm doing as you asked—acknowledging how much I enjoyed being inside you."

He kissed her—and every particle of pretense instantly fell

away. Her lips parted beneath his, her mouth instantly yielded. Inviting, inciting; it was as if he'd waltzed them straight back into the fire that had burned so hotly through the night.

He had his answer, all but immediately. She had been pretending not to be affected; the discovery was balm to his primitive male soul.

Yet he couldn't resist taking the kiss deeper, angling his head and taking more, demanding more. Filling his hands with the bounty of her curves, he lifted her against him, shifted his hips against her, felt her hands grip his head, felt her melt. . . .

Hauling on his reins, he abruptly drew back, staggered that she'd been able to lure him so far so quickly, to so deeply snare him in her sensual web.

A houri, indeed.

Thank God she didn't know how thoroughly he was smitten.

Deliah blinked dazedly up at him. Her lips throbbed, her skin felt heated. She wanted. . . .

Then she remembered where they were. Feeling his hands gripping her bottom, she wriggled—caught her breath at the press of his erection.

Felt marginally better when he cursed through his teeth and set her down.

She was still horrified. "Don't you *dare* do such a thing again—not in public!"

He arched one dark, infuriating brow. "Why not?" His lips lightly curved. "You liked it."

"That's not the point!" She felt flustered to her toes. The same toes that had been curling bare seconds before. Which *was* the point. She clearly couldn't trust herself—her wayward, wanton, according to him hourilike self—to hold to any socially unimpeachable line. Not when it came to him. Not if he touched her, kissed her.

She felt like fanning herself, but it was the middle of winter—a muff wasn't much use. Gritting her teeth, she tried to glare at him.

He merely smiled charmingly, stepped aside and opened the door. "Shall we go on?"

All she could do was elevate her chin and swan through the door back into the room they'd left.

Their watchers were still there; her reappearance interrupted a hasty conference, which abruptly ended.

Ignoring the two men, she led the way on.

They completed their circuit of the Egyptian gallery, then she insisted on looking through the Etruscan rooms as well, which gave her blood time to cool, but otherwise failed to advance their cause. Their watchers simply wouldn't approach them.

Disappointed on that front, they quit the museum, only spotting Tony and Gervase as, a few minutes later, they followed them through the doors.

"Well," she said, settling onto the seat in the hackney Del had hailed, "that gained us nothing."

Sitting beside her, he smiled a knowing, self-satisfied, masculine smile.

She stiffened, waited, but he contented himself with looking out of the window as the hackney ferried them back to Grillon's.

The smile, however, remained on his lips.

They returned to the hotel and repaired to the suite. Minutes later, Tony and Gervase joined them.

"Those two are still watching from down the street," Gervase said. "They come, they go, but they don't go far."

"They have to be the Black Cobra's hirelings." Del grimaced. "Unfortunately, I can't see any benefit in the direct approach. Like the others, they won't know anything."

"The best we can do is follow them this evening and hope to get a bead on the man to whom they report." Tony turned as the door opened. "Ah—luncheon."

They sat and ate. Deliah preserved a certain aloofness. Even she could hear the warning edge to her voice. Neither

Tony nor Gervase could interpret it, but that didn't matter—
he who needed to hear the warning could.

From the look in his eyes when they met hers, Del heard
her message loud and clear, but to her irritation he didn't pay
it any great heed. When, the meal concluded and their plans
for the afternoon confirmed, he and she left the suite on their
next foray—a visit to Hatchards, again shadowed by Tony
and Gervase—in ushering her through the door, he let his
hand linger at the back of her waist.

Rather than respond, she decided to ignore him. And the
reactions he evoked. Nose in the air, she led the way to the
stairs.

Hatchards bookshop wasn't far. Remembering the image
they wished to project, when they stepped out into Albemarle Street and Del offered his arm, she took it. Together
they strolled down the street and into Piccadilly. The day
had remained overcast, the heavy clouds a steel-gray; the
brisk breeze carried the scent of snow, although none had
yet fallen. She'd brought her umbrella just in case; getting
drenched formed no part of her plans.

The bell over Hatchards' door tinkled as Del opened the
door. Deliah walked in; he followed at her heels. "Do you
think they'll come in here?" she murmured.

Pausing, they both took stock of the shop, tightly packed
with bookshelves forming narrow corridors leading into the
depths, with a goodly number of customers excusing themselves to each other as they passed up and down the aisles,
searching the shelves.

"If I were them," Del replied, "I'd stay outside and watch.
There's only one door for customers to use. But still, it's
worth a try—we might lure them in. Pick an aisle, and let's
disappear down it and see what happens."

"Poets, I think." She set off down the third aisle.

Despite the look he cast her, he followed.

"Did you ever read Byron?"

"No. Not my style."

She cast him a glance over her shoulder. "You might be surprised. 'Childe Harold' was quite . . . adventurous."

He merely looked at her.

She smiled and faced forward.

They spent some time loitering deep between the shelves, pretending a spurious interest in this or that, while he kept a weather eye on the others who drifted quietly up and down the aisles.

An assassin would have found the shop very much to his liking. It would have been quite easy to take someone intent on the books unawares. But Del was fast coming to the conclusion that those following them had been hired merely to watch, and nothing else.

Which worried him.

Where was the Black Cobra and his assassins? He couldn't believe there weren't more cultists in England, supporting their evil master. Aside from all else, their evil master was far too canny not to have brought as many men as he could with him. And he'd had days, if not weeks, to build up his troops.

His mind absorbed with speculation, his eyes scanning their surrounds, he didn't see the danger directly before him.

Deliah didn't intend it, and neither did he. She was about to slip past an elderly gentleman when the man turned, blocking the narrow aisle, then, eyes down, stepped toward them. Deliah stopped dead. The gentleman, apparently hard of hearing, and then shocked to find them so close, took a moment to realize and halt—forcing her to hurriedly step back.

Her neatly rounded derriere pressed snugly into Del's groin.

An instant later, realizing the problem courtesy of his inevitable reaction, she tried to shift sideways and succeeded in making matters even worse. Biting back a curse, he closed his hands over her shoulders and forced himself to step back.

Oblivious, the elderly gentleman, with profuse apologies and an attempted bow, excused himself and squeezed past.

Deliah swung to face Del. The look with which she pinned him was full of accusation.

Eyes narrowing, he stepped closer.

She started to edge away. Reaching across, he clamped one hand on the shelf beyond her shoulder, caging her; with his shoulder against the shelf alongside her, his body shielded her from anyone starting down the aisle. There was no one else presently in it.

All points she'd already noted.

He leaned close, met her aggravated gaze. "That wasn't my fault—not in the slightest."

Her lips thinned. Her eyes searched his, then they widened. Her breath hitched. Her gaze lowered to his lips. "Don't you *dare* kiss me—not here."

Part protest, part order, part whispered plea.

For one defined instant, all about them stilled. The very air seemed brittle, charged, all but crackling.

Her breasts rose and fell. His gaze lowered to the tempting mounds, before rising, inevitably, to her lips. . . .

He saw them quiver. He looked up, into her eyes, and realized she was . . . every bit as aroused, as tempted, as he.

But she was frightened, not of him but of what might—would—happen if. . . .

"No. Not here." He straightened, and she sucked in a much-needed breath.

Then she shot him a glance close to a glare. "Good."

Spine stiff, she entirely unnecessarily shook out her skirts, then, nose once more elevated, preceded him up the aisle.

He fell into step behind her, far enough back so he could appreciate the view as they walked back up the long aisle.

That view did nothing for his painfully unsatisfied state, yet the realization that in the aftermath of their earlier kiss—and its as yet unfullfilled promise—she was every bit as exercised as he, every bit as on edge and wanting, went a long way toward easing his temper.

When they stepped out of the shop and the door closed

behind them, he could still feel the charged atmosphere between them, but they were standing in Piccadilly in the middle
of the afternoon. He wasn't surprised when she squared her
shoulders, then, glancing vaguely down the street, said, "It
seems senseless to waste the entire afternoon. I assume they're
still watching—why don't we give them an opportunity they
can't refuse?"

"Such as?"

Deliah bludgeoned her wits to keep them in line, to keep
them focused on his mission and what they were supposed
to be accomplishing, rather than on what they might instead
do if they returned to the hotel.

Her pulse was still tripping, her heart still pounding, but
aside from all else, there were Tony and Gervase to consider.
She couldn't see them, but they would be near, watching,
waiting.

"What about Green Park?" She turned to look down Piccadilly to where, a little way along, leafless trees overhung
the pavement. "I doubt there'll be many nursemaids airing
their charges in this weather."

She cocked a brow Del's way. He hesitated, then, it seemed
with great reluctance, inclined his head. He offered his arm.
Steeling herself, she took it, and let him lead her down the
busy street.

The sky was darkening, the clouds louring, and, as she'd
predicted, there weren't many people strolling under the
large trees in Green Park. A scattering of maids and govern-
esses were gathering toddlers and young children, preparing
to take them home.

To warm hearths and comfort, out of the chill of impending icy rain.

Deliah gave thanks for her thick pelisse. The shiver she
fought to suppress wasn't due to the cold. They were being
followed, she was sure of it, and this time with more definite
intent—although she might be imagining that. She glanced
at Del. "There's more of them, aren't there?"

His features hard, his expression impassive, he nodded. "At least three, but I think there are more."

They strolled on a few paces. "That's good, isn't it?"

Del wasn't sure he agreed. "It's what we wanted to do." To draw the cultists into an attack. Only he didn't think they were cultists, although he still held a faint hope. More importantly, however, he had Deliah beside him—and that went against every tenet in his book.

With every step he took deeper into the park, he felt increasingly torn, one part of him urging him to take Deliah's arm and march her straight back to the safety of the hotel, while the rest of him argued that this was a chance—a chance his mission committed him to take—to engage the enemy's troops and reduce their number. His decoy's mission hinged on that.

And she would fight him every step of the way if he tried to remove her from the action she'd instigated.

They slowed, but remaining apparently oblivious was essential to tempt an attack. Yet the edge of the park drew steadily nearer, and still their pursuers hung back.

"What do we do?" she asked. "Turn and saunter back?"

Mentally reviewing the areas through which they'd passed, he grimaced. "It's too open—they're worried others will see and come to our aid. There's still plenty of people walking along Piccadilly—anyone could glance into the park and see."

"In that case"—with her furled umbrella, she waved ahead—"let's continue on into St James's Park. Lots more bushes under the trees there, and even fewer people."

Let alone the sort who might assist them. With the light fading, and the weather closing in, the denizens left in St. James's Park were more likely to be pickpockets and thieves than upstanding citizens.

Del's jaw set. He didn't want to, but . . . with a stiff nod, he guided her on.

Leaving Green Park, they crossed the end of the Mall, all but deserted, and strolled, apparently nonchalantly, on into the glades of St. James's Park.

The bushes closed around them, and every instinct Del possessed heightened, sharpened.

Beside him, he felt Deliah tense, alert, her senses no doubt reaching out, scanning, as were his.

"Tony and Gervase will be near." He uttered the reassurance beneath his breath.

She tipped her head in acknowledgment, but said nothing.

The attack, when it came, was potentially more deadly than he'd foreseen. They were ambling, outwardly without a care, down a grassed avenue wide enough for three men abreast, when three thugs swung out of the bushes ten paces ahead, and faced them, blocking the way.

Movement to their rear told him there were men there, too; gripping Deliah's arm, he pulled her behind him as he swung to place their backs to a wide tree trunk.

Two more men blocked the path they'd already trod, cutting off any retreat. At that point, the trees and bushes lining the path were too thick to easily push through.

The enemy had chosen a decent setting for their ambush, yet they were all Englishmen. Del inwardly swore as, with a click, he loosened the sword concealed in his stick. Three of the men started forward, two from one end, one from the other, leaving one man standing guard at either end of the short stretch. With a flourishing swish, Del unsheathed his sword. Stepping back, crowding Deliah between the tree and him, he beckoned. "Come on, then."

The sword had given them pause. They already had knives in their hands. They exchanged glances, then looked back at him.

Then they launched a concerted attack.

The fighting was fast and furious, but Del had been in tighter, more dicey situations. He hadn't, however, fought before with a demented female armed with a parasol beside him.

He should have expected it, yet he hadn't. Far from cowering behind him—where she ought to at least have stayed—Deliah slipped out to stand alongside him, with her parasol laying into any of the men who came within beating range.

Her active participation as well as her furious flaying threw the three men facing him off balance.

Before matters got too fraught, and the two thugs standing back thought to intervene, Tony and Gervase slid silently from the bushes, and the two thugs dropped where they stood.

The remaining three suddenly realized that instead of being the ones springing a trap, a trap had been sprung on them.

But it was far too late for escape. With ruthless efficiency, Tony, Gervase and Del subdued them, using their fists, rather than any blades.

Then came silence, broken only by the sound of their breathing.

In the deepening gloom of early twilight, they hauled all five men into a row on the grass, sitting them propped against each other. None were in any state to make a bid for freedom.

The men were still groggy, but they could hear.

"Who sent you?" Gervase began the interrogation.

With short, sharp questions coming from all four of them—Deliah joined in, of course, and as her sharper tone made the men holding their heads wince, Del let her fire away—they soon extracted the expected story. The five had been hired by a man—a suspiciously tanned Englishman with close-cropped dark hair—to stalk them, watch closely, and act on any opportunity to seize either Deliah or Del.

As before, the would-be abductors had been told to bring any baggage they might acquire to a tavern, this time in a seedy alley in Tothill Fields.

Turning to Del, Deliah and Gervase, Tony shook his head. "No point going there—it'll be the same story as last night."

Gervase grunted an assent. He eyed the five figures slumped before them. "What should we do with them?"

While Del, Tony and Gervase evaluated the merits of

turning the men over to the Watch, Deliah stood with her
arms crossed and scowled at their prisoners.

They knew she was watching; none dared meet her eye.
They shifted, but none showed any sign of getting to their
feet and running.

As Del and the other two were in the throes of concluding
they might as well let the five go—no real point in going to
the Watch and having to spend hours explaining why men
continued to attack them—sitting quietly and watching and
waiting was wise.

And that, Deliah thought, illustrated what was different
about these men. They weren't like the lumbering louts of yesterday; these men were harder, smarter, quicker—distinctly
more deadly.

They were quite a different breed.

"Very well." Del turned to the men. "You can—"

"Wait." Deliah shot a glance Del's way. When he raised
a brow but obediently waited, she refocused on the man in
the center of the line. He was, she judged, the oldest, and appeared the most sharply observant. "Before you scurry back
to your sewers, tell me—do you know others like you? Do
you have contacts you can use to get out a warning?"

The man in the center returned her regard steadily. "Might
have. Why?"

"Because you need to understand what's going on here."
Deliah felt Del place a hand on her arm; she nodded slightly
in acknowledgment, but continued, "The man who hired
you—you noticed his tanned skin. He's lately come from
India. He's the servant of a man from India—a fiend who's
been terrorizing the country there, among other things
butchering and torturing Englishmen, English soldiers and
civilians, and even women and children."

She held the man's gaze. "The reason the fiend—he's known
as the Black Cobra—sent his servant to hire you was because
the Colonel here"—with a wave she indicated Del—"and
three others who've yet to land in England are carrying information that must get into the right hands in our government

to bring the fiend down. Naturally, the Black Cobra doesn't want that—he wants to be able to keep killing Englishmen in India. So you might tell all your friends that, if they agree to work for any man, even a gentleman, lately from India, then they're most likely being used as cannon fodder for the Black Cobra, so he can keep killing Englishmen."

The five men on the ground had grown restive as she'd spoken. When she finished, the man in the center exchanged glances with his mates, then looked up at her, nodded. "We'll spread the word. Not many of us hold with working for furriners."

"Good."

"Do any of you know Gallagher?" Tony asked. "Enough to get word to him?"

All five looked wary, but after a moment, the leader allowed, "I could perhaps get word through."

"Tell him Torrington sends his regards, and Dearne—Grantham—is part of this caper, too, just not in London. Pass on all the lady told you. Gallagher will understand."

The men's attitude had undergone a significant shift, from adversaries almost to allies. The leader nodded more definitely. "I'll do that."

He started to rise, then halted, looked at Del.

Del nodded. "Go. And if you've got any English blood in you, spread the word."

With nods, the men clambered to their feet, paused, then bobbed awkward bows to Deliah before lumbering off south toward the nearby slums.

"Well," Gervase said, "that wasn't quite a total loss." He looked at Deliah, and his gaze hardened. "Although, in future, it might help if you would consent to leave the fighting to us. An umbrella is hardly an effective weapon."

Slowly Deliah raised her brows, then she extended the umbrella she still held in one hand, regarded it with approval. "This, I will have you know, is the very latest patented design. It has a steel shaft, a steel frame and mechanism, and, most importantly, it has a steel point." Raising the umbrella, she displayed the steel spike at its tip. "In terms of an unexpected weapon, one a lady might carry, it's ideal—and if you had questioned the man with the red spotted bandana just now, he would have told you that getting jabbed with a steel spike made him think twice about getting closer."

"Yes, *but,*" Tony interceded, "the point is that you're a lady, and we're here, three gentlemen, and having you—"

"Getting in the way?"

"I wasn't going to say that. Having you embroiled in the action," Tony carefully continued, "is seriously distracting."

"For you," Deliah countered. "But for me, what would be totally unacceptable would be for me to meekly cower behind you like some helpless ninny, when in fact, as I just proved, I can perfectly effectively contribute." Her eyes darkened. "I will remind you, gentlemen, that I'm a part of this enterprise whether I wish it or not. That being so, if you think I'm the sort of female to hide behind your coattails and leave all the fighting to you, you will need to think again."

Nose elevating, she swung around—casting a sidelong glance at Del.

He bit his lip and kept his mouth firmly shut. The others would have done better to save their breaths.

Deliah humphed, then looked up at the sky, now a dark slate-gray. "Let's get back to the hotel."

Head high, she led the way, umbrella swinging defiantly.

Disgruntled, disapproving, but with no option for relief, with Gervase and Tony bringing up the rear, Del fell in alongside her.

December 14
Grillon's Hotel

Deliah reached her bedroom in a less than chipper mood.

Stripping off her gloves, then struggling out of her pelisse, she muttered, "They could at least have recognized my contribution. Acknowledged the wisdom of *my* idea to tell the men about the Black Cobra, and hopefully put an end to the supply of local hirelings. But no. They had to harp about me not wilting like a proper gentlewoman."

She was disgusted with them all. Although, to his credit, Del had kept silent.

Not that he'd disagreed. She knew perfectly well he'd felt the same as the other two.

She humphed. Draping the pelisse over a chair, she carried her gloves to the bureau. Pulling open the top drawer, she went to drop the gloves in. Paused.

Her handkerchiefs were jumbled. She frowned, then opened the next drawer down. Her shawls were rumpled.

A quick survey of the dressing table and the armoire convinced her.

She looked up as the door opened.

Bess came in, packages in her hands. "There you are."

"As you see. Has anyone unexpected called?"

"No. Why?"

Deliah cast another glance around. "I can't be absolutely certain, but I think someone has searched through my things."

"What?" Bess bristled. "The only other of our party who's been up to the suite since you left is Sangay, the colonel's boy. He came looking for the colonel's gloves. But I was out for most of the afternoon, shopping for those things you wanted." She raised the packages.

Deliah grimaced. "I don't think anything's missing." She looked at the dressing table. "My silver-backed brushes are still there, and all my jewelry, so it couldn't have been a thief."

She sighed. "Never mind." She focused on the packages. "Let's see what you found."

Seven

December 14
Grillon's Hotel

Feeling sartorially better equipped to face the days to come, Deliah joined the three men for dinner in the suite's sitting room. Tony and Gervase had just joined Del; they all exchanged nods, then took their seats so Cobby and Janay could serve the first course, a delicate chicken broth with small dumplings.

They were silent while they supped. Tension rippled between them—a certain frostiness on Deliah's part, countered by Del's studiously arrogant refusal to notice. Tony and Gervase, meanwhile, were exercised over the mission, as was Del; glancing at their faces, Deliah read their mounting frustration.

When they set down their spoons, Gervase spoke. "We haven't seen anyone who isn't English."

Tony humphed. "We haven't even sighted the man hiring."

"Larkins, from all descriptions," Del said.

"Ferrar's man?" When Del nodded, Tony went on, "I wonder if we'd gain anything by watching Ferrar."

"We'd have to find him first," Gervase pointed out.

"I had Cobby ask if he's been seen at White's." Del grimaced. "They said no, and the address they had for him was from years ago—a lodging house in Jermyn Street. He isn't there, and the landlord hasn't heard from him."

Gervase shrugged. "If he's using Larkins, then watching Ferrar won't help us. And linking Larkins to the hirelings won't materially advance our cause." He nodded at Deliah. "Given you can identify Larkins as the man who shot at Del in Southampton, we can nobble Larkins any time we choose, but unless we can link Larkins and his lethal activities to Ferrar's letter, we have nothing to implicate Ferrar."

"Unless we can prove Larkins is acting under Ferrar's direct orders, then Ferrar will simply deny any knowledge of Larkins's doings, no matter what Larkins says," Tony stated.

"Indeed. And it's Ferrar we want." Leaning back in his chair, Del looked at Gervase, then Tony. "I have to question whether there's any point in us remaining in town."

Cobby and Janay arrived with the next course. They waited while the pair efficiently cleared the table, served them from platters of meats and a tureen of vegetables, then, with everything in order, retreated.

Deliah decided to state the obvious. "London has a large supply of ruffians Larkins can hire to do his master's bidding. Even if those we caught today warn their fellows, it's likely Larkins will be able to find enough men to keep us busy here for at least a few more days."

Del nodded. "And by dallying here, accomplishing nothing beyond running down the stocks of local louts, we give Ferrar time to build up his forces by bringing in more cultists— fighters he'll deploy only when he needs to."

"When we, or more likely our other three couriers, force him to act outside the major towns," Tony said. "Even in the major towns, if the target's moving he won't have time to recruit. He'll need to use his cultists then—they're his only mobile force."

After a moment, Gervase said, "We're getting nowhere here. I vote we send word to Wolverstone, and tomorrow head into Cambridgeshire."

"I second that." Tony straightened. "We move—we force his hand. He must know by now that you're not intending to deliver the letter to anyone in town, but he can't risk you handing it on, so once you're on the road he'll have to make a bid for it, one he won't be able to plan, and for that he'll need his own troops."

Del nodded. "And once we're on the move, his attention will focus on the scroll-holder itself. That's his real goal, the thing he needs to seize."

"True," Gervase said, "but if the opportunity presents, he'll still take either you or Deliah as hostage for the letter." Across the table, Gervase met Deliah's eyes. "You'll need to remain on guard."

She nodded, but added nothing else, instead listening as the three men discussed the possibilities, then made plans to leave the next morning, with Del and Deliah and their combined households making a great and noisy show to ensure they were noted and followed.

"The scroll-holder?" Gervase cocked a brow at Del.

"Is safe."

When Del said nothing more, Tony grinned. "Our journey to Cambridgeshire is sounding more promising by the minute."

Deliah belatedly put two and two together. "I think my room was searched this afternoon." She looked at Del. "Nothing was taken, but perhaps they were looking for the scroll-holder."

"They *who*?" Del's dark eyes pinned her.

The tension, which had waned, ratcheted up again.

"I don't know who. I can't even be sure anyone searched. The things in my drawers were moved, and the bottles on my dressing table, and I'm sure my gowns hanging in the armoire weren't in such disarray. I didn't leave them like that, and Bess—my maid—never would."

"Bess wasn't here while we were out?" Del's expression had turned grim.

"I sent her on some errands." Deliah raised her brows at him. "There was no reason for her to stay in and watch my room—the scroll-holder isn't there."

She, Tony and Gervase looked at Del.

He continued to stare at Deliah, inwardly railing, but helpless. Eventually he answered their unvoiced query. "My room hasn't been searched." Not yet. Cobby would have noticed and told him if it had been.

"Well, then." Tony raised his glass. "To a more productive tomorrow."

They clinked glasses and drank.

The men's conversation turned to military affairs, then to sporting events.

Irritated by the renewed aggravation she sensed coming her way from Del, Deliah seized the moment when Cobby returned with the decanters to excuse herself and retire, denying any wish for tea and wishing them a good night. They all stood as she rose.

"I'll see you in the morning, gentlemen." With a regal nod, she left them.

Del watched the bedroom door close behind her, and felt some of the tension gripping him ease. Not, however, all of it. By no means all.

Resuming his seat, he let himself slide into a discussion of the latest boxing feats. At least outwardly. Inwardly . . .

She'd become an itch under his skin, even more so after last night. And she—it, whatever this was—wasn't any simple sexual itch, one that dissipated after one scratch. Or two.

He doubted three, or even three hundred, instances of having her curvaceous body beneath his would cure his particular affliction.

She made him feel far more than he ever had. No other woman had ever been so provoking. It wasn't simply her refusal to obey his orders, her steadfast antipathy to hiding behind him—her willful insistence on going into danger whenever and wherever she deemed it necessary—although all of that contributed to the emotions roiling through him.

In most situations he could see her point, even sympathize with it, *but . . .*

It was that *but* he wasn't used to, that he had no experience in dealing with, coping with, much less controlling.

He didn't like what she made him feel, didn't approve of it, resented it, railed at it—all of which did no good. He was obsessed with her—and some part of him knew where that obsession was heading. What it was leading him to.

But while his mission was in train, he couldn't think of that. Couldn't think of what came later, after.

Eventually, the conversation died. The other two yawned, then stretched. Together they all rose and left the suite, strolling down the corridor. He halted outside his room. With relaxed good nights, Tony and Gervase went on to their rooms further around the gallery.

Del watched them go, then reached for the doorknob. His hand closed about it, but then he stopped. For what seemed an unending moment, he stared at his hand grasping the knob.

He wasn't thinking—wasn't even debating. He knew he should turn the knob, go inside and fall into his bed.

He couldn't remember why.

Muttering a curse, he released the knob, turned and stalked back to the suite.

The door was still unlocked. He locked it behind him; Deliah's maid would have come and gone via the door between bedroom and corridor.

Deliah should, by now, be abed.

He didn't hesitate but knocked on her bedroom door.

He leaned against the jamb, waited.

Eventually, the door opened.

She stood in the doorway, no sign of surprise on her haughty face. Her hair was down, rumpled dark red tresses caressing the shoulders of the ivory silk wrap she'd flung over a prim white nightgown.

Also of soft, sensuous silk.

Behind her, the bed was disarranged, the pillow dented. She had, indeed, been abed.

Beyond his control, his gaze slid down, over the full mounds of her breasts, nipples peaking, down over the flat of her stomach and the swells of her hips, all the way down her long, long legs, outlined lovingly by the clinging gown. He was immediately, painfully hard. Aching to possess what he knew the silk concealed.

It took a moment to lift his gaze back to her eyes.

She coolly searched his face, then, imperiously, raised her brows. "What do you want?"

Her tone was even, direct, neither encouraging nor discouraging.

He gave her the truth. "You."

For another unending moment, silence reigned.

Then he straightened from the doorjamb, stepped forward.

And she stepped back, allowing him in.

Deliah closed the door behind him.

This was madness, but what was she to do? Tell him no?

She didn't think she could. Didn't think her vocal cords would cooperate in uttering such a very big lie, not when her heart was turning cartwheels of anticipatory delight and her mouth was salivating in expectation.

Turning, she found him waiting. One arm sliding around her waist, he drew her to him.

She looked up, met his eyes as their bodies touched. Awareness streaked through her, but she hid it, suppressed it. Her hands rose, came to rest on his shoulders. Beneath her palms, the tempting warmth, the masculine hardness seduced as she watched his eyes search hers, then drift over her face.

Then lower to her lips.

Parting them, she drew in a shallow breath. There wasn't anything she felt she should say. Nothing she expected him to say, to explain. He was a man of the world, and she . . . she could pretend to be his counterpart.

Would pretend, as his eyes touched hers again and, after a heartbeat's hesitation, he lowered his head, to be taking this all in her stride.

Determinedly pretend, as instinctively she lifted her chin, met his lips as they stooped to hers, that her nerves weren't skittering, that her senses weren't poised to swoon, that her heart wasn't tripping in double time.

He kissed her, and she kissed him. Familiar, yet not. Last night had been so urgent, so heated and driven; tonight, she sensed in him a greater attention, an intention to remain focused . . . on her.

On what he wanted of her.

Quite what that was she didn't know. A thrill of expectation flashed, sharp and bright, through her.

The kiss grew hungrier, more demanding. She met him, matched his claims, his conquest, with her own needs, her own wants.

All entirely instinctive, but she had no other guide. She wasn't innocent, not in the biblical sense, yet she'd never been this way before, had never needed as she now did before.

Had never wanted a man as she wanted him.

That simple; that complicated. Her want was a pattern of needs and desires, and as he wasn't in any hurry tonight, and neither was she, he seemed content to let her explore—those needs, those wants, and him.

He let her undress him. His lips curved when she wrestled his shirt from him and then, the garment sliding from her fingertips, stared in wonder at the muscled expanse of his chest. Eyes wide, she dropped the shirt and spread her hands, palms to his hot skin.

And learned.

She explored like a wanton, freed of restraint, and he let her.

Encouraged her.

Until he stood naked in the moonlight, each heavy bone, the taut line of every muscle, gilded in silver, and she couldn't breathe, yet still she took his member, erect and so flagrantly male, between her hands, stroked, closed her fingers, and lightly squeezed.

He stilled. She sensed the tension in him grow, tighten—to steel, fine and hard and unwavering. Her fingers, her hands, slowed.

His chest swelled as he drew in a breath. Then his hands rose to her shoulders, cupped, tightened—then eased. He drew off the silk wrapper she'd donned over her nightgown.

And slowly, deliberately, turned the tables on her.

He took his time, his lips returning to hers now and again, to sup, to send her senses spinning again. To woo her wits into compliance with his agenda—his needs, his wants, his desires.

His wish to learn of her. To explore her even more intimately, even more thoroughly, than she had him.

His hands traced, outlined, possessed. His touch imperfectly shielded by the fine silk of her nightgown, he cupped, stroked, tantalized.

Eventually—at last!—he divested her of the gown. Stripped it away with maddening ease, and equally maddening slowness.

A slowness that stretched her nerves taut, then set them quivering. That left her lungs seized, her breath a mere sigh, her wits scattered beyond recall.

Her senses were all his. His to command.

Expectation, physical anticipation, had never been so brittlely sharp, so exquisitely honed.

So attuned to his intention, his wish, his desire.

To know her. To have her. Ultimately to possess her.

With hands and fingers, with lips and tongue, he stroked, sampled, caressed. Until her breath shuddered and hitched, until her skin burned, until need was a molten ache low in her belly.

Until reckless abandon pounded in her blood.

When he sank to his knees before her, she had no idea what he planned to do. And no time to wonder, to guess

and mute the shock, before he set his lips, his hot mouth, to
her curls, then, ignoring her breathless gasp, he parted her
thighs, and set his wicked tongue to her softness.

He licked, laved, probed, and her senses reeled. Fingers
tangled in his thick hair, she fought to remain upright while
her legs threatened to give way. He sensed it, caught one of
her knees, bent and lifted it to drape her leg over his broad
shoulder, balancing her there, his large hands cupping her
bottom, the position keeping her thighs wide—opening her
to an even more intimate campaign.

One he wrought with devastating effectiveness.

With ruthless thoroughness.

Experience told.

The assault on her senses stretched her nerves to the
breaking point. Head back, eyes open but unseeing, she was
struggling to even gasp, battling to remain afloat on the tide
of his sensual mastery, and not let the waves of tactile pleasure pull her down and drown her, when, with one last, flagrantly explicit foray, he drew back.

Still supporting her, he fluidly rose.

Before her raised foot even reached the floor, he gripped
her hips and hoisted her.

She only just managed to swallow a shriek. Suspended between his hands, her body felt taut, heated by flames licking
over her skin and a fiery emptiness burning within. Clutching his shoulders, her thighs clamped to his flanks, she
looked down to search his face—but he was looking down
as he drew her hips to his.

In the instant she understood, she felt the broad head of
his erection part her slick folds, and press in.

Surrendering to instinct, she lifted her legs, wrapped them
about his hips. Tilted her hips closer, wanting, needing . . .

She lost her breath as he thrust in.

Arms locked about his shoulders, she let her head tip back,
eyes closed, spine arching as he held her and steadily pressed
deeper to fill her. Tiny thrills skittered over her skin; flicker-

ing showers of bright sensation skated along her nerves. Inexorably, relentless and intent, he drew her hips to him, held her there, locked against him, and pushed deeper still.

And then he was there, hard, hot, and impossibly large, filling her, completing her.

She dragged in a huge breath.

Lost it as, his fingers biting into the lush curves of her derriere, Del lifted her, drawing his rigid erection from the scalding slickness of her sheath, only to slide smoothly home again, to the hilt.

The moan she uttered was music to his ears. He set about gaining more.

Set about discovering how much more she could take. How much more he could take of her before surrendering to the inevitable, to an all-consuming, senses-stealing rapturous release.

She hadn't been a virgin, was twenty-nine, and had lived outside England for a decade. A woman so richly endowed, so attuned to the sexual, so openly embracing and welcoming of the act as she'd proved to be, wouldn't have lived those years in abstinence; there was no reason he need feel constrained by typical English sexual mores.

More need, in fact, given her adventurous nature, to use his experience of exotic lovemaking to lure and hold her.

He didn't need to think further. He walked around the room, jigging her with every stride, making her clutch and moan anew, then he walked to the bed, braced his thighs against the side and set her down on her back on the coverlet.

He straightened. Took a moment to look down at her, hair wild and spread beneath her head and shoulders, her features stamped with blatant desire, her luscious body naked, wracked with passion, her skin delicate rose-tinted ivory, her breasts full and firm, nipples tightly furled, her white thighs spread wide, her long legs wrapped around his hips.

His erection sunk in her sheath.

p, caught a glimpse of jade-bright eyes be-
ashes. Saw her watching him.

her breasts rise as she drew breath.

Sliding deep, snug within her, he set his hands to her
breasts, filled his palms, possessed. Drew her nipples into
throbbing buds, then ran his hands down her body, over her
waist, her bare stomach.

Assessing, branding.

He bent his head and with his mouth, his tongue, swiftly
followed the same path. Made her gasp and squirm.

She arched, lifted to him as he returned to pay appropriate homage to her bountiful breasts. When she was reduced
to desperate, wordlessly pleading need, he straightened and
filled his hands with the firm cheeks of her bottom, her skin
flushed and dewed, heated and damp. Tightening his grip, he
withdrew from the slick clutch of her body until he was almost
free, then thrust deep again, harder, more powerfully.

Holding her hips immobile, he set up a driving, compelling rhythm.

She moaned, then sobbed, threshed her head from side
to side.

He released her hips, unwrapped her legs from his hips
and raised her calves to prop her ankles on his shoulders,
then gripped her hips anew and held her steady as he thrust
repetitively, penetrating even more deeply inside her.

Her breath came in panting gasps, her hands fisting in the
coverlet as the tempo increased and he pounded into her.

She tightened, and tightened, spine bowing, muscles
locking.

Then she came apart.

In a glorious, rippling cascade, release took her, caught
her, wracked her, rocked her, shook her. Deliah had never
felt anything so sensually profound. So primitive. As if her
senses had shattered, disintegrated under the onslaught of
sensation he'd wrought.

But even then he wasn't finished with her. He continued

to move within her, until she reached that curious state of floating.

Then he withdrew, leaving her strangely bereft, but only for an instant.

Shrugging her legs from his shoulders, gripping her hips, he rolled her onto her stomach. He drew her toward him until her hips were at the edge of the high mattress, her legs over the side of the bed, her toes barely touching the floor.

She lay there, boneless, and he filled her from behind.

Her nerves sizzled, stretched.

Passion flared anew as he withdrew and thrust into her. Her senses expanded, greedily taking it all in—the novel sensations of his groin meeting the vulnerable skin of her exposed bottom, his heavy balls brushing the sensitive backs of her naked thighs.

The hot, hard, heavy reality of his erection pushing repeatedly into her.

Excitement melded with a sense of vulnerability as he held her there, pinned, effectively helpless, and filled her body, relentlessly filled her senses and her mind with sensual delight, with mind-melting pleasure.

Desire rose and swamped her; passion erupted in a hot tide and swept through her anew. She wanted to move with him, to contribute, to take him, but his hold was unbreakable and his strength too great; he kept her still, immobile, and thrust ever more powerfully, faster and harder into her.

She tightened about him, instinctively seeking to hold, to caress.

Sensed him shudder.

Through his hands, through the rigid columns of his thighs pressing against hers, she felt the tension holding him tighten, then she heard him drag in a huge, broken breath.

Beneath her skin, fire raced and razed. Closing her eyes, she surrendered to instinct and continued to clamp and ease about him, using her body to intimately caress his as he continued to thrust into her. . . .

He gasped, released her hips and leaned forward. Hands sinking into the coverlet on either side of her shoulders, he hung over her. His breathing was harsh and labored above her. His weight pressed her down as his hips hugged hers, pumped desperately—

And release swept him, took him as she clung, as she tightened about him one last time, and felt herself tipping, falling into the vortex of cataclysmic sensation, too. Into a whirlpool of sharp, bright feeling that coalesced and drew in, tighter and tighter, then exploded in a nova of incandescent heat.

Glory erupted, brilliant and bright, spreading and spinning about them, over them, through them, enfolding them in golden pleasure.

Slowly, inexorably, the glow faded.

His arms gave way and he slumped over her, coming down on his elbows, his chest rising and falling like bellows against her back, his breathing harsh by her ear, his body hot, malleable steel curved protectively over hers. His heart still thundered. She felt the evocative beat against her back, felt it where they joined, in the slick furnace between her thighs, in her still clenching womb. He was in her blood, in her bones, had sunk to her marrow.

The beat gradually slowed as they drifted back to earth.

Eyes closed, thoughts in abeyance, her body more his than hers, her cheek pillowed on the coverlet, she realized she was smiling.

She was a mass of contradictions.

Later, once he'd managed to summon strength enough to disengage and lift her, then draw down the covers and rearrange them both in her bed, Del lay back on the piled pillows, one arm behind his head, the other around Deliah as she slept the sleep of the pleasurably exhausted, her cheek pillowed on his chest.

He stared at the canopy and tried to make sense of her.

Not an easy task, given said contradictions.

Her nightgown, for instance. The style was prim and proper, as befitted a deacon's daughter—her father was a deacon, he recalled. The gown's fabric, on the other hand, was a testament to tactile sensuality. The Indians understood the arousing properties of silk, its inherently sensual nature. So, apparently, did Deliah.

Touching her through the garment—sliding, shifting silk caressing silken skin—had been as arousing for her as it had been for him.

That contradiction mirrored another—her oftimes prim behavior, her insistence on propriety, contrasting sharply with the experienced wanton she was. Or at least appeared to be.

Which left him with the last of the contradictions he'd thus far uncovered. She hadn't been a virgin, yet every instinct he possessed insisted that beyond the basics she was—or at least had been—untutored and untried.

He hadn't been in any condition to think much at the time, but he had noticed. Now he had the leisure to think back . . . she'd been startled—honestly taken aback, even shocked— when he'd used his mouth on her.

She'd been surprised when he'd lifted her, although she'd very quickly grasped the possibilities.

When he'd had her on her back. . . .

Eyes narrowing, he replayed all he could. Accepted that his earlier conclusion regarding her experience had been wrong.

The heat of the moment, her eager, all but molten responses, had veiled the truth. All of the aforesaid—and doubtless all that had come after, too—had been new to her.

The only way he could reconcile the nascent, latent houri he knew her to be, that she'd proved to be in his arms, with the twenty-nine-year-old non-virgin with barely a sexual encounter to her name, was that somewhere in her past lay what was commonly termed "a disappointment."

She'd loved some man, had given herself to him, perhaps only once, but for whatever reason—him dying at Waterloo would fit the timing—no marriage had come of it, resulting in her sojourn in Jamaica, presumably to lift her spirits.

He couldn't imagine her going into a decline, but he hadn't known her all those years ago. Yet given how tight she was, her last sexual episode prior to him was in her dim and very distant past. She'd been with no other man—been tempted by no other man—until, the previous night, she'd lost her temper with him.

She might be a nascent, latent houri, but she was the very opposite of a light-skirted lady.

That, to him, was no contradiction but a reassuring, potentially useful fact. A highly pertinent piece of intelligence given the direction he intended to have them head in—his "later, after."

Regardless of having spent no real time dwelling on it, their mutual destination had already taken definite shape in his mind. That being so. . . .

He glanced at her. Spent some minutes simply drinking in the sight of her, softly flushed in sleep, boneless in the aftermath of intense satiation, curled, trusting, against his side.

Her jade-green eyes were closed. Her luscious ruby lips . . .

Recalling his fantasies involving those sinfully ripe lips, he smiled. Lowering his arm, he slid his hand beneath the covers, found her breast.

Gently fondled, caressed.

And felt her rouse, waken, then sinuously stretch.

Smile deepening, he slid down in the bed.

There was no reason he shouldn't show her more. Indulge her, and himself, further. Educate the houri hidden inside her, to her gratification, and his.

No reason at all that he couldn't open her eyes further, couldn't feed her curiosity.

And simultaneously satisfy his.

December 15
Grillon's Hotel

Del returned to his room before dawn the following morning in a distinctly buoyant mood. Even though nothing about his mission had changed, he felt significantly more positive.

Entering his room, he closed the door, looked at the bed. Considered its neat, pristine state. Inwardly shrugged. Cobby had been with him too long to cozen; he would guess regardless.

Going to the bellpull, he tugged it, then continued to the dresser to set down the gold pin he hadn't bothered replacing in his cravat.

Hand poised over the top of the dresser, he froze. Frowned.

Something wasn't quite right, but he couldn't pinpoint what was triggering the thought, the gut feeling. Lifting his head, he scanned the room.

When Cobby arrived, he was still prowling, frowning.

Closing the door, Cobby paused, brows rising. "Don't rightly know which question I should ask first."

"Don't bother with the obvious. What's bothering me is that . . ." Del looked around again. "I think someone's been in here—that someone's searched." He waved a hand around the room. "See what you think."

Cobby came deeper into the room, looked. Gradually, he, too, frowned. "Things are not quite the way we leave them—either you or me. Take the brushes on the dresser. They aren't in any sort of order. Neither of us leave our weapons like that—even if they aren't exactly weapons."

Del ran a hand through his hair. "So I'm right. Someone has been searching. Who?"

Cobby pursed his lips. "Haven't been many hotel staff about up here—just the maids cleaning, and me and Janay usually hang about then." He darted a glance at Del. "Could it be one of Miss Duncannon's people?"

"I can't see how. She's known them for years, and there's

no way the Black Cobra could have known she and I were going to travel together, that her staff would ever have any chance at the scroll-holder. He wouldn't have had time to put his usual persuasions in place."

The Black Cobra's usual persuasive tactic was to get a family member into his clutches and use their safety to ensure their relative did as he bid them.

"You're right." Cobby nodded. "And I have to say they're a straightforward lot. I haven't had any qualms."

"So it has to have been a member of the hotel's staff. Spread the word to the others—we'll need to stay alert while we prepare to leave."

A tap on the door heralded a lad with a jug of steaming water. Cobby received it, then shut the door. He poured a basinful for Del as he stripped. "So what time are we leaving? You didn't exactly say last night."

Del considered as he washed. "Let's say ten on the steps, ten-thirty away." He towelled his face, then mopped his chest. "Pass the word to Janay. I don't know how long it'll take for Miss Duncannon's household to get ready."

"Oh, we heard we'd be leaving last night, so we're ready. All of us. Just finishing up breakfast, the rest are, so as soon as you and Miss Duncannon give the word, we can go."

"Excellent." It was early, but Del had a definite appetite. "You can leave my clothes out, then go and rustle up breakfast. We'll have it in the suite as usual. I'm starved."

And so, he suspected, would be his charge.

As Cobby rummaged in the wardrobe, Del added to himself, "And then we can start out, and see what the day brings."

December 15
Grillon's Hotel

Sangay felt torn on the one hand, and desperate on the other. From the back of Grillon's foyer, half concealed behind a palm in a big pot, he watched the flurry of activity as the colonel-sahib's and the memsahib's households prepared to depart.

He wished he could go with them. They'd been kind to him, all of them, even though they didn't know him—not really. They'd all accepted him as one of their party. He'd been careful to avoid gatherings where they'd all been together, where one household might have said something to alert the other that he wasn't theirs. That he didn't really belong.

So far, the gods had smiled on him, something he didn't understand. He was not acting honorably—he was being the hand, the tool, of an evil man—yet thus far the gods hadn't struck him down.

Thus far the gods had left him to carry out the evil man's instructions.

He'd searched, he'd done all he was supposed to, but he hadn't laid eyes on any scroll-holder. He could guess what it would look like—his old captain had had similar holders for his maps and orders—but he hadn't seen anything that might be it. And now they were all leaving.

He'd failed.

Despair dragging his heart into his thin slippers, he sucked in a breath and, with one last look at the almost gay commotion surrounding the three carriages lined up outside the hotel, slunk down the side corridor to the alley door.

He slipped out of the door, then cautiously made his way to the corner where he'd met the man before, praying with every step that the man wouldn't simply kill him when he reported his failure. More, that he wouldn't feel moved to have his maataa killed, too.

Nerves at full stretch, he rounded the corner. Nearly lost his brave face when, once again, he all but ran into the man.

"Well? Do you have it?"

Sangay fought not to squirm. He lifted his chin, forced himself to look in the direction of the man's face. "I have searched all the bags, all the rooms, sahib. The scroll-holder isn't there."

The man swore, strings of bad words Sangay had heard often enough on the docks. Stoically, he waited for his punishment, for a blow, or worse. There was no point trying to run.

He felt the man's irate gaze boring into him. Steeled himself. The man's fists were clenched, hanging heavy at his sides.

"What's all the activity?" The man tipped his head toward the front of the hotel. "Where are they going?"

Sangay pulled the answer from his skittering thoughts. "I heard they are going to some big fine house—a Somersham Place—in a country called Cambridgeshire. They hope to reach there by this evening, but they are worried about the weather—they say it is coming on to snow, and fear that that might hold them up, or at least slow them down."

The man's scowl grew blacker. After a moment he asked, "Are the other two men traveling with them?"

"Yes, sahib, but as I understand it, they won't be in the carriages. They'll be riding ahorse."

"I see."

The snarl wasn't encouraging, but the man had made no move to lay a hand on him. Sangay started to wonder if the gods truly were watching over him still, despite all.

"So they're leaving, and you've sighted no scroll-holder, no letter of any kind, and you've searched everywhere?"

"Oh, yes, sahib! I looked everywhere in every room, even the servants' rooms. There was no scroll-holder or letter anywhere."

"So one of them is carrying it with them. Fine." The word was a rough snarl. "Either the Colonel or one of his two men would be my guess. So you stick with them, and you keep a close—a really close—eye on those three. They'll put it down sometime, somewhere. When they do, you snatch it and scarper—got it?"

Sangay risked a frown. "*Scarper,* sahib?"

"Run like the dickens. Like the devil himself was after you—and remember that your precious mother's continuing health depends on you getting away. Wherever you are, you lay your hands on that scroll-holder and you run—I'll be close, watching, waiting. I'll see you, and I'll come and meet you." The man's lips curled. "Just like this." He leaned close, putting his face close to Sangay's. "Understand?"

Eyes like saucers, Sangay couldn't even swallow. "Yes, sahib. I understand." He would rather have faced a real cobra eye to eye.

The man seemed satisfied with what he saw in Sangay's face. He slowly eased back, straightened.

Sangay inwardly trembled, but felt forced to say, "They might not put the holder down this day, sahib, not while they are traveling."

"True enough. More likely they'll put it down once they reach this house. It sounds like someone's country house." The man glanced at him. "Like a palace to you."

"Apparently the man who owns it is a duke."

"Is that so?" The man was silent for a moment, then said, "Likely it'll be huge. You meet me there tonight, at ten o'clock, behind the stable there. There'll be a big stable, for sure." Once again, the man's pale eyes locked on Sangay. "If you get the holder, you bring it there tonight, but even if you don't lay hands on it, you come and meet me there, you hear?"

Sangay hung his head, forced himself to nod even as misery washed over him. His nightmare was still not at an end. "Yes, sahib."

"You wouldn't want anything to happen to your mother, would you?"

He looked up, eyes wide. "No, sahib! I mean, yes—I will be there. I don't want anything to happen to my maataa, sahib."

"Good." The man tipped his head. "Now get back there before they miss you. Go!"

Sangay turned and all but fled. Back down the mews and up the alley, but instead of going through the side door and across the hotel foyer, he followed the alley to the street and peeked around the corner.

The flurry about the carriages was in full swing. Likely

no one had missed him. Mustaf, Kumulay and Cobby each stood on the roof of a different carriage, stowing the bags that an army of footmen, under Janay's directions, handed up. The women in their colored saris, bright shawls wrapped about their heads, stood on the pavement and pointed and directed and argued with Janay and the men over where this bag, that bundle, should go. The colonel and the memsahib stood on the pavement closer to the door, haughtily surveying and waiting.

They all had been so much kinder to Sangay than any other people in his entire life, and yet he'd have to repay their niceness, all their kindnesses, by stealing from the colonel.

Sangay felt as if dirt was being ground into his soul.

But there was no help for it. If it had been only his death to be feared, Sangay hoped he would be brave enough to tell the man no, but he couldn't let his maataa be killed— and killed horribly, too. No good son could have that on his conscience.

Dragging in a breath, Sangay straightened, then, seeing the women start to enter the carriages, he hurried out and quietly joined the melee.

Eight

December 15
Albemarle Street, London

*H*er hand in Del's, Deliah climbed onto the step of the front carriage. Pausing to, from her temporary vantage point, look over the heads at the others entering the two carriages behind, she noticed the young Indian lad—the one Bess called the colonel's boy— scurrying up from around the corner. He spoke to Janay, then conferred with Mustaf, who pointed at the roof of the third carriage. The boy nodded eagerly, and with the agility of a monkey, swarmed up to the roof, settling amid the bags and bundles secured there.

With a quirk of her brows, Deliah ducked and entered the carriage. As she took her seat, she decided she envied the boy. He'd have a good view as they traveled north through London, and with all the luggage around him, he'd have reasonable protection from the elements.

It was a still day, pervasively cold with gray clouds hanging low and a scent in the air that foretold snow. Not yet, however. Once they reached the open countryside, they would get a better sense of what the day might bring.

Del had paused on the pavement to exchange a few words

with the head porter. Deliah settled her skirts, sank into the comforting leather. Del's household and hers had merged into an effective team. The women had banded together and commandeered the second, slightly larger carriage. They would sit and chat and gossip through the journey. The men had been consigned to the third carriage; that no doubt would travel north in greater silence.

The doorway darkened as Del climbed in. He sat beside her, and the head porter, beaming and touching the brim of his hat, shut the door.

The carriage tipped fractionally as Cobby climbed up beside the driver, then a whip cracked, the carriage jerked as the horses leaned into the harness, and they were away, rolling slowly through the streets on their journey into Cambridgeshire.

Deliah glanced at Del. He was looking out of the window at the streetscapes sliding by. Her thoughts returned to the boy. She wondered how he'd come to be part of Del's household, felt sure there would be some story there. It was tempting to ask, but . . . having Del there, seated beside her, reminded her of other things. Other things she really should take the time to think about.

So she did. Let the observations and questions she'd set aside over recent days, that she'd allowed to be overtaken by recent events, finally form in her mind.

Let her thoughts dwell on him, and on what had happened between them, what now existed between them—what label it was most accurate to attach to their . . . liaison.

Chief among her mental questions was how long that liaison would last.

As they rattled and rumbled through the streets of London, a comfortable silence enveloped them, contrasting with the bustle and noisy hustle outside, the buzz of humanity natural in any large city. And London was the largest of them all. It had spread and sprawled since she'd last traveled through it.

They'd chosen not to take the Great North Road, the obvious route to Cambridgeshire. With its constant stream of carriages, coaches and carts, wagons and riders, that route would be no help in tempting the Black Cobra into an attack. They'd opted instead for the lesser road through Royston. They should reach that minor town in the open country beyond London's sprawl by lunchtime.

It was after that, once they'd lunched and taken to the road again, traveling along a straight but less frequented stretch to Godmanchester, then along a series of progressively quieter country roads to Somersham, that they expected their invitation to be accepted and the fiend to stage an ambush.

The view beyond the carriage window was growing more countrified. Deliah stirred, glanced at Del. "This house— Somersham Place. Why are you, and Tony and Gervase, so sure no attack will be made after we reach there?"

His lips curved in clear reminiscence. "You'll understand when you see it. It's a principal ducal residence, and it's huge—massive. You could lose a company in it without effort." He glanced at her, met her eyes. "I visited there years ago—in my school days. I knew houses could be large, but it was a revelation."

"Is it the duke you know from . . . Eton?"

He nodded. "Sylvester Cynster, as he was then, known from the cradle by all as Devil. For good reason."

She arched her brows. "Are you sure—if he was named that from the cradle—that it wasn't simply a case of him living up to the title?"

He smiled. "That, too. Regardless, when the word went out for extra troops, cavalry in particular, in the lead up to Waterloo, Devil and his Cynster cousins joined as a body of six. We'd kept in touch. Through a feat of string-pulling, they were attached to my troop, so we fought together there."

"Side by side?"

"Mostly back to back. It wasn't pretty fighting, that day." His voice, his expression, had turned grim.

She waited.

After a moment, Del shook aside the darker memories, refocused, then smiled again. "You'll meet them—the six cousins. Apparently they're all at Somersham with their wives." That he was waiting to see. The idea of those hellions brought to heel by a pack of ladies . . . he wasn't quite sure he believed it, but he was certainly curious, and looking forward to meeting the ladies involved. "They—the whole family—always gather at Somersham for Christmas, but this year the six families came early so the men could assist with Wolverstone's plan. They know the other three couriers who are ferrying in the scroll-holders almost as well as they know me."

"So it's a reunion of sorts?"

He nodded. "A reunion with the benefit, at least for the Cynsters, of seeing some action again."

"I wonder how their wives feel about that?"

He wondered, too, but didn't reply to the faintly caustic question. "The only other couple who will be there, at least that I know of, is Gyles Rawlings, the Earl of Chillingworth, and his wife. Gyles, Devil, and I were all at Eton in the same year. Devil and Gyles were the friendly foes, and I was the peacemaker."

Deliah glanced at him—an assessing, slightly cynical, but affectionate glance.

He pretended not to notice. "But to answer your question, the reason we consider the Place a safe house, one where no attack is likely after we've settled there, is because once Ferrar or Larkins gets the slightest inkling of the number of ex-military men in the house, they'll pull back. The original idea was to use it as a bolt-hole—a safe place for us to run to once we'd engaged with the cultists, hopefully drawing them along, snapping at our heels, straight into the Cynsters' arms. Whether we manage that or not—" He broke off, lightly shrugged.

After a moment, he went on, "Wolverstone's waiting on one of his estates conveniently nearby, so the Place is ideally situated to be a secondary barracks of sorts. We'll learn more when we get there."

Deliah paused to take mental note. It seemed she was shortly to meet a duchess, a countess, and at least five other ladies of their circle, all most likely a few years younger than she. Certainly a lot more haut ton than she. At least, courtesy of their visit to Madame Latour's salon, she had a suitable wardrobe.

Dismisssing the distracting thought—she'd deal with the ladies when she met them—she refocused on the here and now, on Del and his mission.

With a better picture of the wider plan taking shape in her mind, she murmured, "So once we *reach* Somersham Place, any chance of the cultists mounting an attack on us will be past?"

Del nodded. Folding his arms across his chest, he volunteered nothing more.

He didn't have to; she could read his hopes and fears with ease.

They hadn't sighted a single one of the Black Cobra's own men, except perhaps for the man she'd seen in Southampton, the one Del thought was Ferrar's gentleman's gentleman. Despite their plans for the day—plans she now realized were a final throw of the dice—Tony, Gervase, and even more so Del, were tending glum.

They felt they were failing in their mission—in their decoy's task of drawing out the enemy and reducing his numbers. She could imagine how they were going to feel tonight if they reached the Place without incident.

If they failed to tempt the Black Cobra into the open, into risking his cultists against them.

Relaxing against the seat, she faced forward and thought of their strategy, and of the time they had left.

They were deep in the countryside with signposts to Royston flashing past at every crossroads when she said, "This isn't going to work." Turning her head, she caught Del's eye. "Not if you want to draw out however many of the cultists are following us."

Arms still crossed, he frowned. "We're in slow carriages overburdened with females and luggage, and traveling on increasingly less populated byways. At some point, Ferrar—or Larkins, more likely—will risk his hand. He'll feel he has to."

"Not if he hasn't that many men, and he knows about Tony and Gervase."

He didn't immediately reply. He studied her eyes, then, still frowning, asked, "What do you mean?"

"I mean that at least one of the Black Cobra's men is English—Larkins. It wouldn't have been that hard for him to discover through watching Grillon's that there are two other gentlemen who are also of our party—who breakfasted and dined with us, but who otherwise weren't seen with us. On top of that, we know *someone* searched our rooms. I think it very likely—indeed, we should assume—that the Black Cobra knows about Tony and Gervase, and if he's as colossally clever as you say, he'll have seen through that trap. We should assume he knows that if he attacks our apparently tempting little convoy, he'll have Tony and Gervase to deal with as well."

She paused, assembling her arguments. "You mentioned that the cultists won't use pistols. That puts them at a disadvantage when facing opponents who will." She looked pointedly at the pistol Del had placed on the seat between them.

"That won't deter the Black Cobra. He'll sacrifice foot soldiers without a blink. . . ." Del's voice died away, his eyes widening slightly.

Deliah nodded. "That's my point. He might not yet feel he's in a position to sacrifice any, because he might not yet have enough in the country. You said he—Ferrar—arrived with only his manservant, this Larkins, and only a bare week ahead of you. None of his men on your ship survived. Others presumably would have arrived by now, but surely he's had to spread them about, keeping watch for the other three couriers. He knows who they are, but not where they are, or where they might land, or where they'll go after that, or when. And now we've moved out of London, his men have to follow us, too."

Shifting on the seat, she faced Del. "He won't be able to hire locals for that purpose—which is what we wanted, but conversely, his numbers may well be limited to the point that he'll feel forced to hold back, at least while he knows Tony and Gervase are with us."

Pausing, she frowned, putting herself in the Black Cobra's shoes. "On top of that, he doesn't know where the scroll-holder is. That's why someone searched our rooms at Grillon's." She met Del's eyes. "Until he or one of his men actually sight it, Ferrar can't even be sure you have it with you. That you still have it, decoy or not. It might be with Tony or Gervase. You might have left it in safekeeping in London. If he chances his men now, against our three carriages, it might well be for nought. He knows he'll lose some men, at least, and he might not as yet be able to spare them, especially if he gets no return."

Increasingly convinced she was right, she sat back. "If I'm correct, and he doesn't have enough men to waste on an attack that might prove a worthless trap, when he doesn't even know if the scroll-holder is with us, available to be snatched, then . . ." Eyes narrowing, she went on, "Correct me if I'm wrong, but if all is as I surmise—that he's following us with a limited number of men, and knows Tony and Gervase are near—then the only way for him to successfully get the letter from us is if he swoops in quickly, grabs the letter and runs . . . but he doesn't even know that the letter is definitely with us, let alone which carriage it's in."

She met Del's gaze. "At present, you have him stymied. Frustrated, certainly, which is to our advantage, but as he's so clever, he won't make any move. He can't. The odds aren't in his favor—they're too great that he'll lose vital men and gain nothing in return."

Del couldn't fault her analysis. Slumping back against the seat, he closed his eyes, softly groaned. "You're right." After a moment, he opened his eyes. "In reality we have no chance of luring him into mounting an attack."

An instant of silence followed, then Deliah said, "I didn't say that."

He took a moment to consider, then, feeling his features harden, turned his head and met her gaze. "If you're about to suggest that, in extremis over this, I should countenance you putting yourself in danger—for instance by acting as bait to lure Ferrar or Larkins into the open—then I suggest you think again."

Her brows rose haughtily; she all but looked down her nose. "I wasn't intending to suggest anything of the sort."

She said nothing more, simply held his gaze.

Waited.

Lips thinning, he asked, albeit grudgingly, "What, then?"

With an air of superior nonchalance, she told him.

He didn't like it all that much more, but given their total failure to date, and their otherwise likely failure that day, it was worth a try.

December 15
Royston, Hertfordshire

Still not entirely convinced, he decided to sound out Tony and Gervase over lunch. Reaching Royston, they drove through the town with all due fanfare, then halted at the last inn on the road leading to Godmanchester.

They pulled into the inn yard, and all clambered down. The innkeeper was delighted to see them, and even more so when Del ordered the horses to be taken from the shafts and rested.

Cobby, Mustaf, Janay, and Kumulay all sensed a change in the wind. Del paused to tell them to hold themselves ready for a variation in their plans, but meanwhile to take their ease in the taproom with the womenfolk, then he followed Deliah and the innkeeper inside.

She'd already commandeered the small private parlor, and was giving orders for a repast for four—cold meats, bread, cheese, fruit and ale, with tea for her, to be served as soon as possible.

When she turned to him, Del nodded, took her arm and escorted her into the parlor. There were a few curious locals in the tap, but otherwise the inn was perfect for their purposes.

They settled in the parlor. Deliah drifted toward the window. He called her back. "I don't trust Larkins. If you saw him, he must have seen you, and the Black Cobra is well known for vindictiveness."

She raised her brows, but didn't argue, instead sinking into one of the armchairs by the hearth. The parlor was on the opposite side of the inn to the yard; they couldn't see any arrivals. When the door opened to admit two maids with their meal, Del stepped out of the parlor, scanned the patrons and spotted Tony and Gervase just settling at a table at the rear of the tap. He openly beckoned.

They eyed him for a moment, then rose and joined him.

Tony's brows quirked. "What's happened?"

Del tipped his head to the table being set for four. "Join us and you'll hear."

The maids bustled out, and the four of them sat.

At his suggestion, while they ate, Deliah repeated her rationale of why their original plan was unlikely to work, why it probably wouldn't draw the cultists out and give them a chance to thin the ranks.

He then outlined the plan he'd developed to meet her stipulations of what they needed to do to lure the Black Cobra from hiding, to tempt him to strike.

Tony and Gervase listened to the whole impassively.

When Del fell silent, Tony nodded. "It's worth a try. We'll be at Somersham tonight, and from all Royce has said, the chances of an attack once we're there aren't high. Yet reporting to him without having accounted for even one cultist doesn't appeal. So I vote we try your lure."

Gervase likewise nodded. "There's no harm in dangling it. He'll either bite, or he won't."

Del glanced at Deliah; she raised her brows as if to ask what more he was waiting for.

Suppressing a grimace, he rose, and went out to arrange their departure.

The first carriage—the one he and Deliah were traveling in—was brought around to the front of the inn. Cobby was on the box, the reins in his hand, with Kumulay beside him. Cobby had formed a high opinion of Deliah's bodyguard's abilities, and in such matters, Del trusted Cobby's instincts.

The other two carriages remained in the inn yard, with the six women, Janay, Mustaf and the boy all making a noisy show of reorganizing the luggage. Del stood at the end of the inn's front porch, hands on hips, impatience radiating from him, and watched.

Deliah walked out of the inn's front door and across to join Del. She looked at the two carriages, at their obvious disarray, then sighed and looked at Del. "Do we have to wait?"

They didn't know how close the Black Cobra's men might be, or if they could read lips.

Del frowned. He studied the two carriages again, then stepped down. He crossed the yard to Mustaf and held out one hand. "Give me the scroll-holder."

Mustaf looked at him, then reached under his baggy white shirt and drew the cylinder from the leather pouch strapped around his waist.

Taking it, Del turned, used the holder to wave a farewell as he walked back to Deliah, calling, "We'll see you at Somersham. Don't take too long."

"We'll be after you in no time, sahib." Mustaf turned and, with a frown, chivvied the women on.

Del hoped the Black Cobra was listening. In reality, instead of following his and Deliah's carriage, the other two carriages, now much less well-defended, would head to Somersham via Cambridge, a slower and longer, but much more populated and therefore much safer, route.

Reaching Deliah, Del took her arm. "Come on—we may as well get started. They must have given up and"—he glanced back at the inn's tap—"the other two will be along soon enough."

Gervase's and Tony's horses stood tethered just inside the open stable door, in plain sight.

"Good." Deliah allowed him to lead her to their carriage's door. "I can't wait to have a proper cup of tea."

He helped her climb in. She smiled at Tony and Gervase, slouched low beneath a traveling blanket on the rear-facing seat, then sat. Del followed her in, closing the door behind him. Picking his way between the others' long legs, he sat beside Deliah. "Go!" he called, and Cobby flicked the reins.

The carriage lurched, then rolled slowly away from the inn. After turning into the road, it picked up pace.

Once they were clear of the town and bowling along, Gervase and Tony carefully eased up. They remained slouched, back in the shadows and away from the windows, minimizing any chance of their being spotted, even by someone with a spyglass trained on the swiftly moving carriage.

"According to the innkeep," Gervase said, "the most likely stretch for fun and games is, as we'd thought, between Croydon and Caxton. We've got five miles before Croydon."

"If they wait that long." Shifting carefully, Tony drew a pistol from one pocket. Two long-barreled pistols already lay on the seat between him and Gervase, with another on the seat between Del and Deliah. Tony checked his smaller pistol, then grinned at the others. "Anyone care to wager on the number they'll send against us?"

Deliah guessed eight, Tony nine, Gervase eleven and Del fourteen. Deliah told Del not to be so pessimistic, but as matters transpired, both she *and* he won the wager.

As the innkeeper had predicted, the attack came on the long stretch to Caxton. Their carriage flashed around a stand of trees skirting the slightest of curves and a shot rang out.

Cobby swore, yelled, "Over my head from the trees on the left!" as he hauled on the reins and brought the horses to a plunging halt.

The carriage rocked heavily, crazily, then settled.

As eight dun-clothed figures rushed from the cover of the trees.

Before Deliah could blink, the men had all swung to face the threat. Four shots rang out in quick succession, then the shoulders shifted, and she looked out. Only four cultists remained upright.

The shock of the shots gave them pause, but then they shook their long knives, screamed, and came on.

Gervase was already out of the door on that side, sword in hand. Del, similarly armed, jumped down to join him.

Clutching a long sword, Tony went out of the carriage's other door just as Kumulay dropped from above to join him in meeting the two cultists who'd rushed around the rear of the carriage.

Her heart in her throat, Deliah did as she'd promised. She shifted to the middle of the carriage seat, equidistant from both doors, firmly gripping the small pistol Del had given her, along with strict instructions to shoot any cultist who tried to get in. Otherwise, she was to remain where she was.

Native war-shrieks punctuated the clang and hiss of steel meeting steel. Shoulders swung, shifted; bodies lunged, retreated. Her breathing constricted, Deliah watched wide-eyed, looking this way, then that. She tried to shut her ears to the distracting clamor.

She had every intention of obeying Del's orders to the letter—she wasn't recklessly brave.

Then, with bloodcurdling screams, six more cultists came pelting from the trees.

Deliah sucked in a breath, horror and terror gripping her chest, tight as any vise. Del had warned that the cultists habitually used sheer numbers to win their fights.

That they were finally fighting cultists wasn't in doubt. Their attackers were clothed in traditional Indian garb of loose trousers and tunic, albeit with plaids or blankets fastened about them for warmth. All had turbans of one sort or another wound about their heads, and the faces below were mahogany brown.

The carriage rocked as bodies hit it. The clashes of steel sounded horribly close. Tony and Kumulay now had four cultists ranged against them. As she counted, one staggered and fell.

She looked the other way. Gervase was further from the carriage, sword in hand, slashing at two opponents, with one already prone at his feet.

Del had his back to the carriage door, with three cultists pressing in on him. As Deliah watched, he swore and slashed wildly, and one cultist fell to the ground, shrieking and kicking. Del had to leap clear.

The two remaining cultists drove forward. Resolutely he beat them back.

The opposite carriage door was abruptly wrenched open.

With a start, Deliah turned—and met a horrible smile and fanatically glowing dark eyes. Dark fingers reached for her.

She didn't even think before she fired.

The cultist's eyes flew wide. Sheer shock seized his features. He dropped his long knife. It landed with a clatter on the carriage step as, clutching the patch of red blossoming on his chest, he staggered back, then fell.

The fighting raged on.

Dragging in a breath, telling herself this was no time to succumb to hysterics, Deliah realized she was weaponless. Defenseless should another cultist come for her. Setting the used pistol aside, she reached down and pulled the cultist's knife to her.

It didn't look used.

She picked it up, gripped the hilt. The blade was longish, but not as long as a full-sized sword or a cavalry saber. It wasn't so heavy she couldn't wield it. Use it if need be.

Then someone slammed the open carriage door shut. Tony. He was immediately engaged by a cultist, but he and Kumulay were now fighting one on one. She felt certain both would prevail.

She looked the other way, at Del, then edged toward that door. There were more cultists on that side of the carriage. Gervase was still trading blows with the two before him. Del had done some damage, but still had two vicious opponents attacking him.

Drawn, she inched closer, then, knowing better than to distract him, she crouched down inside the door and silently watched.

With an ear-splitting yell, one of the cultists jabbing at Gervase abruptly whirled and, sword raised high, raced toward Del.

Toward his back, exposed because the other cultists had drawn him to one side.

Fully engaged with the opponents before him, there was no chance he could turn and meet the attack.

Deliah swung the carriage door open and stepped out onto the high step.

The cultist saw her and changed direction.

Eyes alight, he charged toward her.

Desperately she freed the sword from her skirts. Gripping it with both hands, she brought it up to ward him off.

He ran straight onto it.

The shock on his face was mirrored on hers.

Stunned, his mouth still wide open, but with no sound any longer issuing forth, the cultist looked down. Stared at the long blade embedded in his chest. His own knife fell from his nerveless fingers, then his eyes closed and he crumpled, jerking the sword from her slackened grasp.

Her appearance had spurred Gervase and Del to even greater efforts. Cursing, they left their opponents writhing and moaning on the ground, clutching wounds. They exchanged a single glance, then Del whirled and strode for the carriage while Gervase raced around to the other side.

When Del reached Deliah, she was still staring, stunned, at the fallen cultist. Hand to her midriff, he pressed her back. "Sit down."

His tone, the one he used on the battlefield, had her blinking and shuffling back. She dropped onto the seat as he climbed in and slammed the door shut.

From above, Cobby yelled, "All aboard!"

Their agreed signal for "cut and run."

Gervase yanked open the other door and scrambled in. Tony followed on his heels, slamming the door shut behind him as the carriage dipped heavily—Kumulay climbing up again.

Cobby didn't wait for anyone to settle. He sprang the horses, spooked by the rising scent of blood and more than ready to race on.

In a blink, they were away from the trees and thundering out into the open.

For long minutes, they all just sat there, breathing heavily, regaining their sanity.

Eventually, Tony stirred. "How many did we get?"

Deliah swallowed, looked at Del. "Fourteen. All told, there were fourteen."

When he met her gaze, she raised her brows. "Satisfied?"

His eyes were still hard, his jaw still set. "It's a start."

What could he say?

They'd made a respectable dent in the Black Cobra's forces, *but . . .*

She'd been far too involved, too exposed to real danger and death. So much for his careful planning. When he'd glanced across and seen her standing on the carriage step, one of their long knives in her hand with a cultist skewered on the end of it, his blood had run cold.

Not at all helpful in the middle of a fraught clash.

He'd wanted to roar at her for disobeying his strict orders, but if she hadn't . . . he'd have been in much worse strife—possibly not able to roar at her at all.

Certainly not able to ease her back into the carriage and, under cover of her skirts, hold her hand—probably too tightly—all the way to Somersham Place.

He'd contented himself with that—with the simple contact—while the horses had raced on through the increasingly dark afternoon.

A winter storm was massing, roiling and boiling, ready to sweep in from the North Sea. One glance at the horizon, at the color and density of the clouds building there, confirmed snow by nightfall was a certainty.

It was early evening, already full dark, by the time they reached the massive pillars that marked the drive of the Place. Cobby had never been there before, but Del had described the pillars; the carriage slowed, turned into the drive, then continued bowling steadily along.

A welcoming light shone through the bare branches of massive oaks. Then the carriage rounded a corner and the house lay before them, as massive as he remembered, and as welcoming. Lamps on the porch were burning, casting a warm glow down the porch steps, illuminating the couple who walked out, alerted by the rattle of wheels on the gravel.

The gentleman halted at the top of the steps. Del felt his lips curve; Devil looked the same as ever, but the lady who came to stand by his shoulder, linking her arm with his, was new.

The carriage slowed, then rocked to a stop. A footman hurried to open the door and let down the carriage steps. Gervase and Tony waved them on. Del descended first, then turned to give Deliah his hand. She descended, twitched her plum-colored skirts straight, then, head rising, spine straight, allowed him to lead her up the porch steps to where Devil waited with his duchess.

As they neared, Devil's lips curved and his pale green eyes lit. "Del! Welcome, once again, to Somersham."

A spontaneous smile wreathing his face, Del clasped Devil's proferred hand. "It's beyond good to be here again."

Devil hauled him into a brief embrace, clapped his back. "I confess I'm amazed you're still hale and whole—I would have sworn someone would have skewered you by now."

Del made a rude, if muted, noise in reply as they both turned to their respective ladies.

Who hadn't waited for them.

"I'm Honoria—this reprobate's duchess." With an engaging smile for Deliah, Devil's duchess held out her hand.

"Deliah Duncannon." Deliah rose from a curtsy and touched fingers, adding, "I unwittingly became embroiled in Delborough's mission, and so have had to tag along. I hope my unexpected presence, and that of my household—they're following—won't discompose yours."

"Not at all! I'm delighted—and so will all the other ladies be—to welcome you." Honoria's gray eyes testified to her sincerity. "You'll be able to give us a female view on all that's going on."

The duke smiled and smoothly introduced himself—as Devil—to Deliah.

She gave him her hand, and curtsied as he bowed. He was much like Del—tall, starkly handsome, dark-haired and broad-shouldered, with the long, powerful frame of a natural horseman—but in place of Del's military bearing, Devil exuded aristocratic command.

Then Tony and Gervase joined them. Del made the introductions, and discovered Devil had met the other two before.

"At Wolverstone's wedding," Gervase explained. "There was a spot of bother we all helped him tidy up."

"Indeed?" Honoria's finely arched brows rose. She shot a

look at her husband. "I must ask Minerva for the story. Now, however"—she took Deliah's arm—"do come in out of the cold. It's positively frigid out here, and much warmer inside."

Warmer because of the huge fire blazing in the massive hearth at the far end of the long halfpaneled hall, and warmer because of the almost joyous welcome accorded them by the others gathered about the tables and comfortable chairs. Although it was too early for the customary yuletide decorations, here the emotional ambiance of the approaching season seemed already to have taken hold. Deliah felt herself literally thawing, both her flesh and her reservations.

She, Del, Tony and Gervase were taken on a circuit of introductions. The men all either knew each other, or knew of each other. She was the only true newcomer to the group; she'd expected to hang back, to find herself left on the fringe. Instead, as Honoria had foretold, the ladies, one and all, were not just delighted to meet her but keen and eager to hear all she could tell them.

For all their warmth, the couples littering the big hall were an imposing and impressive lot. The males were especially notable. Scandal Cynster, who his wife Catriona called Richard, was clearly Devil's brother, with similar features and build, but cornflower blue eyes. The duke's cousins included Demon Cynster, with wavy blond hair and blue eyes, and his diminuitive wife, Felicity—whom he referred to as Flick—and his older brother, Vane, a harder, quieter man, yet very much in the Cynster physical mold but with brown hair and gray eyes, and his wife, Patience. Then came a Lucifer Cynster, all dark-haired, blue-eyed elegance, and his wife, Phyllida, and a Gabriel Cynster, the epitome of sophistication, brown-haired and hazel-eyed, and his wife, Alathea.

All the Cynster men had fought alongside Del and his three friends—the other three couriers—at Waterloo. In addition, the Earl of Chillingworth—who, from his interaction with Del and Devil, Deliah placed as Gyles Rawlings, the third of the schoolboy trio—was there, with his countess,

Francesca; brown-haired and gray-eyed, he, too, possessed a commanding presence.

Deliah made a mental note to inquire at some point as to how the men had come by their odd names, but even more than the men, she was curious about the women.

Physically they varied dramatically, from Catriona's serene, red-haired beauty, through Phyllida's dark-haired vitality, and Alathea's, Patience's and Honoria's perfectly groomed shades of calm and collected brown, to Flick's blond vivacity and Francesca's black-haired, gypsylike vibrance. In appearance they were widely dissimilar, yet in presence and character, in their attitude to their world, they seemed of one mind. They were confident, assured and assertive, not afraid to state their opinions and make their wishes known.

Not one was the meek, mild or retiring sort. Not one was prim and proper, any more than Deliah was.

Which was something of a social shock.

Other than Alathea, who, Deliah suspected, was a few years older than she, most of the ladies were younger, ranging in age down to Flick, who must have been in her early twenties. These ladies, with their positions, connections and wealth, would be part of the core of the current society-defining generation, the arbiters of social acceptance for the upper class, for the ton.

All her life, Deliah had been lectured on how she needed to behave to be socially accepted, yet these ladies, one and all, were of a vastly different stripe from those she'd always been instructed she should emulate. These ladies were . . .

Like her.

From Honoria, with her rich chestnut hair gleaming in the firelight, her gray eyes alert and all-seeing, to Flick, with her guinea gold curls bouncing and her blue eyes bright with interest, these ladies, each in her own way, were bold, determined and decisive.

Why they were the Cynsters' chosen mates wasn't any great mystery.

To Deliah, with just a few words exchanged recognizing like-minded souls, meeting them was both eye-opening, and an immense relief.

With these ladies, she could be herself.

Honoria turned aside to speak with a majestic butler who had come to hover by her elbow. "Dinner at eight-thirty, I think, Webster. That will give our latest arrivals time to settle in." She glanced to where the men had gradually gravitated into a group halfway up the hall. "And allow the gentlemen time to satisfy their collective curiosity."

On the word, she looked at Deliah, then at the other ladies gathered in the chairs before the fire. "Might I suggest we adjourn to my sitting room? We can sit and chat, and have tea in comfort."

"And greater privacy." With a conspiratorial smile, Francesca stood.

Honoria turned to Webster. "Tea in my sitting room, Webster. And please convey my compliments to Mrs. Hull and tell her and Sligo of Miss Duncannon's arrival, and of the imminent arrival of Miss Duncannon's household, and the colonel's, too."

"Indeed, Your Grace." Webster bowed low and departed.

As the ladies rose, Devil strolled up. He smiled—innocently—at Honoria. "We'll be in the library."

She smiled back, not even feigning innocence. "We'll be in my sitting room." With a wave, she sent the other ladies ahead, then linked her arm in Deliah's and glanced up at her spouse. "We'll see you all at dinner. Eight-thirty."

Deliah grinned as, with that parting shot, she was determinedly led to the stairs.

Strolling beside Devil, Del followed the others along the corridor to the library. Lowering his voice, he said, "I'd forgotten you'd have so many children here. For my peace of mind, I'd appreciate it if you'd post guards around the nursery areas." He met Devil's green gaze. "Just in case."

Devil smiled, but it wasn't a humorous gesture. "It's already taken care of. And now that Sligo has been reinforced by Cobby, I doubt there's any likelihood of anyone getting past their pickets."

Del inclined his head in agreement. Sligo—now Devil's majordomo—had been Devil's batman at Waterloo, just as Cobby had been his. The two batmen had forged a friendship under fire, one just as close as their masters'.

Devil paused by an open door, through which the comforting ambiance of a very male library could be glimpsed. He waved Del through. "Come, sit, and tell us the whole story."

Del preceded him into the luxurious yet comfortable room, and proceeded to do just that.

He told the tale of his mission, from its beginning in the Marquess of Hastings's office months before. Describing the Black Cobra's atrocities while sitting in leather-cushioned luxury, a crystal tumbler filled with the finest malt whiskey in his hand, only made the details doubly stark, and even more disturbing.

There were grim looks all around, and softly muttered curses, when he described James MacFarlane's death.

"He was a good man." Devil drained his glass, then reached for the decanter. His words were echoed as the others did the same.

Del nodded and continued, detailing the events that had led to the four of them—he, Gareth, Logan, and Rafe—leaving Bombay, then described the action he'd seen on his journey, all the way through to that afternoon. Tony and Gervase supplied their observations, and the outcomes of their attempts to gain some clue as to the Black Cobra's lair.

Tony shook his dark head. "Until today, we'd seen nary a sign of any cultist. But clearly they're here—the Lord only knows where he's hiding them. With their peculiar costume, they'll have no hope of blending into the scenery."

Devil met Del's eyes. "That's a point we should convey to Wolverstone. We'll send a rider before dinner. The weather's closing in, so we'd better seize the chance to let him know you've arrived safely, and that there are indeed cultists about."

"How far away is he?" Del asked.

"He's at Elveden Grange, about thirty miles due east." Devil sipped, then went on, "Our orders are to have all three of you remain, for a few days at least, in the hope—distant though it might be—that the Black Cobra will try a sortie. It's possible that, not knowing you were headed here, he won't have had time to do any reconnaissance, and so won't realize how many ex-cavalry there are in the house." He paused, head tilted. "If he could throw fourteen at you on the road, it's possible he might feel he has the numbers for a foray against this place."

Del grimaced. "That's a long shot. On his own ground, he's showy and confident, but he's been careful, watchful and wary over here."

Devil levelled a sharp gaze on him. "Don't disillusion us. You'll have noticed none of us have taken you to task over reducing the enemy by fourteen, all by yourselves? You were supposed to share."

Del hid his curving lips behind his glass. "Sorry. Blame our success on Deliah—if it weren't for her, we'd never have drawn the cultists out."

Demon snorted. "Typical female. And she killed two as well? Haven't you explained that's _our_ job? She's supposed to sit quietly and leave it to us."

Del's brows rose. "I don't suppose you'd like to undertake to explain that to her in words she'll accept?"

Quite a few men choked.

"Once he's worked out how to do that with _his_ wife," Scandal put in, "no doubt he'll oblige."

A heavy sigh sounded, drawing all attention to Vane, who'd been prowling behind Devil's chair. He turned from the window, letting the curtain fall closed. "I hate to further dampen spirits, so to speak, but it's started snowing." He looked at Devil. "You'd better get that rider on his way if you want him to reach Elveden tonight."

There were groans all around.

Devil rose and rang for Sligo.

Del, listening to the others' predictions, recalled that in that season, in that part of the country, the snowfalls could be considerable.

Slumping back, he grimaced. "It doesn't look as if we're going to have much luck in getting the Black Cobra to come to us."

Upstairs in the duchess's sitting room, Deliah had just finished telling the other ladies everything she knew of Del's mission.

Relating the details of the incident that afternoon had left her more shaken than she'd been at the time.

Honoria calmly handed her another cup of tea. "It's often worse reliving it—that's when you realize all the things that might have gone wrong, how much worse it all might have been."

Deliah sipped, met Honoria's eyes, glanced at the others, all nodding sagely. Amazing. Not one of them had paled, let alone looked likely to faint when she'd described shooting a man, then running one through—although technically he'd run himself through. She'd just held the sword.

The tea slid down, warming, comforting—just like the company.

"I believe I speak for all of us"—Catriona glanced around the circle before focusing on Deliah—"in extending my heartfelt thanks to you for reducing the threat. For engineering a situation that successfully reduced this fiend's troops, especially those in this area."

"Indeed." Alathea exchanged a long-suffering look with the others. "We know what our husbands are like."

Felicity set down her empty cup. "We'll have to keep an eye on them." She glanced at Honoria. "A closer eye than usual."

Honoria nodded. "Luckily, it appears the weather has come to our aid." She smiled. "It's snowing."

"Really?"

"At last!"

"Let's see."

Phyllida, Catriona and Flick all rose and went to the wide window. Throwing open the curtains, they peered through the glass.

"It's coming down nicely," Flick reported.

"Wonderful!" Phyllida turned back inside. "Who knows? We might even have a white Christmas. The children will be in alt."

A discussion ensued of the possibilities for keeping their numerous offspring amused. Deliah sat back and listened, smiling at the comments.

For quite the first time in her life wishing she had reason to join in.

The realization was so startling she sobered, blinked.

Just as the sound of a gong resonated through the house.

"Time to dress for dinner." Honoria stood, waited until Deliah set down her cup and rose, too. "Come, I'll show you to your room. Your maid should be there by now."

They dispersed, the others heading down various corridors in groups of twos and threes, heads together, chatting, while she and Honoria headed around the gallery.

"If you get tired of us, do say." Honoria caught her eye and smiled. "I assure you we won't be offended. You've been traveling, while we've been sitting here waiting for something to happen. And you've already done wonders to relieve our boredom."

"That," Deliah replied, "was entirely my pleasure."

And it had been.

Honoria left her at the door of a well-appointed chamber, and went on to her own rooms to change for the evening.

Closing the door, Deliah smiled at Bess. "Everything all right?"

Bess's answering smile was wide. "Lovely place, this. The staff is so friendly. We've all settled in already. Now!" Going to the bed, Bess picked up and displayed the gold satin gown from Madame Latour. "Seeing as this is a duke's house, I thought you might want to wear this."

Deliah studied the deceptively simple, unquestionably elegant evening gown, and gave thanks for Del's insistence that she take it. She nodded. "Yes—that's perfect."

Standing before the mirror, she started pulling the pins from her hair, and reminded herself to extract from him the sum he'd paid for the gowns before they reached home.

For tonight, however, she saw no reason not to take advantage of time, place, and gown.

~ Nine ~

*D*el was standing by the fireplace with Devil when Deliah walked into the drawing room.

The room was abuzz with conversation, yet for him a silence fell.

He was deaf. He felt dazed.

He couldn't drag his eyes from the sight of Deliah in the gold satin gown he remembered so well, standing poised in the doorway—apparently unaware of the havoc she was causing.

Then she moved. His mouth dried as he watched her, lips lightly curved, glide across the room to join Honoria and two of the other ladies standing chatting with Gervase.

Del's chest swelled as he finally managed to drag in a breath and break free of her spell. Instinctively, he looked at Devil. And saw his green gaze also fixed across the room.

Some unfamiliar emotion flared—part irritation, part irrational fear . . . jealousy? He couldn't recall feeling it before, not over a woman, and never so sharply. Tamping it down, he glanced again across the room.

She looked like a golden flame, a beacon of warmth and promise. Gaze circling the room, he confirmed all the other men had noticed. Impossible to hold it against them; they were male, too.

Jaw setting, he turned to Devil, only to meet an amused, but understanding, grin. To his relief, his old friend made no reference to Deliah but instead chose to rib Gyles as he joined them.

Gyles, of course, struck back. Del laughed and felt the years slide away. They no longer stood in Eton's schoolyard, yet beneath the changes of the years, some things—loyalties, friendships—remained the same.

"How's your daughter?" Devil asked Gyles.

"Contrary to my beliefs, she's apparently thriving. Colic, so I've been informed, is something they—and we—have to go through."

Devil grimaced. "I'm still working on developing immunity." His gaze traveled to Honoria, then on to Francesca, standing in another group. "I don't understand how they can, apparently without difficulty, tell the difference between a wail that signifies serious pain and one that merely means they're grumpy."

"Let me know when you've worked it out." Gyles shook his head. "You might have warned me how . . . distracting a wife and family were going to be."

Devil shrugged. "No point—it was in your stars as much as mine. No chance we could have avoided it." He grinned, shot a glance at Gyles. "So we might as well enjoy it."

Gyles laughed, his gaze on Francesca. "True." Then he looked at Del. "So what about you, Del? What lies in your future?"

Neither Gyles nor Devil glanced at Deliah, but Del knew they knew . . . he waved nonchalantly. "I haven't really thought. This mission blew up, and it seemed more appropriate to put consideration of the future off until it's done."

"Sometimes," Devil said, "fate and the future come knocking."

"She certainly did where we were concerned," Gyles said. "No reason it should be any different for you."

Del smiled. "We'll see."

The conversation moved on to different topics, but the

notion of marriage, of having a wife and family, of putting down roots in the rich soil of England and establishing a real home—making Delborough Hall into a real home—continued to drift through his mind, coming to the fore whenever he spoke to the other Cynsters, all men he knew, and he sensed, as he had with Devil and Gyles, their contentment.

A contentment he wanted, one he felt he'd earned.

Again and again, his gaze returned to Deliah.

He wasn't surprised to find they were paired at dinner. He led her in with a believable show of sangfroid, one that deceived neither him nor her.

There was a light in his dark eyes, a warm possessiveness in his touch as his hand grazed the back of her waist when he guided her to her chair. Deliah felt it, on some level reveled in it, even though outwardly she pretended not to notice.

As they sat at the long table and entertained the others with stories of India and Jamaica, she couldn't recall feeling so relaxed . . . ever. For the first time in her adult life she felt free to simply be, to interact without constantly monitoring her words and her behavior.

Free to be herself, because in this company her true self wasn't in any way remarkable. Not shocking, not out of place. In this company, she fitted.

The men had been open in their appreciation of her in Madame Latour's stunning gown. The ladies, one and all, had asked for the modiste's direction. Honoria and Alathea had even inquired if she had more of Madame's creations with her, and whether they might see them.

She'd never shared anything with other women before. Other women had universally regarded her as . . . too much. Too outspoken, too headstrong, too willful—too striking. Too tall, too well curved, too sharp-tongued.

The word *too* had always featured in others' descriptions of her.

Not here. Here, all the *toos* she possessed were accepted,

even encouraged. Certainly these ladies exhibited most of the same, and she couldn't help but note all they'd achieved in their lives—husbands, children, marriages based on love and trust and a great deal more besides.

Ever since the Great Scandal, she'd tried to suppress her inner self, tried to transform herself, cram herself into the mold of a proper English lady, but the mold her parents' had held up for her—one of a lady who clung to convention at every step—had never fitted.

What she saw, what she learned as the conversations flashed and sparked around the dining table, was that there was another mold, one equally socially acceptable. One that fitted her like the proverbial glove.

And that mold was compatible with marriage—with a sort of marriage she could see herself within, one that was more a partnership, a relationship based on sharing.

She wasn't an irredeemable outcast. She'd simply been moving in the wrong circles.

A strange buoyancy gripped her. Seized her. By the time they all rose and, the gentlemen denying any wish for separation, repaired all together to the drawing room to sit and, still very much a large group, continue their conversations, she felt almost giddy.

Freedom, she realized. *This is what it tastes like.*

She smiled up at Del as she sank onto the sofa to which he'd led her.

He looked down at her for a moment, his features set in easy, social lines, yet his eyes . . . then he smiled and turned to sit in the armchair beside her.

Webster circled with port and brandy for the gentlemen. Some of the ladies, too, accepted a glass. Deliah declined. She wanted her wits unclouded so she could continue to notice and absorb all about her. While she was unlikely ever to face the altar, a long-term relationship wasn't out of her cards.

Once everyone was settled, the talk turned to the Black

Cobra cult, then to the incident that afternoon. Together with Tony and Gervase, she and Del remained the center of attention as they described the cultists and their actions.

"So there were *fourteen*?" Honoria looked thoroughly disapproving. She glanced at her husband. "You'd better lay Ferrar by the heels soon, or else this cult of his will be taking over villages and setting up in England."

"Perish the thought." Devil looked at Del. "Did you leave them all dead, or . . . ?"

"We deemed it wiser not to wait and check. We couldn't tell if there were more in the trees, or, even more likely, Larkins with a brace of pistols."

"I, for one," Tony said, "was taken aback that he *had* fourteen men he was willing to send against us. Del warned us, and they did send eight first, then the other six only when needed, but still, committing fourteen men to one such action . . ."

Gervase concluded, "It suggests he has more he can lose."

The talk diverged to considering ways to locate any body of cultists in the surrounding area. That gave the Cynster males something to gnaw on, raising the prospect of some action to ease their disappointment over the unlikelihood of any immediate clash with the cultists.

Del contributed little. He didn't know the county well, and he was exercised by other things.

Other thoughts, other feelings.

Unaccustomed feelings, but they were proving to be strong and thoroughly distracting—stronger and more distracting than he liked.

Recounting the clash that afternoon had called to mind, too vividly, all he'd felt over those fraught minutes. Reevoked the staggeringly intense fear he'd felt on seeing Deliah exposed to danger—a fear of a type that for all his experience of life and death on battlefields around the globe, he'd never felt before.

More intense, reaching deeper, that fear had sunk talons into his very soul.

He hadn't liked it at the time.

Looking back, he liked it even less.

He cast a sidelong glance at the cause of his distress. She sat relaxed on the sofa, a smile of genuine happiness on her face.

The sight of it did nothing to ease his mood. Yes, she was safe, and apparently content. Yet although her well-being was the crux on which his unnerving fear hinged, something within him wasn't appeased. Responsibility for his near-crippling fear lay at her door.

Something he fully intended to point out. To explain. Later. Tonight.

Shifting his gaze forward, he smothered his surging impulses, bit his tongue, and concentrated on shoring up his relaxed façade while inwardly rehearsing a suitable tirade.

December 15
Somersham Place, Cambridgeshire

Shivering uncontrollably, Sangay slogged and slid his way through the layer of icy white stuff that cloaked the rear yard of the very big house. It was as big as a palace, and equally busy, which was a blessing from the gods. No one had paid him too much attention. No one had spoken harshly or questioned him. Instead, they'd given him a small room all to himself, high beneath the roof where it was warm, and Cobby's friend, Sligo, had found him a jacket—he'd called it a page's coat—to put over his tunic.

Hands sunk in the pockets of the coat, the collar turned up and his head ducked against the wind, Sangay awkwardly hurried as fast as he dared toward the massive bulk of the stable.

At the back, the man had said.

The stable was bounded on three sides by high brick walls. Sangay felt his way down one side, then around to the rear, where what looked like a small forest encroached.

He halted in a small clearing midway along the stable's back wall. At least the cold white flakes had ceased falling, but the wind still sliced, and a heavy feeling in the air, as if it were weighed down, suggested the snow would start coming down again soon.

It wasn't inky dark. The white blanket reflected what little light there was and gave Sangay enough illumination to see. Even so, he heard the man's boots crunching through the white crust long before the heavy figure loomed out of the black shadows beneath the trees.

"Have you got it?"

The harsh demand made Sangay tremble beneath his shivering, but he forced himself to shake his head. "But, sahib-sir, I've seen it!"

Larkins eyed the boy dispassionately. "At the inn, when the colonel fetched it?"

"Yes, sahib. I saw it then."

"But have you seen it since?"

"No, sahib, but we've only just got here and the house is very large, but now I know what to look for! And this house is so big no one will notice me! I will be able to search tomorrow and find the scroll-holder, and then I will be bringing it out to you."

Dark eyes wide, trained on Larkins's face, the boy made an effort to disguise his tremors, and look eager and confident.

He didn't fool Larkins, but conversely Larkins knew the boy was his best route to the scroll-holder, and therefore, at present, his most valuable asset.

That was why he'd set this meeting for ten o'clock—not so early the boy would be missed, yet not so late he might attract attention if seen slipping out.

Larkins knew the ways of households like this, knew the routines the servants followed. He'd once been one of them, but it had been a long time since he'd been a lowly servant. Working for the Black Cobra had made him rich. Wealthy beyond his wildest dreams. He was rich enough to have servants himself, if he'd wanted them. But acquiring such chattels didn't bring him pleasure. Nowhere near as much pleasure as dealing in terror did. That was the one thing he most valued about being in the Black Cobra's service—the chance to indulge in the vilest deeds.

He enjoyed terrorizing the innocent. Yet in this case. . . . The failure of the afternoon was acid in his gut. That failure made the boy—getting the boy to deliver the scroll-holder into his hands—even more vital.

He'd never failed his master, but he knew how his master rewarded failure and had no wish to receive such attention.

So he nodded. "Good." He glanced up at the louring sky. "It's going to snow more—probably a lot more. I won't be able to meet you here. So you find the scroll-holder, and the instant you do, you head for the big church." He pointed to the northeast. "There's a big tower you can see for miles. Tomorrow, you look in that direction, and you'll see it. Find the scroll-holder and bring it to me there—inside the cathedral, under the highest tower. I'll be watching. I'll meet you there."

Larkins looked down at the shivering little sod, remembered the value of the letter in the scroll-holder. "Now you listen to me, son—*don't,* under any circumstances, leave the roads. You have to leave here by the drive you came in on, then go around by the roads, staying on them all the way—understand? That country out there"—with one hand he indicated the stretch to the northeast—"it's all fens and swamps. Lots of it looks solid, but you put a foot in the wrong place and it'll swallow you whole. Got that?"

The boy's eyes had grown even rounder. He nodded. "I take the scroll-holder and go by the roads to the big church and meet you there."

"That's right." Larkins narrowed his eyes. "And you won't forget what will happen to your ma if you don't, will you?"

The boy's eyes darkened. His jaw trembled, but he clenched it and shook his head side to side. "No, sahib. I won't forget that. I will find the letter and bring it with all haste."

"Good. Now you better get back before anyone misses you."

"Yes, sahib." Sangay turned and, without looking back, made his way around the stables. Pulling his collar up around his ears, he clutched it closed, then dashed back through a thickening veil of white.

It had started to snow again.

Eventually everyone retired for the night. In the pleasant chamber she'd been given, Deliah held her hands to the cheery fire and gave thanks the day had ended so well.

Straightening, she glanced at the bed, then at Bess, flicking out a nightgown and laying it over a chair. "I'm not sleepy enough for bed yet. I can get out of this gown by myself, and you've had a long day, too. You can go."

Bess grinned. "If you're sure?"

"Yes." Deliah waved at the door. "Off with you."

Bess chuckled, bobbed and went.

Alone, Deliah idly wandered the room, looking at the paintings, at the ornaments on the mantelpiece. Del, she knew, was in a mood. A restless, edgy, and, despite his outward smiles, scowling mood.

She'd felt it, sensed it. She was fairly certain of its cause.

But be damned if she'd apologize for saving his life.

If she hadn't stepped out onto the carriage step . . . just the thought of seeing him cut down sent a sensation of pure ice shafting through her.

The coldness spread until she shivered and shook aside her imagined vision. Bending, she held her hands to the fire again.

Once again, she glanced at the bed. Inwardly frowned at her reluctance to get into it.

Eventually she realized it was the afternoon's incident— the aftermath of it—that was feeding that reluctance.

She hadn't thought the fight had affected her that deeply. She'd been shocked and frightened at the time, but they'd come through it, more or less unscathed. They'd triumphed, they'd won, albeit it on a restricted canvas.

It was all over now, and all was well.

Yet still she didn't want to sleep alone in the big bed.

She was eying the pale blue expanse of the coverlet with increasing self-annoyance, when a soft tap on her door had her whirling.

The door opened, and Del looked in. He glanced once around the room, then slipped in and shut the door.

And locked it.

For one instant, Deliah debated whether to take umbrage at his assumption, but decided she couldn't be that hypocritical. She was far more thankful she wasn't, it seemed, destined to sleep alone.

Del crossed the room and halted directly before her. He'd dropped his mask. He knew his expression was tending grim, but although her eyes calmly searched his face, she didn't seem the least bit intimidated. Not even mildly worried.

He let his inner scowl materialize. "You promised to sit in the middle of the carriage and *not move*."

"And I did. At first."

"We didn't put any time limit on your actions. It was understood you would remain where I'd left you until we quit the scene."

Her eyes narrowed fractionally. "I also understood you didn't intend to die. Or even allow yourself to be mortally wounded."

"I didn't intend—"

"And neither did I." She met his determination with blatant intransigence. "Is there any point to this?"

"Yes!" If only he could figure out how to state it. He searched her eyes, seeking inspiration. "If you can't obey orders—"

"There's really no point in going over this again."

"—then how can I trust that you'll remain safe?" He hauled in a breath. "Damn it, woman, I can't function if I don't know that you'll have the good sense to stay out of the action—"

"And just stand by and watch you get killed?" She came up

on her toes, all but nose to nose. "Permit me to inform you, Colonel, that that's only going to happen in your dreams!"

Her eyes blazed into his.

Lips thin, he met her glare for glare.

Without warning, she clamped her palms about his face, muttered, "Shut up!" and kissed him.

As if she wanted to devour him.

He fought to hold aloof, succeeded for two heartbeats. Then he was with her in her ravenous need; he met her, matched her, an equal participant in the greedy exchange.

He told himself he should use it—the moment, her wildness, her wanting. Her wantonness. That if he was wise, he'd wield her desire like a whip, withholding gratification until she promised—

She pressed against him, into him, and his thought processes stuttered. Stopped.

Evaporated.

She wound her arms about his neck, pressed her breasts to his chest, slid her hips, her belly, sinuously over his erection, and he was lost.

Lost to all pretense that he wasn't as helplessly in thrall to her as, it appeared, she was to him. That he didn't want her as much, didn't need her as much, didn't crave her as desperately as her lips, her mouth, every seductive curve of her body announced she craved him.

Her need was visceral, flagrant and declared. Her wanting was tangible, a giddy purpose scenting the air. Her craving was elemental, a primitive itch that demanded to be scratched.

All she felt resonated within him.

Their kiss was all-consuming, a blatant expression of all that was to come. Her hands slid from his hair to grip his shoulders. She pushed; when he stepped back, she steered. With slow deliberation, she backed him to the bed.

He let her.

Curious to see what her wishes were, he complied when

she pressed down on his shoulders; without breaking the kiss, he sank down to sit on the side of the bed.

She came between his widespread thighs. One hand trailed down from shoulder to chest, to waist. To his groin to cup him.

To fondle with intent.

He mentally gritted his teeth and let her play, while he reached around her and found the laces of her gown. Stripping it from her slowly had been his ambition from the first instant he'd seen her in it, in Madame Latour's salon.

Now he got to, and she allowed him to, realize that ambition. To slowly peel the gold satin from her perfect shoulders, to ease the slinky fabric down, taking her chemise with it, to expose her magnificent breasts.

Then it was his turn to fondle, with educated intent.

Her turn to grow even more heated. Until she moaned and drew back from the kiss. Until her spine bowed and she leaned back in his hands, and he bent his head and set his hot mouth to her flesh.

And ardently possessed.

By the time he consented to draw back, to push her gown down, over the swell of her hips until it slid of its own accord, whispering down her legs to puddle on the floor, her ivory skin was flushed with desire, her nipples tightly peaked, her breasts swollen and firm.

Her lids were so heavy she could barely lift them enough to see as she slipped the buttons at his waist free, and took his rampant erection between her hands.

Then it was his turn to close his eyes, to bite back a moan. To feel her hands possessing until the desire that rose beneath his skin seemed too much for his body to hold.

She leaned in, nipped his earlobe. Gained his attention. "I want you inside me. Now."

She didn't have to ask twice. His hands tightened about her waist and he lifted her, set her down on her knees on the bed, straddling him.

She didn't hesitate, but shifted closer. One small hand wrapped about his shaft, she guided the engorged head between her slick lips.

Then sank down.

Took him in.

The air left Deliah's lungs in a slow exhalation as she sank steadily down and he filled her. Stretched her, completed her.

It felt better than good, even better than blissful, to have the rigid rod of his erection buried so deeply inside her. It felt right. Sublime.

When he nudged deeper, nudged her womb, she reversed direction. She rose upon him, gauging the distance. Just before she lost the fullness of him, she smoothly changed direction and sank down.

Slowly.

She knew the theory of what she, they, were doing, but she'd never before experienced this particular pleasure. Now she was so engaged, she wanted to feel all, learn all, know all there was.

All that might come of loving him like this.

Of using her body to pleasure his like this.

Of taking her pleasure in pleasuring him.

And it was more, much more, than she'd ever imagined. The ride was exhilarating, stupendous, marvelously freeing. She was in charge, and he ceded the reins to her, let her set the pace, let her take him as she would.

Watched her as she did.

Watched as she experimented, then found her rhythm.

Watched as she rode him hard, then harder.

Watched her as she crested, as she rode faster, more desperately, taking him ever deeper as they pushed relentlessly up the final peak.

He held her, his hands tight about her hips, her arms locked about his shoulders, through those last fraught moments when the friction of their joining became a fire that ravaged and consumed.

At the very last moment her eyes locked with his, then she gasped, let her lids fall as she leaned in, and pressed her lips to his. Felt his open.

She slid her tongue between, found his tongue. Stroked, caressed, as the flames erupted, and the world cindered about them.

Del held her, kissed her, felt her sheath clamp tight, all fire and wet heat, about him. Felt her burn between his hands with an incandescent glory.

With a power he couldn't deny.

Then he felt her soar.

Felt the tug, the command, the need to join her flower and sear, and pull him on.

To her promise of paradise. To all he knew awaited him in her arms.

He wanted her, and she wanted him.

Surrender was his only option. He closed his eyes and did.

Later, much, much later, when they'd recovered enough to together remove his clothes and then crawl between her sheets, he lay on his back, one arm behind his head, staring up unseeing as he listened to their tumultuous heartbeats slow, feeling all residual tension fading into sated languor.

Gradually, his mind cleared.

Leaving, etched with crystal-clear clarity, all she'd revealed—everything the most vulnerable part of him had so desperately needed to know.

He hadn't known the question he'd needed to ask, but she'd unstintingly given him the answer.

Glancing down at her, curled against him, her head pillowed on his shoulder, her hair fanned over his chest, he saw she was at peace, floating, but not yet asleep.

Beneath the sheet, he slapped her naked rump, not enough to hurt, enough to claim her attention. "Don't, for the love of God, ever do what you did this afternoon again."

"I won't, as long as you don't attempt to fight three cultists at once in front of me again." She scowled up at him, then pouted as she rubbed her abused posterior. "It would have served you right if I hadn't intervened and saved you. I should have left you to reap your just rewards."

He was, he realized, still smiling inanely. He couldn't seem to stop. He'd just reaped all the rewards he presently needed. Still, with a sense of inner wonder, he stated what he now realized was obvious. "You wouldn't have, couldn't have, sat still and let that happen."

"No, you're right." She snuggled down against him again. "Sadly, I'm too patriotic for my own good."

"So you saved me for the good of the country?"

"Of course."

His smile only broadened, deepened; he felt as if the sun were shining on his soul. He might not appreciate how he felt when she tried to protect him at the expense of her own safety, but at least now he understood why she did.

Understood that she might not be able to refuse the call any more than he could when it came to her.

And, oddly, that felt right. Good. Elementally reassuring.

Fundamentally contradictory, but that seemed the norm for his feelings about her.

His thoughts circled, settled . . . as far as he could see through the haze of pleasure clouding his brain, there was really only one—or maybe two—questions remaining. How should he propose? And when?

He fell asleep before he could decide.

Ten

December 16
Somersham Place, Cambridgeshire

n the wee small hours of the morning, Sangay crept along the corridor on the first floor of the very big house.

He'd seen the colonel take the scroll-holder from Mustaf in the inn yard. He hadn't seen either Mustaf or Cobby take the scroll-holder back. And now he knew what to look for, once they'd all settled in the big house he'd been able to tell that neither Cobby nor Mustaf had been carrying the holder.

Just before the servants had had their dinner in the servants' hall, when Cobby had been sitting with Sligo before the fire there, and Mustaf and Kumulay had been waiting at the big table, Sangay had slipped into first Mustaf's, then Cobby's rooms, and searched. Thoroughly. He was getting very good at searching. But the scroll-holder hadn't been there.

Later still, after he'd come back from speaking with the evil sahib behind the stable, he'd surreptitiously followed Cobby and learned where the colonel's room was.

Now, silent as a ghost, he slipped through the deep shadows. The house was gloomy and dark, but it was almost as if he could hear it breathing—as if the house itself were alive. As if it might wake at any moment and see him. He tried not to think of such fanciful things, but concentrated on retracing his steps to the colonel's room without getting lost.

There were so many rooms down so many different corridors, but he'd noted the steel armor mounted like a metal man on a stand just along from the colonel's door. Finally he saw it, and hurried forward, his slippered feet silent on the rugs. He took a moment to check that it was indeed the right armor, then, going to the door, he opened it, peeked in, then slipped inside.

The colonel spent his nights in the memsahib's bedroom. He was never in his room until close to dawn. So Sangay was free to search.

It was still hours before dawn when he reached into the top drawer of a high chest and his fingers closed around polished wood and brass.

Almost reverently, he drew the holder out. One glance was enough to confirm it was the one the evil sahib sought.

Closing the drawer, Sangay slid the holder up the sleeves of his tunic and the coat he'd donned over it, then, quiet as a mouse, he slipped out of the room and shut the door.

He was downstairs in mere minutes. He paused in the corridor leading to the back door and closed his coat up tight. It would be cold out there—freezing. He hadn't yet had a chance to look for the big church, but the evil sahib had said he had to go back down the carriage drive, and he knew where that was. He would go now and be well away from the house before the other servants stirred. When daylight came, he would be able to see the church tower.

He wondered how long it would take him to reach it. Even going around by the roads, in this country it wouldn't be that far. A few hours, perhaps?

Telling himself to keep his spirits up—he was nearly free of the evil sahib's demands—he reached for the bolts closing the back door, eased them back with barely a sound. Carefully, he lifted the latch, opened the door.

And looked out at a wall of white.

He stared. He could only just see over the top of the white blockage. Hesitantly, he put out a hand. White sand, but cold, and it melted where he touched.

The white stuff slithered, started to slide like sand in through the door. Quickly, he swung the door closed, pushed hard and managed to shut it.

Snow! The white stuff was snow. He'd had no idea it could come like this.

That it could trap him in the house with the scroll-holder.

Stunned, he reclosed the bolts, then looked for a window, saw one over the iron trough in the next room. He hurried over, had to clamber up and balance on the trough to see through. The snow had piled up across the bottom of the window. He couldn't push it open. Looking out, he saw to his amazement that there was plenty of light to see, even though it was still hours until dawn.

A soft, pearly-gray glow bathed the scene, moonlight and starlight reflecting off the snow. Sangay had never imagined the world might look like this—untouched, and so cold. As if there were no people, no animals anywhere. Only the naked trees and the buildings . . . and in the far distance, off to the east, the huge tower of a church spearing up through the white-gray, its stone a solid, deeper gray than the sky behind it.

Three hours at most, Sangay thought, but he couldn't walk through snow that deep.

He looked at the white dunes filling the kitchen yard. Perhaps it might be less on the other sides of the house?

He spent the next hour frantically going from room to room, window to window, but the snow lay everywhere, apparently equally thick. There was no window he could open, no door he could slip through. Everywhere he looked, the snow hemmed him in.

Then he heard the first maids stirring.

Sternly he told himself he couldn't sniffle and cry, that his maataa's life depended on him getting the holder to the evil sahib.

He looked down at the wooden holder, peeking past the edge of his sleeve. He couldn't afford to be found with it, but if he put it back in the colonel's room, he might not be able to fetch it later.

On impulse, he hurried back to the kitchen, slipped into the corridor to the back door, then turned off it into a big storeroom. It was close to the back door, and he'd seen bins there. He found one behind some bags; it was half-filled with wheat. He buried the scroll-holder deep, then, feeling a vise ease from about his chest, drew an easier breath. He went back into the kitchen and curled up in a corner near the fire.

He didn't have long to wait. Three of the kitchen girls came down the servants' stairs. Yawning, laughing, they saw him, smiled and called a good morning, and started taking down pots and plates.

Sangay returned their greetings, then got to his feet. He went to the table, smiled as best he could. "There's lots of snow outside."

The girls exchanged glances, then set down what they held and rushed down the corridor to the window over the iron trough.

Sangay followed them.

"Ooh! Look, Maisie. It's ever so pretty."

"Looks to be dry, too—it won't be thawing today."

"Ah—how long will it last?" Sangay asked.

The girls looked at him, then out at the snow. They pulled measuring faces, then the one called Maisie said, "No one'll be moving for a couple o' days, at least." She flashed Sangay a grin. "Assuming no more comes down, that is."

Sangay felt his eyes grow wide. "Will more come down before this lot goes?"

Maisie shrugged. "Who's to say? In the lap of the gods, that is."

Sangay managed a weak smile. Turning, he left the room. He slipped through the kitchen and went quickly up the stairs. Reaching his room, he quietly shut the door, then climbed into his bed and pulled the blanket over his head.

He tried not to shiver. He wasn't cold. But he didn't know what to do. Desperation clutched his chest, his heart.

What would happen to his maataa?

He believed in the gods. They had sent the snow. They didn't want him to take the holder to the evil sahib, at least not yet.

But was that so? Was there some other route he was meant to take to the big church?

He didn't know. He didn't know this country, and with the snow on the ground, it had only become more alien.

Curling up in the bed, he shivered harder.

Del woke to see a strange, subdued light slanting through a gap in the curtains drawn across the window in Deliah's room.

It took a moment for him to recall what such a light portended.

Deliah slumbered, warm and soft against his side. He glanced at her, then, carefully easing from under the covers, leaving her sleeping, he padded quickly across the room, pushed the curtain aside—and looked out on a scene that embodied the essence of "home" to him.

He looked out on a world covered in white. The thick blanket stretched as far as he could see, the bare branches of trees weighted with an inches-thick coating of soft white. The air was curiously clear. The wind had died during the night, leaving the smothering snow undisturbed, unmarred.

He hadn't seen such a sight for decades.

A soft footfall sounded behind him. Before he could turn, Deliah was there, as naked as he, but she'd brought the counterpane with her; she tossed one end over his bare shoulders as she came to lean against his side.

Her face was alight. "I haven't seen snow for more than seven years!"

The excitement in her voice, innocent and sincere, found an echo inside him. Tugging the counterpane around him, he put his arms around her, held her close. For long moments, they stood snuggling together, looking out on the pristine scene.

"We might even have a white Christmas," she said.

"Much as I, personally, would appreciate that, I hope this will thaw, and soon." When she looked up at him, brows rising, he explained, "The others have yet to get through. Snow will only make them slower—make them easier targets."

She sobered, closed her hand on his arm. "Yes, of course. I hadn't thought of that." Then she frowned. "But there's— what?—nine days to go? They should be here before then, surely?"

"I don't know. Devil hasn't heard anything about the others. We'll have to wait until I see Wolverstone to ask."

They stood silently for some minutes, he thinking about his colleagues, most likely still some way from home. "With luck Gareth will have landed in England by now."

Deliah gave him another moment, then jabbed her elbow into his side. "Let's go down. I haven't thrown a snowball since I left Humberside."

He chuckled. "All right—I challenge you to a snowball duel." Ducking out from under the counterpane, he headed for his clothes.

Trailing the counterpane like a shawl, she went to the wardrobe. "What are the rules?"

"There aren't any." In his trousers and shirt, he slung his coat on. "I need a different coat. I'll meet you in the front hall."

Pulling out a red woolen gown, she nodded. "Five minutes."

He left.

She rushed.

He'd only just reached the front door when she hurried down the stairs, buttoning her pelisse. Breathless, more with excitement and anticipation than exertion, she let her momentum carry her to the door.

Del pulled back the heavy bolts, then reached for the doorknob. He swung the door open, waved Deliah through, then followed her into a world turned white.

Into a world of long-ago childhoods and innocent delights.

The carriage drive had disappeared beneath the tide. The lawns were a blanket of glistening purity, punctured by the skeletal trees, their branches limned with a thick coating of snow.

Shutting the door, he walked forward to join Deliah at the edge of the porch steps. White crust crunched beneath his boots. Their breaths fogged before their faces.

She was testing the snow piled on the steps with the toe of her red halfboot. "Too soft to walk in, and it looks to be more than knee-deep."

He watched as she crouched, then reached out to brush her hand over the snow. She'd put on a pair of knitted gloves. After brushing the surface, she plunged her fingers in. The snow was dry and as yet uncompacted.

She drew out a handful, let it sift through her fingers. Marveled.

He watched her, saw the light in her eyes, the expressions flitting over her face, and felt each resonate within him. "Our snow's usually heavier."

She nodded. "This is so fine. It'll be gone in a few days."

"Not like our weeks of white."

Home for them lay north of the Humber, in the Wolds. Snow often closed them in, blanketing the ground for weeks at a time.

"It's strange how a sight like this—one unseen for years—suddenly takes one back." Looking down, she started gathering snow.

"It reinforces that we're home—that we really *are* home,

because where we were before it never snowed." He strolled to the other side of the porch, hunkered down and started to gather a snowball of his own.

She beat him to it. Her first attempt hit him squarely on the side of his head. It broke in a shower of dry, ice-cold white, dusting his shoulders.

He swung to face her, pelted the ball he'd fashioned at her.

She yelped, dodged, and the ball struck the wall behind her.

Laughing, she bent and quickly gathered more snow for another ball.

Muttering mock-direfully, he did the same.

For the next ten minutes, they were children again, in the snow again, at home again. They shied loose balls of white at each other, laughing, calling insults both adult and childish. There was no one about to hear or see.

Only each other.

By the time she waved and, breathless, called a halt, they were both holding their sides from laughing so much. He looked into her bright eyes, noted the flush on her cheeks, sensed the sheer exuberance that filled her.

Felt the same coursing through him. "Pax," he agreed. The cold was starting to reach through their clothes.

They shook and dusted the powdery snow from their coats, stamped their feet, then headed for the door.

In the front hall, Webster was supervising the rebuilding of the fire in the huge fireplace. Seeing them, he bowed. "Miss Duncannon. Colonel. If you care to go through to the breakfast parlor, we'll be ready to serve you shortly."

Relaxed, still smiling, they ambled down the corridor Webster had indicated. The breakfast parlor proved to be a large room with a series of windows looking south over a terrace, currently lightly covered in snow. A long sideboard hugged the opposite wall, with countless covered chafing dishes lined up along it. A parade of footmen were ferrying hot dishes up from the kitchen to lay beneath the domed covers.

The long table was set. They took seats along one side, facing the view. Coffeepot and teapot appeared before them all but instantly.

Webster brought a rack of fresh toast himself, and extolled the wonders of the offerings on the sideboard, exhorting them to make their selections.

He didn't have to exhort twice. Their impromptu snowball fight had stirred their appetites. Returning to the table, a quite astonishing mound of food on her plate, Deliah suspected their late-night activities had also contributed.

They sat, ate, and shared—long moments of reflective silence as well as comments, most of which centered on their earlier lives in Humberside, but which, in the retelling, highlighted elements each clearly hoped to experience again.

Now they were heading home again.

Now they were close enough to imagine being there.

Now that they were looking their futures in the eyes.

It was apparent neither had any definite vision of what their respective futures would be like.

"You said you wanted to invest in manufacturing." Deliah raised her brows at Del. "Do you have any preferences as to what?"

"I'm not yet sure, but I had thought to look at some of the woolen mills in the West Riding, and perhaps a flour mill in Hull—something along those lines. There's new advances on the horizon which should make great improvements, and it seems somehow fitting that a fortune I—born and raised in Humberside—made protecting our overseas trade should be invested in activities that create jobs in Humberside."

Deliah inclined her head. "A worthy ambition."

"You mentioned the cotton trade."

She nodded. "I think I'll approach the weaving guilds, and see whether there's any interest. Initially I assume I'll remain an absentee grower and importer, supplying the mills rather than investing in them directly. But eventually I may look at investing in the mills, too."

Del seized the moment to ask, "I take it you intend returning to live with your parents at Holme on the Wolds?"

"At first. But I doubt I'll remain there for long."

"Oh? Why?"

She seemed to search for words, then offered, "Consider it along the lines of a clash of personalities. My parents have always expected me to conform to a rigid . . . I suppose you could say mold. A pattern of behavior that allows only the most strictly conservative, prim and proper conduct in all things." She slanted a glance at him. "That mold didn't fit years ago, and while I thought, perhaps, after my years away I might have grown closer to their ideal, sadly . . ." She shook her head and looked down at her plate. "I fear I was fooling myself. So I'll go home, and the instant I do anything outside their expectations—start looking into investments, or, heaven help me, telling them of my interests in cotton and the like—Papa will get on his high horse and forbid it, and I'll refuse, and then I'll feel honor-bound to leave."

"Where will you go?" Del fought to keep his tone even. If she was going to disappear from Humberside, he needed her destination. He couldn't ask her to marry him if he couldn't find her. He didn't want to have to chase her to Jamaica, either.

"I don't know. I'll think of something." She waved her fork. "Courtesy of my highly-disreputable-for-a-lady, as my parents will term it, commercial interests, I'm hardly a pauper."

Footsteps in the corridor heralded the rest of the company. The men came in first, the ladies drifting in later, having been to the nurseries to supervise their offsprings' ablutions and breakfasts.

Within minutes the room was full of bustle and good cheer. The men looked out at the snow and made disparaging comments, disgruntled that the extensive covering effectively put paid to any chance of a Black Cobra attack, at least not that day.

"Or very likely the next." Demon, who owned a racing stud in nearby Newmarket, shook his head. "I can't see us even riding out tomorrow."

"Never mind." Demon's wife, Flick, smiled at him across the table. "You can spend a few hours with your children—that will keep at least them amused."

All the Cynster wives were quick to concur.

All the Cynster males looked horrified.

But that, Deliah soon realized, was all pretense. To a man, the Cynsters, and Chillingworth, too, were exceedingly proud papas. When, later that morning, the nurse-maids brought all the toddlers and babies down to join the company in the long library to which they'd repaired, the men were very ready to jig their offspring on their knees and compare their various putative talents.

Which activity resulted in a great deal of laughter.

Despite the constraint imposed by the weather, the day rolled on in relaxed, good-humored, pleasantly comfortable style.

December 16
Bury St. Edmunds, Suffolk

Alex led the way through the reception rooms of the house the Black Cobra had commandeered. "This will do nicely. So helpful of the owners, whoever they are, to have vacated it just when we need a headquarters in this area."

When Delborough had left London, scroll-holder still in his keeping, and headed into Cambridgeshire, it had become clear that whoever he intended delivering the scroll-holder to wasn't in town. Hardly surprising, given there were so few people of power left in the capital that close to Christmas.

When Larkins had sent word that Delborough had stopped at Somersham, so close to the many great houses of the truly powerful scattered throughout northern Suffolk and neighboring Norfolk, Alex had given orders to shift their base from Shrewton House—pleasantly satisfying though their stay there had been—to some place better situated to block the couriers' access to those "truly powerful."

Bury St. Edmunds was perfectly positioned. Thus far the town was proving exceedingly accommodating.

"Creighton heard the owners had gone to stay with family in the north for Christmas, so he came to take a look." Following Alex into the sitting room, Daniel sprawled on the holland-covered sofa, putting his feet up on the low table before it. Creighton was his gentleman's gentleman. "The back door apparently opened very easily."

"Well, we couldn't have stayed at an inn," Alex said. "Can you imagine the talk once the locals laid eyes on M'wallah and the others?"

"Especially the others," Daniel replied.

They'd assembled a select body of cultists—assassins and foot soldiers both—to act as bodyguards for them under the command of M'wallah, Alex's fanatically loyal Indian houseman. The same cultists would also serve as a well-trained force should they need to deploy men from their base. Their preference, however, was, as always, to act from a distance by sending cultists from groups not directly connected to their households to do their bidding.

Concealing the Black Cobra's identity had become second nature to them all.

Roderick drifted in, looking around, assessing. Seeing a sideboard along one wall, he walked to it and tried the cupboard doors. Finding them locked, he smiled, drew a lockpick from his pocket and crouched before them.

An instant later, the doors popped open. Sliding the pick back in his pocket, Roderick pulled out a bottle, held it up to read the label. "Whoever he is, the owner has a nice taste in brandy. Lucky for us." Putting the bottle back, he rose.

At the far end of the sitting room, Alex had parted the curtains covering the front window to peer outside. "With the house built into these old arches, we can even have the curtains open during the day. The front façade is so shadowed and gloomy, no one will be able to see in from the street."

The house was one of a short row built into the massive arches along the west face of the ruined Abbey Church.

"So Delborough's taken refuge at Somersham." Daniel looked at Roderick. "Why there?"

"Not Somersham the village, but Somersham Place. It's the principal residence of the Duke of St. Ives—Devil Cynster."

"Doesn't ring a bell." Alex returned to join Daniel on the sofa. "Could St. Ives be Delborough's contact? Is St. Ives in a position to bring us down?"

Shaking his head, Roderick dropped into an armchair facing the other two. "It's a mystery why Delborough's chosen to go there. St. Ives is eminently well-connected within the ton, very much haut ton, but he's not a political heavyweight, at least not in foreign matters. Papa would simply shrug off any accusation St. Ives made, then bury it. I really don't think we need to worry about St. Ives. Besides, Larkins believes Delborough hasn't handed over the scroll-holder but has it still in his keeping, which suggests Somersham is merely a staging point—a safe house, perhaps—from which Delborough will make the last push to his ultimate destination."

"Any guesses as to where that 'ultimate destination' is?" Alex asked. "I assume the other couriers will make for the same place."

"I think we can count on that," Roderick returned. "There has to be one person behind this—someone is the puppetmaster pulling all the strings. The big question is: who?"

Alex nodded. "Whoever they are, *they* are the person we need to worry about—to counter. And the safest and easiest way is by ensuring the original letter never makes it into their hands."

The other two nodded in agreement.

"So what did Larkins report?" Daniel asked.

Roderick had made a detour to meet Larkins in Newmarket. "His thief is inside the house, still undetected, still free to move. Unfortunately, the snow was particularly heavy in that part of the country. When Larkins spoke to the little beggar last night, he—the boy—was confident he could find the scroll-holder and bring it out to Larkins, but now with the snow so deep, even if he has filched the scroll-holder he'll have to wait for the thaw to bring it out."

"I assume Larkins was wise enough to arrange to meet this boy-thief at a distance?" Alex asked.

Lips curving, Roderick nodded. "He's picked a place anyone can find—Ely Cathedral."

"Oh, I do approve." Alex smiled back. "Not so much appropriate as . . . contemptuous. Very much in keeping with the Black Cobra style."

"Larkins thought you'd be pleased."

"I am, but . . . I have to say, thus far Larkins isn't living up to his usual efficiency." Alex met Roderick's eyes. "Delborough, after all, still lives, and we're still waiting for his scroll-holder."

Roderick shrugged. "You can hardly blame Larkins. If it hadn't been for that damned redhead, we'd have done for Delborough in Southampton. And got the scroll-holder, too. As you'd predicted, after the attacks by the two cultists we put on board his ship at Capetown, the good colonel had fallen into the habit of assuming he only had knives to fear."

"While it's nice to be proved correct," Alex dryly replied, "we sacrificed two good men, and we still have Delborough alive and running around Cambridgeshire with his scroll-holder."

Alex never liked losing cultists.

Roderick sighed. "We've lost more than two, now."

"What?" The sharp question came from both Alex and Daniel.

"That's the rest of what Larkins had to report. If you recall, we'd ordered him to, if an opportunity presented, seize Delborough alive, and the scroll-holder, too. He was to exercise caution, and not go against a superior force, but if the chance was there, he was to take it. What looked like such a chance—and yes, it was engineered deliberately to look that way—occurred, and Larkins felt obliged to risk his force. He sent only eight out initially, but when the strength of the opposition became clear, he sent in the rest of the cultists he had with him—six more—trying to tip the scales." Roderick grimaced. "They failed."

"So . . . we lost another fourteen." Alex's eyes glittered. "And we can lay that at Delborough's door."

"Indeed." Daniel looked at Roderick. "So Larkins is now alone?"

Roderick nodded. "I told him we couldn't spare more men to him, not when all he's doing is waiting for this boy-thief. As things stand at present, there's nothing else he can do, not with the snow and Delborough staying put in the ducal mansion."

"Any chance we can overrun said mansion?" Alex asked.

Roderick shook his head. "I wouldn't advise attempting it. I vaguely recall that the Cynsters hold a family gathering there every Christmas. And the duke and his five cousins were all in the Guards, and all fought at Waterloo."

"That must be how Delborough knows them," Alex said. "He was in the Guards and fought at Waterloo, too."

"As did the other four—the three other couriers and MacFarlane," Daniel added.

"So we now know the connection between Cynster and Delborough and the others. Somersham Place might be a staging post for all of them, or some of them." Alex grimaced. "Or only Delborough."

They pondered that, then Alex continued, "This is turning out to be rather more involved than we expected. I was right in predicting the colonel would lead the charge home, and while it's a pity we've missed our chance to capture, or even harm, him, it's the original letter we really want . . . and I have to say, given his actions since landing, I'm increasingly inclined to think he's carrying a copy."

Roderick opened his mouth. Alex silenced him with an

upraised hand and went on, "However, we can't make that assumption safely, so we need the scroll-holder the colonel's carrying. If we could seize him, too, I'm sure we could persuade him to tell us which of his friends has the real letter, and which port he'll be coming through."

Daniel shifted. "Delborough would be no easy nut to crack."

"True." Alex smiled coldly. "But I would love a chance to break him. Unfortunately, I agree our seizing him now seems remote—not unless we can lay our hands on the redheaded female, and perhaps not even then. There's no telling how much she means to him, but regardless, I'm getting a very bad feeling about this puppetmaster."

Roderick frowned. "How so?"

"It's occurred to me that Delborough and his cohorts are not the sort to put their faith—and their lives and their mission—into the hands of another, not unless he commands their absolute respect."

"And someone who commands such respect," Daniel said, "is someone we should perhaps fear?"

"Not fear." Alex dismissed the notion with contempt. "But we should treat this puppetmaster with due caution. This is starting to feel like a game—a chess match, almost. Even us moving here—we're not on the box seat but are having to respond to . . . the puppetmaster's plan. We need to think more carefully—we need to allow for an enemy with brains. Take Delborough's actions, the reason I believe he's a decoy. When you look at his going to London, it makes no sense—not unless his mission was to draw our fire. To make us send our men after him so he could engage and reduce their number. He's clearing the field, and the other two decoys will do the same. However, because of my newfound respect for this puppetmaster, I agree we can't assume, based on behavior, who is decoy and who is not. So until we find the original letter, we need to concentrate on that—the letter—rather than being drawn into unnecessary skirmishes. And, of course, always covering our tracks. Speaking of which." Alex looked at Roderick. "I assume Larkins will kill his boy-thief once he has the scroll-holder? Not that I imagine an Indian boy being all that much of a threat, but we might as well be thorough."

"Of course," Roderick replied. "It's only Larkins the boy has seen. Larkins knows whose head is in the noose should the boy—somehow—be believed."

"Excellent. Now if only we knew where and to whom Delborough and his friends are ferrying the letter." Alex looked at the other two. "If the decoys are trying to draw our fire, then I believe we can assume it's someone with an estate in this area, someone powerful enough, well-connected enough politically to make a charge against Roderick stick. So who might that someone be?"

Roderick shrugged. "Norfolk is littered with the discreet mansions of the truly wealthy, the seriously powerful— houses many of those gentlemen use over winter, even when their principal estates are elsewhere. It could be anyone."

"No," Alex corrected, "it has to be someone with the clout to stand against our dear father."

"They wouldn't be making for Shrewton himself, would they?" Daniel looked at Roderick. "He winters on his estate outside Norwich, doesn't he?"

"Yes, but that hardly makes sense—he's not the puppet-master, and anyone could guess he'll simply destroy the letter." Roderick shook his head. "As Alex says, Delborough and his colleagues must be planning to get the letter into the hands of someone willing and able to do something with it, or what's the point?"

"Indeed," Alex said. "And sadly there are quite a few powerful men around here."

December 16
Somersham Place, Cambridgeshire

Del sprawled in an armchair by Devil's library fire, legs stretched before him, a glass of brandy in his hand, and laughed.

He'd laughed more today, been more genuinely amused than he had been in decades. A sad reflection on how lacking his life had been. A hint, a prod, as to what he wanted, even needed of his future, of his life yet to come.

Despite the snow, the day had been truly relaxing. There'd even been a glimmer of sunshine to lighten it, but then the clouds had closed in, the wind had picked up, and blizzard-like conditions had set in.

Night had fallen like a pall. There'd been no letup in the wind, presently howling, bansheelike, about the eaves. Outside, snow was swirling thick and fast, mostly scoured from what had fallen earlier, but inside, the heavy curtains had been drawn and the fires built up to cheering blazes.

With so many gathered in it, and the fire roaring, the library felt like a cozy cave. A very comfortable and luxurious cave, safe from the elements.

Dinner was over, and the children had just been recaptured and carried off by their nursemaids. The company had spent the last hour swapping tales of childhood exploits—not so much of the young ones rolling and crawling about the floor or toddling awkwardly on short stubby legs, but of their parents. Tales of family, of shared adventures, of kinship in the true sense.

From the padded comfort of the armchair, Del watched Deliah, seated on the chaise opposite, drinking in the ambiance, noted that she, like he, was drawn to the stories of childhood daring and thrills.

He and she were the exotics in the room. They were both only children; neither had had siblings with whom to share. But it wasn't only that that drew them to the stories the Cynsters had in abundance. The tales epitomized normal English life, life in this country, their homeland—a life neither he nor she had experienced for many years. If ever.

The Cynsters' experience hadn't been theirs.

Yet.

There was no reason it couldn't be, that together they couldn't make a bid to have just that sort of life, those sorts of experiences. Have similar family stories to tell, perhaps not of themselves, but of their children.

He felt an inner tug at the thought.

His gaze traveled her face, saw laughter light her fine eyes at some comment. He wanted to spend the rest of his life with her. To marry her, and try his hand at creating a real family at Delborough Hall.

But what did she want?

He was who he was; he couldn't help but approach the task of gaining her hand—her agreement to wed him—as a campaign.

The easiest way to get her to fall into line was to discover what she wanted of her life, her future, and couch his proposal in a way that best paralleled that. That supported that.

Not that he intended accepting any reply other than a "yes." Preferably a "yes, please." What he was more concerned with was the speed, the rapidity with which he could secure that correct response, thus minimizing any cost to himself, to his pride by way of any revelations required to convince her to utter that small word.

His decision to wait until his mission was concluded still seemed the wisest course, but her comment that morning about leaving her Humberside home for parts unknown had sounded a warning. Once his mission was ended, it wouldn't be wise to let her have her head for long.

Indeed, with every hour that passed, he was more inclined to refine his plan. The instant his mission was ended, before he surrendered her to her parents, he would offer for her hand, and be accepted, thus reducing the separation that would naturally occur between returning her to her home and her coming to live permanently with him.

He wasn't of a mind to let her go, not even for a day. Somehow simply having her about, in the same house, knowing she was there, made him feel more settled. More complete.

As if he'd found his future purpose and she was an instrinsic part.

He was too seasoned a campaigner not to pay attention to instinct.

So what did she want? How could he tempt her?

At that moment, despite her outward appearance of content, Deliah was feeling distinctly downhearted.

Not that she had any reason to be; she kept telling herself that, but it didn't help.

For the first time in her life, she'd experienced a day in the company of genuine friends, women and men who saw her as she was yet did not consider her—the real her—as in any way beyond their pale. Throughout the day, little incidents had underscored that in this company, she—her character, her traits—were the norm. In the world the Cynsters and Chillingworth inhabited, ladies were life partners, not cyphers, their existences significantly more than mere adjuncts to their husbands' lives.

The events of the day had conspired to educate and show her, to lay before her in all its glory the precise type of life she might have had had her Great Scandal not derailed her. A life she would even now sell her soul to seize and enjoy— if she could.

If any gentleman of similar ilk to the Cynsters, one with similar expectations of his wife, could be prevailed on to offer for her hand.

If Del would.

But he wouldn't.

He'd taken her as his lover—she'd accepted him as hers. And that was that. As she'd years ago proved, and as she'd been lectured about ad nauseam in the aftermath of the scandal, gentlemen did not marry their lovers.

More specifically, no gentleman would ever marry her.

Her spirits sank lower as the thought floated blackly through her mind. Its darkness, its intensity, made her wonder—made her look more closely at what she felt. And why. . . .

She managed to keep a smile on her face, or at least keep her lips curved, her expression relaxed, while inwardly she berated herself. How unutterably foolish. How unforgivably silly. How inexcusably willful.

She'd done it again—fallen in love, again.

No. She caught herself, looked anew, reconsidered. She'd fallen in love, really, truly, head over heels forevermore in love, for the first time. What she felt for Del was oceans apart from the mild emotion she'd felt for that bastard Griffiths. Then, in her innocence, her naïveté, she'd convinced herself that what she'd felt was love; she hadn't at the time known enough to know the difference.

Now she did.

She knew she loved Del.

To the absolute bottom of her foolish, foolish heart.

Bad enough. She would not—could not—allow herself to compound her stupidity by even imagining that there was even the slightest hope that he might feel the same for her, let alone that he might see her as an eligible lady. One he might marry.

As she'd been told from adolescence on, she wasn't the marriageable kind. The kind of lady gentlemen wanted to marry.

She was too bossy. Too headstrong, too opinionated. Too willful.

Regardless, even if Del were different, and might have considered her for the position of his wife, he wouldn't now, now that they were lovers.

The wash of deadening, dismal feelings that flowed through her threatened to sink her.

Still smiling, but inwardly desperate for escape, for distraction, she looked around—and met Del's eyes.

He'd been watching her. Some part of her had registered it—she'd felt the telltale warmth—but she'd been too engrossed in her black thoughts to respond.

He smiled, and slowly—with his signature languid grace—drew in his long legs and rose.

She swallowed as he crossed to the chaise. Instinct brought her to her feet as he neared.

His eyes met hers. "You look like you need to escape. We could walk in the long gallery, if you like." His dark gaze was rich and warm. Enfolding.

"Ah . . ." It was herself she wanted to escape. Herself and her deadening, desolating reality. She glanced around. The others were mingling, chatting in groups. She looked back at him. "Actually, I have a headache."

A frown came into his eyes.

She hurried on, "Just a mild one—nothing too bad. But . . . I think I'll go up now."

Summoning the smile she'd let drop, she turned to Catriona, on the chaise beside her, then let her gaze travel on to the other ladies. "I'm going to retire. I'm feeling rather jaded. A good night's sleep will no doubt see me right."

Catriona smiled her madonna's smile and touched Deliah's hand. "We'll see you in the morning."

Deliah nodded a smiling good night to the others, at the last inclined her head to Del—still standing by her side, eyes too shrewd for her liking fixed on her face—murmured, "Good night," then walked from the room.

Del watched her go and wondered what was wrong. She was . . . upset. Discomposed, disturbed, but in a strange way, one he couldn't explain. His immediate impulse was to follow her, to ask, learn, and put right. But . . . she'd seemed unusually uncertain herself. Perhaps he'd give her a little time.

Fifteen minutes, maybe.

If she'd thought her comment about getting a good night's sleep would keep him from her bed, she would need to think again. If she truly did have a headache, she could sleep in his arms.

With an easy smile for Catriona, who returned the gesture serenely, he ambled across the room to join Gyles and Gabriel in discussing sheep.

The party broke up shortly after Deliah's retreat. Del went to his room, paced for ten minutes—not so much thinking as imagining what might be going on in her red head—then, with a muttered curse against anyone still hovering in the corridors, he opened his door and stalked to hers.

He tapped once, then opened the door. Walking in, he saw her, still gowned and coiffed, drawing the curtains over the window through which she'd clearly been staring.

Shutting the door, he snibbed the lock, then strolled toward her. He tipped his head at the window. "What did you see?"

"Snow. It's still blizzarding."

She'd been waiting for him, that much was clear. Why was less so, given she'd remained fully dressed.

Halting before her, he held her gaze, was about to reach for her when she looked away.

Moved away.

"I really do have a slight headache, you know. Besides"— she waved airily—"I'm sure it's not necessary for us to live quite so much in each other's pockets."

He caught the hand she'd waved before she could drift further. Used it to anchor her as he turned and came up behind her. So she couldn't see his face, couldn't read the confusion, the sudden, leaping need to seize and hold.

Just the suggestion—the faint hint—that she might be trying to draw back, away from him, had been enough to spark it. That rattled him; it seemed the emotional sand was shifting beneath his feet, but he knew in his heart that wasn't truly so.

Something was going on.

In her red head, not necessarily anywhere else.

Heaven only knew what. He didn't, but doubted she would consent to explain.

Shifting his hold, he laced his fingers with hers, felt hers grip unconsciously, without thought. He breathed in, deeply, and the perfume of her hair, of her skin, wreathed through his brain. On some elemental level, reassured.

She was here, in his hold.

Raising their linked hands, sliding them around her waist,

he lowered his head, and murmured by her ear, "Contrary to general belief, sexual indulgence is almost guaranteed to relieve a headache."

"It is?" Distraction and interest, immediate, quite definite, resonated in her voice, but then she cleared her throat and said, "But perhaps we should try abstinence for a change—just to vary our interactions. Perhaps heighten expectations for later."

"That won't work. At least, not for me."

"It won't?"

They could circle all night. He swung into the attack. "Why are you suddenly so skittish? You haven't lost interest, have you?"

"Lost interest? Ah . . ."

"It was a rhetorical question." Raising his other hand, he brushed his palm boldly across the fullness of her breast. Feeling the nipple instantly bead beneath his palm, he cupped the full swell, gently kneaded. "The answer's transparently clear."

Thank heaven.

She'd stiffened, trying to hold firm, but as he continued to fondle, evocatively knead, her spine softened. She leaned back against him. "Perhaps we might experiment, and see." He rolled her nipple between finger and thumb, lightly squeezed. Spine bowing, she gasped, "About my headache, I mean. Whether it goes, or stays."

He touched his lips to her temple. "We can experiment as much as you like." Turning her, lowering their linked hands, he drew hers down. "Because I haven't lost interest in you." He molded her palm to his erection. "To having you—multiple times."

Her eyes widened. "Oh." Then her lids lowered, and those jade eyes grew sultry. Her tongue slipped out to moisten her lower lip. "I see. . . ."

The absentminded murmur was filled with speculation.

"No, you feel." Bending his head, he took her lips, her mouth, kissed her long, lingeringly, hungrily, but not ravenously. When he raised his head, her lids were down, her eyes concealed. "So what do you feel? What do I make you feel?"

She felt as if she were stepping off a cliff. Deliah raised her heavy lids enough to see his face, to note the intentness in his expression, his absolute focus on her.

How long would it last? When would it fade?

How was she going to feel when it did?

Worse, when they returned to Humberside and went their separate ways, and she heard on the grapevine that he'd married? Married some entirely eligible country miss with no scandal in her background, and a soft, sweet disposition. A lady totally unlike her.

She hadn't thought of those questions before today—until half an hour ago. She'd tried to step back, but . . . he was here, in her bedroom, and she was in his arms.

And he was all she'd ever wanted.

How did he make her feel?

Chin firming, she closed her hand. "Wanton. Abandoned. You make me feel . . ." *Desirable.* "Lustful."

His lips curved, sculpted, utterly mesmerizing. "Good. That's how I want you to feel. Wanton, abandoned, and"— he bent his head—"helplessly lusting for me."

❧ Eleven ❧

The kiss ripped her wits away, left her heated and
yearning. There was nothing relaxed about the
exchange, nothing languid, nothing tentative. His
tongue found hers, stroked heavily, probed, dueled when she
responded, then he settled to vanquish and claim.

Straightforward, blatant, direct.

Genuine, honest, and true.

A true expression of what he wanted from her. How he
wanted her.

A declaration of possession, passionate and intense.

She sank her hands in his hair, gripped, clung, held him to
her as her wits reeled and her senses spun.

His fingers found her laces, then her bodice sagged. His
hands claimed her breasts, hard palms kneading, mold-
ing. Fingers clamping, squeezing, sent sensation searing
through her.

Then he broke from the kiss and set his mouth to her
flesh.

And devoured.

As she gasped and drank in each evocative caress, every
provocative, possessive touch.

As her wanton self savored, wallowed and rejoiced.

There was no hesitation—not on her part or his—when,

heated beyond bearing, they broke from the embrace to dispense with their clothes. No barriers, no shields. In seconds they were naked, a heartbeat later skin to skin.

Two heartbeats later, he lifted her and they joined.

She sobbed her joy, wrapped her arms about his shoulders, locked her legs about his hips and let him fill her. Let him stand before the fire and move her upon him until she thought she'd lose her mind.

Then she did, in a scintillating cascade of sensation.

Before it ended, he'd walked to the bed and tumbled them both upon it.

Before she caught her breath, he rose over her. His hips wedged between her widespread thighs, he thrust heavily, deeply, into her.

Then he rode her, fast, hard, determined.

Determined to wring every last gasp of surrender from her.

To take her, complete her, possess her, brand her.

With his passion, his need, his irresistible desire.

His desire for her.

Simple, intense, so strong it stole her breath.

So demanding, so commanding, she could do no other than yield.

Completely, absolutely.

To the depths of her soul.

Del looked down at her face, wracked with rapture as ecstasy claimed her. Felt her let go, felt her fly.

Felt her vulnerable and accepting beneath him.

And he took. Seized and claimed in the most fundamental way. Thrust deep, then yet deeper, driven by a lust more primitive and compelling than he'd ever known.

A lust more commanding, and fulfilling.

A lust driven by an emotion even more powerful, one that subjugated all he was, that made him the supplicant and she the conqueror as he threw his head back and, on a long groan, gave himself, commited all he was and ever would be, to her.

December 17
Somersham Place, Cambridgeshire

Del entered the breakfast parlor early the next morning to find most of the other men already there.

Everyone, it seemed, had hearty appetites.

Taking the chair next to Devil, at the table's head, Del joined them in assuaging his immediate need.

Devil glanced at Del's plate, piled high with ham, kedgeree, two sausages, bacon, mushrooms, onions and a portion of roast beef, and grinned. "You didn't eat so much at dinner. I take it the activities of your night exceeded those of yesterday."

Del grunted.

Already finished, Gyles, sitting opposite, pushed aside his plate. "So, what are your plans for the lovely Miss Duncannon?"

Del frowned at his plate, poked at a mushroom. "Women—ladies in particular—are damned confusing."

The others, to a man, laughed.

"There's nothing you can tell us about that," Demon stated.

"Mind you," Richard said, "they do have a logic of their own."

"Indubitably." Gervase nodded. "It's just that it's so alien—"

"Not to mention convoluted," Tony interjected.

"That it's devilishly hard to recognize," Gervase continued, "and near impossible to follow."

"My advice," Vane said, "such as it is, is not to try. Perseverance, in my experience, usually wins."

Devil scoffed. "And your wife is called what? Patience."

Vane grinned, and responded.

Del let the resulting exchange of jocular insults fly past him. The night had been eventful, although matters hadn't gone quite as he'd planned—something that happened frequently when Deliah was involved.

Something had made her uncertain, tempted her to play safe and try to back away from him, to play down their relationship, yet the night's interludes had left him even more convinced that not only was she the lady for him—the one and only lady he wanted by his side, a helpmate and partner as they constructed their joint future—but, all uncertainties aside, that he was the man for her.

What had caused her uncertainty and made her unsure, he didn't know, but how she could miss, not see, not correctly interpret her own passionate response, her own strength and inner fierceness as she'd clung to him, soft and giving and so elementally all he would ever want in a bride, he couldn't understand.

She was his.

He'd set out to prove that last night. To demonstrate it in actions impossible to misconstrue or misinterpret. But it had been she who had proved his point. She who, at the end, had conquered him by being everything his soul wanted, and all his heart desired.

She'd proved that he was hers.

Regardless, she didn't seem to view their relationship with the clarity he did. With the conviction, the absolute acceptance. Presumably, she hadn't yet thought things through to the same extent he had. She would, he assumed, but the question was when. How long would it take her to realize . . . ?

He wasn't of a mind to give her too long, to wait too long to formally claim her. His response to her retreat—the intense vulnerability that had reared its head and left *him* uncertain, unsure . . . almost wounded—wasn't a feeling he wished to feel again. It had affected him on a level on which he hadn't known he was susceptible, and left him beyond uneasy.

He wouldn't have peace of mind, would not function at his best, if he was distracted by the prospect of her slipping through his fingers and somehow becoming "not his."

That was a prospect he wasn't willing to consider, let alone countenance.

Chasing the last of his kedgeree around his plate, he made up his mind. His original plan had been to wait until his mission was complete before he made an offer, but the hallmark of a good commander was an ability to rescript plans on the run, whenever circumstances changed.

Looking up, he discovered the others had progressed to discussing the likely hunting in coming months. He waited for a lull, then turned to Devil. "What do you know of Wolverstone?"

Devil arched his brows, sat back, and gave him a potted history of the man Del had heard of only as Dalziel. Devil wasn't given to exaggeration, yet his description painted a picture of a nobleman of imposing abilities, a man of action like them, yet one who had, through necessity, been equally active in the political field.

Tony and Gervase volunteered their own views, colored by a closer professional acquaintance.

"I'd trust him with my life," Gervase concluded. "And even more telling, with Madeline's and my children's lives."

Tony merely nodded. "Your mission couldn't be in better, safer, or more effective hands."

Devil added a short description of Minerva, Wolverstone's duchess, and ended with a word sketch of Elveden Grange, Wolverstone's nearby estate. "It's thirty miles due east, this side of Thetford. His visits there are frequent, but irregular—the family normally spend Christmas at Wolverstone Castle in Northumbria."

"So there's no reason Ferrar, even if he knows of him, will expect Wolverstone to be at Elveden," Del said.

Devil nodded. "As soon as the snow thaws enough, I'll send a rider to Elveden to ask Royce what he wants us to do next. Presumably that'll rest at least in part on whether your other friends have reached our shores." He looked at Demon. "Possibly tomorrow, do you think, if we get no more falls?"

Demon, living at Newmarket, knew the area in question

best. He nodded. "I should be able to make it across tomorrow. Not sure I'd trust anyone else to do it, but I'm happy to go."

Gabriel snorted. "You just want to escape another morning with your brats."

Demon grinned. "And I can."

A footstep sounded on the floor above. They all exchanged glances, then Devil pushed back from the table. "That sounds like our other halves are up and about. Might I suggest we retire to the billiard room?"

Chairs scraping on the floor was all the answer the others made. In a general exodus, they made their way out of the door.

Passing through it beside Del, Lucifer caught his eye. "Any chance of examining that scroll-holder? I'm curious as to the construction—it sounds unlike anything I've seen."

Del had heard that Lucifer was now something of an expert on antiques and curios. He nodded. "I'll fetch it and meet you in the billiard room."

Lucifer inclined his head.

Del went with the others down the corridor, then parted from them and went up a secondary stair to his room.

Ten minutes later, Del strode into the billiard room. At the sound of his footsteps, all conversation ceased. Gyles, bent over the billiard table, about to place a shot, froze, then straightened. Devil and Richard, standing by the table, cues in hand, swung around, alerted.

All eyes locked on Del as he halted just inside the doorway.

Grim-faced, he met their questioning gazes. "The scroll-holder's gone."

There was silence for a moment, then Devil asked, "How?"

When Del shook his head, Lucifer asked, "Where was it?"

"In the top drawer of the tallboy in my room. It's not there, nor anywhere else in the room now, and Cobby hasn't seen it since yesterday." One hand rising to his hip, Del plowed the other through his hair. "Before, until Royston, either Cobby or Mustaf—one of my staff—carried it with them, strapped to their body. Once we reached here, there didn't seem any reason not to leave it in the room." He looked at Devil. "How in all Hades did the Black Cobra reach it?"

"Are we sure it's him?" Gabriel asked. "Could the scroll-holder itself have attracted a thief?"

"Unlikely," Gervase replied. "I wouldn't have said it's all that special."

"It isn't," Del said. "It's at best a curiosity. I don't think anyone would imagine it had any intrinsic value."

"So the letter is the only attraction." Gyles met Del's gaze. "But who could have taken it? Could someone unknown have slipped inside?"

"Given the snow, I doubt it." Vane looked at Devil. "But before we go further, perhaps we should check?"

Devil nodded. "Let's go up to the tower and see." Laying down his cue, he headed for the door.

His cousins fell in in his wake. Del, Tony, Gyles, and Gervase all exchanged mystified glances, but the Cynsters strode forward with purpose, so they followed.

Into the central part of the mansion, then up a narrow spiral stair that led up and up, eventually opening into a small square room. Del looked around as he stepped out of the stairwell, and realized they were at the top of the tower that stood high above the Somersham Place roofs. The wide windows on all sides gave magnificent views over the surrounding lands.

It was a tight fit with all nine of them in the tower room. They stood shoulder to shoulder, and looked out. Over an unbroken blanket of white.

"The snow fell the night before last." Devil stood at the windows facing south. "Anyone see any tracks, footprints, signs of a horse?"

"None to the east," Demon said.

"Nor the west," Gabriel said.

"The north is untrammeled, too." Vane glanced at Del. "Whoever took the scroll-holder, they arrived before or on the same night you did, and, most importantly—"

"They haven't left." Devil swung to meet Del's eyes, and smiled in wolfish anticipation. "Buck up, lads—the scroll-holder's still here, and now we get to go hunting."

They repaired to the library to consider the suspects and plan their strategy.

Del paced before the fire. "It has to be one of the staff. The Black Cobra is inventive, relentless, and entirely without morals—the thief might be someone we would normally trust, but they've been threatened, or, as is more frequently the case, their family has been threatened. That's the Black Cobra's style."

"Let's start with the obvious," Gervase said. "How well do you know Miss Duncannon?"

Del stopped pacing, stared at Gervase, then shook his head. "No—it can't be her. Her part in this, her appearance in Southampton, had to have been in train, passage booked at least, before MacFarlane even found the letter."

"But are you sure she is in fact Miss Duncannon?" Tony asked. "The lady you were supposed to meet?"

Del thought of all the snippets of their past lives they'd shared, her intimate knowledge of Humberside and the Wolds. "Yes, it's her. I've known her family since childhood, and I even recall her, albeit distantly, and everything about her fits my picture of what she should be like too closely for her to be an imposter."

"Very well. Not her, then," Gervase said. "If she is who she's supposed to be, then the enemy couldn't have had any knowledge of her before you met her in Southampton, and so couldn't have had any chance of subverting her."

"By the same standard of when the opposition would have known about people currently under this roof," Tony said, "we can exclude all those who traveled here with the various Cynster families—" He broke off, looked at Devil. "But that assumes there was no chance our enemy could have learned the role Somersham Place was to play in Royce's plans earlier—in time to arrange to bring pressure to bear on someone here, or someone who has traveled here. How sound is that assumption?"

"What you're effectively asking," Devil said, "is how secure Wolverstone's plans are, and you'd know that better than I."

Tony grimaced. "More secure than the Crown jewels."

"And in organizing all this"—Devil waved at those gathered around—"nothing was written down. Wolverstone rode over with Minerva—outwardly one of the occasional social visits we exchange when they're in residence in Suffolk. Nothing to alert anyone, even had they been watching, but how the Black Cobra could have guessed what was going on months ago . . ." Devil looked at Del.

Who shook his head. "That's drawing an altogether-too-long a bow. Wolverstone communicated with me by letter, but that was long before we found Ferrar's letter."

"And as for Royce's security," Gervase said, "while he'd be the first to tell us not to count on anything, he was the one we—all his operatives—constantly relied on for absolute secrecy, and he never let any of us down. Why his security would be breached now, by someone who, no matter how brutal, is really not in his league experience-wise . . ." He shook his head. "I really can't see it." He met Del's eyes. "We'll have to look elsewhere for our thief."

"I agree." Tony looked at Del, too. "That leaves your staffs—yours and Deliah's. Let's take yours first. How can you be sure none of them have been subverted?"

Del's impulse was to shrug the question aside, but the matter was too grave. He forced himself to consider what to him was the unthinkable. "Cobby . . . he's been with me for years, from long before Waterloo. I don't think anyone here could imagine him being subverted by the enemy, in this case an enemy of England."

He started pacing again. "Other than him, there's only Mustaf and his wife, Amaya, and Mustaf has been carrying the scroll-holder for much of our journey here. If he'd wanted to, he could have opened the holder, seen the letter wasn't the original, and reported that to the enemy long ago—in which case I seriously doubt the Black Cobra would have been chasing us through Cambridgeshire. The same applies to Amaya—she would have had opportunity aplenty to act before now. No reason for either of them to wait until we're trapped here. And in terms of the cult's usual means of bringing pressure to bear, namely through family members, Mustaf and Amaya hail from a region of India entirely free of the Black Cobra's influence."

Gervase nodded. "So not them. What about the girl?"

"Alia?" Del paused, then allowed, "Normally I would count her as a likely prospect, but she's an orphan, and her only living relatives are Mustaf and Amaya. And Amaya keeps a very close eye on her—she's very protective, worse than any mother hen. It's part of their culture to keep girls close, almost cloistered."

"So no obvious chance there," Richard concluded. "What of Deliah's staff? Do you know much about them?"

Del opened his mouth to reply just as the double doors to the library were sent swinging wide.

Honoria stood in the doorway, eyes narrowing as she surveyed the gathering. "So this is where you're all hiding."

The other ladies ranged at her back.

Devil smiled. "Just in time. Come and join us. Developments have occurred, we have questions, and would value your sage counsel."

Honoria humphed, bent a steely, disapproving look on her spouse, but consented to lead the ladies in.

"We weren't hiding," Demon said, shifting his legs so Flick could sit on the sofa beside him.

Flick poked his shoulder. "Of course not. You'd just forgotten your appointment to entertain your children in the nursery. But never mind. You can fill in the time after their afternoon naps."

The fond papas exchanged glances, but didn't dare moan.

"Now." Honoria had settled in an armchair by Devil's desk. She fixed her imperious gaze on Del. "What are these developments?"

Gabriel caught Del's gaze. "Allow me." At Del's nod, Gabriel swiftly and succinctly summarized the recent happenings.

The ladies were predictably horrified, none more so than Deliah.

She stared all but openmouthed at Del. "You left it in a drawer?"

He shrugged. "It seemed safe enough."

Before Deliah could respond, Tony smoothly cut in. "We've been considering whether any of the staff might have been subverted."

Del leapt in to explain the Black Cobra's usual tactics. "Could any of your staff have been pressured like that?"

"They would have to have been approached either at Southampton, or after we left there," Tony said. "Before then, the Black Cobra couldn't have known that you might be traveling with Del."

Deliah was already frowning. "Bess is English and has been with me most of my life. She's very patriotic, too. I don't think there's any likelihood the Black Cobra could persuade her to anything—she'd be much more likely to report any approach to me, or Del, or you two." With a nod she indicated Tony and Gervase. "As for the others, Kumulay has been with me since I landed in Jamaica—my uncle recommended him as my bodyguard." For the benefit of the others, she explained, "My uncle is the Chief Magistrate of Jamaica. He'd be unlikely to recommend anyone whose integrity wasn't beyond question."

She looked at Del, still standing before the hearth. "Like Kumulay, although they've only been on my payroll for the last few years, Janay and Matara were in my uncle's household for over a decade. They left India long ago and have no family left there."

"Ferrar created the Black Cobra sometime after he landed in India. The cult first surfaced in '19." Del shook his head. "Hard to see how there could be any connection."

"No. I'm sure there's not." Deliah forced herself to consider all the possibilities, no matter how far-fetched. The scroll-holder was too important, not just to Del but to England, too. "The girls—Essa and Muna, Janay and Matara's daughters—would be easy to threaten, but I've seen them both over the last days, and they've been their usual, giggling, bright-eyed selves." She met Del's gaze, then glanced at Tony and Gervase. "You've seen them—you know what they're like. If there's anything the least bit wrong in their lives, no matter how inconsequential, it instantly shows in their faces, in their demeanors. Of everyone here, they'd be the last two to be *able to* carry out any secret or subversive mission."

She looked at Del. "So in answer to your question, no, I don't think any of my people are involved."

Del started to nod, then stopped. "What about the boy?"

"Sangay? What about him?"

Del frowned. "What's his background? Where does he come from? What do you know of him?"

Deliah frowned back. "I don't know where he comes from—I know nothing about him. He's your staff, not mine."

Del froze. "He's not mine." When Deliah blinked, he added, "I—and my people—thought he was yours."

She stared at him. "My people thought the reverse."

"Aha!" Devil rose and, grim-faced, crossed to the bellpull. "It sounds like we've identified our thief."

Webster answered the summons remarkably quickly.

"Tell Sligo and Cobby to report here," Devil said.

"And Mustaf, too." Del glanced at Devil. "He might know more."

"And please ask Janay and Kumulay to come up, too," Deliah added. She met Del's gaze. "They've all been talking to him."

Webster bowed and departed on his mission.

"When did you first notice the boy?" Gyles asked.

Del and Deliah looked at each other.

"He was with us in London," Deliah said.

Del nodded. "I can't recall seeing him before then, but he might have joined us at Southampton."

"That would make more sense," Deliah pointed out. "Our respective households knew each other by the time we reached London. But we left Southampton in a rush—if he was suddenly among them then, they would have assumed, as they did, that he belonged to the other household."

Devil raised his brows. "Quick thinking on his part, if that was so."

A tap on the door heralded those summoned. Sligo led the others in. "Y'r Graces." He bowed, and the others followed suit.

"Colonel Delborough has a few questions about the boy, Sangay." Devil arched a brow at Del.

Briefly, concisely, Del explained the situation—the missing scroll-holder, and the recent realization that Sangay did not belong to either his or Deliah's household.

"He doesn't?" Cobby gave voice to the astonishment lighting his, Mustaf's, Janay's, and Kumulay's faces.

Sligo growled, "The little beggar."

"Wait before you judge, Sligo," Del recommended. "The boy's likely to be a victim in all this." He glanced at Cobby and Mustaf. "You two know how the Black Cobra operates. Any thoughts?"

After a moment, Mustaf volunteered, "I did think he— Sangay—seemed . . ." He waggled a hand, pulled a face. "Oddly quiet for a boy of his years, his background."

Kumulay nodded. "I originally thought he must have been an orphan—that he'd lost his family. He seemed . . . reserved, you would say, and quietly sad. But then I heard him praying for his maataa." He glanced around the company. "His mother."

Del and Deliah exchanged a glance.

"Could the Black Cobra be holding Sangay's mother as a hostage against him stealing the scroll-holder?" she asked.

Del frowned. "I can't see how Ferrar might have arranged that—to be already holding her—not unless, foreseeing a need he couldn't possibly have foreseen, he brought Sangay with him from India." He looked inquiringly at Cobby.

Cobby shook his head. "No Indian boy on the ship Ferrar and Larkins arrived on. Not in any capacity."

"So Ferrar—or more likely Larkins—must have picked him up in Southampton, or even in London. Plenty of East Indiamen in the Pool of London on any given day." Del's face hardened. "And just because the Black Cobra recruited Sangay here in England doesn't mean that Sangay doesn't believe his mother is in dire and imminent peril back in India."

Cobby was nodding, his expression grim. "Young, impressionable, and well out of his league—not even in his own country. Sangay'd be an easy target for anyone who knew what levers to pull."

"Indeed. And the Black Cobra certainly knows." Del looked at Mustaf. "Where is Sangay?"

"He was in the servants' hall when we left to come here."

"I'll go and bring him up," Cobby said.

Del nodded. He dismissed the others with a word of thanks, and they all trooped out on Cobby's heels.

A murmur of light voices filled the silence as the ladies asked questions, seeking clarification on the Black Cobra's heinous tactics. Minutes passed while they listened, then, shocked, exclaimed.

Del inwardly grimaced, and paced before the hearth.

After a while, he frowned, halted, and looked at Devil. Caught his eye. "Perhaps—"

A tap on the door interrupted his suggestion that they ring to find out what was going on. Cobby had been far too long.

At Devil's "Come!" the door opened. Sligo and Cobby walked heavily in. Sligo met Del's gaze, then Devil's, and nodded grimly. "You've guessed it. He's gone."

"Where?" Devil asked.

"That's just it." Cobby looked at Del. "We don't think he's left the house."

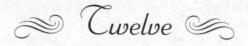

Twelve

*V*erbal pandemonium ensued.

Ignoring all the questions and exclamations, suppositions and speculations, Devil dispatched Vane and Demon, along with Cobby and Sligo, to the tower.

Vane and Demon returned ten minutes later, confirming that the blanket of snow surrounding the house remained unbroken.

"No one's come in, and no one's left." Vane dropped back into his chair. "Cobby and Sligo have gone down to do a quick reconnoiter of the nether regions."

The pair of erstwhile batmen returned fifteen minutes later to report. By then, the rest of them had beaten all the suppositions to death and been left with a large handful of unanswered, and as yet unanswerable, questions.

"Have to say it's dreadful outside," Sligo said. "Not fit for man nor beast. Freeze your . . . toes off, it would, and Sangay wouldn't be used to cold like that, would he? Any roads, the scullery maids said they've found him looking out the scullery window on and off since yesterday morning. That window looks onto the rear yard, and the snow is undisturbed out that way."

"Mustaf and I searched his room in the attic," Cobby reported. "There was nothing there. Literally nothing beyond a comb he'd borrowed from Matara saying he'd lost his own. Sligo found him a page's coat once we got here—poor lad was shivering and said he had nothing warmer to wear. That wasn't in the room, nor was Sangay."

"He's got the scroll-holder and is worried about being caught," Deliah said. "So he's hiding."

Del met her eyes, nodded. "He's quick—he must be to have got this far without any of us suspecting. He must have got the wind up when we called the others up here, and gone off to find a safe place to hide." Del looked at Devil. "The question is: where?"

Devil returned his gaze, then raised his brows. "Strange to say, despite its long past, I don't believe anyone has ever tried to search this house."

"Hardly surprising," Vane said. "The place is immense."

"Well, there's a first time for everything." Honoria looked at Devil. "Ring for Webster. We'll need to confer."

Devil nodded. Richard, the closest, rose and tugged the bellpull.

Demon had returned to the sofa beside Flick. "It's still blowing a gale outside, but there's no snow falling, and the clouds aren't promising more. However, the wind is scouring what's already fallen and blowing it about like the worst sort of sleet. Not even a desperate boy would try to leave just yet. It might be possible by tomorrow, depending on his level of desperation and if it ices over, but today not even Goliath would get twenty yards."

"That's something," Devil said. "So we'll have at least all day to find him and the scroll-holder."

"And we'll most likely need every minute." Gabriel looked cynically resigned. Alathea poked him. He looked at her. "Just being realistic."

"Try being encouraging instead."

Webster arrived, and the talk turned to how best to quarter such a very large house. All the ladies joined in, which drew their menfolk to offer helpful, and in some cases less helpful, suggestions.

At an early point in the proceedings, Devil sent Sligo up to the nursery. He returned to report that all was quiet up there. "The footmen and nursemaids haven't seen or heard anything—most haven't sighted Sangay at all—but now they know, they'll keep their eyes open, and their ears, too, in case he tries to hide somewhere up there."

Still seated behind his desk, Devil nodded, continuing to jot notes on a piece of paper as, with Webster standing behind him, Gyles perched on the desk to his left, Del in similar position on his right, and Sligo and Cobby hovering near, they thrashed out the basic skeleton of an effective search.

Eventually, Devil reached for a heavy paperweight and banged it on his blotter. "Quiet!"

Everyone fell silent. All heads turned his way.

"Thank you." He inclined his head to Honoria, then went on, "We've come up with a reasonable plan of campaign. Webster and Sligo will coordinate a search of the lower levels, and all the servants' domains belowstairs. They'll do that now, first. Once those areas are known to be clear, we'll seal them off by placing footmen or stable lads at all the relevant doors and on all the stairs. There's only so many routes that connect abovestairs with below. By blocking those, we can ensure Sangay can't slip past and get behind the searchers."

Devil glanced around at the attentive faces. "There's no sense in being anything but methodical. Once belowstairs is cleared and sealed off, then all those who normally have business abovestairs and so know the basic layout of the house will start searching, working from the ground floor up. We'll go floor by floor, all the way to the third floor—the attics—if need be. As each floor is cleared, we'll put watchers on the stairs so Sangay can't slip through our net." Devil laid down his notes, looked at the others. "That seems the only way to efficiently and effectively search this place, and we'll need all hands on deck to help."

"Well, of course," Honoria said.

No one disagreed.

"However," Honoria continued, "I suggest that when it comes to us"—a wave of her hand indicated them all—"we should search in pairs. A lady will think to look in places a gentleman won't, and vice versa."

"So we search as couples?" When Honoria nodded, and the other ladies mirrored the gesture, Devil glanced at the males scattered about the room, then smiled in mild acceptance. "That sounds like an eminently . . . sensible idea."

Honoria narrowed her eyes at him.

Devil pretended not to notice.

They decided to have an early lunch while the areas beyond the green baize doors were searched. Cobby and Sligo took charge, leaving Webster to supervise the serving of the meal.

The seating was impromptu, resulting in the ladies congregating at one end, flanking Honoria, with the men at the other, on either side of Devil. There was much discussion in both groups. The ladies' attention centered on the life Sangay must have led to that point, which resulted in a discussion of conditions in India and elsewhere in the colonies. Deliah found herself peppered with questions, most of which she could answer, either from her own experience, or her uncle's, or Del's. Over the past days, she'd picked up quite a lot about the Black Cobra and his nefarious ways.

The ladies' sympathies were all for Sangay. Other than Deliah, all were mothers, and all had baby boys.

They were just finishing the fruit course, a degree of mild excitement burgeoning, when Cobby and Sligo presented themselves. In keeping with the campaignlike atmosphere, they both stood to attention.

"He's not anywhere belowstairs." Sligo sounded unshakably confident.

"We've cleared the attics, as well, Your Graces." Cobby nodded respectfully to the table at large. "It was easy enough to open the doors and see the dust hadn't been disturbed. We left some stable lads to guard the attic doors, just in case, once he hears us searching, Sangay thinks to slip up there."

"Excellent." Devil sat back. "You've done your bit—you can stand down and hold your lines while we do ours." He looked around the table. "So here's what we'll do."

It was a massive house, and they would have only so long before the gray light faded. Searching by candlelight would be that much harder; with that prospect hovering, they were committed to searching thoroughly, yet as quickly as they could.

They'd agreed each floor had to be declared clear before any of them moved on to the next. On the ground floor, Del walked beside Deliah as she bustled down the corridor into the middle section of the wing to which they'd been assigned. Following them, Richard and Catriona were to search the rooms further along, to the wing's end, while Vane and Patience had already disappeared into the room nearest the front hall.

The other couples were likewise spread throughout the house, down each of the main wings, and through the central section around the massive stairs.

Many footmen, all the parlor maids and housemaids, all the ladies' maids and gentleman's gentlemen—anyone familiar with the rooms abovestairs—were assisting, searching the smaller rooms, the service rooms, storage areas and cupboards hidden behind paneling or tucked between the main rooms. Grooms and stable lads, meanwhile, were positioned on all the stairs.

Reaching their appointed position along the wing, Del saluted Richard and Catriona, then followed Deliah into the billiard room.

She'd halted beside the massive table that dominated the room, looking around, taking stock. "There doesn't seem all that many places to hide in here."

"There's cupboards along the side walls." Del pointed out the doors cunningly set into the paneling. "They're deep enough to hide a scrawny boy."

Deliah nodded. "I'll take this side."

Del headed for the other side of the room. Although the billiard table currently held pride of place, this room had originally been a general indoor games room. The cupboards held boards, stacks of cards and assorted paraphernalia associated with various games popular with the aristocracy over the last . . . Del thought it must be something like a century. Some of the cupboards certainly held enough dust.

Across the room, Deliah sneezed, then muttered, "Ugh—there are spiders."

A moment later, she reached the end of her wall of cupboards. Straightening, she noticed the heavy velvet curtains looped back with cords framing each of the wide windows. Each swag of gathered curtain was wide enough to hide a boy.

Walking to the windows, she patted and poked the first curtain, then continued along, subjecting the other curtains to the same treatment.

"No boy." Turning, she arched a brow at Del. "Shall we move on?"

Before he rose, Del looked under the billiard table itself, then he nodded and straightened. "He's definitely not in here."

They only had two rooms to search on this level. The next proved to be a minor sitting room adjacent to the conservatory. The room was relatively small and contained no concealed cupboards. The two sideboards it did contain were easy to search, the few pieces of furniture easy to check beneath or behind.

"He's not here either." Through the window, Deliah could see Vane and Patience going down the avenues between the plants in the well-stocked conservatory. Every so often, one would duck to look under this palm, or behind that plant;

when next she straightened, Patience flung a frowning glance over her shoulder at her spouse. "Perhaps we should help in the conservatory."

Del came to stand beside Deliah. His lips curved as he looked into the glass-roofed room. "I think Vane has it in hand."

Arching her brows, Deliah turned away. "In that case, we may as well wait in the corridor."

As the searchers finished their allotted tasks, all returned to the wide corridors, shaking their heads when others looked inquiringly. Deliah considered the line of people gradually assembling along the wing. Richard and Catriona were strolling back to join them.

Gaze rising, she looked upward, thinking of the bedrooms, sitting rooms, bathing chambers and dressing rooms above. "If I were Sangay, I'd curl up in some unlikely spot—one that might be overlooked."

Del nodded. "I'd wager that's exactly what he's done. And the rooms upstairs provide more scope for that."

Vane and Patience emerged from the conservatory. Vane shook his head. Patience looked down, straightening her gown.

In the distance, Devil's voice rang out. "All clear?"

Vane called back from their wing. They heard Gabriel reply from the other. Sangay wasn't on the ground floor.

"Right, then!" Devil called. "Everyone back to the front hall, then it's up to the first floor."

Like well-ordered troops, they all headed for the hall.

Searching thoroughly ate the minutes; the light was starting to fade by the time Deliah and Del, along with all the others, trudged up the main stairs to the second floor.

All the men were starting to look a trifle grim.

Casting a glance at Del as she went past him into the first room they were due to search—a good-sized bedchamber—Deliah inwardly humphed. "I have to say that, quite aside from seeing a room through different eyes, Honoria was very wise in suggesting we search in pairs." She halted by the foot of the four-poster bed and, hands on hips, surveyed the bedchamber. "At least this way there's a lady with every overpowering man."

Del threw her an uncomprehending frown as he walked to the armoire standing against one wall. "We aren't overpowering."

"Oh, yes, you are—even you. Or at least you'll appear that way to a young boy who knows you're after him." She started with the bed, bending to check beneath it, then patting the pile of pillows and bolsters at its head.

Even though Sangay had some knowledge of Del, Del was still a man of action—a hard, military man. Even though he'd been out of uniform the entire time she'd known him, there was absolutely no chance of mistaking his bearing. Those shoulders, the way he moved.

As if seeking to refresh her memory, without conscious thought she glanced across the room.

Turning from the armoire, he caught her gaze. Held it for an instant, then slowly arched a brow. "What?"

She waved. "Nothing." Suddenly feeling unaccountably warm, she turned and went to the window.

Del watched her pat down the cushions covering the wide window seat, then focus her attention on the swagged curtains. Noted the way her hands fluttered as she fussed. That glance she'd cast him . . . no matter what she said, it meant something. Said something.

Of how she saw him.

Given his resolution of the morning, put in abeyance but only postponed by the search, that—how she saw him—was something he wanted to know. Needed to know.

And, unlike every other couple he'd laid eyes on, he and she had yet to take a break from their searching to investigate other things.

Rounding the bed on silent feet, he closed in on her.

Finished with the window and its accoutrements, she turned—into his arms.

She started, startled, but her body knew his and softened immediately his arms closed around her.

Her widening eyes darted to the door.

Her lips parted—on what protest he didn't need to know.

He swooped and covered them with his, took them in a long, lingering, searching kiss. With slow deliberation he filled her mouth, her mind, her senses, with something he wanted her to think about instead—him.

He kissed, and persuaded. Lured her into the silent communion, then used it.

Used the caress as a means to show her, to reveal and explain and cajole. He let all that he intended, all that he felt, well and flow through the interaction.

From him, to her.

This was what he felt for her, this was what he wanted, what he needed from her. The comfort, the inexpressible closeness, the simple joy.

The pleasure, yes, but beneath that, more important than that, he wanted and needed . . . her.

Just her, being there.

Just her, in his arms.

Just her lips against his and her body surrendered.

Her commitment. To simply being there.

For him.

Deliah couldn't mistake the tenor of his kiss, the truth, the simple honesty, the directness. As if barriers had fallen, as if he'd set some shield aside, she felt immeasurably closer, more linked.

More a part of him.

Sensed that he would be—wanted to be—more a part of her.

Myriad images whirled through her mind. The faint color in Patience's cheeks as she'd left the conservatory, the glint of something in Catriona's fine eyes—and the devilish look in her husband's—when they'd finally congregated on the floor below . . . was this what they'd been doing?

And was that what she and Del were doing now?

Simply being together, a couple together, acknowledging what lay between them . . .

Admitting what lay between them.

Yes, that was it.

She knew it was unwise, but as his lips moved on hers, as his tongue caressed hers, she sank into the kiss, sank her hands into his hair and gave herself over to it. Gave herself up to it. Surrendered.

To the simple communion of two people who shared.

The caress stretched, warm, real. They'd reached some plateau—of reality, of understanding—and lingered there for some time, long enough to feel settled, before, with obvious reluctance, he drew back.

It was with real regret that she relinquished his lips and, with a sigh, returned to the mundane world.

Opening her eyes, she looked into his. Dark, rich, inexpressibly warm, his gaze held her.

Told her. Spoke to her. Reminded her of all they'd just shared.

He'd meant it, she realized. Meant her to see, to sense, to know. To experience and understand how he felt for her.

Her heart swelled with the knowledge that she felt the same for him.

For long moments, they stood locked in each other's gaze, communing silently as they had through the kiss.

A noise—a stealthy shuffle of leather on wood—had her blinking.

Had Del frowning. Raising a finger, he laid it across his lips, then hers.

She nodded. They remained as they were, unmoving and silent. Earlier, locked in the kiss, they must have been all but soundless and motionless for minutes—five, or even more. Long enough for someone hidden to have assumed they'd gone.

But where the devil was he?

Slowly, she turned her head, visually searched one side of the room while Del did the same for the other.

She didn't immediately see it, not even when another slight sound reached her ears. But the sound fixed her attention on the window . . . on the window seat.

Del had turned, too. He studied the seat, then glanced at her.

They exchanged a look, then he nodded.

His arms fell from her. Together they turned and silently crept across the floor to the window.

It was a bay window. Without touching anything, she peered around and out, looking through the side panel along the wall of the house. She saw the window of the next bedchamber along—another bay. It would be identical to the window they were studying, and it told her what she needed to know.

Groping blindly, she grasped Del's sleeve, tugged. Glancing at him, she pointed out of the side window, then silently stepped back.

He looked, saw, but when he turned back to her, incomprehension lit his eyes.

With her hands, she sketched in the air what he'd seen—the protrusion of the bay beyond the wall. It didn't stop at the bottom of the window, as some bays did, nor did it stop at the level of the window seat. The built-out section continued to floor level, including the area between the seat and the floor.

There was a cavity of some kind beneath the seat.

Understanding dawned; Del pointed below the seat, and she nodded.

Carefully, they lifted the cushions off the wooden seat. Del felt with his fingers, and located the hinges set in the wooden top near the wall.

He glanced at her, and reached for the edge of the window seat.

She did the same, grasping the wooden edge.

She drew breath, then together they swung the seat back.

And looked down into a shadowed box, and a pair of stunned dark eyes.

"Aii-yii!" Sangay let out a wail, struggled to his feet, and tried to leap from the box.

Del caught him, initially by the collar, but when Sangay, head down, flailed at him, he grabbed one thin arm, then the other, swung Sangay around and, pinning his arms to his body, hoisted him out of the window seat and stood him on his feet on the floor.

Trapped with his back to Del, Sangay wriggled, squirmed, then tried to kick.

"Sangay!" Deliah loaded the word with command, and was relieved when the boy slowed his struggles to glance at her. "Stop it. You'll only hurt yourself. The colonel doesn't want to hurt you—no one will hurt you if you'll just stand still."

Eyes huge, he stared at her, sniffed.

Then his face crumpled. "Oh, no, miss—you don't understand. The man—the evil sahib—he will hurt my maataa if I don't—" He caught his breath on a giant sob. "If I don't, he will . . ."

Overcome, Sangay opened his mouth to wail again.

"No, he won't." Releasing Sangay's arms, Del dropped a hand on his bony shoulder, gripped firmly. "The evil-sahibs won't be able to hurt your maataa, Sangay."

Very slowly, Sangay turned his head to look up at Del. The dawning, all but disbelieving hope in his eyes was painful to see. "They won't?"

Del shook his head. "I don't think they'll be able to. But to be sure, you'll need to tell us your tale—where you come from, and how you came to be working for the evil-sahibs."

Sangay swallowed, his eyes locked on Del's face. "Only one, colonel-sahib. I have seen only one evil-sahib."

Del nodded solemnly. "I see."

"I didn't want to be working for him," Sangay replied, equally solemn.

"We know that, Sangay," Deliah said. "He told you that he'd hurt your mother if you didn't bring him the colonel's scroll-holder. Is that right?"

Sangay, all round eyes, nodded. "Yes, miss. That is it exactly."

"Where were you when the evil-sahib found you?" she asked.

"I was in London, at the East India Docks. My captain—I was on a ship from India, you understand. First cabin boy, I was, until . . ." Sangay blinked. "My captain sent me to fetch him some tobacco from the shop near the docks. The evil-sahib saw me. He took hold of me and dragged me aside, into an alley. He told me his men had my maataa and she would die a terrible death if I didn't do what he wanted."

Eyes like bruised brown pansies, Sangay shrugged. "So I had to go with him, and he took me in a coach to some other town with ships—then he sent me into the inn where you were staying to find the scroll-holder." Sangay paused, then went on, "Then there was the pistol shot, and then there was the panic, and because I had to search the luggage Cobby put in the carriage, I went with it." He looked up at Deliah, then Del. "With you."

Sangay studied Del's face, then swallowed. In a small voice, he asked, "If I tell you all I know of the evil-sahib, will you let me go, and let me give to the sahib this scroll-holder so he will not kill my maataa?" He shifted, looked down, straightened the sleeve of the page's coat he wore. "I know you don't think he will be able to do that last, but how can you be sure? And"—dragging in a deep breath, Sangay looked up again, into Del's face—"you see, I must be sure."

Del looked down into the boy's big eyes, read the tortured uncertainty that held him. Crouching down so his eyes were level with Sangay's, he said, "We're going to find a way to keep you safe, and also to ensure—make absolutely sure—that your maataa is safe, too. I don't know at this stage exactly how we'll do it, but we'll make a good plan, and we'll make sure." Del searched Sangay's dark eyes, then added, "I'm thinking that killing the evil-sahib would be a good first step. What do you think?"

Sangay's eyes fired, finally came alive with a hint of the

vitality that should be in any boy's eyes. "Oh, yes, sahib. That sounds an excellent plan. That one—the evil-sahib—is definitely by way of needing killing."

"Good. Then that's what we'll do." Rising, Del looked at Deliah, then glanced down at Sangay. "So now we need to go downstairs and talk to the duke and his cousins and all the others, and together we'll work out a good plan."

Sangay actually smiled.

"Well, then." Deliah looked at Del. "I think it's time we told the others they can all stop searching."

Everyone reassembled in the library, including Sligo and Cobby.

"It might help to have the rest of our staffs in, too," Deliah suggested to Del. "Not the girls, but the others. They'll need to understand."

Del nodded, looked at Cobby.

Cobby saluted. "I'll fetch them."

As they resettled on the sofas, chaises and armchairs, two footmen briskly restoked the fire into a roaring blaze while maids bustled about, drawing the curtains. Then Mrs. Hull arrived, supervising a trolley laden with teacups, saucers, and plates piled with biscuits and pieces of cake—and a glass of milk for Sangay. Seated on a straightbacked chair beside Devil's desk, he accepted it gratefully.

The rest of them accepted cups of tea from Honoria, and made their selections from the cakes and biscuits.

From her position on one chaise, Deliah noticed that San-gay's feet didn't even reach the floor, and that he sat with his knees pressed tight, head ducked, as if to quell knocking knees and make himself invisible. She hesitated, then leaned forward, picked up one of Mrs. Hull's justifiably famous jam tarts, rose, and went to give it to Sangay.

He looked up at her, surprised, but then took it with a mur-mured word of thanks.

The tart was gone, every last crumb, before Deliah resumed her seat. She thought it likely Sangay hadn't eaten at all that day.

Then Cobby arrived, ushering in her senior staff and Del's. Both Matara and Amaya stopped by Sangay's chair. Straining her ears, Deliah heard them telling him to be a good boy and answer the sahibs' questions directly—by which they meant truthfully—and all would be well.

As Deliah had suspected, Sangay was comforted by the other servants' presence. Still . . . he remained very much alone on his chair by the desk.

Surrendering to impulse, she rose, set down her teacup and crossed to where another straightbacked chair stood against the wall. She started to lift it. Vane came to help. She directed him to set it next to Sangay's chair.

Once he had, she thanked him with a smile, and sat, then reached out and patted Sangay's thin hand. "All you have to do is what Matara and Amaya told you. Just answer the questions, and everything will be all right."

Sangay met her eyes for a moment, then bobbed his head.

Devil chose that moment to call the gathering to order. "Now we've found our missing young man, let's hear what he has to say." He smiled at Sangay, perfectly innocuously, but Sangay no longer trusted the smiles of powerful men, and there was nothing wrong with his instincts. Deliah sensed the tension holding him increase.

But then Del came around the front of Devil's desk. He relaxed against it and smiled at Sangay.

Sangay looked back. He didn't smile, but his tension eased.

"Sangay, we need to tell these people where you came from, and all that you know of the evil-sahib, the man who bullied you into stealing the scroll-holder." Del paused, then asked, "Incidentally, where is it?"

"In one of the bins in the big storeroom near to the back door, sahib. The bin nearest the back of the room." Sangay started to slide off the chair, but Del waved at him to stay and looked at Sligo and Cobby instead.

"That's the pantry," Sligo said.

"I'll fetch it." Cobby headed for the door.

Del turned back to Sangay. "Meanwhile—"

With a series of simple questions, Del led Sangay through his story. He didn't rush, didn't let the ladies' sympathetic murmurs and outraged exclamations distract him or the boy. Sangay's answers came haltingly at first, but with each point he relaxed and grew more confident, until, when Del asked for a description of Sangay's evil-sahib, an excellent word picture tripped off the boy's tongue.

Del glanced at Devil, seated silently behind the desk. "Larkins."

Devil frowned. "Why so sure?"

"The deeply tanned skin plus the close-cropped hair—not many Englishmen would fit that description."

Devil conceded that with a nod.

Turning back to Sangay, Del saw the question in the boy's face. "I think the evil-sahib's name is Larkins."

Sangay nodded solemnly, and they continued with their questions and answers.

When it came to the man's instructions, and the place where Sangay was to meet him to hand over the scroll-holder, Devil and Demon, the two locals, were unequivocal in their interpretation.

"The big church with the big tower to the northwest can only be Ely Cathedral," Devil said. "And Larkins was wise to warn Sangay not to attempt to get there across country but to stick to the roads. The fenland between here and there is treacherous."

"So," Del said, his gaze on Devil's face, "Larkins definitely wouldn't expect Sangay to arrive at the church until after the snow melts—at least enough to make travel by road possible?"

Both Devil and Demon nodded. "Clearly he knows," Devil said, "that there's no chance Sangay can make it to the church before at least the day after tomorrow."

Del hid a smile. "Just so." The little play had been for

Sangay's benefit. He looked at the boy. "So we have time to make a very good plan."

Sangay said nothing. He shifted, bit his lip. Looked down.

Deliah glanced at him, then looked up at Del.

Del crouched so his head was level with the boy's. "Sangay?"

Sangay lifted his gaze only briefly to Del's face. He spoke in a bare whisper. "I'm afraid, sahib—not for me, but for my maataa. What if the evil-sahib gets angry because I don't come, and then he might think I have failed, and been caught, and so. . . ."

Del welcomed the reassuring noises the ladies made; they seemed to soothe Sangay.

"Listen to me, Sangay. The evil-sahib is a servant for a much more evil man, *but* that much more evil man is here, in England, so he can't give any orders to make anything happen to your maataa. Just think—as neither the evil-sahib nor his master knew it was you they were going to pick to be their thief, they can't have already seized your maataa. You know how long it takes to get letters back to India—you've sailed back and forth many times yourself, haven't you?"

Sangay nodded, but his eyes remained filled with uncertainty. If there was one thing Del was sure of, it was that they—his mission—would need Sangay as a part of any "very good plan," so he persevered. "The master of the evil-sahib won't have sent any word back to India yet—there's been no need, because you've been doing what the evil-sahib wanted. And all those here"—he gestured to those around them—"and lots of others who are helping with this mission, are going to make sure that the evil-sahib's master is too busy to worry about sending any message, no matter what happens with you."

Del could see from Sangay's dark eyes—feel from the intensity of Deliah's regard—that he hadn't yet succeeded in allaying all fear. "And Sangay—regardless of what happens, I'll make sure your maataa is safe. I'm a colonel, you know that?" When Sangay nodded, Del continued, "So, being a colonel, I can send a message back to India, to the Governor-General, who is the man I'm working for, and ask him to make sure that your maataa is safe." He looked into Sangay's eyes. "All right?"

Sangay's fear dissolved into abject relief. "Oh, yes, please, Colonel-sahib. That would be very very good." He hesitated, then said, his dark eyes locked with Del's, "If you will do that for me and my maataa, I will do anything I can to help you capture the evil-sahib and his very evil master."

Feeling relieved himself, Del allowed his features to ease into a smile, and rose. "That's good—very good. Now"—he glanced at the other servants standing by the wall—"these gentlemen and I will need to sit down and make our plan. While we do, you can go down with the others to the servants' hall. You must be hungry."

"Oh, yes, Colonel-sahib. I am famished." Smiling, Sangay slipped off the chair. He turned, and Matara waved him on ahead of her. With a little bow to Del, then another to the company, Sangay hurried to join the other servants as, with welcoming smiles for him, they filed out.

When the door shut behind Sligo, Del looked at Devil. "It's not hard to see what we should do."

Steepling his long fingers, Devil inclined his head. "If the Black Cobra or one of his senior henchman is going to be waiting in Ely Cathedral for Sangay to bring him the scroll-holder, I suggest we give him what he's expecting." He smiled, all teeth. "And just a little bit more."

Del smiled back, equally predatorially. "My thoughts exactly."

There were nothing but assenting sounds from the other men. The ladies, too, led by Deliah and Honoria, were in a distinctly bloodthirsty mood.

Of necessity they had to allow for the weather, but ultimately their plan wasn't that hard to formulate.

Execution, however, was another matter.

❧ Thirteen ❧

December 18
Somersham Place, Cambridgeshire

he next day went in preparation.

At first light Demon, rugged up to the teeth against the bitter cold, rode out on the strongest horse in the stables—Devil's Sulieman. Anyone who knew Demon would expect him to ride into Newmarket to check on his racing stables. That was his overt goal, his initial destination.

Once he was certain he wasn't being followed, he would continue on to Elveden Grange to alert Royce to the developments and report their plan. If possible, Demon would return that evening in time to join the group going to the cathedral.

After an early breakfast, all the other men adjourned to the library. All the Cynsters were familiar with the cathedral, but Tony, Gervase, Del, and Gyles didn't know the interior. Defining exactly where each of them would hide once inside, given they had to both protect Sangay and block all the numerous exits, wasn't straightforward. In the end, Devil drew a detailed plan.

"As you can see"—he turned the sketch so the others,

gathered about his desk, could more easily view it—"the cathedral's both large and complex. The nave runs west to east. It's extremely long, the longest in England, and the only place inside from which you can see all the principal doors is from the center of the octagon under the tower, which is where the altar sits. In other words, there isn't any single concealed position that will allow us to cover even the main entrances. In addition, there's umpteen smaller rooms off the various transepts, and some of them have external doors."

He pointed to various areas on the sketch. "There's a lady chapel and two chantry chapels at the east end. We have a presbytery here, and choir stalls separated from the nave by a screen. There are stalls between four pairs of pillars in the octagon. In the south transept, we have the cathedral library on one side and the vestries on the other. The north transept contains two chapels on one side and another chantry chapel at the end. And right at the east end of the cathedral we have the chapel of St. Etheldreda. The prior's door—here, off the south aisle of the nave—is one example of the many unexpected entrances."

"So our evil-sahib chose well." Gyles glanced at Del. "That suggests he knows the area."

"He's probably visited," Del said. "As Ferrar's gentleman's gentleman, he would have stayed from time to time with Ferrar's father's household. I've heard the Earl of Shrewton spends his winters on an estate at Wymondham, outside Norwich."

"So Ferrar himself would be familiar with the place?" Lucifer asked.

"Almost certainly. He was born at Wymondham."

At that point, the ladies, having risen somewhat later from their beds, joined them. They asked questions, glanced at the sketch, reiterated that Sangay had to be kept safe, then subsided in various chairs and sofas around the room. Many had brought pieces of sewing, knitting, embroidery and the like to keep their hands busy while they listened.

The men all looked at them.

Honoria waved a haughty hand. "Carry on."

The men exchanged glances, then turned back to the desk and got down to business, placing themselves like pieces on a game board, then assessing how well the arrangement satisfied their criteria.

"Not easy," Tony concluded. "Covering all the exits is difficult enough, but because of this octagon with the altar at its center, to sufficiently protect Sangay we'll need at least three men close in—inside the octagon, or within a few steps of it."

They all looked at the sketch.

"The octagon's definitely the place to stage the handover," Devil said. "It gives us the best chance of catching whoever comes to get the scroll-holder, Larkins, Ferrar, or both. Anywhere else is more problematical."

"True," Richard allowed. "But Tony's right—we need three men to cover that area. And there's no way to have three men that close without them being seen."

"Disguises." Gervase glanced at Devil. "I don't suppose there's any chance of laying our hands on some monk's robes?"

Devil met his gaze, then looked down the room at Honoria. "Monk's robes?"

She raised both brows. "We have some, certainly. In the costume box, I think." She rose. "I'll go and hunt them out."

"I'll help." Catriona rose, too.

"Three would be useful," Devil called.

Honoria waved as she headed for the door.

Del studied the sketch. "Let's assume we can place three men in monk's robes close. Where, exactly?"

They worked that out, then, once Honoria and Catriona had returned with three passable monk's robes and they'd been tried on and approved, with those three deployments settled, they made final judgments on their other positions. Lastly, they worked out who would go where.

They each had their strengths. In the end, it was decided

Tony, Gervase, and Gyles would be the monks. Their primary aim would be to protect Sangay. With a glance toward the ladies, Del added, "At all costs."

All the rest had only one aim, one goal. "We concentrate on apprehending whoever comes to fetch the scroll-holder."

Gabriel frowned. "What are the odds Ferrar, or even Larkins, sends a foot soldier? All that's required is to pick up a scroll-holder from a boy, after all. No urgent need to risk getting caught themselves." He looked around at the others. "Surely by now Ferrar has realized that the critical point in Wolverstone's plan is to tempt him to show his hand, and through that action to connect himself irrevocably with the scroll-holder, and therefore with the letter it supposedly contains?"

Del forced himself to weigh the chances, but then shook his head. "No. It'll be Larkins who comes. He'll definitely be there. Whether Ferrar will come, too, is anyone's guess. Consider. Larkins has been the one throughout to deal with Sangay. He told Sangay he'd be there, and I'm sure he will be if for no other reason than to make sure Sangay hands the scroll-holder over and doesn't get confused by someone he doesn't recognize and instead slip away.

"In addition to that, Ferrar knows the letter—the real one—is damning. He won't risk such a thing falling into the hands even of one of his cultists. He'll send someone he trusts implicitly—Larkins—or he'll come himself."

After a pause during which they digested that, Vane asked, "So what are our chances of getting Larkins—presuming it's he we catch in our trap—to point the finger at Ferrar?"

"Reasonable," Del said. "Larkins has been with Ferrar for years, and has relished his time in the upper echelons of the Black Cobra cult. But when faced with the choice between a rope or transportation? I'd say it's more likely he'll cooperate than he won't."

Del looked down at Devil's sketch, at their planning represented by the crosses and notes marked on it. "If we can hobble the Black Cobra before the others have to wrestle through his coils, I'll be more than content."

"As will we all," Devil said.

An "indeed," followed by soft "hear, hears" from the sofas, chaises and armchairs further down the room had the men exchanging uneasy glances. They were planning a dangerous foray, and their ladies were listening. All were aware of the looming problem. Only Tony and Gervase were immune.

But they had to make their plans, and there was no point trying to hide that—or the plans themselves—from the ladies.

Devil and Del studied the sketch of the cathedral yet again.

"Even though there'll be ten of us—assuming Demon makes it back in time—we'll be spread thin," Del noted.

"True," Devil returned. "But at least there are plenty of places to hide once we move away from the altar and that end of the nave."

"One eventuality we haven't considered," Tony said. "What if he comes in force?"

Standing beside Devil, his fingertips brushing the desk, Del considered, eventually said, "I can't see it. If I had to wager on it, I'd say he'll come alone, or with only one, or two, others. More, and he'll risk attracting attention—"

"Given the cultists are Indian," Deliah put in from the nearest sofa, "it's likely he won't want them seen. They create too much notice. People will look, and remember which way they go."

"Indeed." Devil sat back, looked up at Del. "So we assume we'll be facing no more than a handful, all most likely Englishmen."

Del nodded. There seemed nothing more to add to their plan of action for inside the cathedral. Talk veered to the logistics of getting into position without alerting the enemy.

"A night march." Lucifer sighed resignedly. "I'd hoped I'd left such horrors behind me."

"At least," Gabriel said, "there won't be a bloody battle-field at the end of it."

Ultimately they agreed they would leave at four o'clock

the next morning. Despite the hideous hour, they would still have to travel by a circuitous route to make sure they didn't inadvertently pass the enemy's bolt-hole, wherever that might be.

"In order to circumnavigate the fens"—Devil pointed to the areas on a map he'd spread on his desk—"Chatteris, Horseley, and Langwood Fens, we'll need to go up to Chatteris, then toward Sutton, but turn off onto minor lanes before we reach the village, and then progress by minor routes until we reach Ely and come down to the cathedral from the north."

"What about Sangay?" Honoria asked. "You can't seriously be thinking of having him walk that distance, not in this weather."

"He'll catch his death," Catriona stated.

No one argued.

"I've thought of that." Del turned to face the ladies. "We'll have Sligo and Cobby dress as laborers and drive a loaded cart away from the place, apparently heading for the market in Ely. Sangay can hide in the back beneath a blanket, as if he's stowed away. They'll take the obvious route via Earith, Sutton, and then the main road directly east to Ely. That way they'll approach the main street from the south. There'll be an inn there they can stop at. Cobby and Sligo will go in as if for a late breakfast, leaving Sangay to slip out of the cart and over the lawns into the cathedral."

"With the scroll-holder," Gervase added.

Del nodded. "Exactly. If Larkins is watching for him as he said he will be, he'll see him, then he'll follow him inside."

"That will work," Devil confirmed. "There's an inn perfectly situated across from the cathedral, and the area between the street and the main cathedral door is open ground—easy to spot a boy scampering across, especially one dressed as Sangay will be."

The men glanced at the ladies. As a group, they nodded approvingly.

"And once inside the cathedral, there'll be three of you

watching over him—all within easy reach?" Deliah arched a brow at Del.

He nodded. "He won't be alone, and he'll know that."

Inclining her head, appeased, she transferred her attention to the ball of yarn she was rolling.

Interpreting the ladies' subsequent silence as permission to proceed, the men huddled closer and quickly revisited the details of their plan one last time. Then, at a look and a nod from Devil, Vane stepped back from the desk, with a glance enlisted Richard, Lucifer, and Gabriel, then the four strolled the short distance to stand in a line, chatting with the ladies.

Distracting them as Devil, Del, Gyles, Tony, and Gervase left the room.

As the five men made their way to Devil's study, Gyles sighed. "Honoria noticed."

"So did Francesca," Devil returned.

Gyles pulled a face. "Fifteen minutes, do you think, before they hunt us down?"

"If we're lucky."

They wanted to work with Sangay, to rehearse him in his role, without the distraction of the ladies. Not that the women would distract Sangay that much. The evasion was more in the nature of self-preservation.

Gaining the study, Devil sent Webster to fetch Sligo, Cobby, and Sangay. When the three presented themselves, expectant and eager to learn of their roles, Del took them through the plan, explaining their strategy, then settled to take them, step by step, through the parts the three of them would play.

He'd reached the point where the cart with Sangay hidden in the back reached the outskirts of Ely, when he was interrupted by a light rap on the door.

They all looked at the innocent panels.

Although Devil didn't respond, after an instant's hesitation the knob turned, the door opened, and Deliah walked in.

After one comprehensive sweep of the room, her gaze settled on Sangay. "Are you all right, Sangay?"

Del managed not to roll his eyes.

Sangay's innocent reply did more good. Bright-eyed, he nodded excitedly. "Oh, yes, miss. I'm to be a part of the plan, too. The colonel-sahib was just telling me."

Switching his gaze back to Del, Sangay waited, eager and attentive.

Del looked at Deliah.

She looked back, eyes narrowing a fraction, then closed the door and came forward to sit in a chair near Sangay's. "I'll just listen, too."

Sangay looked perfectly happy. Del squelched his own reaction, and calmly continued with his rehearsal of their plan.

When he got to the point of Cobby and Sligo leaving the cart and going into the inn, and Sangay slipping out and on his own going into the cathedral, Deliah frowned . . . but, thank heaven, kept her lips shut and allowed him to continue.

Del was at pains to stress to Sangay—and therefore to Deliah, representative of the ladies as she indubitably was—that once he set foot in the cathedral, Sangay would have numerous men protecting him, three of whom would be devoted to ensuring he came to no harm. Del was permitted to continue outlining the plan to the point where Sangay handed the scroll-holder to the evil-sahib, or whoever came to fetch it from him.

"And then," Del said, holding the boy's dark gaze, "you run. As if the devil was on your heels. You run to one of these three gentlemen." He pointed to Tony, Gervase, and Gyles. "They'll be dressed in these robes."

Gyles held up one robe, displaying it. "We'll look like monks, and have the hoods up, but you'll know it'll be us."

Sangay nodded, eyes wide as he surveyed the three large men. He turned to Del. "So they are to be my body-guards?"

Recollecting that in India, people of high rank often had bodyguards as a mark of status, Del smiled. "Exactly. Just like a maharajah, you'll have your very own bodyguards."

Sangay was clearly beyond delighted.

"And," Gervase said, "just like all those who have bodyguards, when in a dangerous situation, you must do exactly as your bodyguards tell you."

Round-eyed, Sangay nodded eagerly. "Oh, yes, sahib. I will do exactly as you and my other two bodyguard-sahibs say."

Gervase inclined his head, endeavoring to keep his lips reasonably straight.

"Good." Del reclaimed the stage. "Now you should go downstairs with the others. There's nothing more you need to do today. Cobby will wake you in the morning when it's time to leave. He'll have the scroll-holder for you to take."

"Yes, sahib." Abruptly assuming a serious mien, Sangay wriggled down from the chair, then bowed solemnly to Del, then Devil, and lastly the other three men.

Then, his smile blooming anew, he hurried to join Cobby.

Grinning himself, with a neat bow for the company, Cobby led the boy from the room. Sligo followed, closing the door.

Del had been watching Deliah. She was still frowning slightly.

He was trying to predict why, what part of their plan failed to meet with feminine approval, but just as she raised her gaze to his face, the first gong for dinner echoed through the house.

Gyles stepped in. With a charming smile, he gave her his hand to rise, and, with a wink over her head for Del, bowed her out of the door.

Demon walked into the dining room just as they were preparing to address the main course. He grinned, paused to drop a kiss on his wife's upturned cheek, then slid into the chair beside her. Helping himself from the platter of roast beef Webster immediately offered, Demon informed them, "It was very dirty riding, but the sky looks to be clear of snow. Temperatures are up. The roads will be passable and people will be on the move as usual tomorrow."

"Excellent." Devil smiled. "So our plan can go ahead."

"What did Wolverstone say?" Del asked.

Demon grinned wolfishly. "Short and sweet. By all means proceed, then we're to come on to Elveden with whatever prey we manage to trap. He'll be waiting."

Del felt satisfied expectation bloom in his chest. A familiar feeling, one he'd often experienced on learning he'd see action soon. "Any word on the other three couriers?"

"Yes, and no," Demon replied. "You'll be the first to reach Elveden, but another of your comrades, Hamilton, has landed in England. He's in Surrey at a safe house there."

"Probably Trentham's estate," Gervase said.

Demon nodded, swallowed. "That was the name." He looked at Del. "Now that Royce knows you're about to land on his doorstep, he's sent word to Hamilton and his escort to come on. According to Trentham, Hamilton has a Miss Ensworth with him."

Del choked, coughed, then managed to wheeze, "The governor's niece? How the deuce did she come to be with Hamilton?"

Demon shrugged. "Royce doesn't know the details. Sounds an interesting tale. Apparently she's been with him since Aden. He came up through Alexandria, then Marseille to Boulogne, where apparently they ran into quite a bit of action, but eventually they got to Dover, where two of your crew"—Demon nodded to Gervase and Tony—"nabbed them and whisked them into hiding."

"Hamilton's a good man," Del said. "Any word of the other two?"

"Not that Royce mentioned," Demon replied. "I took it to mean he hasn't yet heard."

After dinner, the men gathered in the billiard room.

Devil looked up as Vane, the last to join them, came in and closed the door. "How are we situated?"

Vane gave him a wry grin. "We're safe enough for the moment. They've got their heads together, doubtless planning an early morning jaunt."

Del had been wondering if Deliah might attempt such a thing. Now he looked his horror. "Not all of them?"

Devil just looked at him as all the others with wives nodded. "Every last one, which brings us to what we need to plan now. How to stop them."

"We only need to delay them for a few hours," Richard pointed out. "Long enough to make sure they can't reach the cathedral in time."

"We could lock them in their rooms," Demon suggested.

"Alathea can pick locks," Gabriel said.

"So can Francesca, I think," Gyles put in. "Whatever we do has to hobble all of them, and effectively, or those who get loose will release the rest."

"What about blocking their access to transport—in this case, horses?" Lucifer suggested. "Order the stable staff to sleep in. The ladies can't follow us if they can't get beasts saddled or horses put to."

Demon humphed. "Flick can saddle anything with four feet. And she's perfectly capable of organizing the others to put horses to gigs."

"Catriona can, too," Richard said. "Forget that tack."

They all thought. Hard. Some of their suggestions were wildly fanciful. By and large, all were impractical.

Devil drummed his fingers on the billiard table. "We only need to stop them from following us and arriving early morning, before or during the action. It would be useful, in fact, if they arrived at Ely after the excitement, say by ten or so. That way we could go on to Elveden all together—an inclusion to salvage some hope of our continuing felicitous matrimonial existence."

There was silence for a moment, then Vane admitted, "That's a serious consideration. No need to court unnecessary retribution by excluding them from sharing whatever triumph we reap."

"What we need," Gyles stated, his gaze locking with Devil's, "is to stop them from leaving their beds before dawn."

Lucifer waggled his brows. "Surely *we* can manage that."

Gabriel snorted. "Sadly, determination can overcome a great deal. We can't rely on exhaustion to accomplish what we need. We have to have something more certain."

"Indeed." Devil's tone was decisive. "And as we've just demonstrated, when it comes down to it, there really is only one way."

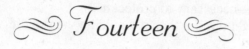

Fourteen

December 18
Somersham Place, Cambridgeshire

L ater that evening, Del made his way to Deliah's bedchamber, Devil's strategy for dealing with the pending problem posed by the ladies wishing to join them circling in his brain.

It was, by any measure, an outrageous proposition, yet it would work, and he couldn't think of anything else that might.

Every male linked with one of the aforesaid ladies had sworn to do their part. Only Tony and Gervase were excused. Yet while all the others—being married to their respective ladies—were in a sound position to weather the resultant and inevitable storm, he stood on significantly less firm footing.

Unless he took steps to shore up his position *before* he put Devil's plan into action, he would risk losing all. Losing her. That was not something he wished to contemplate. It was certainly not a situation he would accept.

Ergo, it was now imperative that he take the necessary steps—to offer for her and secure her, and through that gain the right to protect her at all costs. Once she'd agreed to be his, she couldn't argue with him doing everything—and anything—necessary to protect her.

She might try, but then it would be she standing on shaky ground.

Reaching her door, he paused, conscious at some deeper, rarely stirred level that, aside from all else, it was somehow now fundamentally important for him to know she was unquestionably his—declared to be his—and that she was safe. He needed her to somehow balance him; she was now essential to the framework of the life he wanted to live.

She was crucial to his future, and not having her agreement to be that critical and necessary part of it wasn't a situation he could any longer accept.

Before he went out to face the Black Cobra, he needed to know she would be there—his—when he got back.

Determination hardening to resolution, he reached for the knob and opened the door.

Firelight flickered inside. A single candle was burning on the table by the bed. Beyond its glow, the rest of the room lay in deep shadow.

Deliah was waiting, already in her nightgown with a warm shawl draped about her shoulders to defeat the winter chill. Arms folded, she'd been standing before the hearth gazing at the fire. She turned as he entered, and smiled.

That smile embodied everything he wanted, not just for tonight but for every night for the rest of his life.

He returned it as he crossed to halt before her. He looked into her eyes as he drew her into his arms.

She held his gaze. Searched it.

Read something in his eyes—saw something of his resolution, his purpose. Head tilting, she parted her lips—

He bent his head and kissed her. Gathered her closer as, after an instant's surprise, she responded. Ardent as always, instantly willing to follow his lead, to waltz into the fire and the flames with him.

To let mutual passions flare and burn.

The last thing he needed was for her to ask questions—not yet, not now. So he kissed her to distract her.

Then he realized, and kissed her to persuade.

To convince.

To woo.

She was supple and giving in his arms, all feminine curves and lush challenge. Raising her arms, she wound them about his neck and kissed him back, enticing and provoking. His arms locked as she pressed against him, into him, and his world narrowed and condensed.

To just this. To her, and all he'd found in her arms.

To her, and all he felt for her.

Sunk in her mouth, his tongue dueling with hers, he seized the moment, used it to show her.

What she meant to him.

How much he needed her, wanted her, desired her.

Deliah read his message with ease, but when he lingered, holding her in the kiss, letting the exchange stretch until her wits and senses spun, some part of her wondered.

Some tiny rational part of her mind looked, and saw. Sensed and felt with every heartbeat something deeper. Some element she hadn't seen, or hadn't noticed, hadn't felt before. It didn't feel new, just . . . more.

Even as she sensed it, and wondered, he pressed deeper, tasting her, inciting her to taste him, to drown in the flavors she now knew so well—him, all heady masculinity and passion, strength, desire, and the promise of possession.

All there, all familiar, yet there was a deeper thread running beneath all. A powerful current that fed all the rest, that gave the rest life.

For the first time she could touch it.

Stroke it, know it.

Welcome it as his hand closed over her breast and, pulling back from the kiss, she gasped.

Eyes closed, head back, she drew that novel power in with every racing beat of her heart as his hands, hard, possessive, sculpted her curves. Arousing, yet not driving.

This was lovemaking with a different slant. With something else in the mix. Something he was letting rise up and fill him, and pour into her.

It was glory of a different degree. It took desire and passion, hunger and need, and gilded them. Made them shimmer with meaning, with purpose.

She drank it in, focused on each and every caress. Every explicit act of claiming. Reveled in the heat, the deeper warmth that suffused every inch of skin, and sank to her bones.

Raising her heavy lids, from beneath her lashes she studied his face. His features were set, harshly passion-etched, his lips a firm, unyielding line, yet his eyes as he surveyed the bounty of her breast, filling one of his hands, held an expression of . . . reverence.

Possession, too, but there was a deeper joy, a deeper appreciation beneath.

Before she could concentrate and identify the impression, he saw her watching him. He bent his head and took her lips again.

Again swept her away on the familiar tide . . . but slowly.

As if their heartbeats were counting the bars, marking time.

He waltzed her to the bed, but before he could tug away her shawl, she stopped him with a hand on his chest. He paused, but didn't break the kiss.

She seized the moment, and slowly—still keeping to that deeper, slower, compulsive beat—pushed his coat off his shoulders. Unwound his cravat and let it fall from her fingers, unbuttoned his waistcoat and pushed it away. Spread her hands over the fine linen of his shirt, traced, unlaced, then pulled the tails from his waistband, slid her hands beneath to find his heated skin, and stroked, caressed.

Del broke from the kiss, and drew the shirt off over his head. Watched as her eyes fastened on his chest, watched them gleam, watched her lips curve with feminine greed and blatant anticipation.

She touched him. Spread her small hands and possessed.

He let her, captive to some compulsion he didn't fully understand, yet he was the one who had let it free. His pulse drummed in a slow cadence—powerful, controlled, all passion and driving need held subservient to that greater force.

Together, they dispensed with his trousers, his stockings, his shoes, until he stood naked before her.

He reached for her, needing the promise of her body against his. She came, but with one hand on his chest, stayed him from locking her against him. Looking down, she closed her other hand about his jutting staff.

Caressed, possessed.

Deliah traced his heavy erection, took it in her palm and stroked down, up, then she ran her fingertips around the bulbous head.

And he shuddered.

She glanced up, and their eyes met. Gaze to gaze in the candlelit gloom, the dark pools of his eyes drew her in. Held her. Even as she cradled him. Then she felt him tug at her shawl; this time she let it go. Let him divest her of shawl and nightgown, let him pull back the covers, lift her and lay her down, and join her.

He drew the covers over them, creating a cocoon of warmth, a cave, a place that, with the firelight flickering over the walls, was safe and theirs. She'd expected him to join with her immediately, but he propped himself on his elbow beside her, leaned over her, captured her mouth once more with his, filled it, her mind and her senses, then set his hands once more to her body.

Stroked, caressed . . . worshipped.

There was no other word to describe what she felt, what she sensed through his touch. He'd never made her feel less than desired. This night he made her feel . . .

Loved.

Cherished.

Desired not just in a physical sense but on some deeper emotional plane. While one part of her mind scoffed at such thoughts, at such an interpretation of his motives, another part saw, and knew.

She felt it in her heart, recognized it in every slow beat of his.

Sensed it in the rise of their pulses as desire thundered anew.

As passion rose and claimed them, and he lifted over her, spread her thighs with his, and filled her.

Completed her.

As she took him in and gloried.

Del wasn't holding the reins. He'd given them over, ceded all control, surrendered to the compulsive force that was the reality of what he felt for her.

That was the reality of why he needed her.

Giving that reality free rein had been easier than he'd thought—showing her, letting her see. But now it whipped them both, raged through them both, leaving them blind, deaf and consumed, victims to the fire raging in their blood. To the molten heat, to the need to be one, caught in the inexorable drive to consummation.

Their blood pounded in their veins, and glory beckoned.

Desire lifted them on a wave of raw, exquisite, mind-numbing sensation.

Ecstacy sharpened, heightened, brightened, then exploded.

And they shattered, fragmented.

She screamed his name as she clung and fell.

He smothered a roar in the curve of her throat as he followed.

They spiralled back to earth through the fading brightness, to the comfort of that familiar golden sea, to satiation and completeness.

And, he suspected—he hoped—to a deeper understanding.

Never had he felt so utterly wracked with pleasure.

Never had the act been so deeply fulfilling.

Never had he felt so vulnerable—as if he'd placed his heart and his soul in her hands.

* * *

Deliah didn't immediately sink into sated slumber. Sated she was, to her toes, yet . . . curiosity niggled. What had changed? And, more importantly, why?

He'd dropped his guard completely, lowered all inner shields, and given her honesty—emotional honesty. With a compelling sincerity he'd shown her what he felt.

But why? Or rather, why now?

From the depths of her mind surfaced the thought that tomorrow might well see the end of his mission. If, as she suspected he would, he decided to stay in Cambridgeshire to wait for his friends to reach safety, he might well send her north with an escort.

Once his mission was over, there would no longer be any further danger to her, no further need to keep her with him.

Was this—tonight—their last time? The last night they would share?

A species of dark panic bloomed inside; she felt it grip her throat, black and strangling.

His fingers touched, traced her forehead, her temple, her cheek.

She opened her eyes, and fell into his.

Searched them frantically. Waited, breath bated, for him to tell her their time together was over.

His gaze remained unwavering, rock-steady and sure.

"I want you to marry me."

She opened her mouth, arguments jostling on her tongue— then his words registered.

And her world spun.

She blinked at him. "W-what?"

He frowned, then tried, not entirely successfully, to banish the expression. "You heard me. You can hardly be surprised . . ." His frown deepened as he studied her face, her eyes. His jaw firmed. "I want to offer for your hand— whatever the correct form of words is, consider it said."

She gaped at him.

Del gave up trying to lighten his frown. "Why the devil are you so surprised?"

Surprise, shock—utter astonishment—were writ large in her eyes and invested every line of her face.

"Ah . . ." Finally she found her tongue enough to say, "I wasn't expecting you to propose—that's all."

"All?" He blinked at her. If she hadn't been expecting . . . his frown turned to a scowl, and he came up on one elbow so he could glare down at her. "We've been sharing a bed for nearly a week. What sort of gentleman do you take me for?"

"The usual sort."

He stiffened, but then she waved as if to erase the words. "No—wait. Let me explain."

"Please. Do." He bit off the words.

He felt almost insulted when, wriggling up on the pillows the better to meet his glare, she vaguely patted his chest as if to calm him.

She stared down the bed, unseeing for a moment, then slanted him a glance—one filled with such uncertainty, such vulnerability, that he nearly weakened and gathered her to him to comfort her.

But he needed to hear what she was going to say. Needed an explanation. Needed her answer to his offer.

Needed to make sure she accepted.

"What?" he prompted.

She bit her lower lip—such an un-Deliahlike action that he nearly broke. "Are you really . . . I mean, did you really mean . . . what you just said? That you want me as your wife?"

There was some problem; he could see it in her eyes. Feeling grimmer by the second, he nodded. "I wouldn't have uttered the words if I didn't. Why?"

She drew in a breath. Held it for a second, then in a rush said, "Are you sure?"

"Deliah—" He held on to his frustration with an effort. Nodded again. "Yes, I'm sure."

"Oh."

When she stared at him, perplexed, he drew patience to

him. "Earlier, you said you thought I was the usual sort of gentleman—implying that the usual sort of gentleman wouldn't want to marry you. Why did you say that?"

"Because they don't. Gentlemen—the usual sort—never marry ladies like me. I've been told that more times than I can count. And—"

"Who told you? Your parents?" Her parents, as he recalled, were strict and highly conservative—and she'd been the bane of her mother's life.

"My parents, my aunts, my cousins—everyone."

"Meaning everyone in a tiny pocket of the Wolds north of the Humber." He caught her eyes. "That's a very small, isolated, and, in this regard, narrow-minded part of the world."

She held his gaze, then her lashes flickered and she looked away. "There's more."

She was already married. She was a convicted murderess. She . . . clinging to patience, he asked, "What?"

Looking down, she picked at the coverlet lying over her breasts. "You know I wasn't a virgin."

He'd noticed, in passing as it were, and been cravenly thankful he hadn't had to mute his lust, or hers, to ease her through her first time. "You're what? Twenty-nine? I would have been more surprised if you had been."

She flicked him a frown. "It was only a few times with one young man, when I was twenty-one." Her gaze grew distant; then she looked down. "He was the younger son of a viscount, on a repairing lease, although I didn't know that until later. He was dashing, and charming, and I thought . . ."

"You thought he loved you?"

She nodded. "And I thought I loved him. I didn't—I know that now—but I was young and naïve and I thought . . . so when he wanted me, I agreed. I thought it was all part of our courtship."

"Only it wasn't?"

"No. A week later—after quarter day had come—I

heard he was leaving, going south again." She dragged in a tight breath. "I asked him about us—what would happen. He laughed." Her voice grew bleaker. "He told me I was a fool—that no gentleman in his right mind would ever marry a lady like me. I was a Long Meg, I was too sharp-tongued, too headstrong, too independent. I was too *everything*—no one would ever have me."

"He was wrong." Del made the statement unequivocally. She'd lived with that judgment, that belief, for eight long years. A species of fury boiled up inside him. "What is this younger son of a viscount's name?"

"The Honorable Melvin Griffiths. But he's dead now—he died at Waterloo."

Sparing Del the need to beat the bastard bloody. "Good."

Her lips twisted; she glanced at him. "That's what I thought, too."

He nodded. When she said nothing more, he asked, "Is that all?"

She met his gaze, surprise in hers. "Isn't that enough?"

"To make me change my mind about marrying you?" He shook his head. "So, will you marry me, Deliah Duncannon?"

She held his gaze for a long moment. Hope and uncertainty warred in her eyes. Then, in a small voice she asked, "Why do you want to marry me?"

He could see all sorts of reasons, surmises, hovering in her mind—waiting for him to confirm them. That he felt he should because he'd ruined her in the eyes of his friends by sharing her bed. That he felt he owed it to her parents—and his aunts—to make an honest woman of her. That . . . there were dozens of reasons she would consider more likely than the simple truth.

Some part of him was horrified, but he didn't hesitate.

"I want to marry you because I love you." Cupping her face in one palm, he looked into her eyes, held her gaze steadily. "I love you, and want you and only you as my wife precisely because you're not the common sort of lady. You're more. You're everything I need, everything I want, everything I must have to build the future I want—a future I couldn't even see until we met."

He paused, watched dawning belief lift the clouds from her jade eyes. "We belong together, you and I. Marry me, and together we'll create a future that's ours, that's rich and vibrant, exciting and fulfilling."

She raised a hand, touched the back of his. "You make me believe."

"Because I believe—that I love you, and that you love me." The twin facts were enshrined in his heart. Set in stone and immutable, they simply were. "So—will you do it? Throw your lot in with mine and see what we can make of life together?"

Her lips slowly curved. To his horror, tears filled her eyes.

But she was smiling.

"Yes." She blinked, blotted her cheeks as the tears overflowed, then laughed at the look on his face. "I told you I didn't love Griffiths—I know I didn't because what I felt for him was nothing, simply nothing, to what I feel for you."

She sniffed delicately, then smiled mistily up at him. "So yes, I'll marry you. I'll put my hand in yours"—she suited the action to the words—"and see where life takes us."

He stared at her for a moment, then the wondrous reality finally impinged. "Thank God," he said.

And kissed her.

She laughed through the kiss, wound her arms around his neck—and kissed him back.

December 19
Somersham Place, Cambridgeshire

He was still freely thanking all beneficent deities when, in the wee small hours by the faint light of a waning moon, he stetched an arm from beneath the covers and managed to snag his coat from where they'd left it lying on the floor. Deliah slept on, warm and snug beside him. Quietly going ockets, he withdrew the silk scarves he'd poked

pping the coat, he turned to her.

She murmured sleepily when he reached over her to tie one long scarf to the bedhead on that side. He dropped a kiss on her temple, another on her bare shoulder as he drew back.

To anchor the second scarf more or less above where his head had been, it was easier to move over her and settle between her thighs—they parted welcomingly, her hips cradling him instinctively.

He reached up, secured the second tether.

Instinctively rocked his hips against her, the head of his erection seeking, finding, sliding into scalding wetness, penetrating her a fraction as he tugged the scarves tight.

After that, it was easier to slide slowly home. To feel her come awake beneath him as he filled her.

To feel her softness fully surrendered, and to instinctively take what was offered.

To bend his head and, as he rocked, find her lips with his. Cover them. Fill her mouth, helplessly yielded, and take that, too.

To lay claim. In the quiet of the night with the dark enfolding them, to love her.

Slowly, silently, she crested beneath him, her cries as she fell from the peak muffled by his lips. He felt the inexorable tug, the clenching of her sheath along his length, but this time resisted the call.

This time waited until she slumped, boneless and spent, beneath him.

Then he withdrew from her.

It was the work of a moment to lash both her wrists, one in each scarf. Dazed, still floating, she turned her head and watched him secure the second, then she looked at him.

Even in the dimness, he could sense her question.

In answer, he reared back on his knees, grasped her hips

and flipped her. He drew her down the bed just enough for the scarves to pull taut, enough to keep her arms extended, her wrists higher than her head.

Then he lifted her hips, rearranged her long legs so she was kneeling on the bed, too, bent over her knees, her arms stretched before her.

He touched between her thighs, found her wet and weeping, set his groin to the luscious curves of her bottom, guided his erection to her entrance, then thrust powerfully into the scalding slickness.

And let instinct rule.

He took her as he wished, hard and deep, slow and thorough, until passion rose and swamped him. Until it drove him, ruthless, relentless, to, with his hands sunk into the bedding on either side of her shoulders, pump into her and fill her.

She shattered again, her strangled cry fracturing the silver silence of the night.

Her body clutched, spasmed, caressed. Lured . . .

He let go, let her take him. With a roar he muffled in her hair, let ecstacy wrack him.

Until he slumped, as boneless as she, over her.

He couldn't move, had no strength he could yet command to lift from her. Freeing one hand, he brushed her hair from her face, glanced down at her features.

Noted their softness, the satisfied—sated—curve of her lips.

He remained where he was, savoring the lingering clutch of her body, until he had full command of his limbs. Then he gently drew back from her, reached over her head and tested his restraints, then he slid from beneath the covers, letting them resettle over her.

She woke as his weight left the bed. Watched in silence as he rapidly gathered his clothes. Frowned as he started donning them. "Where are you—" She blinked; straightening her legs, she slid around to fully face him, the scarves twisting as she did. She peered at the window. "Is it time to go?"

He glanced at his fob-watch, then slid it back into his waist-coat pocket, reached for his coat. "It's nearly four o'clock."

She tried to sit up, but the scarves held her back. Frowning even more, she looked at them, tugged. "You forgot to untie me."

He stepped into his shoes, and didn't say anything.

Slowly, she turned her head and looked at him, suspicion dawning in her face, her breasts swelling in incipient outrage, mounding above the upper edge of the covers.

"It was that, or lock you all in your rooms. We thought you'd prefer this way, so Bess—and the other lady's maids—can release you when they come up, and you can join us at Ely once the action's over." Voice low, he hurried on, "We thought you'd like to see what the outcome was, and go with us to Elveden."

"Well, of course we want that, but . . ." She tugged at the bonds. "We were supposed to go with you—as you well know."

"No, you weren't." He took a step back.

It wasn't just outrage that lit her face. "You can't leave me tied up like this!"

"Not just you—all the ladies."

She stopped struggling, stared again. "All?"

He saluted and backed another step. "Every last one. So there's no point shrieking or calling for help. Everyone left on this level will be tied up, too."

Turning, he had his hand on the doorknob when she said, "Delborough, so help me, if you leave me here like this, I'll . . . I'll . . ."

On a muttered curse he swung back into the room. Returned to the bed, leaned over her—and kissed her soundly.

"Be good." He was at the door before she'd managed to draw breath. With a last salute, he opened it. "I'll see you at Ely." He walked out and shut the door behind him.

Listened. An ominous silence was all he heard.

Lips twisting, reassured by her promise to be his wife, he strode down the corridor.

Returning to his room, he quickly changed into breeches, boots and donned a heavier coat, then rendezvoused as arranged with the other men at the bottom of the main stairs. Devil was the last to join them, still shrugging on his coat as he came, a grin still lingering about his mobile lips. He waved them all on, then fell into step beside Del.

There was a strong sense of déjà vu as they strode out to the stables and saddled up. They'd done this before, he and Devil at the head of a group of men, many of whom were Cynsters, going out to face an enemy.

And bring him down.

They led their horses out to the stable yard, mounted, all but oblivious to the icy breeze, the crisp crust on the cobbles, the coldness of the white drifts all around. Cobby and Sligo had come out to see them on their way.

In his saddle, Del looked up at the window behind which Deliah lay.

Sated, but almost certainly stewing.

Very likely planning retribution.

But that was for later.

With everyone mounted, Devil looked at Del. Grinned. "Lead on, Colonel."

With an answering grin, Del wheeled his horse and smartly led the way out.

December 19
Ely, Cambridgeshire

In an icy misery of overwhelming dampness carried by a desolate, sleeting wind, the group reached Ely in the last of the long night.

Leaving their horses tethered in a field outside the town, they slipped through the shadows in twos and threes, approaching the massive bulk of the cathedral from the north, as planned.

The main doors would be unlocked, but they didn't want to risk being seen. Gabriel picked the lock on one of the side doors, and they slid quietly inside.

To Del, who had been inside only once decades before, the cathedral, with its soaring arches and massive walls, felt like the belly of a sleeping stone giant. They all walked slowly around, getting their bearings and familiarizing themselves with the layout, with the numerous corridors, major and minor, the rooms giving off them, and, most importantly, the location of the doors that led outside.

Finally, wraithlike, they drifted to their assigned places.

The soft slap of their footsteps on the stone floor ceased.

They settled in for a long wait.

Silence descended.

Fifteen

December 19
Somersham Place, Cambridgeshire

$\mathcal{D}$ eliah roused from a fitful sleep to find Bess supervising one of the housemaids making up the fire. A glance at the window, at the narrow slit between the curtains, showed the faintest trace of gray light outside; it was barely dawn.

Courtesy of her earlier, futile efforts to loosen Del's silken bonds, the pillows now hid said bonds from view. She'd look as if she'd simply fallen asleep with her arms splayed out. Which was what, furious and defeated, she'd eventually done.

She feigned sleep until the housemaid left. Then she called Bess. "Don't ask questions—just come and untie me."

"*Untie* you?" Eyes wide, Bess hurried over.

Deliah raised her arms, displaying the scarves wound about her wrists.

Bess's eyes widened even more. "Oh, my."

"No questions." Deliah waggled one wrist.

Bess fell to picking apart the knot securing it.

Del had gauged the bonds so while she'd had some play in

her arms, she hadn't been able to reach one hand to her other wrist, and undo the knot herself. She'd tried every contortion possible, to no avail.

When Bess had both her wrists free, she nodded with what dignity she could muster. "Thank you."

Sitting up against the pillows, she rubbed her wrists, then noticed Bess was frowning. "What?"

Her expression disapproving, Bess gathered the scarves and set them on the dresser. "I don't know as I hold with tying up, no matter the reason. I had thought the colonel quite gentlemanly." Bess was quite a few years older than Deliah, and occasionally, when she deemed it necessary, could become quite motherly on Deliah's behalf.

Deliah waved Bess to her robe. "If you must know, he tied me up so I couldn't go with him, or follow him to the cathedral. Not until all the action is over—then, mind you, I'm supposed to join him. Huh!"

"Oh." Returning to the bed with the robe, Bess looked thoughtful. "So he was protecting you—that's why he tied you up." She held up the robe as Deliah slid from the bed. "If that's the case, I don't suppose I can hold it against him."

Belting the robe, Deliah leveled a narrow-eyed look at her maid. "You don't have to. *I'm* holding it against him enough for us both."

With a frustrated humph, she headed for her washstand. "Incidentally, apparently it wasn't only me who was tied up. You might slip downstairs and make sure all the other lady's maids have gone up to free their mistresses."

Bess had followed her. Deliah heard a smothered giggle from behind her, then Bess said, "Yes, miss. I'll just slip down, if you don't need me for a moment?"

With haughty grace, Deliah inclined her head.

Left alone, she washed, then poked in her armoire, wondering what to wear.

Wondering how she felt.

Her principal conclusion was that she felt far too much.

Elated because she and Del were to marry—that he loved

her, actually *loved* her! Her, the lady with so many character flaws that no gentleman was supposed to be able to overlook them.

But perhaps that was what love was, what it did? Presumably it was love that made Del overlook all her flaws . . . no. He'd said he loved her *because of,* not in spite of, her unconventional traits.

Even better. The fiend.

He loved her, and he'd made her love him—set her free to openly love him. She'd already loved him before, but now . . .

Now she loved him unreservedly.

And now she was worried. Now she was afraid.

For him. The damned man had gone off to face who knew what without her to watch his back. No her to step out of a carriage with a sword this time. So who was going to distract the enemy for him today?

She pulled out a forest-green pelisse, frogged with gold braid, that she'd yet to wear. That he'd paid an exorbitant sum for it was a point in its favor. Tossing it on the bed and resuming her hunt for a gown to go beneath it, she reminded herself that Del had the other men with him.

Presumably Devil and the others would watch his back, as she had no doubt he would theirs.

But . . . this loving someone, being free to love someone and therefore fall victim to all the accompanying feelings, was new to her.

Fear for another—another who now meant a very great deal to her—was new to her.

And she wasn't at all sure she liked it.

She pulled out an elegant gown in pale green wool. It had long sleeves and was closed to the throat. If she was to go to the cathedral, she would need all the warmth she could wear, and hadn't he said something about going on to Wolverstone's residence afterward? In which case, she'd need the elegance, too. Laying the gown on the bed, she went to find underclothes.

Bess returned, breathless. Deliah suspected it was from laughing, not running.

"All the other maids have gone up and freed their mistresses. The duchess has called a meeting in the breakfast parlor as soon as maybe—they're rushing to serve breakfast now—so we'd better get you dressed and ready." Bess hurried to help her tie off her petticoat, then lifted the gown over her head.

Gowned and laced, Deliah sat at the dressing table, let Bess brush and braid her hair, and wondered what the other ladies thought. She strongly suspected they'd be as unimpressed with their spouses' actions as she was with her spouse-to-be's.

While she'd lain in the bed tied to the headboard waiting for dawn to arrive, she'd had plenty of time to consider the timing of Del's offer for her hand. Being a spouse-to-be gave him certain rights—one of which he'd claimed mere hours later.

Had he made the offer so he would have the right to do what he felt he had to to protect her? Was that why he'd offered for her hand?

The uncertainty tried to insinuate itself into her mind. She considered it, but rejected it. Felt confident enough to reject it. Del was too practical a man to, as it were, sacrifice his future merely to protect a woman he considered to be in his charge—a woman he had no real feelings for. He could have tied her up without her promise to marry him, risking her wrath and subsequent alienation, if he'd had no feelings for her. If he hadn't wanted a future with her.

She remembered enough of his words, his declarations of the night. He'd been sincere and absolute in his wishes and wants, his view of them together as the cornerstone of his future.

And the very fact that he'd gone to exceedingly domineering lengths to protect her was an irrefutable indication that he did, indeed, harbor strong feelings for her.

But she didn't like being tied up, helpless to help him.

That, she was going to make very clear, simply would not do.

"There." Bess slid the last pin into place. She glanced at the pelisse. "Will you be going out later?"

"Yes." Deliah rose, tweaked her gown straight. "And I suspect it will be sooner rather than later."

Turning, she headed for the door and the breakfast parlor. "I'm going to see what the other ladies think."

On more than one front.

"So he proposed, and then he tied you up? Congratulations!" Eyes twinkling, Alathea beamed at Deliah. "On the proposal front, I mean. As for the rest." Wryly, she glanced around the table. "Welcome to the club."

Deliah glanced at the other ladies gathered about the long table in the breakfast parlor. All seemed to share Alathea's sentiments. "So we really were *all* tied up?"

Nods and affirmations came from every occupied seat. It transpired their men had been rather inventive in their choice of restraints—silk scarves, cravats, silk curtain cords, even silk stockings.

"And," Honoria said, eying them all from her position at the end of the table, "not one of us got free. For that, they'll all have to pay."

"Hear, hear," echoed around the table.

Having discovered, the instant she'd smelled food, that she was ravenous, Deliah made steady inroads into the selections she'd heaped on her plate, and tried to assess the other ladies' thoughts and intentions. In the end, she simply asked, "What do you mean by pay?"

Honoria's fine gray eyes came to rest on her face. "After behaving in such a high-handed fashion, they'll expect us to react. They'll be expecting us to extract our ounce of flesh"—she paused to smile—"in one way or another. And, of course, we will, not least because we would never want them to believe we'd grown resigned, or, heaven help us, were no longer annoyed by said high-handed ways."

"If they ever thought that, we'd be in dire straits." Patience sipped her tea.

"But," Deliah allowed her inner frown to show, "you don't seem all that annoyed. You *do* seem rather resigned. Much more so than I. When Del first left, I was furious."

"That's because you're new to this . . . for want of a better description, emotional game." Phyllida toasted Deliah with her teacup.

"The emotional game of being married to a strong, dominant, possessive—and protective—gentleman," Flick added. "Sadly, you can't take the protective-to-a-serious-fault characteristic out of the mix. It's an inescapable part of who they are—the sort of men they are."

"Exactly." Chin propped in one hand, Alathea nodded. "If we want all their other characteristics exactly as they are—as we do—then we have to accept their sometimes overactive protectiveness."

"Especially," Catriona said, "when you realize that that protectiveness, and its sometimes extreme nature, is a direct reflection of how much we mean to them." She smiled at Deliah. "They're really quite simple and straightforward in that way."

"Mind you." Honoria set down her teacup with a definite click. "That docs not mean that they get to exercise that protectiveness to the extreme without paying us our due." She met Deliah's eyes. "Over the years, we've grown increasingly shrewd. Anything you ask—and if you're wise you can extend the boon time to quite a few days—he'll feel forced to grant."

"To make up for his high-handedness," Flick explained. "I once managed to get Demon to take me to a horse fair he never would have countenanced me attending otherwise."

Alathea nodded. "I've managed to get Gabriel to more than one ball on the strength of an overprotective incident."

Catriona smiled serenely. "And then there's the other, more personal benefits."

All the ladies smiled in what was clearly fond memory, and equally fond anticipation.

Deliah blinked, imagined. . . . "I see."

"Indeed." Honoria folded her napkin and laid it beside her plate. "And, of course, they're all together."

"We would be much more exercised if it was any of them alone," Phyllida told Deliah, "or even just two of them against unknown others."

"In this case," Honoria said, "we don't need to actually worry for their safety—they're as safe as they could be even were we there to watch over them. However, while I will admit us being anywhere near the cathedral while they're dealing with this Black Cobra person would distract them utterly—and we don't want to forget they have Sangay to protect—there's no reason I can see that we shouldn't arrive the instant the action's over."

"Which by my calculation," Patience said, "means we should leave as soon as possible."

"My thoughts exactly." Flick glanced around the table. "So—how many horses, how many gigs?"

Del sat on the floor of one of the stalls around the octagon in Ely Cathedral and prayed he wouldn't get a cramp. At least the stall floor was timber, not stone. The cathedral—so much massive stone in the depths of winter—was as cold as the proverbial tomb.

Waiting for time to pass—it was exactly like being on picket duty. Not that he'd been a picket all that often, let alone recently, yet at least in war, there was an element of omnipresent danger to help keep one alert. Here . . . they all knew nothing would happen until after Sangay arrived.

Which would be shortly, Del hoped. Shifting silently in the confined space, he pulled out his fob-watch. It was almost nine o'clock. Outside the stained-glass windows of the octagonal tower, it was full daylight—or as full as the light was going to be that day.

Settling back into his hunched position, he found himself staring at the hilt of his sword. The sheathed blade lay on the floor beside him. He had a loaded pistol, too. Many of them had elected to carry one, just in case Larkins resorted to firearms. The cultists, thank heaven, abjured such weapons on some convoluted religious grounds, which was all to the good. He had no doubt that, regardless of how many came to the cathedral, his side would see victory, at least of a sorts, that day.

He was in a mood for victories. Succeeding in gaining Deliah's promise to marry him had meant more to him than he'd thought it would. He'd intended to ask her regardless and had told himself he'd been asking then because of the necessity of his mission—because he'd needed the right to ensure she didn't arrive at the cathedral too soon.

While all of that had been true, he'd needed to know she was his on some much more crucial, personal plane. Knowing she'd agreed had filled him with a . . . certainty. A jubilation, an assurance and an absolute conviction that this—all of this—was proceeding exactly as fate decreed. Exactly as it was supposed to be.

His only remaining uncertainty was a small, tiny, niggling one. He hoped his and Deliah's exchange of promises would be strong enough to stand against the inevitable ramifications of his morning's actions. He hoped she'd understand that he'd simply had to do it, that given what she meant to him, he'd had no choice.

Regardless, he thought, as he shifted awkwardly again, he couldn't regret tying her to the bed. She was safe, and in his new world—the future he'd taken his first steps into last night—that, to him, was the most important thing.

A loud creak had him raising his head, listening, straining his ears.

Light shafted above his head, then slowly faded as the sound of a heavy door closing reached him.

Someone had just entered through the main doors at the end of the nave. Sangay? Or someone else?

Carefully shifting into a crouch, he slowly raised his head, until he could look out over the front lip of the stall. His line of sight was across the octagon, past the altar, and down the nave. He could see Gervase in his borrowed monk's robe seated halfway along a pew three rows from the front, head bowed, apparently deep in prayer. Glancing to his right, Del saw Tony, also garbed as a monk, all but invisible, seated at prayer in the shadows of one of the stalls across the octagon from Del's position. Gyles, the other monk, Del couldn't see, but he knew Gyles was sitting or kneeling in prayerful attitude beyond one of the columns on the other side of the nave.

Whoever had entered had hesitated at the far end of the nave. Thinking of how awestruck Sangay would feel in an edifice that struck awe into the hearts of grown men, Del prayed the boy would remember his instructions.

Assuming it was he.

Finally, on slippered feet, the newcomer crept slowly up the central aisle. It was Sangay.

Del exhaled. Watched as the boy, still wary, but with increasing assurance—presumably he'd sighted his bodyguards—made his way to the second pew from the front, and slid into it to perch at the end by the aisle.

Everything was in place. No matter how he strained his ears, Del could hear not even a shuffle to give away the presence of the other men concealed at various points inside the cathedral. Even the monks were as still and silent as statues; in their gray robes in the shadows, they were difficult to see unless one looked directly at them.

Sangay looked around, scroll-holder in clear view in one hand. Seeing no one frightening, the boy settled on the pew.

He didn't have long to wait. As they'd surmised, the Black Cobra had had someone watching the cathedral, too wise to get trapped inside. Less than two minutes had passed when a door somewhere opened and shut, then footsteps—confident and assured—came striding in. They were coming from the south transept, past the vestries.

Whoever had come to fetch the scroll-holder would appear through the massive archway on Del's left. He ducked down, peered through a narrow gap he'd found in the front paneling of the stall.

Held his breath.

A man—large, heavy, close-cropped dark hair—Larkins!—strode into the octagon.

Del looked at Sangay. The boy's eyes had widened, locking on Larkins. To his credit, Sangay didn't do the one thing that might give their game away—he didn't glance at any of his bodyguards.

Instead, even though he was visibly trembling, he gamely stood and slipped out of the pew. And halted, waited. There, at the top of the long nave, in the middle of the central aisle, the scroll-holder clutched in one thin hand.

As they'd hoped, Larkins saw no reason not to go to Sangay. The boy was the epitome of unthreatening. Larkins slowed, but didn't break stride, almost swaggering as he crossed to halt before the boy, towering over him.

Watching Larkins from behind the man's back, Del couldn't see his face, but he saw no evidence of a glance to either side, no indication Larkins had even noticed the monks. None of them had been, or were, in his immediate line of vision.

Larkins looked down at Sangay. "Well?" His voice was rough, dark with suppressed menace.

Sangay ducked his head respectfully. "I have brought the scroll-holder as you wanted, sahib." Sangay offered it up, balanced across both his palms.

Unseen by Larkins, Tony slid silently from the stall in which he'd been sitting and, sword in hand, glided to the altar. Gyles appeared, hovering just behind the column to Larkins's right. Gervase held his position, apparently as yet unseen, but he was closest to Sangay—he would be the last to move.

"Good." Reaching out, Larkins took the scroll-holder. He turned it in his hands, examining it. Then his fingers flicked and tugged, releasing the six levers. Opening the unlocked holder, Larkins slid the single sheet of parchment from within.

Ignoring Sangay, still standing before him, Larkins unrolled the letter. The decoy copy. Half turning so the light from the tower windows above fell on the sheet, Larkins quickly perused it. Then he smiled.

Del caught the satisfaction in that smile—also saw the evil anticipation infusing Larkins's features. He tightened his grip on the hilt of his sword, felt his body tense.

Still turned away from Sangay, Larkins slid the letter back into the scroll-holder, closed and locked it, then put it into the pocket of the heavy coat he wore.

Focused on securing the letter and holder, Larkins missed seeing the three monks draw closer.

Focused on Larkins, Del didn't miss the glint of light along the blade the bastard drew from the pocket into which he'd dropped the holder.

"Run, Sangay!"

The order rang out from multiple points around the octagon as Larkins turned and lunged for the boy, but Sangay had already yelped and danced sideways, avoiding Larkins's grasping hand and his deadly knife.

Leaving Larkins momentarily off-balance.

Before the heavy man could recover, Sangay shrieked, *"Ai-ai-ai!"* and fled—flew—past him, straight to Tony, rounding the altar some paces beyond Larkins.

Larkins whirled with a roar—then gaped. Froze at the sight of Tony, monk's robe thrown back over his shoulder, sword raised, his other arm clamped protectively around Sangay's shivering shoulders.

Larkins's eyes widened. He looked to the left, toward the north transept, and saw Gyles move out from behind the column.

Larkins whirled to face down the nave.

Only to find Gervase waiting, sword in hand, in the middle of the aisle, with Vane coming up behind him.

Larkins took a step back, then swung to the south—to the corridor through which he'd entered. He'd already taken a step before he registered that Del stood there, blocking that route of escape. Demon hovered in the shadows behind him.

Meeting Larkins's eyes, Del saw recognition flare—felt grim retribution curve his lips as Larkins stared.

Then Larkins glanced around, and bolted.

Tony had grasped the moments of Larkins's distraction to draw Sangay back to safety beyond the choir screen. Larkins thought that meant the east corridor was unguarded—mistakenly.

He ran into Gabriel and Lucifer, avenging angels with swords in their hands. Larkins saw them a few steps before it would have been too late. He slid to a halt, then reversed direction and came pelting back toward the altar.

One glance down the north transept revealed Devil and Richard, coming up fast to corner him.

With a scrape and a hiss, Larkins drew a long cutlass from beneath his coat, then swung to put his back to the altar, facing them all, menacing them all, a snarl distorting his features.

None of them were impressed.

"No need for any heroics." Del stepped forward. They had Larkins exactly where they wanted him, trapped in the octagon. Their plan was to take him alive so he could talk about his master. And none of them were all that keen to even wound him literally on the altar.

However, Del doubted Larkins possessed any such reciprocal sensibility.

Larkins had one hand on the altar as, head slightly lowered, he stood watching Del. Larkins could possibly vault onto the altar. Standing atop it, he'd have something of an advantage, but, regardless, he couldn't—wouldn't—escape them.

Rather than prolong the standoff until Larkins sensed their reluctance, Del switched his sword to his left hand, intending to make use of his pistol to capture Larkins.

Larkins saw the move. Desperate, he thought to capitalize. Raising his sword high, he uttered a bellow—

"Good *gracious*! What's going on?"

All of them jolted. All of them swung to look.

At the two middle-aged ladies who had appeared behind Devil and Richard. Both ladies had huge flower-filled urns in their arms.

Between them, a pace behind them, stood a cleric, the vicar. He'd halted, blinking myopically toward the altar. "Great heavens! Is that a sword?"

Behind the vicar, the door through which the trio had come stood open.

The next actions happened in the blink of an eye, but to Del, viewing them, time slowed.

Like all of them, Larkins had swung to face the intruders. As Del saw the open door, so did he.

Del saw Larkins's body shift, knew what he was going to do. With a muttered curse, he stopped reaching for the pistol in his pocket, grasped his sword in his right hand and started forward.

Just as Larkins's sword arm started to rise again.

Larkins raised his sword above his head, with a roar swung it wildly—and charged.

Devil and Richard had no choice. They turned. Ducking one shoulder, each grabbed one of the women, and in a shower of water, flowers and urns, to ear-splitting screams they hoisted them and rushed them back down the corridor, beyond the door through which they'd come, to safety.

His way cleared, Gyles leapt in and hauled the vicar to him, sword raised, sparks flashing down its length as he used it to ward off Larkins's roundhouse slash.

Then Larkins was through, past, and racing for the open door.

Del raced after him, but wasn't close enough. Larkins barreled through the door, then whirled and slammed it shut.

Just before his shoulder hit the panel, Del heard a key grate in the lock.

The door was like the cathedral—solid. The heavy iron hinges were even more so.

Together with Gabriel, Del rammed his shoulder to the panel, but it didn't so much as shake.

"Wait—wait! I have a key." The vicar, visibly shaking, came shuffling up, hauling a massive key ring from his robe. There were at least twenty keys on it. "Now . . . which one is it?"

The keys jingled as he sorted through them.

Del shifted his weight, glanced at the others. "Go out and around." Because of the risk of being seen, they hadn't dared post anyone outside.

Gervase, Vane, Lucifer, and Demon rapidly headed out, through the octagon and down the nave—the fastest way to the outside of that part of the cathedral.

Devil came up, sword in hand. "Reverend, is there an external door in that room?"

The vicar glanced up, blinked, then smiled. "Why, my goodness. St. Ives, isn't it?"

"Yes," Devil said, unsmiling. "Is there an external door in there?"

The vicar glanced at the door. "Well, of course. That's how we came in."

Someone muttered a poorly smothered expletive. Richard and Gabriel started after the others.

The vicar glanced their way. "But there's no need to worry—I locked it after us. I had no idea you were chasing a madman, but he won't be able to leave by that door."

Richard and Gabriel halted, then slowly came back.

"I always lock that door," the vicar said, returning to his keys. "It's the parish office, you see. I wouldn't want just anyone poking around in there—ah!" He held up a key. "This is it."

"Allow me." Devil took the key, fitted it in the lock, turned it. They all heard the bolt click back.

The vicar obligingly stepped to the rear.

Devil exchanged a glance with Del, who came to stand by his shoulder.

Devil's lips quirked. "Just like old times."

Sword in one hand, with a twist of his wrist Devil opened the door and sent it swinging wide. Del stepped through first. Devil followed on his heels to stand shoulder to shoulder with him, blocking the doorway.

Del's first thought was that there was no one in the room. All he saw was the open window alongside the locked outer door.

A large casement window fully open, the gap was more than wide enough for a man, even one as large as Larkins, to easily escape through.

Then Del's gaze lowered, and he realized Larkins hadn't got away.

What in his peripheral vision he'd seen as a shadow on the floor before the window was in fact a body.

Larkins, on his back in an unnatural sprawl.

Both Del and Devil had seen death often enough to know Larkins was dead even before they reached him.

As they did, Vane appeared in the window. He looked in, swore softly.

"Search," Del told him. "Whoever did this has only just left."

Vane met his eyes. "We saw the open window. The others are already looking. I'll pass the word, but so far we haven't had sight nor sound of anyone beating a hasty retreat."

With that, Vane went, leaving Del to look down at Larkins, at the ivory-handled dagger jutting out of his chest.

"Whoever did that knew what he was doing." Devil nodded at the knife, then stepped over Larkins's legs to the window.

"Oh, yes." Del crouched, laid his sword aside. "The Black Cobra is exquisitely well-versed in dealing death."

"So Ferrar, do you think?" Devil asked, examining the window ledge.

"He would be my guess." Methodically, Del went through Larkins's pockets, shifting the big man to check every section of the heavy coat.

Devil humphed. "Well, it's clear enough what happened.

Ferrar, if it was he, was watching. He saw Larkins come to this window. Before Larkins could climb through, Ferrar got here."

Del rose. "Most likely Ferrar watched the action from outside—easy to peer through those small segments of clear glass set between the stained glass. With the light so weak outside, we wouldn't have seen him even if we'd looked, but he would have seen all that happened inside."

He glanced down at the body. "He saw Larkins accept the scroll-holder and try to kill Sangay—in front of all of us. All of us saw, all could bear witness. We saw Larkins attempt to kill while trying to retrieve a letter from the Black Cobra sealed with his master's personal seal."

Del circled the body, studying Larkins's coarse-featured face. "What would be the odds that Larkins, given the choice between the hangman and transportation in return for his testimony, would have implicated Ferrar?"

Devil joined him. "High, I would say. If you trust a ravening dog, it'll turn on you someday."

"Just so. I think Ferrar thought that, too." Del bent and retrieved his sword. "So he killed Larkins—sacrificed him to save his own skin."

Gervase appeared at the window, Vane, Demon, and Lucifer at his back. "No sightings," Gervase grimly reported. "The closest we got . . ." He glanced at Demon.

Who looked disgusted. "On the west side, heading south. I heard hoofbeats, already distant, fading rapidly. Too far away, and going too fast for us to have any chance of following. And there'll be no tracks—the roads that way are churned to slush."

Devil looked down at Larkins's body. "So the Black Cobra got away, but gave up his right-hand man."

Del finished a slow perusal of the room, then looked at the others. "And the scroll-holder's gone."

⟪ Sixteen ⟫

December 19
Elveden Grange, Suffolk

*Y*our letter was a copy, a decoy. Sacrificing it to take out his right-hand man, with a chance at Ferrar himself, was the right decision." Royce Varisey, Duke of Wolverstone, erstwhile government spymaster, with his black hair, dark eyes, chiseled features and long, powerful frame the very epitome of a darkly dangerous nobleman of Norman descent, kept his compelling gaze fixed on Del.

The entire company, ladies included, were congregated in the large drawing room of Elveden Grange, a sprawling Jacobean manor house set amid extensive gardens in a forested area a little way from the village of that name. The ambiance was soothing, and very English. The instant Del had set eyes on the house—two low stories with attics set under a many-gabled roof—he'd suspected what he would find inside. Lots of oak, on the floors, in the linen-fold paneling and ornate woodwork, even in some of the ceilings. The furniture, too, all lovingly polished until it glowed with a honey-gold patina.

Outside, there were ramblers festooning the walls, bare

branches now, but he could imagine what they would be like in summer, blossoms nodding in the breeze. Inside, a similar sensual luxury abounded, with richly painted artworks and exquisite ornaments, velvet and satin-striped fabrics, and the jewel tones of precious Eastern carpets.

The result was both colorful and comfortably restful.

Royce stood to one side of the hearth, by the chair his duchess, Minerva—a calm, graceful, and ineffably capable blond beauty—had claimed.

Del stood in a similar position by the chair in which Deliah sat.

Both ladies, of course, were avidly—and openly—listening.

Del grimaced. "It's an anticlimax to know we almost certainly succeeded in drawing Ferrar into the action himself, but that we missed him by minutes."

"I'm more than happy simply to know he's definitely engaged." Royce's lips curved. "I didn't actually expect you to accomplish that. Reducing the cultists by fourteen more than fulfilled my expectations of what we might reasonably achieve from your mission. But by attempting to use the boy as a thief, Ferrar gave us a weapon—by seizing it, we've achieved a great deal more than I, for one, anticipated."

"Yet he escaped." Del was still irritated by that. To have come so close. . . .

"True, but he's chanced his hand—he's dealt himself personally into the game. It was a bold act, to step in and kill Larkins like that, with all of you so close. From all you've told me, that was characteristic in its arrogance, but *un*characteristic in that it was massive risk. Trust me, he's rattled. We'll keep tempting him—taunting him—with the others as they come in. Eventually, one way or another, we'll have him."

"Speaking of having him." Devil strolled up to join them, Vane by his side. "Is there anything useful we can do with Larkins's body?"

They'd conveyed the body to the magistrate in Ely

with the recommendation he wait on further orders from Wolverstone—a name that carried quite amazing weight. Given it was Devil—St. Ives—making the recommendation, the magistrate had been only too happy to await developments.

The ladies had arrived very soon after the end of the action, much to the men's unfeigned delight; they'd been able to hand the two hysterical local women into gentler clutches to be soothed and calmed. Eventually, Devil had nudged the vicar in the same direction.

As Del had been quick to later acknowledge, the ladies had contributed in a very real way to the success of their mission.

Sangay had been thrilled, especially when he'd seen Larkins's dead body. When Sligo and Cobby had arrived, he'd happily recited every second of his ordeal, every last detail of all he'd witnessed. He'd still been chattering when they'd reached the Grange. Being introduced to Royce had abruptly sealed his lips. Wide-eyed, he'd bowed low, and accepted a commendation for his bravery in stunned silence. Despite the assembled ladies' kind words and reassuring smiles, he'd been perfectly happy to be dispatched with Cobby and Sligo to the kitchens.

"I've been wondering the same thing." Gervase strolled up, his wife, Madeline, on his arm. He and Tony had been stunned to discover their wives and families—in both cases their wives had much younger brothers as well as their own young children with them—in residence at the Grange. Minerva, it transpired, had made plans of her own.

"It does seem as if," Tony said as he and his wife, Alicia, joined the group, "a dead Larkins ought to be worth something—that his body is a weapon we could use in some way."

"Perhaps," Royce said, "but not yet, I think."

"I heard that Shrewton—Ferrar's father—is in residence at Wymondham, as he usually is at this time of year." Demon, with Flick, joined them. "Wymondham's this side of Norwich, not all that far from here." Demon arched a brow at Royce. "I assume that's one reason you're using this as your base."

Royce smiled. "That, and knowing I had all you Cynsters I could call on as additional troops."

"We've still got three men—three couriers—to come in," Del said.

"Which is why I think we might wait and see what comes next before deciding how best to use Larkins's body." Royce glanced at Devil, then Vane and Demon. "In case you haven't yet realized, your roles in this game are far from over. All the couriers are to make their way here, and this is home territory for you."

Devil, Vane, and Demon looked delighted.

Honoria had come up beside Devil in time to hear Royce's words, and to witness her husband's reaction. She poked him in the arm. "Which, of course, means *our* roles in this game are not yet over, either." As she exchanged a partner-like nod with Minerva on the words, there was no doubt that her *"our"* meant the assembled ladies.

All the wives—and Deliah. A funny little frisson of happiness went through her to know she was included in that company.

Honoria raised her eyes to Royce's face. "Which leads me to ask, what does this letter say, exactly? I assume"—she glanced at Del—"that you have a copy?"

Del exchanged a glance with Royce.

Royce didn't frown, but the expression filled his eyes. "No. We don't." He glanced again at Del. "Unless you made another?"

Lips twisting wryly, Del shook his head. "I never imagined the Black Cobra would succeed in stealing the copy I was carrying, so no, I didn't make another."

Minerva looked at Del, then twisted in her chair to look up at her husband. "So you still don't know exactly what's in this letter? I thought you said there was a chance there might be more in it than Del and his colleagues had seen?"

Lips firming, Royce nodded. "I did." After a moment, he added, "I'll send a messenger to Trentham and ask him to ensure a copy is made from the decoy Hamilton's carrying, in case, as with Del's, they decide to sacrifice it."

Minerva and Honoria approved the action with identical imperious nods. Turning back in her chair, Minerva saw their butler appear in the doorway. "However"—she rose—"you'll have to wait until after dinner to send your messenger. Dinner is ready to be served, and tonight, we're celebrating."

No one was game enough to attempt to gainsay the Duchess of Wolverstone, least of all her arrogantly powerful husband. The company duly fell into line, husbands unfashionably, and with all due attention, escorting their wives; the majority had yet to be informed of the penance they would have to pay for their rabid protectiveness, and not one of them had forgotten it.

Del offered Deliah his arm, and they went in with the others, all chatting and commenting in relaxed and easy camaraderie, all glad the day was ending so well. While it might not have yielded the ultimate victory they wanted— not yet—a definite blow had been struck, and they'd all come away without hurt or harm.

Once the glasses were charged, at the head of the table Royce rose to address them. An expectant hush fell over the room. He looked down the long board, lips lightly curving as he included them all. "We've drawn first blood. In the last days, we've won a number of skirmishes and, this morning, the first battle. Yes, we haven't yet won our war, but we've made an excellent start."

He raised his glass to Del, seated halfway down the table. "To Delborough, and the successful conclusion of his part in this mission."

They all cheered and drank.

Del smiled and inclined his head in acknowledgment.

"The next engagement," Royce continued, "will be on us soon—as Hamilton draws near, which, with any luck, will be tomorrow."

Cheers from all the men greeted that news.

"However," Royce went on, his gaze returning to Del, "tonight is for celebrating the success of today. For that, and for all that's to come, I give you a toast." He raised his glass high. "To justice for all who deserve it. And death to the Black Cobra."

"Hear, hear!" came from all around. The men all rose, raised their glasses high and drank. The ladies drank, too. Not one shied from the sentiment declared.

Then everyone subsided, and the meal began.

Excellent food, excellent wine, and excellent company. Free-flowing conversations and the warmth of good cheer wrapped Deliah in their comfort, welcomed and reassured. As the meal progressed, she became increasingly aware of the quiet happiness welling within her. Content beyond measure, she glanced at Del, seated beside her, and saw the same appreciation in his eyes.

They shared a smile, knew without speaking what was in the other's mind. This was home—at last, they were here. For both of them the journey had been long, but they were there now; at last they knew what their future would hold.

His eyes still locked with hers, Del found her hand, raised it, placed a kiss in her palm, then closed his hand over her fingers. He turned his head to answer a question from Devil.

Deliah studied his profile, let her happiness continue to well.

Home is where the heart is.

She'd heard the phrase before.

Now she understood it.

All their ladies *seemed* to have taken being tied up that morning relatively well.

Later that evening, back at Somersham Place, Del followed Deliah up the stairs to her room—just as all the other men were following their wives, metaphorically trotting penitently at their heels to face whatever penance was to be theirs.

And just like all the other men, he had to fight to keep a smile from his face.

In his case, the only thing that had marred his day was Ferrar escaping, but as he hadn't really expected the bastard to even be there, he couldn't repine too much. Tomorrow, as Royce had intimated, was another day.

Overall, as Deliah halted before her door and he reached around her to open it, he was feeling distinctly . . . mellow. It had been such a long time since he'd felt that way that the word took a moment to come to his mind.

Following Deliah into the room, he shut the door behind them. She was unbuttoning her pelisse. He crossed to lift it from her shoulders.

The pale green gown she wore beneath, another of Madame Latour's creations, fitted Deliah's lush curves exceedingly well; he'd admired the result throughout the evening. He vaguely recalled paying a pretty penny for the gown, and considered it money well spent.

He laid her pelisse over a chair. Her back to him, she glanced at him over her shoulder, then glided into the room.

"This morning . . ." She said nothing more, but crossed to the dresser. On its top, he saw the two colorful scarves he'd used to secure her to the bed. She picked them up, slowly ran the silk through her fingers as she turned to, across the dimly lit room, regard him.

She tilted her head. "You tied me up."

Despite his conviction that all was well, more than well, and settled—definitely settled—between them, his stomach contracted at her distant and chilly tone. But . . . lips thinning, he nodded. "I had to. If you'd been at the cathedral when the fiend, or even Larkins, was there . . ."

He inwardly shuddered at the thought even now.

Her brows rose. "I would have distracted you?"

He nodded. "I would have been thinking about you—focusing on you, and not on what I was doing."

"Hmm . . . that's what the others said."

"The other ladies?"

When she nodded, he eased out a breath, and walked forward, closing the distance to halt just before her.

She studied his face. "They also said you . . . *fussing* protectively over me was a measure of how much I mean to you. Were they right in that, too?"

Some part of him squirmed, literally squirmed at the thought that she—and the other ladies—saw through him so easily. But he forced himself to nod, albeit curtly. "Yes."

She smiled. "In that case, all else they said on that subject is presumably correct, too." She pulled the scarves taut between her hands.

He suddenly felt exceedingly wary. "What else did they say?"

"Actually, it was Minerva who recommended the . . . procedure. As you might imagine, we spent some time after dinner discussing what recompense would be most appropriate to demand for your high-handedness in tying us all to our beds. A piece of male arrogance that, as you might expect, we were not, individually or collectively, inclined to let pass unanswered. Unremarked on. Unpaid for."

He was perfectly sure he didn't want to know the answer, but had to ask, "What is this procedure?"

"It's very simple." Her smile was the epitome of feminine triumph. "It's along the lines of, 'What's sauce for the goose is also sauce for the gander.' "

"Ah." He looked down at the scarves she kept tugging taut between her hands. "I . . . see."

"I'm told it works best if you first remove your boots and stockings, coat, waistcoat and cravat." Stepping back, she gestured with a wave to the bed. "So if you will?"

He eyed the bed, glanced briefly her way, then reluctantly shrugged out of his coat. Laying it aside, he set his fingers to the buttons of his waistcoat, rapidly assessing her tack, her options, the likely outcome.

It wasn't all bad.

Dispensing with his waistcoat, he caught her eye. "Just

promise me one thing—you won't leave me tied naked to your bed in the morning."

She laughed, a distinctly sultry sound. "We'll have to see how well you perform in fulfilling your penance." She turned to survey the bed, as if measuring him lying upon it. Then she walked toward it. "Just console yourself with the thought that every man who sinned is paying the same price."

"They are?"

"Well, of course."

That cast the matter in a completely different light. Del inwardly grinned, wondering what comments he, Devil, and the others would be sharing tomorrow morning.

Tossing his cravat aside, he followed her to the bed, where she was lacing the scarves through the ornate headboard, just as he had that morning.

She straightened and turned as he neared.

He caught her in one arm, bent his head and kissed her soundly.

Lifting his head, he looked into her jade eyes, already hazed with rising passion. "I'll do anything you ask of me—anything and everything—just as long as, come the morning, you'll still be mine."

She looked into his eyes, studied them, then smiled. "Always." Her smile deepened. She raised a hand, laid her palm to his cheek. "Always and forever."

A heartbeat passed, then she lightly patted his cheek. "Now get on the bed."

He did, and gave himself up to her torment.

To giving his all, and accepting hers in return.

The night rolled on as passion roiled about them, as desire surged, then, sated, waned. Only to wax anew, and take them again.

They found new ways to use the scarves, experimented and laughed, then fell silent as desire and joy twined again, crested again, wracked them again.

At the end they lay entwined, his arms around her, their legs tangled, and traded whispers and hopes, thoughts and ideas of what their joint life would be like once the Black Cobra was brought down.

Ultimately, sleep crept in on quiet wings and enfolded them.

Deliah's last thought was that for her part in Del's mission she'd gained a reward far greater than she ever would have—ever could have—imagined. She'd gained the love of an honorable, courageous, handsome, and passionate gentleman—something she'd been so often told, and had for so long believed, she could never have.

He was with her now, hers now, and she was his forevermore.

She closed her eyes, hugged that glorious truth close, and let sleep claim her.

Del listened to her breathing slow, felt her warmth filling his arms, and knew he'd already gained the greatest reward he could possibly expect from this mission. He'd defined and secured his future—their future.

It lay waiting for them, just ahead on their road, a shared life in which she would be his—his wife, his lover, his helpmate, his heart—while he would be hers, her husband, her protector.

Even if he had to pay a penance every time he exercised the latter right.

His lips curved as sleep tugged him down. He surrendered as one last thought slid through his mind.

Home.

He was finally there.

Home for him lay in Deliah's arms.

December 19
Bury St. Edmunds, Suffolk

In the darkest hour of the long night, Roderick Ferrar strode up to the back door of the house in Bury St. Edmunds that the cult had made its own.

The door opened before he reached it. He strode in, fighting to keep the shivers that racked him at bay. He went straight through the house to the drawing room, barely noticing the silks now draping the walls, the incense permeating the air, the servants and cultists who bowed low as he passed.

Alex and Daniel were waiting, playing cards at a small table set between two armchairs angled before the hearth. They looked up as he entered. Stiffly, he walked to the hearth, and bent to warm his icy hands at the blaze.

One look at Roderick's face, and all expression leached from Alex's. "You're exceedingly late. What happened?"

Roderick straightened, drew a tight breath, then faced them. "It was a trap. They turned Larkins's brilliant plan into a trap, and Larkins walked right into it."

Alex blinked, slowly. "Where is Larkins?"

Roderick snorted. Gripped the mantelpiece. "He's dead. He'd been seen by a bevy of them—St. Ives was there, for heaven's sake! And Chillingworth. And a host of others of that ilk—including Delborough, of course. They all saw Larkins take the scroll-holder, open it, read the letter, then pocket it—then, of course, he moved to silence the boy. That's when they showed themselves. There were a dozen of them, maybe more. I didn't wait to count. I had to get to Larkins, had to kill him. They had more than enough testimony to take him up, to prove he was after the letter with my seal. And once they had him—"

"He would have given us up to save his miserable hide." Daniel nodded. "I take it you managed to eliminate Larkins without being seen yourself?"

Roderick wiped a hand over his mouth. "Just. It was a near-run thing, but I got clean away." He looked at Alex. "That's why I'm so late. I stopped in Newmarket—in a tavern—to make sure I wasn't followed."

"Sound thinking." Alex leaned back in the armchair.

Roderick started to pace before the fire. "This is *unbelievably* irritating. Where the hell am I to find someone to replace Larkins? Someone who understands our needs, knows how the cult operates, is willing and able to do what's required, and above all, given these damned couriers and our present need, is an Englishman?"

The other two exchanged a glance, but neither leapt to answer.

Eventually, Daniel murmured, "Larkins did have his uses."

"I didn't want to kill him." Roderick ran a hand through his hair. "Lord knows, he's been with me for decades."

"You did the right thing," Alex reassured him, in a voice of infinite, collected calm. "If he'd been taken up, as inevitably he would have been—impossible to hide him forever—he would have given you, and us, up. There's no doubt of that. You would have been a fool to wager your neck on his loyalty. You had to act as you did."

Alex's words had the desired effect. Roderick calmed, grew less agitated.

"There's too much at stake in this game," Daniel said. "We have to play to win."

"Indeed, " Alex concurred. "Those who are weak enough to get caught . . . have to be eliminated."

Neither Roderick nor Daniel argued.

After a pause, Alex continued, "You mentioned Delborough's scroll-holder. What happened to it?"

"Larkins's last useful act. He had it when he met me." Roderick felt in the pockets of the greatcoat he still wore, pulled out the scroll-holder, and handed it to Alex. "I checked. It's a copy, not the original."

Alex's lips twisted wryly. "So I was right. Delborough was a decoy."

"Your prescience is not much use after the fact," Roderick said. "But at least we now know why Delborough went to Somersham Place. What better reinforcements than a whole troop of Cynsters?"

Daniel shrugged. "So they rattle their sabers around these parts. We'll just make sure all the action henceforth takes place far from here."

"Exactly." Alex looked at Roderick. "So where is Hamilton?"

Roderick gave a brief report. "So in the matter of the major, we've done all we can—put everything in place—that we can to this point. But Hamilton and Miss Ensworth are already at Chelmsford. They appear to be heading this way." He glanced at Alex and Daniel. "The question is, are they heading to Somersham Place as well, or somewhere else?"

"It's possible, of course, that they're heading to Somersham." There was a frown etched on Alex's face. "I just wish we'd known about the damned Cynsters in time to act earlier, at least to keep Hamilton from getting this close."

"Too late for that now," Daniel observed. "He's virtually on our doorstep."

"True," Alex allowed. "But what worries me more is these others our puppetmaster has drawn into this fight. We're not, as we thought we would be, facing only the colonel and his three friends. We've the Cynsters getting in our way up here, and bodyguards escorting our pigeons from the moment they land. Delborough had two, and now you say Hamilton has another two—a different two—who were waiting for him when he landed."

Head slowly shaking, Alex met Roderick's, then Daniel's eyes. "This is all too expertly organized. We're facing an enemy more able than we'd thought, and being forced to fight on a front far wider than we'd anticipated."

When Alex fell silent, Daniel prompted, "So?"

Alex pulled a face. "I just wish I knew who was behind this. It's much easier to triumph over an enemy if you know who that enemy is. How else can you learn his weaknesses?"

Neither of the other two answered.

Roderick shifted his weight. "What we do know is that, whoever he is, he poses a very real danger to us—or will if the original letter gets through to him."

Alex examined the scroll-holder Larkins had died for. "The usual contraption." The cult used similar devices to transport sensitive communications.

With quick flicks, Alex manipulated the levers, unlocked

the scroll-holder, opened it, and drew out the single sheet of parchment it held.

Daniel looked at Roderick. "While our men are taking Hamilton down, we should put more effort into identifying who our puppetmaster is. Chances are it's someone with links both to the Cynsters and to these other men—the ones acting as bodyguards. What do you know of them? Are they from some arm of the services, or . . . ?"

"At this point," Roderick said, "I don't even know who they are."

While Daniel and Roderick discussed ways and means to identify their unexpected opponents, Alex unrolled the letter and, after checking—just to make sure—that it was indeed a copy with no incriminating seal, idly scanned the contents.

The rumble of the others' voices filled the night's silence. Alex's eyes traveled the sheet, then halted.

Neither Alex nor Daniel had previously seen the letter. Neither had had any idea of its full contents.

A long moment passed. Alex's eyes remained locked on the letter, on a single line. Roderick and Daniel continued to talk.

Abruptly, Alex looked up. *"You used my name."*

The words resonated with accusation and incipient black fury.

Roderick looked at Alex, frowned. "Of course I mentioned you. If you recall, I was trying to persuade that bastard, Govind Holkar, to commit more deeply—men and money. We'd discussed mentioning you visiting Poona as an incentive—you knew I'd be mentioning it."

"That's not what I mean." Alex bit off each word, gaze boring into Roderick. "You used my *real* name."

Both Roderick and Daniel blinked. Then both froze.

In a movement redolent with rage, eyes narrowed to glittering shards, Alex tossed the letter on the table. "And just what do you think, brother-mine, will happen if our dear father is shown this letter? Even a *copy* of this letter?" The words were vicious, lashing, scathing as Alex's voice rose.

"You don't think, perhaps, that he might be tempted to throw me and Daniel to the wolves to save you? To save the honor of his house?" Eyes blazing, Alex pushed upright. *"Of course he will!"*

Alex shouldered past Roderick and fell to pacing, a great deal more violently than Roderick had.

Daniel reached for the letter. It took him only a moment to find the relevant line. Lips tightening, he tossed the letter back on the table. Sitting back, he caught Roderick's eye. "My name, too, *brother-mine*. And just when were you going to remember to tell us?"

"I didn't know—I *swear* I didn't know." Pale, looking suddenly ill, Roderick raked a hand through his hair. He glanced at Alex, who shot him a murderous look, then he hauled in a huge breath. "We don't need this. We need to concentrate. I was in a rush when I wrote the damned thing—remember? I didn't even register that I'd used your real names."

"Make no mistake," Alex scoffed. "Our father *will* register that, if he's ever shown it."

"So we make sure he never sees the damned thing." Roderick swung to Daniel, who was leaning back in his armchair, his face a mask. "We'll intercept *all* the letters—the copies as well as the original. Chances were we would have had to do that anyway in order to seize the original."

Roderick glanced at Alex, still pacing viciously, then looked back at Daniel. "So—Hamilton's next." Roderick stole another glance at Alex. "What are we going to do about him?"

"Not we. *You!*" Swinging around, Alex pointed a finger at Roderick. "You asked before where you might find a man to replace Larkins. His replacement, Roderick, is you!" Another jab of Alex's finger emphasized the word. *"You* take on Larkins's role, and *you* get those damned letters back—*every* copy, every last one!"

Roderick's eyes narrowed to shards of blue ice. "All right." Face set, he nodded. "I will."

Look for the next installment in

The Black Cobra Quartet

The Elusive Bride

17 September, 1822
My cabin aboard the Mary Alice

Dear Diary,

As usual, I will endeavor to record my thoughts at five o'clock every afternoon, before I dress for dinner. This morning I departed Bombay, and I understand we are making good time as the Mary Alice slices its way through the waves to Aden.

And yes, I acknowledge that it's undeniably bold to be pursuing a gentleman as I'm pursuing Major Hamilton, but as we all know, fortune favors the bold. Indeed, even my parents should accept the necessity. They sent me to Bombay because I dragged my heels over choosing any of the young men who offered, opting instead to wait for my "one," as all my sisters—and I suspect my sisters-in-law, too—did. I have always maintained that it was simply a matter of waiting for the right man to appear, and if Major Hamilton proves to be my right man, then at the ripe old age of twenty and four, I doubt anyone would argue against me pursuing him.

Of course, I have yet to determine if he truly is my "one," but I can only decide that after meeting him again.

Speaking of which . . . he and his party are two days ahead of me.

I wonder how fast a sloop can go?

E.

1 October, 1822
My cabin aboard the Mary Alice

Dear Diary,

The answer to my last question is: quite amazingly fast when all sail is risked. My being extra-charming to the captain and challenging him to demonstrate how fast his ship can go has paid a handsome dividend. We passed the Egret, *the sloop carrying the major and his household, sometime last night. With luck and continuing fair winds, I will disembark in Aden before him, and he will have no reason to suspect I set out on this journey to follow him.*

E.

October 2, 1822
Aden

"What the . . . ?" Gareth Hamilton stood in the bow of the *Egret* and stared incredulously at the pale pink parasol bobbing through the crowd on the wharf alongside.

They'd followed another of the company sloops into the harbor and had had to wait for that vessel, the *Mary Alice*, to be unloaded first.

His bags, along with the minimal luggage carried by his small but efficient household—his batman, Bister; his houseman, Mooktu, an ex-sepoy; and Mooktu's wife, Arnia—were being stacked that very minute on the wooden wharf, but that wasn't the cause of the consternation—to put it mildly— that had seized him.

He'd noticed the parasol bobbing down the gangway of the *Mary Alice*, tied up almost at the end of the long wharf. He'd watched the bearer, a lady in matching pale pink skirts, tack and weave through the crowd. She and the contingent of staff following at her heels, with one heavily muscled man clearing a path through the noisy, jostling throng ahead of her, had to pass along the wharf beside the *Egret* in order to enter the town.

Until a moment ago, he hadn't been able to see the parasol holder's face. But passing the *Egret*, she'd tipped the parasol aside and glanced up—and he'd glimpsed . . . a face he hadn't expected to see again.

A face that, for the last few weeks, had haunted his dreams.

Yet all but immediately, the bloody parasol had come up and re-obscured his view.

"Damn!" One part of his mind was calmly telling him that it couldn't possibly be she, that he was seeing things he wanted to see . . . some other part, a more visceral part, was already sure.

He hesitated, waiting to see again—to know for sure.

Movement in the crowd behind the parasol caught his eye.

Cultists.

His blood literally ran cold. He'd known they'd be waiting for him—he and his people were expecting a welcome.

But Emily Ensworth and her people weren't.

He'd vaulted the railing on the thought. He landed on the wharf, his gaze locked on her.

He came up from his crouch with considerable momentum, cleaving his way bodily through the crowd.

He came up with her just in time to grab her and haul her away from the blade a cultist thrust at her.

Her gasp was drowned beneath a cacophony of sounds—exclamations, shrieks, shouts. Others had seen the menacing sword, but even as the crowd turned and garrulously searched, the cultists melted away. Taller than most, Gareth saw them pull back. Over the heads, one cultist—an older, black-bearded man—met his eye. Even across the distance, Gareth felt the malevolence in the man's gaze. Then the man turned and was swallowed by the crowd.

Mooktu appeared by Gareth's shoulder. "Should we follow?"

Bister was already further afield, scouting.

Gareth's instincts screamed *follow*, to pursue and deal appropriately with any cultist he could find. But . . . he glanced down at the woman he still held, his hands locked about her upper arms.

Her parasol now askew, he looked down into wide, moss-hazel eyes. Into a face that was as perfect as he recalled, but pale. She was stunned.

At least she wasn't screaming.

"No." He glanced at Mooktu. "We have to get away from here—off the docks—quickly."

Mooktu nodded. "I'll get the others."

He was gone on the word, leaving Gareth to set Miss Ensworth back on her feet.

Gently, as if she were porcelain and might shatter at any instant.

"Are you all right?"

As the warmth—the heat—of his hard hands fell from her, Emily managed to blink. "Y-yes." This must be what shock felt like.

Indeed, she was amazed she hadn't swooned. He'd seized her, dragged her from danger, then held her close, effectively plastered to the side of his body. His brick-wall hard, excessively warm—not to say hot—body.

She didn't think she'd ever be the same.

"Ah . . ." *Where was a fan when one needed one?* She glanced around and noise suddenly assaulted her ears. Everyone was talking in several different languages.

Hamilton hadn't moved. He stood like a rock amid the sea of surging humanity. She wasn't too proud to shelter in his lee.

She finally located Mullins—her grizzly ex-soldier guard—as he came stumping back through the crowd. Just before the attack a wave of bodies had pushed him ahead and separated them—then her attacker had stepped between her and Watson, her courier-guide, who'd been following on her heels.

Her people were armed, but having lost her assailant in the melee, they gradually returned. Mullins recognized Hamilton as a solider even though he wasn't in uniform and raised a hand in an abbreviated salute. "Thanking you, sir—don't know what we'd've done without you."

Emily noted the way Hamilton's lips tightened. She was grateful he didn't state the obvious—if not for his intervention, she'd be dead.

The rest of her party gathered, and without prompting, she quickly put names and roles to their worried faces—Mullins; Watson; Jimmy, Watson's young nephew; and Dorcas, her very English maid.

Hamilton acknowledged the information with a

nod, then looked from her to Watson. "Where were you planning to stay?"

Hamilton and his people—a batman, in his mid-twenties but with experience etched in his face, and a fierce Pashtun warrior and his equally fierce wife—escorted her party off the docks, then, with their combined luggage in a wooden cart, continued through the streets of Aden to the edge of the diplomatic quarter and the quietly fashionable hotel her uncle had recommended.

Hamilton halted in the street outside, studied the building, then simply stated, "No." He glanced at her, then past her to Mullins. "You can't stay there. There're too many entrances."

Stunned anew—and she still hadn't managed to marshal her senses enough to think through the implications of the cultist attack—she looked at Mullins to discover him nodding his grizzled head.

"You're right," Mullins allowed. "Death trap, that is." He glanced at her, and added, "In the circumstances."

Before she could argue, Hamilton smoothly continued, "For the moment, at least, I'm afraid our parties will need to stay together."

She looked at him again.

He caught her eye. "We need to find somewhere a lot less . . . obvious."

Welcome to
the World of

STEPHANIE
LAURENS

Dear Reader,

I'm delighted to welcome you to the World of Stephanie Laurens. Why "the World"? Because that's the most accurate way of describing how my books relate to one another—each is a separate window onto the same largely fictional world.

Family and friendships are what make any world go around, at least on the personal and emotional plane. Consequently, although each of my books focuses on two principal characters—the hero and heroine—as neither exist in a vacuum, their brothers, sisters and other family members, or their close friends, appear in their story, and in return the hero and heroine of one book are very likely to waltz past in the background of one of their sibling's or friend's books.

My world is a part of the haut ton of Regency England, a specific social strata peopled by the "upper ten thousand," the aristocratic families and their connected offshoots. My characters all belong to this relatively small group of people, so it's unsurprising that some characters, such as the fabled Lady Osbaldestone and Helena, Dowager Duchess of St. Ives, appear in many stories, lending their wisdom and guidance as ladies of their age and experience tend to do. Similarly, various characters from the Cynster novels swan past in the backgrounds of the Bastion Club novels, and vice versa.

So each book, although focusing on one or other couple, gives you another glimpse into the lives of the same larger group in society.

I hope you enjoy visiting my world through my books already published, as well as the works to come. Read on to discover more—answers to questions about the world's structure, what's real, what's not, and numerous other issues readers love to know.

Have fun!

Stephanie
Laurens

SPECIFIC QUESTIONS READERS OFTEN WANT TO KNOW

Why aren't the books always in chronological order?

I've always resisted labelling my works a "series," because to readers "series" implies one of two things—the books are written in a fixed chronological order, and/or the plots are such that you must read the books in a fixed order, namely the order in which they were published. With my works, neither of those is true. The *only* aspect that links every book into the group is the characters. Each book can be read entirely on its own, without loss of meaning.

Much confusion is generated when readers assume that a long-running group of novels is necessarily written in chronological order. Since the release of *The Taste of Innocence,* I've been innundated by emails from readers wishing to point out that in that volume, Simon Cynster and Portia are not wed. "But they were married in book number ten!" the readers cry. "Ah," say I. "But have you noticed that *The Taste of Innocence* is set more than two years *before* the events of *The Perfect Lover?*" So no, Simon and Portia are not yet married in *The Taste of Innocence.*

Why jump around in time? Because of characters' ages. There's a gap of nine years between *The Perfect Lover* and the book before it, *On a Wicked Dawn.* But after *On a Wicked Dawn,* readers wanted to hear Simon and Portia's story straightaway, as the next volume, and because of their respective ages in *On A Wicked Dawn,* that meant jumping from 1825 to 1835.

The following Cynster novel, *The Ideal Bride*, then had to step back to 1825, to pick up the story of Michael Anstruther-Wetherby immediately after he'd left a wedding breakfast that occurred midway through *On a Wicked Dawn*.

The subsequent Cynster novels were about a group of friends who were also Cynster connections, and were set in 1831, 1831, then 1833, followed by *Where the Heart Leads*, set in November 1835–the first book to be set after *The Perfect Lover*. And yes, Simon and Portia are married in that.

And now we've swung back again, to 1825 for the story of Jonas Tallent in *Temptation and Surrender*, and in years to come we'll advance through time once more as we move through the romances of the five as-yet-unwed Cynster girls. Again, the year in which each of their stories are set will be determined by their ages. The month and year in which each novel commences is always stated at the start of chapter one.

How real are the Cynsters? And their houses?

Not real at all. The Cynsters are not based on any family that actually existed. Some readers are convinced I'm working from some family's archives, but no—Cynsters, Bastion Club members and all others are entirely figments of my imagination. The only characters in my novels who ever existed are historical figures such as the Prince Regent, the patronesses of Almack's and a few social and/or political figures mentioned in passing, like Wellington. Real people are never central characters in my works.

Likewise their houses. No, you cannot go on a tour of England viewing the various "Cynster" houses—they don't exist, and never have. They are not even modeled on houses that exist, or have ever existed. That said, I lived in England for four years and visited many stately homes, so my imaginary houses are "conglomerates" of houses I've walked through—the bedroom from here, the Adam fireplace from there—all mixed up and swirled together in the melting pot of my memory.

So what is real?

In my works, the geography mapwise is accurate—roads are where I say they are, and go from this town to the next as I say they do, and yes, it would take a curricle that long to travel that distance. My streets of London really are the streets of London, and the relative affluence of the various areas is as pertained during Regency times.

However, my topography is fictional—if I need a hill with a certain view along this particular road at that point, then that's where the hill will be. I'm describing views that are known to exist in the neighborhood, and which in many cases I've observed firsthand, but the precise location of that lookout is my creation.

As mentioned above, all known historical figures are accurately portrayed.

Otherwise . . . one point to bear in mind when reading the works of storytellers is that we are writing to entertain you, not to educate you. Consequently, while we necessarily must use sufficient historical accuracy to create the right ambiance and atmosphere for whatever period we're using, getting buried in historical detail isn't entertaining, nor is adhering to historical detail to the detriment of the story. If there's a point where *minor* historical detail gets in the way of telling a good story, then history has to give way to storytelling, because it's you, the reader, we have to satisfy, not the history police.

As an example of that last point, think of men's shirts. Buttons down the front of men's shirts were not widely used until the early 1830s. However, I've decided that my Cynster and Bastion Club novel male characters all went to a shirtmaker who was ahead of his time—logically there must have been at least one shirtmaker who started the trend; they'd had buttons for some time. So my male characters' shirts often have buttons down the front. Why? Because all my heroines are significantly shorter than their respective heroes, and there is no way on earth a shorter female can divest a taller, much broader male of a shirt that doesn't have buttons down the front. And believe me, there are only so many ways you can write a love scene where the hero has to break away, step back, and pull his shirt off over his head. Yes, you can do it well once or twice, but routinely, shirts without buttons down the front are . . . limiting.

On the other hand, what I write about society and its mores, social strictures and boundaries is real—a fairly accurate portrayal of what went on in the upper echelons of society at that time. For those who are Austen fans and fondly believe she depicted how all English society behaved in terms of marriage and courtship—think again. Austen only wrote of one aristrocrat in all her works (Lady de Bourgh in *Pride and Prejudice*), and that picture is widely accepted by Austen scholars as a caricature. Austen's works are socially accurate, but she wisely limited the social class of which she wrote to her own. She was a country vicar's daughter and had no experience of, and so never attempted to write of, the aristocracy—the haut ton to which all my characters belong. And all the factual evidence suggests that in wider society, and especially the higher echelons of the upper classes, then as now, intercourse was considered an integral and normal part of courtship, albeit serious courtship; it was not something left to the wedding night except in unusual circumstances. The average age at which women married varied between twenty-two and twenty-four throughout this period.

On matters such as politics, commerce, police and military actions, and so on—for instance the Peninsula War battles referred to in many of my novels, or the investment in building of railways in *The Taste of Innocence*—the actions described either did happen, or could have happened, at the time and in the way I have described them.

Overall, I adhere to the one guiding rule any author writing historical fiction should follow: whatever you describe has to be possible. It may not be common, obvious, or even all that probable, but it absolutely has to be possible.

Why are there so many historical romances, including all of mine, set in Regency England?

Most books set in England between 1800 and 1840 have a "Regency" feel. The reason that era is so useful for romance authors stems from the wide-ranging social changes that were occurring over that time, and the parallels, or echoes, those create with our time, and the lives of our readers.

To summarize these:

a) Whether it was the influence of the romantic poets (late 1700s) or simply the passage of years, by the early 1800s it was becoming increasingly acceptable for aristocratic couples to marry for love, as distinct from what prior to that period had been considered the right and proper and indeed only acceptable reason for marriage for them—the transfer of property and the getting of an heir.

So for the first time, aristocratic heroes and heroines were faced with a real choice—to marry for love, or not. That is a choice that resonates with today's readers—to marry for love, or not.

b) Aristrocratic females had a greater degree of freedom provided they were wealthy enough and remained unwed. Or married a man amenable to allowing them their independence. In other words, aristocratic females, unlike their more lowly born peers, could be sufficiently independent to create their own lives—like Phoebe Malleson in *To Distraction,* and Sarah Conningham in *The Taste of Innocence.* Such women could create lives that did not revolve around marriage, yet still remain accepted within their social circle. Some, like Penelope Ashford, could be quite eccentric, but because of their social standing and that of their families, remain accepted by the ton.

Sadly, this relative freedom did not long survive Victoria's marriage to Albert, hence the "Regency" period is something of a window for independent women, and again, that independence, the search for their own lives outside of or beyond marriage, resonates powerfully with women today.

c) The haut ton—the upper echelon of society—lived in a fabulous, glittering world, with massive houses, expensive clothes, dashing carriages. The background to stories set in the haut ton is attractive to readers—a glimpse into a glamorous world of wealth and consequence. Just as the lives of wealthy modern-day celebrities exerts a powerful attraction for readers, so too do the lives of their historical counterparts.

d) There was a great deal of social upheaval going on throughout the wider Regency period, leading to the emergence of social and political conscience that went further than *noblesse oblige*. This creates a background with a wide range of potential avenues to exploit for story plots—such as employment agencies, orphanages and investment schemes—as well as adding edge to the more usual intra-family plots.

Why are heroes and often heroines usually wealthy aristocrats?

The answer lies above. It was only those belonging to the haut ton who were faced with the question to marry for love or not—and who were free to do so and could decide either way. In all other social strata, the reason for marriage had for centuries been largely because of physical attraction. In Regency times, the middle class had not yet come into being. Below the aristocracy, there came various levels of gentry, then those involved in commerce, and the shopkeepers and traders, and then the workers and peasantry. As Austen's works demonstrate, within the gentry, even if there was a token nod toward wealth and family standing as criteria, liking for a partner played the major role in determining marriages.

Not so for the members of the haut ton—for them, this period is the first when they, free of all other constraints as no other class could be, came to face the question: To marry for love, or not?

Today that is still the crucial question in any romance.

So it's the characters and the social world of the aristorcracy that most strongly resonate with modern-day readers and the questions and challenges modern readers face. This is why in Regency-set novels, the aristocratic world is the favored setting.

The Cynsters

The Cynster Family Tree

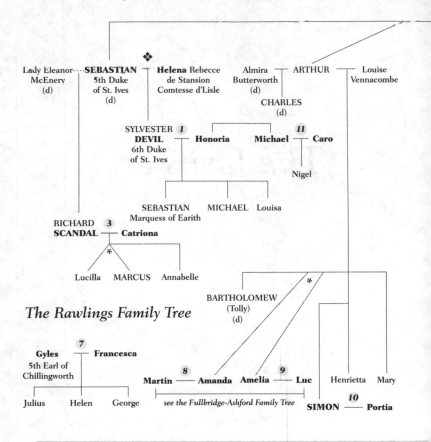

The Rawlings Family Tree

THE CYNSTER NOVELS

1. *Devil's Bride*
2. *A Rake's Vow*
3. *Scandal's Bride*

❖ *Special—The Promise in a Kiss*

4. *A Rogue's Proposal*
5. *A Secret Love*
6. *All About Love*

7. *All About Passion*
8. *On a Wild Night*
9. *On a Wicked Dawn*
10. *The Perfect Lover*

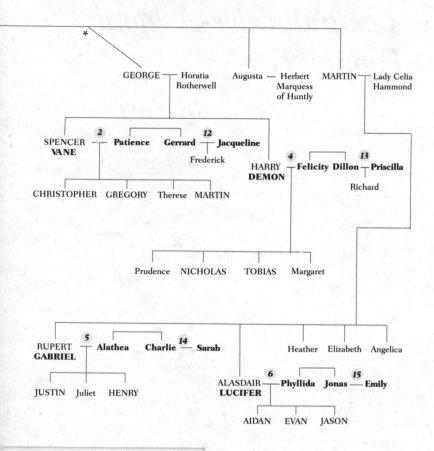

GEORGE — Horatia Rotherwell   Augusta — Herbert Marquess of Huntly   MARTIN — Lady Celia Hammond

SPENCER VANE — **2** **Patience**   **Gerrard** — **12** **Jacqueline** Frederick   HARRY DEMON — **4** **Felicity**   Dillon — **13** **Priscilla** Richard

CHRISTOPHER   GREGORY   Therese   MARTIN

Prudence   NICHOLAS   TOBIAS   Margaret

RUPERT GABRIEL — **5** **Alathea**   **Charlie** — **14** **Sarah**   Heather   Elizabeth   Angelica

JUSTIN   Juliet   HENRY

ALASDAIR LUCIFER — **6** **Phyllida**   Jonas — **15** **Emily**

AIDAN   EVAN   JASON

11. *The Ideal Bride*
12. *The Truth About Love*
13. *What Price Love?*
14. *The Taste of Innocence*
15. *Temptation and Surrender*

MALE Cynsters in capitals
* denotes twins

The Fulbridge-Ashford Family Tree

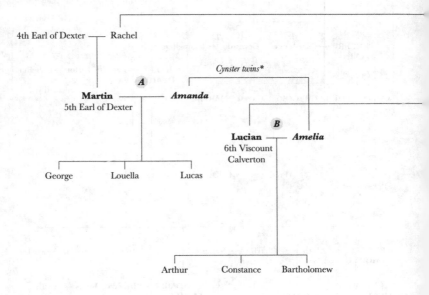

4th Earl of Dexter —— Rachel

Cynster twins*

Martin —— *A* —— *Amanda*
5th Earl of Dexter

Lucian —— *B* —— *Amelia*
6th Viscount
Calverton

George   Louella   Lucas

Arthur   Constance   Bartholomew

THE RELEVANT NOVELS

A. *On a Wild Night*   **D.** *Lost & Found* (novella in anthology *Hero, Come Back*)
B. *On a Wicked Dawn*   **E.** *Where the Heart Leads*
C. *The Perfect Lover*

Connections to Cynsters noted*

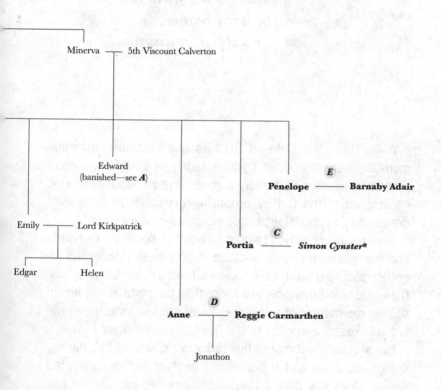

Minerva —— 5th Viscount Calverton

Edward
(banished—see **A**)

Penelope —— **Barnaby Adair** *E*

Emily —— Lord Kirkpatrick

Portia —— *Simon Cynster** *C*

Edgar   Helen

Anne —— **Reggie Carmarthen** *D*

Jonathon

*See Cynster Family Tree

Devil's Bride

First published March 1998

*Was he the husband
of her dreams . . .
or a devil in disguise?*

When Devil, the Duke of St. Ives and the most infamous member of the notorious Cynster family, is caught in a compromising position with plucky governess Honoria Wetherby, he astonishes the ton by proposing marriage. No one ever dreamed this scandalous rogue would ever take a bride!

Honoria, however, isn't about to bend to society's demands and marry a man simply because they've been discovered together unchaperoned. She craves adventure and longs to see the world—and though she's more than happy to assist him in solving the murder of a young Cynster cousin, once the crime is put to rest she intends to bid Devil farewell forever.

But she underestimates the seductive power of this daring, dangerous man, and the scalding heat of her own unsated desire. Does she dare let passion carry her into Devil's embrace . . . and into the most perilous, rapturous adventure of them all?

Peek at the Book

Her heart in her throat, Honoria lifted her gaze to the rider's face—and met his eyes. Even in the dimness, she was sure of their color. Pale, lucent green, they seemed ancient, all-seeing. Large, set deep under strongly arched black brows, they were the dominant feature in an impressively strong face. Their glance was penetrating, mesmerizing—unearthly. In that instant, Honoria was sure that the devil had come to claim one of his own. And her, too.

Then the air about her turned blue.

SETTING
1818 England

CHARACTERS
Devil Cynster
Honoria Anstruther-Wetherby

RECURRING CHARACTERS
Members of the Bar Cynster
Gyles Rawlings, Earl of Chillingworth
Helena, Dowager Duchess of St. Ives

A Rake's Vow

First published October 1998

He vowed never to marry.
She vowed no man would
trap her. But some vows are
meant to be broken. . . .

Vane Cynster greatly enjoys his dalliances, but he's always remained aloof when other Cynster men stepped up to the altar. Resolved to *never* submit to being leg-shackled to *any* woman, he believes he's found the ideal temporary refuge from London's infuriating husband hunters at Bellamy Hall. But an encounter with the irresistible Patience Debbington has his head—and his heart—spinning . . . and soon he has more than mere seduction on his mind.

But Patience is not about to succumb to arrogant, presumptuous Vane's sensuous propositions. Certainly his kisses leave her weak, his caresses leave her flushed and burning with desire. But he is bound to be unfaithful—just like every other man—and despite his assurances, she will not trust the handsome, elegant rogue with her heart.

But can a promise to resist temptation stand firm when passion demands otherwise?

Peek at the Book

Patience looked up and met the stranger's hooded gaze. As she watched, his grey eyes darkened. The expression they contained—intensely concentrated—sent a most peculiar thrill through her.

She blinked; her gaze fell—to the man's lips. Long, thin yet beautifully proportioned, they'd been sculpted with a view to fascination. They certainly fascinated her; she couldn't drag her gaze away. The mesmerizing contours shifted, almost imperceptibly softening; her own lips tingled. She swallowed, and dragged in much needed breath.

SETTING
1819 Northampshire

CHARACTERS
Vane Cynster
Patience Debbington

RECURRING CHARACTERS
Therese, Lady Osbaldestone
Minnie, Lady Bellamy & Timms
Gerrard Debbington

On A Wild Night

First published April 2002

*Where are all the exciting
men in London?*

After years spent in the glittering ballrooms of the ton, Amanda Cynster is utterly bored by the current crop of colorless suitors. One night, determined to take matters into her own hands, she shockingly goes where no respectable lady ever should, but where many an intriguing gentleman might be found.

Quite suddenly out of her depth, a panicked Amanda looks for help—and is unexpectedly rescued by Martin Fulbridge, the Earl of Dexter. Lean, sensuous, and mysterious—the epitome of the boldly passionate gentleman Amanda has been searching for—Martin has delayed reentering society, preferring instead a more interesting existence on its fringes. And his sensuous touch makes it eminently clear that he would be happy to educate her in the arts of love.

Now Amanda has to wonder: can such a masterful rake be sufficiently tamed into the ways of marriage?

Peek at the Book

Hauling her gaze from it, she looked up at him. It took a moment to get enough breath to even gasp, "You're *Dexter?*"

The rakish, rumored-to-be-profligate, elusively mysterious Martin Fulbridge, fifth Earl of Dexter. She certainly knew of him, of his reputation, but tonight was the first time she'd set eyes on him.

When, stunned, she continued to stare, he raised one brow, cynical, yes, but world-weary as well. "Who else?"

SETTING
1825 London

CHARACTERS
Amanda Cynster
Martin Fulbridge, Earl of Dexter

RECURRING CHARACTERS
Amelia Cynster
Reggie Carmarthen
Luc Ashford

On A Wicked Dawn

First published May 2002

*"Marrying you will be
entirely my pleasure."*

Amelia Cynster hears these words from the handsome, enigmatic Lucien Ashford and is stunned. It's near dawn and she's
risked scandal by lying in wait for him just outside his London
house. But he agrees to her outrageous marriage proposal—
just prior to passing out at her feet. Amelia's torn between astounded relief and indignant affront, then decides she doesn't
care. She has always loved him—no other man will do—and,
frankly, she's tired of waiting.

Sometimes a young lady needs to take matters into her own
hands.

But matters of the heart are never that simple. The first
hitch in Amelia's plans comes when Luc refuses to agree to a
hasty wedding but insists on properly wooing her . . . in public
and private. Soon she longs for those moments away from
the watchful gaze of the ton, in which she can learn all about
seduction from a master. But unbeknown to Amelia, Luc has a
very good reason for wooing her. Every wicked gentleman has
his price.

Peek at the Book

That brief human contact, deadened by layers of fabric though it was, sent sensation rushing through him, and told Luc unequivocally who the dervish was. Amelia Cynster.

The wall behind his shoulders was the only thing keeping him upright. He stared astounded, utterly bemused . . . waited for the effect of her touch to subside . . .

SETTING
1825 London

CHARACTERS
Amelia Cynster
Lucien Ashford

RECURRING CHARACTERS
Portia Ashford
Penelope Ashford
Anne Ashford
Helena, Dowager Duchess of St. Ives

The Ideal Bride

First published March 2004

Who is this man's ideal bride?

Michael Anstruther-Wetherby is a rising member of Parliament, a man who has everything . . . except a wife. So he begins the search for his ideal bride—a malleable, gently bred young lady, and thinks he has met the perfect match. However, he finds an obstacle in his path, the young lady's beautiful, strong-minded aunt, Caroline Sutcliffe.

Once one of London's foremost diplomatic hostesses, Caro has style and status—and she realizes her young niece is all wrong for Michael. This handsome, aristocratic man needs someone with strength, wit, and sensuality by his side . . . someone more like her.

Suddenly Michael senses he has found his ideal bride—in Caro! Persuading her to accept his hand in marriage will take every ounce of his seductive charm. He tempts and tantalizes Caro beyond all reason—but can he convince her that becoming his wife will bring her all her heart desires . . . and more?

Peek at the Book

There were only five years between them, yet although they'd known each other since childhood and had spent their formative years growing up in this restricted area of the New Forest, he didn't truly know her at all.

He certainly didn't know the elegant and assured lady she'd become.

She looked at him—caught him looking at her—and smiled easily, as if acknowledging a mutual curiosity.

The temptation to assuage it grew.

SETTING
1825 England

CHARACTERS
Michael Anstruther-Wetherby
Caroline Sutcliffe

RECURRING CHARACTERS
Devil, Duke of St. Ives
Honoria, Duchess of St. Ives
Timothy, Viscount Breckenridge

The Truth About Love

First published March 2005

Bold, passionate and possessive, the Cynster men let nothing stand in their way when it comes to claiming the women of their hearts.

Gerrard Debbington, Vane Cynster's brother-in-law, is one of London's most eligible gentlemen. Uninterested in marriage, his driving passion is to paint the fabled gardens of Lord Tregonning's Hellebore Hall—an opportunity that is now at hand . . . *if* Gerrard agrees to create an honest portrait of Tregonning's daughter as well.

Gerrard chafes at wasting his talents on some simpering miss, only to discover that Jacqueline Tregonning stirs him as no other does. Certainly, she is beautiful, but it is her passionate nature that strikes sparks with Gerrard's own, igniting desire and sweeping them into each other's arms, convincing Gerrard that he has found his ideal soul mate—the lady he must have as his wife.

But something is horribly wrong at Hellebore Hall. Evil and lies are reaching out to ensnare Jacqueline—and Gerrard will have to move Heaven and Earth to protect the remarkable woman who, for him, personifies the truth about love. . . .

Peek at the Book

Pushing back from the rock, he straightened and turned.

Only to discover Jacqueline had leaned toward him, fighting to hold her hair with one hand.

They were suddenly very close, their faces only inches apart. Her eyes widened. Her lips were parted; she'd leaned close to say something.

Beyond his control, his gaze dropped to her lips. Soft, intensely feminine, shaped for passion, and mere inches away.

SETTING
1831 England

CHARACTERS
Gerrard Debbington
Jacqueline Treggoning

RECURRING CHARACTERS
Barnaby Adair
Amelia Cynster
Amanda Cynster

Lost and Found in
Hero, Come Back

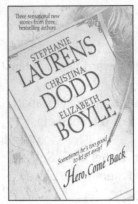

In an innovative new twist comes the story of a secondary character from a previous book, starring in his own story. Revisit your favorite Lost Heroes, and see old friends from your favorite books.

A resourceful beauty's determination to locate the true father of a poor foundling sets off a society scandal—and ignites a fire in handsome Reggie Carmarthen's world-weary, aristocratic heart, in the unforgettable . . . *Lost and Found.*

Peek at the Book

Stepping back again, she locked her eyes on his.

"Thomas now knows—and Hugh hasn't forgotten, so—"

"All is well on the Benjy front. Quite."

On the last, ferociously clipped word, Reggie stepped forward again—and her back hit the wall. She didn't dare blink. He had to be able to see her reaction, yet he took still another step. Deliberately crowding her, leaving her not an inch to breathe.

She'd expected panic to overwhelm her, but it wasn't fear that raced down her veins. She'd never felt excitement, expectation— exhilaration—to match this.

His eyes, furious, cloudy, roiling with anger, held her gaze mercilessly. "All, however," he enunciated softly, "is not right— nowhere near right—on the *Reggie* front."

SETTING
1834 London

CHARACTERS
Reggie Carmarthen
Anne Ashford

What Price Love?

First published March 2006

*A passionate man and
a daring woman confront
the ultimate question—
what price love?*

Dillon Caxton, protégé of Demon Cynster, is disillusioned with love. Blessed with wealth, status and stunning good looks, he has no time for marriage-hungry misses. As a guardian of the "Sport of Kings," he has a daring criminal scheme to thwart—one that threatens to wreak havoc on the thoroughbred racing world.

Enter ravishingly beautiful Lady Priscilla Dalloway. She, too, has no time for romance—she has to rescue her horse-mad twin brother from the dangerous swindle in which he's become embroiled. But the man holding the key to finding her twin is Dillon—who allows her to believe he is immune to her charms.

The lady is Dillon's only lead to the criminals, and Pris will do *anything* to save her twin, including seducing the said-to-be unseducible. Linked in a journey riddled with danger and passion, they find themselves facing that terrifying question: *what price love?*

Peek at the Book

He drew close enough to see the expression in her eyes. There was temper there—an Irish temper to match her accent. It was presently leashed, but she was definitely irritated and annoyed with him.

Because she hadn't been able to bend him to her will.

He felt his lips curve, saw annoyance coalesce and intensify in her eyes. She really ought to have known just by looking that he wasn't likely to fall victim to her charms.

Manifold and very real though they were.

SETTING
1831 Newmarket

CHARACTERS
Dillon Caxton
Priscilla Dalloway

RECURRING CHARACTERS
Barnaby Adair
Demon Cynster
Felicity Cynster

NEW YORK TIMES BESTSELLER
Stephanie
LAURENS

The Taste of Innocence
A CYNSTER NOVEL

The Taste of Innocence

First published March 2007

He knows all too well how dangerous love can be. . . .

Charles Morwellan, eighth Earl of Meredith, has seen many happy, successful Cynster unions, but he also watched his father's obsessive love nearly destroy their family, a mistake he has sworn he will not repeat. But he also knows his duty, so he has chosen a bride. Sarah Conningham is beautiful enough to grace his arm and intelligent enough to know the value of his offer. Imagine his shock when she refuses to wed for anything less than intense, unbridled, unbounded love.

Now he's determined to win her! In a tantalizing game of pleasure and persuasion, Charles courts Sarah with excruciating propriety during the day, but each night spirits her away into the lush, moonlit gardens, where he tutors her in the arts of passion. Sensual embraces soon turn to searing kisses, and much, much more. Yet after their wedding, his polite mask returns, leaving Sarah wondering which man she actually married: the controlled aristocrat, or the lover whose touch leaves her gasping. But then Sarah's life is threatened, and Charles is forced to confront his own truths—when he discovers just how much he is willing to surrender to protect . . . the taste of innocence.

Peek at the Book

Now he was talking to her, with her, no longer on any formal plane but on an increasingly personal one; his tone had deepened, becoming more private. More intimate.

She quelled a tiny shiver; at that lower note his voice reverberated through her. She'd wanted to increase the space between them for several minutes, but there was something in the way he looked at her, the way his gaze held her, that made her hesitate, as if to edge back would be tantamount to admitting weakness.

His eyes held hers. Although he didn't move, she felt as if he leaned closer. . . .

SETTING
1833 Somerset

CHARACTERS
Charles Morwellan, Earl of Meredith
Sarah Conningham

RECURRING CHARACTERS
Barnaby Adair
Gabriel Cynster
Alathea Cynster
Inspector Basil Stokes

Temptation And Surrender

First published March 2009

When a gentleman is restless, bored with the careless pleasures of London society, he needs to discover a new diversion, and if that diversion is a beautiful woman, so much the better.

Jonas Tallent, who has masterfully taken the reins of his family's estate, never expected a delectable morsel like Miss Emily Beauregard to step into his library, but he certainly isn't about to hire her as manager for the village inn. A lady as tempting as Emily belongs in a ballroom, or a bedroom—preferably his.

Emily herself hadn't expected her current circumstances, but she has her reasons, and doesn't plan to share them, even with someone as seductive as Jonas. Yet he can be so devilishly persuasive. But a villain knows her secret, and soon danger threatens—Em, her family, and the powerful love she and Jonas have found in each other's arms.

Peek at the Book

Jonas released the note. She took it, tucked it in her reticule, then looked up, met his eyes—and smiled.

Just like that, she scrambled his brains.

That's what it felt like as, still beaming, she rose—and he did, too, driven purely by instinct given none of his faculties were operating. Emily left with her head high and a spring in her step, but didn't look back.

For long moments after she'd disappeared, Jonas stood staring at the empty doorway while his mind slowly reassembled.

His first coherent thought was a fervent thanks to the deity that she hadn't smiled at him when she'd first arrived.

SETTING
1825 Devon

CHARACTERS
Jonas Tallent
Miss Emily Beauregard

RECURRING CHARACTERS
Lucifer and Phyllida Cynster and family
The Reverend Joshua Filing
The Villagers of Colyton

Where The Heart Leads

First published February 2008

Handsome, enigmatic and deliciously dangerous, Barnaby Adair has made his name by solving crimes within the ton. When Penelope Ashford appeals for his aid, he is moved by her plight—and captivated by her lush beauty.

More than a pretty face in a satin gown, Penelope has devoted her will and intelligence to caring for London's orphans. But now her charges are disappearing. She turns to Adair for help, never dreaming she'll discover in him a man who matches her appetite for life and passion.

As Barnaby and Penelope unravel the mystery of the missing children, they uncover a shocking trail that leads to the upper echelons of society, and a ruthless criminal who is ready to destroy all they hold dear, including their newfound understanding of the irresistible intrigues of the heart.

Peek at the Book

Barnaby listened while she outlined an eminently rational strategy that would expose him to the basic facts, enough to ascertain where an investigation might lead, and consequently, how best to proceed.

Watching the sensible, logical words fall from her ruby lips—still lush and ripe, still distracting—only confirmed that Penelope Ashford was dangerous. Every bit as dangerous as her reputation suggested, possibly more.

In his case undoubtedly more, given his fascination with her lips.

SETTING
1835 London

CHARACTERS
Barnaby Adair
Penelope Ashford

RECURRING CHARACTERS
Inspector Basil Stokes
Griselda Martin
Heathcote Montague
Lord and Lady Paignton

The Honorable Barnaby Adair's Investigations Involving Cynster Connections

Cornwall, June 1831—Hellebore Hall
Assisting Gerrard Debbington, brother of Patience
Cynster, brother-in-law of Vane Cynster, and Miss
Jacqueline Tregonning
In: *The Truth About Love*

Newmarket, August 1831—The Jockey Club
Assisting Dillon Caxton, cousin of Felicity Cynster,
brother-in-law of Demon Cynster,
and Lady Priscilla Dalloway
In: *What Price Love?*

Somerset, February 1833—Morwellan Park
Assisting Lord Charles Morwellan, Earl of
Meredith, brother of Alathea Cynster, brother-in-law
of Gabriel Cynster, and Miss Sarah Conningham
In: *The Taste of Innocence*

*London, November 1835—The Foundling House,
Scotland Yard & the East End*
Assisting Miss Penelope Ashford, sister of Luc,
Viscount Calverton, sister-in-law of Amelia Cynster
In: *Where the Heart Leads*

The Bastion Club

"a last bastion against the matchmakers of the ton"

The Bastion Club
∽ MEMBERS ∾

Christian Allardyce, Marquess of Dearne (7)
Lady Letitia Randall

Anthony Blake, Viscount Torrington (2)
Alicia "Carrington" Pevensey

Jocelyn Deverell, Viscount Paignton (5)
Phoebe Malleson

Charles St. Austell, Earl of Lostwithiel (3)
Lady Penelope Selborne

Gervase Tregarth, Earl of Crowhurst (6)
Madeline Gascoigne

Jack Warnefleet, Baron Warnefleet of Minchinbury (4)
Lady Clarice Altwood

Tristan Wemyss, Earl of Trentham (1)
Leonora Carling

Honorary Member: Royce Varisey aka Dalziel, Duke of Wolverstone (8)
Minerva Chesterton

1. *The Lady Chosen*
2. *A Gentleman's Honor*
3. *A Lady of His Own*
4. *A Fine Passion*
5. *To Distraction*
6. *Beyond Seduction*
7. *The Edge of Desire*
8. *Mastered By Love*

The Lady Chosen

First published September 2003

Seven of London's most eligible—and adventurous— bachelors have banded together to form the Bastion Club, an elite society of gentlemen dedicated to determining their own futures when it comes to marriage.

Tristan Wemyss, Earl of Trentham, never expected he'd have to wed within a year or forfeit his inheritance. But he won't bow to the ton's matchmaking mamas. Instead, he'll marry someone of his own choosing—specifically his enchanting neighbor, Miss Leonora Carling. The lady has beauty, spirit and passion—qualities Tristan seeks in a mate. Matrimony, however, is the last thing on her mind. . . .

Once bitten, forever shy—never again will Leonora allow *any* man to capture her heart and break it. But Tristan is a seasoned campaigner who will not accept defeat, especially when a mysterious blackguard with dark designs on Leonora's family home gives him the perfect excuse to come to the lady's aid—as her protector, confidant, seducer . . . and husband.

Peek at the Book

With a wave, he invited her to walk with him the few steps back to the gate.

She turned, only then realized her acquiescence was a tacit acknowledgement that she'd come racing out purely to meet him. She glanced up, caught his gaze—knew he'd seen the action for the admission it was. Bad enough. The glint she glimpsed in his hazel eyes, a flash that made her senses seize, her breath catch, was infinitely more disturbing.

SETTING
1815 London

CHARACTERS
Tristan Wemyss, Earl of Trentham
Miss Leonora Carling

RECURRING CHARACTERS
Deverell, Viscount Paignton
Charles St. Austell, Earl of Lostwithiel
Dalziel

A Gentleman's Honor

First published October 2003

The season has yet to begin, and Bastion Club member Anthony Blake, Viscount Torrington, is already a target for every matchmaking mama in London. But there is only one lady who sparks his interest. . . .

Desperate and penniless, but determined, Alicia *will* make a spectacular match for her ravishing younger sister! Masquerading as the widowed "Mrs. Carrington"—the perfect society chaperone—Alicia intends to boldly launch her sibling into the ton. But fashionable ladies are not normally accused of murder. . . .

Every instinct Tony Blake possesses tells him that Alicia—the exquisite, distraught beauty he discovers standing over a dead body in his godmother's garden—is innocent of serious wrongdoing. His connections will allow him to take control of the investigation, his social prominence will certainly provide her public support.

But it is more than honor alone that compels Tony to protect this remarkable, imperiled beauty—and he will do everything in his seductive power to make Alicia his.

Peek at the Book

The tableau exploded into Tony's vision as he gained the top of the steps. Senses instantly alert, fully deployed, he paused.

Slim, svelte, gowned for the evening in silk, her dark hair piled high, with a silvery shawl wrapped about her shoulders and clutched tight with one hand, the lady slowly, very slowly, rose. In her other hand, she held a long, scalloped stiletto; a streak of blood beaded on the wicked blade.

She held the dagger by the hilt, loosely grasped between her fingers, pointing downward. She stared at the blade as if it were a snake.

A drop of dark liquid fell from the dagger's point.

SETTING
1816 London

CHARACTERS
Anthony Blake, Viscount Torrington
Miss Alicia Pevensey

RECURRING CHARACTERS
Jack, Lord Hendon, and Kit
Helena, Duchess of St. Ives
Dalziel

A Lady of His Own

First published October 2004

After years of dedicated service to the Crown, the seven members of the Bastion Club have banded together to support each other through the most perilous mission of all: finding a bride.

Impatient to find his bride-to-be yet appalled by the damsels of the ton, Charles St. Austell seeks refuge in his castle—and discovers Lady Penelope Selborne walking the deserted corridors at midnight. Years ago, they'd consummated their youthful passion on one unforgettable afternoon. And while the ardent interlude haunts Charles still, Penny wants nothing more to do with him.

But resisting a stronger, battle-hardened Charles proves difficult, even though Penny has vowed she won't settle for anything less than true love. And when a traitorous intrigue threatens them both, she discovers that her first love—a man who will not rest until he has made her his own—is her fated champion and protector.

Peek at the Book

Charles wished the light was better or the chair closer to the bed; he couldn't see Penny's eyes and her expressions— the real ones—were too fleeting to read in the dimness. He'd chosen the safe distance of the chair to avoid aggravating their mutually twitching nerves. That moment in the corridor had been enough; the urge to seize her, to have his hands on her again, had been so strong, so unexpectedly intense, it had taken every ounce of his will to resist.

He still felt off-balance, just a touch insane. . . .

SETTING
1816 Cornwall

CHARACTERS
Charles St. Austell, Earl of Lostwithiel
Lady Penelope Selborne

RECURRING CHARACTERS
Jack, Baron Warnefleet
Gervase Tregarth, Earl of Crowhurst
Dalziel

A Fine Passion

First published September 2005

The men of the Bastion Club are powerful, loyal, and not averse to overcoming danger if they must. Now, after years of loyal service to the Crown, they each—one by one—must face that greatest danger of all . . . love.

The last of his line, Jack, Baron Warnefleet, has fled London after nearly being compromised into marrying a *dreadful* female. Turning his back on the entire notion of marriage, he rides home to the estate he has not seen for years, determined to set in motion an alternative course of action.

But then in the lane before his gate, Jack rescues a startlingly beautiful lady from a menacing, unmanageable horse. However, while he begins by taking command, the lady continues by taking it back. Lady Clarice Altwood is no meek and mild miss. She is the very antithesis of the wooly-headed young ladies Jack has rejected as not for him. Clarice is delectably attractive, beyond eligible, undeniably capable, and completely unforgettable. Why on earth is she rusticating in the country?

That enigma is compounded by mystery, and it's quickly clear that Clarice is in danger. Jack must use every ounce of his cunning and wit to protect this highly independent and richly passionate woman . . . who has so quickly stolen his heart.

Peek at the Book

Jack shot a glance at the lady. Riding up, all he'd seen was her back—that she had a wealth of dark mahogany hair worn in an elegantly plaited and coiled chignon, was wearing a plum-colored walking dress, and was uncommonly tall.

Sprawled on her back on the bank beyond the ditch, she struggled onto her elbows. Across the ditch, their gazes locked.

Her face was classically beautiful.

Her dark gaze was a fulminating glare.

SETTING
1816 Gloucestershire

CHARACTERS
Jack, Baron Warnefleet
Lady Clarice Altwood

RECURRING CHARACTERS
Lady Osbaldestone
Deverell, Viscount Paignton
Dalziel

To Distraction

First published September 2006

The gentlemen of the Bastion club have proven their courage while fighting England's enemies, but nothing has prepared them for dealing with that most formidable of challenges: the opposite sex.

Deverell, Viscount Paignton, is in desperate need of a wife. Unmoved by the matchmaking "herd," he seeks help from his aunt, who directs him to a lady she vows is perfect for him. Dispatched to a country house party to look the lady over, he discovers her not swanning about among the guests but with her nose buried in a book in the library.

Phoebe Malleson is tempted to distraction by Deverell, but marrying him isn't part of her plan. Moved by an incident in her past, Phoebe has a secret cause to which she's committed. Unfortunately, telling Deverell to go away doesn't work, and he quickly learns of her secret. But someone powerful has her cause targeted for destruction—and her in their sights. Phoebe must accept Deverell's help . . . though the cost to them both might be dear—and deadly.

Peek at the Book

Fascinating green eyes . . . and a direct gaze that was, even more to her surprise, frankly disconcerting. She wanted to look away, to break the contact, yet some part of her didn't dare . . .

Who the devil was he?

More to the point, her inner self whispered, *what* was he?

SETTING
1816 London

CHARACTERS
Jocelyn Deverell, Viscount Paignton
Miss Phoebe Malleson

RECURRING CHARACTERS
Gervase Tregarth, Earl of Crowhurst
Christian Allardyce, Marquess of Dearne
Dalziel

Beyond Seduction

First published September 2007

A little bit wild and undeniably brave, the gentlemen of the Bastion Club have pursued adventures far and wide. But their exploits at home could prove to be the riskiest of all as they hunt an elusive target: the perfect bride.

In a moment of recklessness, Gervase Tregarth, sixth Earl of Crowhurst, swears he'll marry the next eligible lady to cross his path. Cloistered at his ancestral castle in Cornwall, with nary a suitable woman for miles, he never expects he'll have to fulfill his pledge, at least not until the London Season begins. But then he meets his neighbor, the *very* appealing Madeline Gascoigne.

Years of secret service to the Crown have taught Gervase the value of always having a loophole; there will be no wedding if he and Madeline are incompatible in *any* way. So he sets out to prove that they would make a most *dreadful* match . . . by luring her into his arms and, ultimately, his bed. From their very first kiss, Gervase discovers that the headstrong and independent Madeline is no meek country miss . . . and that the fire between them will burn long beyond that first seduction.

Peek at the Book

Gervase was curious—and just a little intrigued. He rather liked tall women, but more than that, Madeline possessed a certain vitality—an open, honest and straightforward appreciation of life—that he found attractive in a surprisingly visceral way.

She'd enjoyed their ride, and he'd felt drawn to her in that, as if the fleeting moment had been a shared illicit joy.

The memory held him for some minutes; when his mind circled back to the present, he realized a smile was curving his lips.

SETTING
1816 Cornwall

CHARACTERS
Gervase Tregarth, Earl of Crowhurst
Madeline Gascoigne

RECURRING CHARACTERS
Charles and Penelope, Earl and Countess of Lostwithiel
Christian Allardyce, Marquess of Dearne
Dalziel

The Edge of Desire

First published September 2008

They proved their bravery fighting for His Majesty's Secret Service and were rewarded with brides of great beauty and breeding. But one member of the Bastion Club has remained a bachelor . . . until now.

"Christian, I need your help. There is no one else I can turn to . . . L."

When Christian Allardyce, sixth Marquess of Dearne, reads those words, his world turns upside down. Lady Letitia Randall is a woman like no other, and the day he left her behind to fight for king and country was the most difficult of his life. He never forgot the feel of her lips against his, but he never expects to see her again. Yet now she seeks his help, and Christian knows he will not resist her plea.

Letitia believes that Christian abandoned her when she needed him most, and she hates to call on his aid. But to clear her brother's name, she has sworn to use every weapon at her command, even if it means seducing her ex-lover. Yet all the while, Christian is waging a war of his own—a campaign of pure pleasure and sweet revenge that will take them both beyond the edge of desire.

Peek at the Book

Letitia hadn't been this close to him for twelve long years. Her decision to keep her distance when he'd reappeared among the ton had clearly been wise; even with a good six feet separating them, she could feel her rib cage tightening, enough to affect her breathing.

Enough to make her feel just a touch giddy. To have her nerves stretching in telltale anticipation.

An anticipation that would never be fulfilled.

Not now.

SETTING
1816 London

CHARACTERS
**Christian Allardyce, Marquess of Dearne
Lady Letitia Randall**

RECURRING CHARACTERS
Anthony Blake, Viscount Torrington
Tristan Wemyss, Earl of Trentham
Dalziel
Lady Osbaldestone

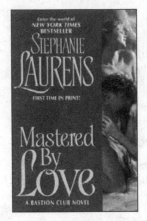

Mastered By Love

First published August 2009

The men of the Bastion Club proved their bravery secretly fighting for their country. Now their leader faces that most dangerous mission of all: finding a bride.

As the mysterious leader of the Bastion Club known as "Dalziel," Royce Varisey, tenth Duke of Wolverstone, served his country for decades, facing dangers untold. But as the holder of one of England's most august noble titles, he must now take on that gravest duty of all: marriage.

Yet the young ladies the grand dames would have him consider are predictably boring. Far more tempting is his castle's willful and determinedly aloof chatelaine, Minerva Chesterton. Beneath her serene façade lies a woman of smoldering sensuality, one who will fill his days with comfort and his nights with sheer pleasure. Determined to claim her, he embarks on a seduction to prove his mastery over every inch of her body . . . and every bit of her heart.

Peek at the Book

The passing years had honed and polished him, revealing rather than concealing the sleekly powerful, infinitely predatory male he was. If anything, that reality seemed enhanced.

Royce continued to stand twenty feet away, frowning as he studied her, making no move to come closer, giving her witless, swooning, drooling senses even more time to slaver over him.

Minerva thought she'd outgrown her infatuation with him. Sixteen years of separation should surely have seen it dead.

Apparently not.

SETTING
1816 Northumbria

CHARACTERS
Royce Varisey, Duke of Wolverstone, a.k.a. Dalziel
Minerva Chesterton

RECURRING CHARACTERS
All Bastion Club members and their wives
Devil Cynster, Duke of St. Ives
Lady Osbaldestone
Jack, Lord Hendon and Kit

Novellas

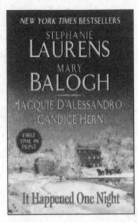

The Fall of Rogue Gerrard in
It Happened One Night

First published in October 2008

Once upon a time, four superstar storytellers came up with a delicious idea. What if they each wrote a story about a proper young lady stranded at a remote inn away from society's constraints? What would happen? And how long would it take for her to give in to desire?

Robert "Rogue" Gerrard is London's most notorious rake. But he once did everything in his power to protect Lydia Makepeace, igniting a yearning that persists to the day they are trapped alone at an inn. Fueled by desire, Lydia is determined to finally have Robert for her own delight. . . .

Peek at the Book

Across the room, a lady whisked into the parlor, turned and shut the door. Swinging back into the room, looking down, shaking rain from an umbrella, she walked a few paces, then halted.

She was swathed in a heavy cloak, the lower foot of which was wet through and muddy, but she'd pushed back the hood, revealing hair the color of burnished walnut neatly secured in a chignon, and a small oval face with delicate features.

Features Ro recognized, that still held the power to stop the breath in his chest.

She hadn't seen him; she was patently unaware he was there.

He frowned. "What the *devil* are you doing here?"

CHARACTERS
Robert Gerrard, fifth Viscount Gerrard
Lydia Makepeace